RELENTLESS HEART

The Relentless Series Book 1

JENNIFER CARY

Also by Jennifer Cary

The Patriarch: The Crockett Chronicles: Book 1

The Sojourners: The Crockett Chronicles: Book 2

The Prodigal: The Crockett Chronicles: Book 3

Tales of the Hob Nob Annex

The Relentless Series:

Relentless Heart

Wedding Bell Blues (September 2020)

Relentless Joy (November 2020)

Prologue

The Oval Office, May 24, 2068

HE'S READY FOR YOU."

Natalia Alaniz stood. Her heart pounded as she brushed a wrinkle from her skirt. After all the strides of this twenty-first century, why had no one invented a method to keep clothes from wrinkling? Did she look professional? She brushed the thought away with one more swipe and followed the secretary.

Breathless, Natalia pinched herself. Since childhood, she'd dreamed of this room. Old and new media often used this setting for broadcasts and photos. Yet standing in this place bathed her in surreal almost as much as the sunlight filtering through the floor-to ceiling windows. Her eyes roved from the ornate desk to the curved walls, landing on the Seal of the United States, emblazoned on the carpet at her feet.

"Your first time, I see."

Startled, she spun as another voice, the one in her ear, spoke, "Don't be too much the fan. Remember, you're the professional."

She held out her hand. "Mr. President. Thank you for seeing me."

Mr. David Joshua Salem, President of the United States,

shook her hand, and guided her to the chairs set up, all in one motion. Natalia's mind screamed like a teenage groupie—*I'll never wash this hand again!*—while the voice in her ear brought her back to earth. "Breathe, smile, and make nice."

"You're correct, sir. This is my first assigned interview on-site outside of the Press Corps room. I'm sure it shows all over my face."

"Not at all. You are doing fine. You'd never believe how I behaved the first alone moment I had in here."

"Would you like to tell me about it?" She'd have an exclusive.

He shook his head and chuckled. "You are good. Almost let that secret out of the bag." He winked, taking the other chair.

"Well perhaps we can get started." She double checked her right earring. Her producer's voice came through loud and clear. Next, she touched the statement necklace that held the camera, waiting a second to hear the "looks good."

Last, she handed the tie clip to President Salem. He put it on. She gave him a thumbs-up as her producer expressed approval for the wireless reception.

"We're set." She paused, ignored her thumping heart, and began. "This is Natalia Alaniz, correspondent with CBS *Sunday Morning*, streaming live from the Oval Office. My guest today is President Salem. Good morning, Mr. President."

He leaned back, ever so slightly. "Good morning, Ms. Alaniz." Open, friendly.

One last glance at her bracelet of notes. For months she dreamed of and prepped for this moment. Now here it was. She took a breath. "You are concluding your first term in office and gearing up for a second. Overall, the American people seem to think they know you. Is that accurate?"

"Pretty much, yes, that is accurate. In this day and age, not much is hidden. The opposition has tried to expose my sins or faults. But what you see is what you get. I'd say I'm fairly transparent."

"Your military career is of public record, along with the heroic actions for which you received the Medal of Honor while serving in the Sudan War. I understand you come from a long line of warriors."

President Salem crossed his legs. "I guess you might say that. My father, grandfather, and great-grandfather all served in the military."

"How did their service impact you and your new program, Plows of Peace? How does it impact you as Commander-in-Chief?"

He chuckled. "I am who I am because of their choices as much as my own. The nucleus of Plows of Peace started many years ago in my family, eventually growing to include others from my hometown. We believed the time was ripe to present it on a bigger stage."

"Do you view Plows of Peace to be the Peace Corps of the twenty-first century? In some ways that might put you on level with President John Kennedy, wouldn't it?"

He sat straighter. "I don't see that. I just know POP, as we affectionately call it, has served many. By championing it with a national platform, the number of people helped grows exponentially."

"So, what was the nucleus for POP? How did this get started?"

He smiled. Memories twinkled in his eyes. "There was another warrior. She inspired the idea."

"Another? Who was she?"

He nodded and held out his hand. "Come, I'll show you." He led Natalia to a table behind his desk, picking up an old-fashioned double frame from a group of digital photos, two five-by-sevens hinged together. The left held a shot of an elderly Asian woman. Her smile tired, but gentle, nearly closed her eyes to thin lines. Strands of silver hair wisped about her face while the rest was pulled to the back. She appeared to be... Natalia couldn't guess. Her only thought was ancient.

The one in the other frame included the woman, though one could see she sat in a rolling chair—what they used to call a wheelchair. Now her smile was wide. A small child, perhaps preschool age, pushed the chair from behind. "This is my *Bà*." He rubbed his thumb over the rolling chair picture. "My great-grandmother." Pointing to the boy, he added, "That's my son, David Junior."

"He met his great, great-grandmother?" How could that be?

"Yes." He sighed. "She passed away not long after this. Bà lived to be 104 years old. I remember when it was taken. DJ says he remembers, too, though I'm not sure that it's her or the photo he recalls, but yes, they were great buddies."

This was something new. Excitement bubbled from her toes. And he seemed to want to talk. So, she nudged. "She's lovely, very sage like."

"She was. And she was more than determined. Not ruthless or anything negative, but her faith, the way she loved, it was strong, tenacious. You could say relentless." He replaced the frames.

"How do you mean?"

Mr. Salem motioned to the chairs. "To understand, you must go back one hundred years to a city once called Saigon."

Viet Nam

ONE

How Can I Be Sure

Saigon, Viet Nam January 1, 1968

Hien gazed square into the eyes of the man whose hands held hers, the man whose eyes captured her heart. The heart that was about to pound out of her chest if his eyes didn't hold her captive. If she blinked, it would all fall apart.

And so would she.

"Michael Ryan Wheaten, do you take this woman to be your lawfully wedded wife? To have and to hold from this day forth, for richer or for poorer, in sickness and in health, 'til death do you part?"

"I do."

He said I do! *Heart, calm down!*

"Nguyen Han Hien, do you take this man to be your lawfully wedded husband? To have and to hold from this day forth, for richer or for poorer, in sickness and in health, 'til death do you part?"

Michael squeezed her hand.

She squeezed back. "I do." A tear etched its way down her cheek, plopping in a warm, wet blob on her new red *ao dai*, the traditional Vietnamese dress she bought for today.

Tears welled in his blue eyes too. He looked so handsome in his Air Force dress uniform.

"By the power vested in me by the United States of America, I now pronounce you man and wife. You may kiss your bride."

Michael's lips were on hers before she caught a breath. But how sweet to faint in those arms. More than a peck but not so much as to be embarrassing, they broke off the kiss together. He swept her off her feet.

"Oh! Michael."

He spun her around before planting her feet back on the ground.

Heat flooded her cheeks. Hien glanced at the man who performed the ceremony. The officer grinned. So did Michael's parents. Apparently, it was not too embarrassing.

His father, Minister Ernest Wheaten, a retired colonel, pulled her into an embrace. "Welcome to the family, Hien. You are now Hien Wheaten. Think you might get used to being a Wheaten?"

Hien nodded, whispering her new name in her brain. Yes, she could get used to anything with Michael by her side.

His mother, Melanie, hugged her, not as effusively as his father, but still warmly. "We're so happy for you two."

Then she was back in his arms.

With a new name.

And a new home.

So much new. But she could figure it all out with Michael.

THAT EVENING she lay curled in her husband's arms. He tucked a few wayward strands of long hair behind her ear. "We can't tell my mom yet. Dad plans this big surprise once we get out. Brother Charlie's enlistment won't be up for a while. He's already told me he wants to reenlist. He and Lai might settle down here, with her teaching and all. They're not sure." He sighed. "I'm rattling on."

"No, Michael. I love the sound of your voice. I want to just listen. Tell me more plans." Her finger made lazy circles on his sternum.

"You sure?"

She nodded, nuzzling next to his neck. His words flowed softer than the moonlight, filtered by the cherry tree leaves, through their balcony window. Their bed in the room he kept at his parents' in the embassy villa was only a single, but she had no complaints about sharing it tonight. Or any night.

"Okay, so the farm is near a little town called Breadville in Indiana. It's a few miles from Bunker Hill Air Force Base. Kokomo would be the nearest bigger town, I suppose. Peru's not far either. Mom and Dad came for a visit one time while I was stationed there, and we got talking about the future. Dad has wanted to retire to a farm like where he grew up, and I suppose I've always listened to his stories, because he's got me thinking that way too. We found this place close to some of Mom's family. The farmhouse is in good shape. It has all sorts of possibilities. My cousin is caring for it until we can get there. He lives close by, so he said he didn't mind. It will still need work, though."

Hien nodded into Michael's shoulder. She could do anything if they did it together.

"But here's the part you can't tell Mom." His finger made a slow trace from her temple to the base of her throat. "Dad is signing the farmhouse over to you and me as a wedding gift. He plans to build her a new house on another part of the property, but this way we won't have to inherit the farm. It'll be ours when we move back. Think you might enjoy being an Indiana farmer's wife?"

She nodded and nibbled his ear. As much as she loved his voice, it was time to stop talking.

"Morning, Hien! Glad you're back. Where've you been?" Nick Jones, a correspondent for a small newspaper in upstate New York, threw out the soliloquy as he dashed past. Hien figured out awhile back that he did not want answers unless he was sure it led to a story. If he wanted answers, he would pause to give you the opportunity. No pause, no real interest.

Today he didn't slow down. "Morning!" She plunged herself into the atmosphere of stale coffee and keyboard clacks and headed for her desk.

To call it a desk was a kind misnomer. Rather it was a disintegrating school desk with the attached seat removed. A metal pipe protruded where it once had been. However, it was perfect to stow any immediate work and a few belongings—a box of Kleenex tissues, two Bic pens, a stenographers pad, an extra tube of Slickers lip gloss (the only makeup she allowed herself because Michael liked how it tasted).

Hien did not mind. Her camera always stayed with her. Two or three spare rolls of film lay hidden in the Kleenex box, and that, as well as the rest of her treasures, remained stashed beneath the lift-up plywood board which served as a desktop, though it barely held on by the grace of one tiny hinge.

Unused film disappeared faster than they could replace it, unless you had the backing of a big media outlet. Hien's photos were for the independent market. There was no telling who might buy them. Film was a precious commodity not to be wasted. Out of habit, she felt inside the tissue box. The canisters were where she'd hid them.

She started with the Corps as a translator. Her English was fluent. In truth, it was extremely fluent, thanks to the Catholic school nuns who drilled the language into her and her brother. She gained a reputation for accuracy and an awareness of semantic subtleties.

One day, she brought her camera to an interview and

snapped a shot. No other cameras were available. The correspondent she assisted grew excited for the photo. He did not care how amateurish it turned out.

It turned out better than amateurish. Hien's life changed.

Tony Bennett crooned from someone's radio, extolling that for once in his life he had love and hope. Hein understood. He sang her story.

Had it only been a year since she left her family in Huê? One year. She went from a daughter to a working woman, from translator to photographer, from single to married. Her two-week-old ring glittered like the candle in the little paper boat she sent sailing down the Houng River last Tet, filled with wishes for the new life she would start the following week in Saigon. The river gleamed that night with all the tiny New Year boats sailing off into the future.

Funny, in two weeks it again would be the New Year—Tet. What would this New Year bring? Perhaps she would become a mother. She and Michael might start their family. Four more weeks and he would be done flying sorties over jungles. They could leave Viet Nam. She would say goodbye to everything familiar, more than when she left Huê´ for Saigon. But the excitement tantalized. Her destiny lay on the other side of the ocean. She was sure.

Indiana, what a strange name! She shook her head.

Hien checked the schedule for the darkroom. Someone got there before her. Too much daydreaming. She knocked, inquiring how long the wait.

Of course, she could fly to Huê´. When she lived there, she built her own darkroom in the bathroom of her parents' apartment building. People knocked on the door there too. But it was a four-hour flight.

She missed that world—her family, the city, her home. Never did she expect to return to it. Yet, her family was there.

Her family.

She sighed. Her family had not attended her wedding. They sent word that it was too dangerous to travel.

At least, that is the reason they gave.

Hien shrugged and knocked again.

"Almost done. Five minutes."

"Okay." What could she do but wait? She leaned against a table cluttered with dirty paper coffee cups, crumbs, and dried smeared something.

Mat Morrissey shouldered past to grab the schedule clipboard, grunted as he perused, and tossed it back onto the file cabinet. "Hien, you gotta let me in ahead of you. I think I've got something. Something big."

"Like what?"

"I'm not sure. You know that niggle when you know something, but you're unsure what it is?"

Hien nodded. She did not know, but she knew Mat. He could not let go of this any more than her brother's dog could let go of a bone. "Fine, you may come in with me. I will share my time, but you must tell me what you learned."

Mat hesitated. "Deal. But I've got the scoop. Right?"

"Deal."

Mat checked his watch, then pounded on the door. "C'mon, Riley! You're holding up the show!"

The voice behind the door called back. "Gimme a sec, Morrissey! Geez Louise!" Usually the language was saltier, but Hien was sure Steve Riley realized she was there and controlled himself.

Finally, the lock clicked, and the door opened.

"About time, man!" Mat pushed through.

"Hey, you can't rush perfection!" Steve waved a sheaf of photos. "And, you're welcome."

"You coming, Hien?"

"Coming, Mat." She smiled at Steve as she hurried past and shut the door fixing the lock which would keep others from coming in and destroying their work. Steve left the safe light on. "Where were you shooting?"

Mat opened the small film canisters. "I was over by Huế last evening. Just got back. There's this feel in the air. Something's not right. That city used to be so beautiful, even the atmosphere. The one place the war overlooked. Now it's like walking into the opening of a suspense movie."

"What do you mean?"

He shrugged, the red glow casting eerie shadows on his face. "Like nothing is out of place, yet something is. It's a sensation I can't shake. I swear, if Alfred Hitchcock stepped out from behind a tree, I wouldn't have been surprised. Terrified, yeah, but surprised, no."

Hien's heart climbed its way up her throat. "My family is there."

"Oh, sorry." Mat's gaze met hers and then returned to his work. He was reconsidering his bargain.

"I remember the area well. Perhaps I can see something."

"Perhaps." He didn't raise his head.

They worked in silence until Mat had his second roll developed. "Man, I thought for sure there was something. I'm just not seeing it."

"Let me look." Hien started with the first photo hanging from the drying line. A teenage girl on a bicycle. She studied the next. Then the next. Bicycle girl was not the only human photographed, but the manner in which she showed in different places… and she was only in maybe eight shots? But Hien could see it, rather sense whatever it was Mat meant. But she could not put a name to it either. "The city looks weird, different." The fear she had pushed away reared.

"Yeah. There's a curfew in effect for the locals. They don't get far from home that late in the evening. This isn't even inside the Citadel. I took these in the Triangle district, just south of the river. Still, I can't shake the eeriness. What does it mean? Have they gone underground or are they following orders? And why was that girl in those places?

Hien shook her head, reviewing each shot. It was where she grew up. It was where her mother lived. Mat developed sixty photos altogether and only eight of the girl—a girl she had never seen—but in a different locale each time. Who was she? What happened to her beautiful city? "What is this?"

Mat searched where she showed.

The girl did something near a doorway. What? "Hand me a magnifying glass, please."

He grabbed one from the table.

She peered closer, pointing to a shadow in the doorway next to the girl. Was she talking with someone? Was it supposed to be secret? It made no sense. Huế was beloved by both the north and the south. Battles raged near it, but neither side wanted to desecrate the Imperial City. Plus, the cease fire for Tet was just around the corner.

She must see for herself. "Can you get me there?"

"Not a good idea."

"I must go. I need to see this."

Mat shook his head. "I can't take you there. Not without some kind of security team. Your new husband would kill me deader than dead."

"If you will not take me, I will go on my own." New husband or not, she almost added. Michael was on call for a flight today, anyway. He would not learn of this before she returned tonight.

Mat paused. His eyes gave him away before he spoke. "This is against my better judgment, but there's a guy who owes me. Let's go."

Hien returned her film canisters to her purse for another time and grabbed her camera before Mat changed his mind.

"C'mon, Hien, the sooner we leave, the sooner we can get back to Saigon."

THE IMMENSE CARGO hold of the C-130 Hercules allowed no room for conversation. The plane's four engines roared loud enough to silence the most talkative. That left Hien running scenarios in her mind and asking herself questions she had no information with which to answer. Mat appeared calm, from the waist up. The rhythm of his right knee bouncing the entire flight belied him.

The second they rolled to a stop, he was out of his seat, heading for the cockpit.

"When do you need to take off?"

The pilot, Capt. Juan Andrade, shrugged. "This is a turn-around flight. Just long enough to unload."

"Can you give us an hour?"

"An hour, yeah, I'll stretch it that far. But, if you're not back, I'm not waiting."

Hien grabbed Mat's arm, speaking in his ear. "Tell him not to leave us!"

"She says don't leave us."

Juan shrugged again. "Then be back in an hour." He returned his attention to the controls.

"We'd better move. I'll get a vehicle." Mat climbed out and ran for the operations shack, leaving Hien to dismount the plane on her own.

She followed, only to have him return, running with keys in hand.

"Let's go." He grabbed her elbow, steering her toward a jeep on the edge of the runway. They both jumped in, he started it up, and they were on their way into the city. Hien gave him directions to her parents' apartment building. That was the easiest place to start.

Fifteen minutes later, they pulled in front. Everything looked the same, though different. The tree outside her old bedroom window appeared taller. The flowers in the pot beside the door bore a different color. A neighbor she did not recognize swept the stoop of the adjacent building. Her heart did a little twist. This must be the definition of bittersweet.

Clambering out, she motioned for Mat to follow, and ran to her parents' door, what used to be her door. She tried her old key, but it did not work. She reinserted it, trying again. It would not turn. Hien left the key in the lock and knocked. "*Mẹ, chính là con.*" She called to her mother. Now she heard her brother's dog, Bao, barking from the back of the apartment. Surely someone was there. Bao grew quiet. She knocked again. "I do not understand, Mat. Mother should be here."

Mat tapped her shoulder, put his finger to his lips, and pointed down.

A small piece of paper stuck from the threshold. The folded sheet moved, sliding further out. She stooped to retrieve and opened it. Only three scrawled words.

Rời khỏi, Nguy

TWO

Love Is Blue

R# ɪ ᴋʜ# i, Nɢᴜʏ

Leave, faker!

Hien stared at her mother's handwriting. The noisy four-hour return trip brought no understanding. Every time she stared at the paper, Hien could hear her mother speak the daggered words. That slur hurt the most. Nguy. The Viet Cong saved that for South Vietnamese government collaborators.

Or Americans.

Her father worked with the French during the civil war, sent her to all the right schools to prepare her to help on the side of the South Vietnamese. Her family believed in democracy as much as they hated communism. What changed?

During the entire walk from the Press Corp that question rolled around her brain like a bee-bee searching for its place to land. Once home, she showed her ID pass to the guards at the Embassy and headed for the Wheaten villa. She was positive she beat Michael home. The more she considered it, the better she liked it. She wanted time with her new father-in-law. Maybe he could help her sort this out.

Laughter over music greeted her. Patti Page sang "The Tennessee Waltz," while Hien's in-laws danced. Minister

Wheaten—she could not bring herself to call him Ernest or Father, not yet—twirled and dipped Mrs. Wheaten. The thought crossed Hien's mind that Michael was much like his father.

It was too personal to interrupt. Hien slipped upstairs and changed out of her work clothes. When she returned, her in-laws had moved on. Mrs. Wheaten in the kitchen. The door to her father-in-law's office was mostly closed, though incandescent light escaped through the crack.

Hien took in a breath and slowly exhaled. The incident in Huế left her gun-shy about door-knocking. But she summoned her courage and tapped. Her touch made the door open enough to see the Minister on the phone, motioning her in.

"Let me call you back, Bruce." He hung up and smiled. "Hien, how can I help you?"

This is silly. He has no time for my imaginings. But she was here. Michael often said, in for a penny, in for a pound. "Do you have a moment, sir?"

"For you? Of course, Hien. Have a seat. What's going on?" He motioned to the chair in front of his desk, waiting for her to sit before seating himself.

Hien shared about the day—Mat Morrissey's photos, the trip to Huế, and her mother's note. She even pulled the paper out of her pocket and handed it to him.

He listened, not interrupting once with questions, but he made a notation on a pad at one point. When she finished, he seemed deep in thought. Finally, he stood, came around the desk and sat on the edge. "You've had one heck of a day, Hien. Please tell me more about the photos."

Hien told him everything she could think of, how they made her feel, and what she remembered about them, the locale and the strange girl. "But sir, what bothers me most is what my mother wrote on the note. She would never use that kind of language, especially not to me. I do not understand."

"Is it possible she was protecting you, wanting you to leave? Could you have been in danger if you stayed?"

She had not considered that possibility. And it made sense. That was something her mother might do. The thought made her fearful for her. "Yes, thank you, sir. I had not thought of that."

"Hien, we are family now. I hope you will soon be comfortable enough to call me Dad, or at least, Ernest. I want you to know I'm here for you too. Not just for Michael."

Hien nodded and smiled. It would take more than one talk to become that comfortable. But she was a few steps closer.

He stood as she did and walked her to the door. "Hien, do you mind if I keep the note?" It was still on his desk, so she nodded and returned to her room.

Before she could get too deep in her thoughts, she heard Michael arrive. Racing to his arms, she hugged him, hoping he would spin her around again. He did, ending with a kiss that took her breath away.

"Oh, I am so glad you are home."

"Me too." His whisper tickled her ear. One more hug and then he pulled away, took her hand and led her to their room, calling out "Hi, Mom!" over his shoulder.

His mother's "Hi, sweetie!" followed them up the stairs into their room before he closed the door.

Once inside, Michael kissed Hien's cheek before starting to peel out of his clothes. "Thought we might go out tonight. A few drinks, a little dancing, let's have some fun!"

His mind was made up. It did not matter anyway. They would be together. And wasn't that the point? "Sure. Where shall we go?" They could talk later.

"I was thinking the Jade Pagoda. Some guys mentioned it."

The Jade Pagoda was the newest nightclub in the heart of the city. She had not been there, but coworkers mentioned it. The ones who liked hangovers and lost weekends. Press boys and fighter pilots had one thing in common: They were adrenaline junkies. The Jade Pagoda supposedly catered to all kinds of junkies.

"Are you sure about that place? I have heard—"

"I wouldn't put too much stock into rumors. Besides, you'll be with me and three or four other fly boys. You'll be as safe as in your mama's arms, baby."

A poor choice of words. Hien turned away. If he only knew.

Michael was too busy to notice her distress. Good. It gave her time to gain self-control. And he was right, the danger was minimal if they were together. This was Saigon, for goodness sakes (as her new mother-in-law would say). The war was farther north, not a problem tonight.

"Get all dolled up, baby, while I go grab a shower, and we'll paint this town." He again pecked her cheek as he breezed past toward the bathroom. All at once he turned on his heel, pulled her into a passionate kiss. "Hmmm. We're not going to act like an old married couple after two weeks." He pinched her bottom. "By the way, that blue number is my favorite." And he left for the shower.

It was only a playful pinch, but not something Hien liked. She rubbed the spot before pulling the dress from the closet. It was new and made her feel sophisticated the way it flowed— from the satin reverse collar to a sleeveless, lacy A-line.

She stood facing the mirror, holding the dress in front of her. Her eyes seemed tiny. She studied her reflection. Who was she kidding? All of her was tiny. At almost five feet, in just her socks, she often felt like a child in the middle of all the tall Americans she encountered. One more reason she had taken to wearing her hair in a bun at her nape—when her thick, long curtain of hair hung down, she appeared too waiflike. Once, a new guy at the Press Corps called her China Doll. She ignored it, but later learned Steve Riley "set the guy straight." No one explained, but she never had another problem with the guy.

She also never again wore her hair down at work.

By the time Michael returned from the shower, she was dressed and putting on her pumps. His clean scent lingered after he passed to the closet. "That's my girl!" He grinned, taking his shirt from the hanger.

She warmed to the idea that she had pleased him. "I will wait in the other room. We should tell your mother we are going out."

"You tell her. I'll be out in a minute."

She gathered her coat and purse. Then, just as her fingers touched the doorknob, he added, "I really like it when you wear your hair down." He followed with the look, the one that convinced her to do whatever he asked.

Something deep inside whispered trouble, but she went to the mirror and took down her chignon, brushed her hair free and then pulled the top center back into a barrette. At least her hair should stay out of her eyes. She brushed a kiss against his cheek and left the room.

Hien passed through the dining room noting the maid set the table for six. A second later, familiar voices rang from the living room. Charlie and Lai were here for dinner. She dreaded seeing her mother-in-law's face when word got out that she and Michael were leaving.

"Hien, how pretty you are!" Mrs. Wheaten beamed until her eyes locked on something behind Hien. Michael.

"Hey, Mom, tell MiVu not to set places for us. Hien and I are headed out to meet some friends."

"Oh, but I thought I'd have my family together tonight. It's been so long since we've even shared a meal. I just—"

"Mom, we'll do it another time, I promise. Love you." Michael whispered something that made her giggle before giving her a peck on the cheek. Oh, he could charm.

"You're just lucky I love you too. Have fun."

Charlie punched Michael on the arm. "Don't worry, baby brother. You just keep on and I'll win the favorite son prize."

"Sure, you will, Charlie, you keep dreaming. Hey, Lai!" Michael gave his sister-in-law a quick hug, turned to wink at his mom and then motioned for Hien to follow.

Which she did. Because when all was said and done, she would follow Michael anywhere, including to the Jade Pagoda. Even across the world to a strange land called Indiana.

~

THE EMBASSY LIMO let them out in front of the building. The Jade Pagoda was neither made of jade nor shaped like a pagoda. Someone put oriental sounding English words together to make something that might draw off-duty American military personnel into the establishment. Michael spoke to the driver before escorting Hien toward the worse-for-wear double doors. A guy resembling a Japanese sumo wrestler in street clothes checked them up and down before allowing them inside. Once inside, the place was smoky. And loud. And dirty. And, had she mentioned smoky?

Michael guided her to a cluster of tables shoved together, cluttered with glass mugs, a couple pitchers—one empty and one half full of what might be beer—and three ceramic ashtrays, overflowing and smoldering. Burnt tobacco and stale alcohol assailed her. Chairs were pulled up to the mess, four taken and two waiting for her and Michael.

"About time you got here, Artemus. Been saving seats for you and your lady." With that, the slouching redheaded speaker in the Hawaiian shirt kicked a chair out toward Michael without changing his position.

"It takes time to look this good. But how would you know? Besides, we wanted to make an entrance." Michael took the chair, spun it around, and straddled it before motioning to her to sit in the next one. "Honey, this slob is my wingman, Slick. Real name is Curt Miner, but we just call him Slick. The guy sitting next to him, that's Rags, or Rick Lee. Then we have Prof, Jim Wayne and last, but not least, Fabian, whose real name is Fabian Martinelli. Guys, this is my wife, Hien."

Prof and Fabian stood and offered their hands. Rags waved.

Slick grunted. "Well, I guess you were telling the truth. You really got married and to someone way out of your league." He leaned in toward her, his breath tinged by cigarettes and beer. "How do you put up with him? I tell you it's all we can do to stand the guy."

She tried to smile but then stared at her hands. What did he mean? Perhaps it was funny, but it made no sense. "May I ask a question, please?"

"Sure." It sounded like a chorus, all saying it at once.

"Why do you call my husband Art… Arte… mis?"

Slick sat straighter. "Artemus you mean?"

Hien nodded.

"Because he's like Artemus Gordon on *The Wild Wild West.*" He must have seen she did not understand. "*The Wild Wild West.* It's a TV show back home. Artemus Gordon is a master of disguise and is always trying out new ideas, like our Mikey here, so we call him Artie or Artemus. I'm Slick because I'm just so cool." He wagged his head and smiled, "And Ricky here is Rags because he's jumped from not one, but two planes to avoid crashing and burning with them—rags, parachutes." He held up two fingers and studied her face before continuing. "Jimmy boy is book smart. Real smart. Hence Prof, short for—"

"Professor!" Now Hien understood.

"Give the little lady a cigar! And Fabian, well, he's so pretty." Slick pinched Fabian's cheek while the subject batted his hand away. "He's loved by the girls and has the perfect name already. That's our story." He slapped the table. "Waiter!" He waved the empty pitcher in the air. A boy dressed in black came and traded him for a full one. "We need two more glasses too."

The guys jumped into conversation, so Hien took the opportunity to view her surroundings. Her in-law's living room was bigger than this place. The bar stood to the right of where they sat, but the stage was straight ahead. American rock-and-roll blared when they entered, but now stopped as a balding man in his late forties, maybe early fifties, waddled out with a microphone. He set the pole down, pulled the mic free, and blew into it a couple times.

"Can you hear me out there?" He must have decided they could because he kept speaking. "On this stage tonight, we have three beautiful ladies who, if you close your eyes, you'll swear they're The Supremes! Let's give them a warm hand!" Two people close to the front clapped while the curtains parted. A trio of Vietnamese girls in beehives, wearing colorful mini dresses and big, white hoop earrings thrust out their right arms and burst into "Stop in the Name of Love."

Hien remembered the song from the radio. They did not sound like The Supremes, no matter how tight she closed her eyes. She continued to survey the place.

The door opened. Someone familiar wandered to the bar. Hien watched him order a beer and turn around. She knew the second Mat Morrissey glimpsed her. He strode for her table, mug in hand.

"Hey, Hien, did you talk with your father-in-law yet?" That was Mat, straight to the point. No courteous filler.

"Hello to you too, Mat."

The exchange halted the other conversation. Michael rose to his feet.

She did as well. "Mat, this is my husband, Michael. Michael, this is my colleague, Mat Morrissey. He is an investigative reporter and photographer with Press Corps." Hien's throat constricted with the tension emanating from Michael. Then he stuck out his hand, and she could breathe.

"Sure, Morrissey. I remember Hien mentioning you. Nice to meet you." He turned his focus on her. "What's this about talking with Dad? Was he able to help you?"

"I spoke with…" How did she refer to her father-in-law at this point? "with your father—" her hand on Michael's chestand then her attention back to Mat— "and he will do some checking for us."

"Did you tell him what we saw?" Mat continued, clueless to what he had started.

"Yes, I explained about the photos and gave him the note. He needs some time, but I hope to speak with him again tomorrow." She could see Michael hung on every word and not because she was so cute.

"Okay. I think I'll head back in the morning. Plan to leave early. Gonna try a different time of day. Wanna tag along?"

"Where?" Michael's eyes bored into her.

"Huê."

Did Michael grow taller? "No. Absolutely not. I won't allow it."

Hien's backbone lengthened, indignation stretching her. "You will not allow it? Michael, I have a job. And this is no strange place. It is my home."

"I'll take care of that. You don't need to work. You're my wife. We're leaving here in a month, anyway. Quit now."

Hien's face steamed as anger turned to embarrassment. She could feel the gaze of every male in the vicinity absorbing the whole scene. "This is a private conversation, Michael." Her voice hissed at his ear. "We can discuss it at home. Excuse me, please." She pushed past her husband, searching for the ladies' room.

It had to be somewhere. She spotted a small alcove with a payphone. A door inside to the right opened on one dirty toilet and a cracked sink. It smelled bad enough to stop her advance. She only wanted to escape the situation, anyway. The alcove would work though the stench still emanated. With her head against the wall, Hien tried to slow her heart from pounding to death. Oh, timing was everything. She had planned to tell Michael about her trip, especially about the note. If she could have quietly explained while they held each other in bed, surely he would understand. *Mat, you have a big mouth.*

"I'm sorry."

Hien spun around at the touch on her shoulder. It was not her Michael.

She tried to smile. "I know, Mat. We had no chance to speak." She swiped an angry tear from her cheek.

"He's with his buddies."

She nodded. That was likely it. Stupid, but likely. "Well, I have no intention of quitting. I have a small stubborn streak."

He chuckled. "Yeah, I've had that impression more than once. Hey, don't worry about it. Go home and talk it out. If you end up quitting, you still know how to reach me if you learn anything from your father-in-law."

Hien nodded. "You are right. Be careful tomorrow. Please, let me know."

"Deal. Now I'm gonna enjoy this so-called beer and then get some sleep. Later gator." Mat wandered to the bar, chugged his mug, and left.

Hien took a breath. Through the open restroom door, her reflection stared back in a large shard of mirror over the cracked sink. Her eyes appeared puffy, but what could she do? She ran her knuckles beneath her lower lashes, disposing of the last of her tears, and started back to Michael.

The airmen all rose as she arrived at the table. Including Michael, who helped her to her chair before they all again seated themselves. Even Slick sat straighter. Michael's chair was turned to the table.

"Honey, I'm sorry. This isn't the place for that conversation. I embarrassed you, as these slobs were quick to point out. So, since I did that in front of them, I'm apologizing. In front of them. Can you forgive me?"

"Oh, Michael." She embraced his neck. He always said the right thing. She could never stay angry at him.

But there was tension in his muscles. She could feel it. This was not finished. Her heart clenched, and she relaxed the embrace. "Thank you. I forgive you." *But do you forgive me?*

A Vietnamese teen took the stage, mic in hand, and began "To Sir, with Love." Her hair was cut pixie style and bleached white blonde. Multiple layers of false eyelashes, whose sole purpose was to make her eyes as enormous looking as Twiggy's, in reality obscured her real eyes. Long gold triangle earrings dangled down to her shoulders, and her orange mini dress barely covered her crotch. The saddest part was that she had a beautiful voice, young and pure, but Hien knew this fifteen-ish child would be hundreds of years older in another month. Between the whole thing with Michael, the words of the song, and watching the waif, a tear escaped.

Michael noticed and pushed a handkerchief into her hand. Maybe it would be okay after all. As he rested his arm on the back of her chair, hope filled her once more.

The teen left the stage. The bald, fat announcer returned with one of the faux Supremes. He placed a stool center stage and sat while the girl draped a bangled arm over his shoulder. The music started and the tone-deaf wannabe Sinatra sang of lovely nights and stupid words while the other part of the duo tried to stay on key with her part. If it had not hurt her ears so much, it might have been the funniest version of "Somethin' Stupid" ever.

It must have bothered Michael's ears and those of his friends. They all stood, each leaving some bills on the table. Michael held her chair, helped with her coat, and escorted her through the door.

Once outside, the sweet-blossomed air cleansed her lungs of the smoky debris. Her ears rejoiced in relief. The guys said their see-you–in–the-mornings, and Michael hailed their driver.

But in the limo, the tension grew. Well, she would not start this conversation. It could be avoided until they were alone. She waited for him to put his arm around her shoulders, but he did not. Usually, he pulled her close. Now there was a gap big enough to accommodate another person, one as large as that announcer. The darkened windows of the embassy car blocked much of the city lights, but Hien knew Michael's chin was set like stone. She tipped hers a smidge higher. He must make the first move.

Silence reigned the entire ride and the walk to the villa. Hien remained quiet as Michael held the door for her. A small light gleamed from the kitchen to welcome them.

While Michael went in to flip the switch, Hien dashed upstairs. She switched on their bedroom light and undressed for bed.

"Hien, Mom, help me!" Michael's voice carried terror.

Hien ran from the room, shoving her arms into the sleeves of her robe as she followed the sound of his calls. She found him in his father's office. His mother arrived an instant later, wrapping her robe about her.

"Michael?" It took a second, but she realized why Michael was on the floor. Behind the desk, her father-in-law lay crumpled in a heap.

"Call for help." Mrs. Wheaten pushed past to her husband. "Is he… breathing?"

Hien overheard Michael's "yes" as she grabbed for the office phone. With the embassy operator on the line, she explained the situation, "It is Minister Wheaten. He is unconscious in the Mission Coordinator's Residence. Send help." She stayed on the line while the medical team was notified.

"Help is on the way." The operator sounded so calm, so strong. It squashed a piece of fear rising to attack.

"I will wait for the team." Hien realized they did not hear, but no matter. It was better for her to go. She slipped from the room, hurried to the front door, and pulled it open. The team arrived an eternity, or five minutes, later.

She led them to the office but stepped aside, remaining in the hall for fear of being in the way. Michael and his mother stood in the doorway, giving the team space to work. It was hard to see anything with the two of them standing in front of her, so she listened.

Words like "cardiac arrest" and "nitro" floated back to her. Then the doctor spoke to Michael's father. "Sir, can you hear me? Sir, we're taking you to the hospital. It looks like you had a heart attack. We'll stabilize you and then send you on to the ER. If you understand me, don't bother talking, just squeeze my hand." A pause, then over his shoulder he explained to Michael and his mother. "He squeezed. Good sign. We'll get him situated. You may follow us. Get dressed while we do that." And then, he returned to his patient.

Michael had not changed out of his clothes, but his mother scurried to her bedroom. Hien turned toward the stairs when Michael grabbed her elbow. "Hien, I know we need to talk, but right now—"

"I know, Michael." She kissed his cheek and raced upstairs. Pulling on jeans and a poor boy top, she finished by drawing her hair in a ponytail, and slipping into a pair of boots. Michael waited in the living room as she emerged. Her mother-in-law soon followed.

"I sent word to Charlie and Lai. They will meet us there."

"Thank you, honey. It didn't occur to me." Mrs. Wheaten glanced toward the office. "Are they about ready to leave? I want to ride with him."

Michael put an arm around his mother. "The ambulance is coming, but I don't think there's room for you in it. Once they get Dad, the doctor and the rest in there, it will be tight."

Hien longed to offer comfort, though she didn't know what to say. Michael was so good with words. "May I get you anything? Something you might want to bring?"

"Hien, thank you. That's thoughtful but… wait, yes. Ernest's Bible. It's on his desk in the office. Do you think you can get it?"

Hien hustled, slipping in without disturbing the team. The book sat on the corner closest to the doorway, so she was in and out before anyone spotted her. It was a good thing the word Bible gleamed in large gold letters on the front cover. From her days in the Catholic school she knew what a Bible was, but she had never touched one before this moment. The black leather was cracked and worn, from use or age or both, and some folded papers were tucked at the back. It occurred to Hien it must be well-loved. If she retrieved it, might it be her way to bring comfort? That thought brought her comfort.

Hien returned to the living room, handing the book to her mother-in-law.

She wrapped it in her arms. Michael sat with her on the sofa, his arm about her shoulders.

"Do you want your pocketbook?"

Surprise shadowed the older woman's face. "I suppose I will need that. Good thinking, Hien." She sighed. "It should be on my dresser."

Again, Hien raced, this time upstairs and down the hall, finding the pocketbook where it was supposed to be. She stopped by her own room to grab her purse, too, and returned in time to see the ambulance personnel arrive with a stretcher.

"It won't be long now, Mom. They'll get him to the hospital, and once he is under their care, he'll be good as new." Michael gave his mom a squeeze.

"Oh, Michael, I hope you're right. I have no idea what I would do without him." A sob escaped. She turned to cry on his chest.

"Mom, Mom, don't worry. He's gonna be fine. You wait and see."

Hien felt like a voyeur. An outsider. An intruder. She longed to be part of the family, to be of help, to be accepted.

Mrs. Wheaten pulled back and patted his knee. "I know. I mustn't borrow trouble. He'll be fine, and that's that."

Hien sat next to her mother-in-law. "Yes, he will be fine. He was already responding to the doctor, and at the hospital they can help him more. He will be fine."

The older woman wrapped Hien in a sudden hug, "Oh, Hien, you are a gift. I am so glad Michael found you."

Hien returned the embrace, her heart overflowing so much it made her eyes leak.

At that, Michael stood. "One minute." He left only to return waving handkerchiefs in each hand. "I'm surrendering my last clean hankies to you ladies. Looks like you need them." And they laughed, all three of them. Together. Like family.

THREE HOURS LATER, 2:17 a.m. to be exact, the minister was admitted to Grall Hospital and slept in his room. He was to rest —absolute bed rest for the next five days, after which he was to add some movement, like frequent but brief walks about the courtyard. An intravenous Heparin drip was added, and it was determined that as long as his blood pressure numbers didn't go past his age plus one hundred over one hundred, his body would handle it. Hien translated everything the French nurse explained, even though the nurse's English was passable.

The French continued to staff the hospital they built at the latter end of the nineteenth century despite leaving Viet Nam in the 1950s. Because of the medical discoveries and advances that took place there, it was written into the agreement that the French remained in this one spot. Hien had never appreciated that forethought until tonight.

She wrote notes to help with the translation and to make sure she remembered the instructions and information. Her mother-in-law asked her question after question—often the same one five minutes after she just answered it. By writing it down, she could show also that she knew what she was saying.

Hien yawned.

"Honey, why don't you get some sleep?" Michael sat next to her in the hallway and pulled her close. "It's all waiting now."

"I know, but your mother needs me. I cannot let her down."

"I should have asked Lai to stay. She's fluent in French and could translate."

"No, I would rather do it. This way I learn what happens. And it helps to bring your mother and me closer." Hien's stomach growled.

Michael chuckled.

Hien tried to give him the look that he often gave her, the one that always made her do his bidding. "I could use something to eat."

"That's right. We missed out on dinner. I'd planned to take you to Howard Johnson's after the Jade Pagoda. Thought you might like to try food you'll find in Indiana." He kissed the top of her head and stood. "I'll see what I can discover. Be back soon."

She watched him go to his father's door and realized he was asking if his mother wanted anything. This thoughtful man, this was the Michael she knew, the one with whom she fell in love. The other man she experienced tonight, or rather this past evening, was someone she did not know. Maybe Slick was correct. Maybe Michael had disguises, or personalities he wore to fit the moment.

Maybe weariness and hunger clouded her judgment.

Not the time to wonder about this. She shoved the thought to another part of her brain and started reading through the notes she had taken. The doctor's English was fluent, but the nurse supplied more information. They were cautiously hopeful that with complete bed rest for five days followed by mild activity, five-minute walks every hour or two, and so on, there was a good chance the minister could fly home in a month. He was expected to check in at Walter Reed Medical Center, and when they gave the green light, he and Mrs. Wheaten could go on to Indiana and wait there for Hien and Michael to follow. The doctor was clear, however. There would be no more embassy work. Either Mr. Wheaten took it easy or his heart would not allow him to continue.

Hien could tell the news hurt. Not devastated, but there was pain. The plan was to leave in another month, anyway. Perhaps that was why. But he could not be part of the physical labor on the farm nor handle any stressful parts of the business. That would mean more on Michael's shoulders.

She raised her head in time to spot him rounding the corner, a small pack of Lay's potato chips in each hand. "Grabbed the last bags in the snack machine."

Hien's tummy growled in anticipation as she caught the pack he tossed to her and tore it open. "What about your mother?"

He returned to his place next to her and opened the other bag. "She wasn't hungry. I think she's too keyed up to eat. Bet you can't eat just one." He winked at her.

"I intend to eat the whole bag."

"You don't get it. It's a commercial from the States. A kid comes out and says, 'Bet you can't eat just one,' and the other guy can't stop eating them."

"Oh, okay. There must be much TV there." She munched another chip and could not remember when the snack had tasted so good.

"Most homes have one these days. Sometimes I miss it, a little, but as long as I have the radio for music, I'm fine." He popped three at once in his mouth.

"We owned a television set in Huế. Not too many programming choices, but I have watched television. Tell me more about what is different." Hien wanted to be prepared.

"I'm not sure how to describe it. You are used to living in apartments. We'll have a whole house to ourselves, after Mom and Dad's new one is built. The kitchen will be larger. More appliances." He chewed. "Machinery on the farm will be different. And the crops will be different."

"How? How are they unusual?"

"Well, corn. Like they grow rice here? They grow corn there, everywhere. Lots of corn. And soybeans. Plus, it's a lot less crowded. Especially in the country, but you will notice it most in the city. More cars and fewer bicycles. Even the busy cities feel less packed. In Saigon, there are times it is almost claustrophobic." Michael tipped his bag to his mouth, pouring in the crumbs before wadding it into a ball and tossing it at the trash can at the end of their bench. "Two points." He stood, holding out his hand. "Let's go check on the boss."

Hien shoved her chip bag and notes into her purse and took his hand.

Together, nearly on tiptoe, they entered the minister's room. Michael's mother sat in a chair on the far side, near the window, while his father slept in the hospital bed in the middle of the tiny room. She put her finger to her lips, motioning them to her.

Michael leaned next to his mother and whispered, "Is there anything you need us to do?"

She shook her head.

"Then we're going to grab some sleep. We'll be back in a few hours to relieve you. Plan on heading home to rest then."

His stern face didn't secure a promise. Instead she whispered, "We'll see."

He wagged his finger at her, then kissed her cheek.

Hien kissed her other cheek before she followed him from of the room. They laced their fingers together and ambled through the corridors to the entrance. The embassy car waited. The driver held the rear door while they piled in. This time Michael drew her close. She started to drift with her head on his shoulder. How different this ride was from the one mere hours earlier. They were loving and comfortable again, even if still silent. This was nice, peaceful…

"Hien, baby, we're here." Michael's voice pulled her back.

She opened her eyes. They had stopped moving. Straightening, she yawned and slid toward the open door. The driver held out his hand.

Michael followed, guiding her to the villa. Good thing or she might have seated herself on the walkway and fallen back asleep.

She stayed awake long enough to get out of her clothes and into her nightgown before plopping in bed and curling up with him.

The next thing she knew, sunshine streamed through the window. Hien stretched and realized she was alone. When she sat up, she noticed a note taped to the mirror.

Baby,

Didn't want to wake you. Need to report in at MACV. Be back by noon. We can grab a fast lunch and then go to the hospital.

I love you!

Michael

Noon. What time was it now? Eleven twenty-five?

Hien phoned the Press Corps room to report she would not be in due to a family emergency. They must not get a scoop from her on her father-in-law, so she couched her words but assured them she would phone later to say when she would be back. Since she was freelance, there was no problem. She raced to the shower and into some clothes.

Her work attire would be fitting enough for the hospital. A brown plaid skirt suit with another poor boy top, this one in off-white, was an easy grab. Nylons and two-toned flats, Mary Jane style, finished the ensemble. She thought of adding her dark tan billed cap with the high crown, but that had been a spur-of-the-moment buy. She had yet to find the gumption to wear it. Even though her hair was still wet, she pulled it into a chignon at her nape, and returned the hat to her closet. She had just closed the door when she heard Michael's voice.

"Hey, baby, I'm back. You ready?"

Hien charged out from the bedroom, down the stairs, into his embrace.

He spun her around, as she hoped, then stepped back and whistled. "Yep, you're ready. Pretty snazzy, like Dad would say." The sun shining through the window chose that moment to hide behind a cloud, reflecting the sudden change in Michael's expression.

"He will be okay, Michael. You will see."

He squeezed her again as Hien hoped harder than ever that her words were true.

"That's just it, baby. C'mere." He took her by the hand, leading her to the sofa. "There's a troop buildup in Khe Sanh. The brass is sure that's where the trouble will be, expecting a breach of the upcoming Tet truce. They're moving me up to the field in Da Nang so I can fly interference. Supposedly only for a couple weeks."

The fear that gripped Hien's heart must have glistened in her eyes. Michael squeezed her hands tighter.

"Don't worry. We've been lucky to be so far from the fighting. I fly a sortie during the day, and come home to you at night, like ordinary married people. My buddies are so jealous. It's only fair I take my turn. But right after Tet, you watch. Things will go back to normal. The NVA will realize it is useless to try to grab Khe Sanh. We'll shove them so deep behind the DMZ they'll be worried Hanoi might fall!" He drew her close. "And remember, we have only thirty-five more days until we're Indiana bound. No more war, no more fear, just you, me and cornfields. Okay?"

The way he said *cornfields* made her giggle. She raised her face, and he swiped a tear away before kissing her. A kiss she felt to her toes and back. This was her Michael. Her husband. The man she loved.

"Can you do me a favor?"

Anything. She would do anything for him.

"Would you take care of my mother?" He captured her with his gaze, and she knew what he was asking. At least he was asking, not demanding. "If you are there to relieve her, and listen to her, and help with the translations, I won't have to worry. And I know Dad won't fret as much if he knows she has you, and that will help him heal."

She nodded. "Yes, Michael. They are my family now too. Do not worry. I will take care of your parents." And, with that, it was decided. Her family to tend. Her job to let go. Her husband to wait for and support. Her path had developed another curve, but she would keep walking.

THREE

Tell It Like It Is

____

HIEN STOOD IN THE HOSPITAL CORRIDOR, LISTENING AT the doorway. The words her mother-in-law read floated out to her. There was a vague familiarity, something one of the nuns or priests probably recited while she was in elementary school. Her Catholic schooling had not changed her family's claim of Buddhist faith, though education and social advantages may have subdued the ardor of daily devotion.

"And lead us not into temptation, but deliver us from evil: For thine is the kingdom, and the power, and the glory, forever, Amen. For if ye forgive men their trespasses, your heavenly Father will also forgive you: But if ye forgive not men their trespasses, neither will your Father forgive your trespasses." Mrs. Wheaten raised her head. "Oh, Hien, please come in. Don't wait in the hall." She stood, putting the book on her chair.

Hien crossed the room and hugged the older woman.

"Hey, what's a guy got to do for some attention?"

The grin on her father-in-law's face at once improved her outlook. She planted a kiss on his cheek and patted the hand not hooked to an IV. "You look improved."

"So where is Michael? Didn't he come with you?" Michael's mother chose that moment to check the corridor.

This would be harder than expected. "No, Michael received some news this morning." Hien took a breath while the intensity of their stares tried to steal her air. "They have rotated his team up to Da Nang. He says it is a temporary assignment, just until we are through Tet. He says not to worry, that he will be back to make you crazy before you know it."

Mrs. Wheaten grew pale, but the minister winked. "That sounds like Mike. Don't worry, either of you. He'll return very soon. You wait and see."

"Ernest, might you call someone, and have him reassigned here?"

Hien's hope began an upward arc.

"Now, Mellie, we can't. Mike would be embarrassed if his old man pulled strings. I've pulled enough for him and Charlie without putting them in bad situations. Other people's sons and husbands haven't gotten the same consideration. There's a point where we need to trust."

The hope rocket started its downward projection.

"I know, Ernest, I know. My head understands, but my heart still says that's my baby boy you're talking about." Michael's mother returned to the chair, hugging the book to her, that Bible.

"He's mine, too, though I don't expect he'd appreciate us calling him that. I'm sure Hien prefers to consider him an adult." He winked at her again.

She liked his sense of humor and winked back.

"Oh, you two. You're ganging up on me. Just for that, you can read to him, Hien, while I take a stroll to the restroom." Mrs. Wheaten stood, handed the book to her, and made a point of winking at them both before leaving the room.

Hien sat in the vacated chair. "Where shall I begin?"

"My dear, how about we talk for a bit before you read?"

"Okay." A small piece of panic caused her fingers to twitch, so she folded them on top of the Bible.

"You may not realize this, but I listen. You're still having trouble with what to call us."

Hien nodded, staring at her hands.

"I'm sorry this is hard for you. I've thought about it and can see how calling me by my first name might be uncomfortable. And you have your own father. Then, I remembered about a guy from my hometown, Gibson City. Everyone there, his sons and their friends, called him Pop. How about you call me Pop? Would that work?"

Pop. She chuckled. That she could do. "Yes. Pop. You are now my Pop. Oh, thank you for understanding and for finding a solution!" She squeezed his hand.

"Well, that's half the battle. We need a name for your mother-in-law. I think I might have an answer. Mother-in-law. M I L. If I'm Pop, could she be Mil?"

Hien mulled it a moment. "How does she feel about it?"

"How does who feel about what?" Her MIL was back.

"I suggested that Hien call you Mil. You are her mother-in-law."

It was quiet for too long. Her nerves grew taut. Had she done something disrespectful?

"I think… I think that would be okay. Yes, Mil, I like it! Plus is sounds like how you, Ernest, sometimes call me Mel. Oh, I like it." Mil laughed. Then Pop laughed too. Hien joined them. She had a Pop and Mil. She had a family.

Sometime later, Mil agreed to allow the driver to take her home for a rest. The fact that she agreed made Hien feel all the more trusted, though citing a need for a shower seemed to be her main reason. Would how long Mil stayed away would determine how much she trusted her?

Hien kept the Bible on her lap, ready to read whatever Pop wanted. However, he continued the conversation wanting her to tell more about her life before Michael and the Press Corps and Saigon. He appeared to have a real interest and asked several deep questions, questions that made her go to times long buried.

"Huế is all I knew. My family was not wealthy like those who live in the Citadel by the palace. My parents were thrifty. That is the correct word? We lived in a nice apartment and attended private schools. Education was very important to my father. He believed in a democratic Viet Nam. He'd fought on the side of the French and later taught civics classes at the University in Huế. From an early age, he expected my brother and me to become fluent in French and English. He said if we could communicate well in both of those languages, we could go anywhere in the world and do whatever we wanted, though I am pretty sure he hoped we would stay to help make South Viet Nam into a strong democracy. My brother stayed in Huế. He works at *Mang Ca* as a coordinator with MACV. I guess that is why my mother's note so hurt me. She did not just call me a slur; she cut off all my father tried to build, everything for which my brother and father fought."

"Where is your father now?"

A tear slipped free. "He died when I was at university. I was supposed to spend a semester abroad in Paris, but when he passed, I realized I could not yet leave my mother. Two years later I left for Saigon. I believed my brother would be there for her. I do not believe that now. Why would she have written the note?"

His hand covered hers. "I don't know, Hien. Could your brother have moved to live on base at Mang Ca?"

"That's possible." Something, something struggled to break the surface of her memory. Something... "Bao!"

"What?"

"Bao. My brother's dog. He barked when I went there. Why was Bao there? Where was my brother?" Though Pop's hand-squeeze brought comfort, it did not bring answers. Would she ever have answers?

The nurse entered.

Hien stood with her notepad, ready to record all information.

Pop opened his mouth for the thermometer and lifted his wrist for the nurse to take his pulse. After which, she added the blood pressure cuff to his arm and began pumping the bulb.

Hien wrote each number recited and any comments in regards, though those were few.

"*Le docteur sera de vous voir ce soir.*"

"Merci," Hien said before translating. "The doctor will see you this evening."

Pop nodded and the nurse left.

"Looks like most things are good. You do not have a fever, and your pulse is normal. She said that your blood pressure is somewhat elevated."

"Doc said not to worry about that. Said it was perfectly natural to have high blood pressure at my age."

Hien also heard that, though something did not seem correct. She was not the doctor, however. What did she know?

"While I am up, I shall make a trip to the restroom. I will be right back. No getting up or running around while I am gone. Okay?" She wagged her finger at him.

Pop laughed and promised.

The guest bathroom was downstairs. She took the stairs to the lobby. It was located to the left of the front desk. On her return via the stairs, she glanced out the window. The rain clouds she hoped would hold off until after Tet were gathering.

Familiar faces caught her gaze as Charlie and Lai came through the entrance. "Hien!"

She smiled and greeted them.

"Hey, how's the old man doing? Have you been here all night?"

"He is improving but will need to remain in bed for several more days. And no, Michael and I went home early this morning. I returned after lunch."

Charlie glanced around, "Yeah, where is Mike, by the way?"

The question brought it all back. "He checked in at the field today. He is to be rotated to Da Nang until after Tet."

"I'm sorry." As quiet as Lai was, she was also intuitive. Hien had no doubt she understood.

"That's gonna make my news even harder." Charlie glanced at Lai, who studied the floor tiles. "My copter crew is getting attached to the hospital ship *USNS Sanctuary*. They need us ready to evac any wounded once the fighting there picks up, like they keep telling us it will."

"This is not good timing." She clearly felt her in-laws' pain. "When do you leave?"

"In about three hours, I report to MACV Saigon and head out. We want time together, but Dad's here. We had to stop."

Hien nodded. There was nothing else to say. They climbed the stairs in silence and found their way to Pop's room. At the door, she paused. "You two go in. I will wait here. The room is small and—"

"Nonsense. You're family. Get in here." Charlie gently shoved her through while Lai entwined arms with her.

Still, she retreated to a corner.

Charlie and Lai hugged Pop, putting on smiles and cracking silly one-liners.

"Boy, oh, boy, what a guy's gotta do to get attention from his kids."

"Gee, Dad, if I'd known you were craving my attention, I'd have been here sooner. You shouldn't have gone to all this trouble on my account." Both men chuckled. "Seriously, Dad, what are they saying?"

"You best ask Hien. She takes notes every time the nurse comes in the room. She can show you the data."

All eyes peered in her direction. She pulled out her notepad and read through the basics. "His blood pressure is 160 over 101, his pulse is 65 resting. He has not shown signs of fever. The doctor says that he needs complete bed rest for five to seven days and then at least two weeks of light activity. He will still be in the hospital but may take daily walks to the courtyard. They have discussed moving him to the lower level so he will not have to deal with stairs."

"That's kinda high numbers, right? For blood pressure, I mean. What's the doc say about that?" Both Charlie and Lai shared a glance.

Pop dismissed their concern. "The way the doctor tells it, we older folks are supposed to have higher blood pressure. It's just how life is."

"I think I'd rather get you stable and then off to Walter Reed or Bethesda for some expert opinions."

"Son, Grall Hospital is world renown, especially on the Pacific side. Don't worry. Your old man is in good hands." The smile Pop radiated all but convinced even Hien not to worry, and she held the written data.

"If you say so, Dad. You don't mind if I worry a little, though, hmm?" Charlie sat on the edge of his father's bed. "And, I don't want you to worry, but I need to tell you that I won't be up to see you for a bit."

Pop's expression didn't change, but a light dimmed in his eyes.

"My evac team is getting sent to the *USNS Sanctuary* to be on alert. Shouldn't be gone too long."

"Near Da Nang, is it? Probably need you ready to evac wounded from Khe Sanh." Pop grew quiet.

"You okay, Dad?"

"Yeah, son. Just wondering. Are we putting too much focus on Khe Sanh, and not enough… elsewhere?" Hien caught Pop's glance her way. She knew he was thinking of Huế. That tightened her stomach all the more.

"General Westmoreland seems to think the Tet truce will be broken at Khe Sanh, so he's got the place on high alert."

"I know, I've been cussin' and discussin' this since Christmas. Something in my gut tells me Westy's wrong. That's he's missing something. I just can't find what it is, and without proof, it's only my gut. Look where that's landed me." His laugh lacked humor. "Keep your head down and be alert."

"Cause the world needs more lerts." Charlie grinned.

This time Pop's laugh was genuine.

The men shook hands. Lai slipped in and kissed his cheek.

"Promise you'll stop to see your mother before you leave. I'll catch all sorts of you-know-what if you don't."

"Promise, Dad." Charlie wove his fingers with Lai's, waved to Pop with his other hand, and they left.

The silence made Hien's eardrums pound.

Pop cleared his throat. "Hien, would you mind reading to me for a bit? I think I'd like to hear the twenty-third Psalm."

She scanned in the front of the Bible, locating the table of contents. The chapter called Psalms started on page 610. Once opened to there, she realized what she titled a chapter was labeled as The Book of Psalms, and that every so many paragraphs, there was a subtitle with the word Psalm and a number. She turned pages until she found the psalm numbered twenty-three. "A psalm of David. The Lord is my shepherd; I shall not want. Two He maketh me to lie down in green pastures: he leadeth me beside the still waters. Three He restoreth my—"

"Hien, have you ever read from the Bible?" Pop had a strange expression on his face, as if he was puzzled. Or wanted to laugh.

"No, sir. I understand that a Bible is a special book to Christians. I heard words from it from the nuns in school. But I have never read it. Did I do something wrong?"

"Nothing bad. No, I shouldn't have assumed. When you read, you don't need to say the numbers. They reference the verses in each chapter."

"I thought Psalms was the chapter, but the heading called it a book."

Pop nodded. "The Bible has two parts, called testaments. Each testament has books, each book has chapters, and each chapter has verses. Sounds like a lot, but it makes looking things up easier. At least, once you crack the code." He winked at her.

"Would you like me to go on?"

"Yes, please. Continue."

"I will leave out the numbers and start at… verse? three. He restoreth my soul: he leadeth me in the paths of righteousness for his name's sake." She paused to remember, no numbers. "Yea, though I walk through the valley of the shadow of death, I will fear no evil: for thou art with me; thy rod and thy staff they comfort me. Thou preparest a table before me in the presence of mine enemies: thou anointest my head with oil; my cup runneth over. Surely goodness and mercy shall follow me all the days of my life: and I will dwell in the house of the Lord forever." By the time she was half through, he was reciting with her. When she finished, he leaned deep into his pillow, closed his eyes and sighed.

"Do you understand what you were reading, Hien?"

"Words of comfort for you, but I do not know to what they referred."

"This is an ancient song from Israel's most beloved king, King David. Even though he had been anointed King, he had to fight to take his rightful place. It wasn't easy. There was a king, Saul, who disobeyed God. He lost the right to rule. This king's son, who should become the next king, was David's best friend. King Saul chased David all over the countryside to hunt him down and kill him. David once was in a position to kill Saul but chose not to, saying he could not kill the Lord's anointed. God must make it right. When He did, David became the king. In the meantime, David would fight to protect Israel, and do whatever God required. He would follow God, his shepherd, and trust Him to supply all his needs, knowing God would lift him above his enemies' grasp, and lead him to where God wanted him to be at the perfect time."

"I saw other… psalms that were called a psalm of David. Did he write many?" She thought the poetry lovely.

"Can't remember how many but he wrote several. That's the most familiar, I think."

"These words, they bring you comfort?"

Pop smiled, not a wide grin, but soft, pensive. "Comfort, yes, and peace."

"Peace," she echoed. Some peace would be nice right now.

HIEN CLOSED the leather-clad book and let it lie on her lap. Pop had drifted off. The window's light dimmed, leaving the room in darkening shadow. Since he was asleep, she stopped reading. It was too hard to see now anyway.

Mil must have taken a nap while she was home. She had been gone a few hours.

Hien stood, stretched, and meandered to the window. The view included the courtyard—a courtyard which concealed the city from those in need of respite. However, from her vantage point several feet above, she could see the metropolis lights gleam.

Saigon, the largest city in South Viet Nam, glowed like a crown of jewels in the darkening night. Even though she grew up in the second largest city in South Viet Nam, Huế was aesthetically older, more royal, for lack of a better word. Saigon, on the other hand, was modern, at least where the tourists and camera crews tended to film. There were pockets of cheap, garish nightlife, such as the Jade Pagoda, and there were miles of the poorest of the poor living in refugee villages around the outskirts. These areas sprouted overnight, making Saigon not only one of the biggest, fastest growing cities in the world, land-wise, but one of the most crowded. Hien saw the squalor when she photographed families shoved together into cardboard and tin lean-to shacks, hiding from the elements, praying they picked the right side of the fight. Her latest photos were in those film canisters still in her purse. She had taken them before the wedding, planning to develop them the day she and Mat got sidetracked into a trip to Huế.

Was that only yesterday?

Mil returned, yarn bag over her shoulder. She put her finger to her lips.

Hien tiptoed to her. "He drifted off about twenty minutes ago."

Mil whispered back, "Thank you. Now it's your turn to go."

"Are you certain? I do not mind staying."

Mil kissed her cheek. "I'm positive. He is a captive audience. I finally get his full attention." She winked.

"Anything I can do? Might I bring you something?"

Mil shook her head, aiming her at the door.

"Oh, my purse." Hien grabbed her bag before retreating to the hall. The lights there were much brighter. It took a second for her eyes to adjust.

The driver waited for her.

She appreciated that more than words could express. To walk or catch a cab this time of evening was not a safe idea.

Though hungry, she dreaded being alone at the villa. MiVu was long gone. Not that she needed help to fix a bite, but company would be nice. Company who spoke Vietnamese would be extra nice. But none of that mattered.

The driver let her off. As he helped her from the car, a thought hit. "Please pick me up in an hour?"

He nodded and tipped his cap.

She thanked him and crossed the courtyard to the villa. Mil left the lights on. Again, she was grateful. She dropped her purse on her bed and washed her face. It revived her. Then, in the kitchen, she found leftover pot roast. She heated some rice and cut a cold slice of the meat for dinner before eating and cleaning after herself.

This time, returning upstairs for her purse, she noticed a paper sticking out from the pillow.

My love,

I wish we'd had more time before I left. I want to hold you again. Kiss you goodbye again. Never leave you again. We will be together, soon and then we'll go to Indiana, and we'll be a normal married couple with a never-ending honeymoon. Until then, remember I love you. Carry on, for my parents, for me.

Yours,

Michael

The floor gave way. Hien fell in a heap, sobs choking her breath. She'd held in the fear and pain while with her in-laws. Now, in private, there were no barriers. She let it out. All of it. Until there was no more. Air returned to her lungs.

Then she picked herself up.

She brushed away the tears and left the precious note on the bed while she rewashed her face in the coldest water she could get.

It was time.

～

"WHAT ARE YOU DOING HERE?"

Hien hugged the now-awake Pop before answering. "I realized you must need the car, too. Plus, I must be here to translate. The doctor should be here soon. I am guessing, but I think he will send us both home when he comes, so I can leave with you." She hugged Mil and whispered, "It is lonely there all alone."

Mil smiled. She did not argue. "Do you return to work tomorrow?"

"They understand I will be absent until further notice. I go there to be available and hope they choose me, but I do not have a set schedule. Others will receive their turn to translate now that I am unavailable."

"I see."

"My photographs help get me more jobs. I am a bonus for the smaller media outlets."

Pop and Mil nodded. She realized they had never seen her photographs. They did not understand what she did.

"I brought a deck of Pinochle cards. We could play three-handed. Do you know how to play, Hien?" Mil reached into her bag, pulling out a small box.

She shook her head.

"It's okay, we'll teach you. Could you raise me a tad?" Pop squirmed.

Mil jumped to adjust his pillows, while Hien moved to the foot of the bed to turn the crank. She was careful to only raise his head a small bit.

Mil moved his rolling table over in front of him and began to shuffle.

Hien found an extra chair in the hallway, pulling it next to the other side of Pop's bed, opposite Mil.

Together, Pop and Mil explained the game, finishing each other's sentences. Though this was a fun diversion for both of them, Hien struggled with the point system, the ideas of a meld and a trump.

Mil dealt. The first hand was practice. That way Pop and Mil could demonstrate.

Just as it started to make sense, the doctor entered the room. He peeked at her hand, *tsked*, and shook his head. "I would fold if I were you," he added in a thick French accent.

Mil and Pop laughed as she laid her cards on the tray.

"Maybe next time."

The doctor shook hands with Pop and then reached across to shake hands with Mil. "Minister Wheaten, you appear much better than when I last saw you. How are you feeling?"

"I have no pain. I also don't have a lot of energy, but other than tired, I'm fine."

"That is good." Dr. Baleau nodded, flipping through his clip-board of charts. "I like how you have responded. That is all good. How old are you again, sir?"

"I'll be sixty-four next month."

The doctor tapped his chin. "We will watch your blood pressure. It is still in the safe numbers, barely, so we'll watch. Do you have questions?"

Pop glanced over at Mil and Hien. "Can you convince these two mother hens that it is fine to go back to the embassy? They seemed think I can't handle a night here alone."

"Ah." Dr. Baleau nodded. "Ladies. The visiting hours will end soon. The nurses expect you to leave so they do not worry about you too."

"I won't get in the way," Mil protested, though it was obvious she knew the battle was lost.

"He is in good hands. You need not worry." Something about his accent gave Dr. Baleau more authority, as if his words bounced and bubbled away fear. "I will check in again tomorrow. I believe a few more days here and then we can move you to the first floor where you may begin some small activity." He shook hands with everyone, even Hien, and left.

She caught the glance that passed between her in-laws. "I will wait for you downstairs, Mil. I need to use the restroom." She kissed Pop on the cheek and promised to come read more tomorrow before heading for the stairwell.

Mil entered the lobby moments after she exited the lavatory. "Thank you for that, Hien."

She was uncertain what she did but was glad it was correct.

One more silent ride in the back seat of the embassy car. This time there was no angry strain and no loving ease or sleepy exhaustion. This time deep sorrow tinged the tension swirling about them. She had entered a long tunnel of sadness with no idea how far it stretched before her or how deeply dark the sadness might become before she found some light. She only knew this was a beginning. It would not end right away. And, she was not alone on this sad journey.

Again, at home, she followed Mil into the Mission Coordinator residence, and put her purse in her bedroom. The past forty-eight hours wore on her, so Hien turned in early. But when she pulled out her nightgown, she glimpsed one of Michael's T-shirts sticking out from his drawer. The soft material called to her until she had it wadded in her hands with her face buried into it. His scent took hold of her senses. She was washed in the moment, almost feeling him, almost touching him, almost hearing him. Almost…

She shoved her nightgown back in the drawer and put on the shirt. It fit like a mini dress. She added her robe and went to say goodnight to Mil.

Hien heard her before she saw her. Mil's bedroom door at the end of the hall stood open a crack, but the wracking sobs seeped through. She nudged the door further. Taking a seat on the edge of the bed, she pulled Mil into her arms and held her. As her mother-in-law cried against her shoulder, her own tears dripped onto Mil's back. Did she cry for Mil, or herself, or both? The sadness weighed heavy.

After a bit, Mil calmed and sat back. "Hien, you become dearer to me each day. I'm sorry to burden you."

"It is no bother. I weep too. This is difficult. Plus, we had little sleep last night. We are tired."

Mil cradled her cheek in her hand. Such a simple gesture, but it filled something in Hien's heart.

"Then perhaps we need to call it a night. Sweet dreams, Hien. I think if Michael had not been smart enough to have married you, I would have wanted to adopt you." Mil kissed her forehead.

"I think I would have liked to have been adopted by you. Good night, Mil."

Mil climbed into bed. Hien flipped the light as she left the room. She turned off the lights in the rest of the upstairs and then crawled into her bed and turned off the nightstand lamp.

MORNING CAME EARLY, even without the alarm. The foggy gray light of day brought no cheer, but neither could it dim the hope that somehow she would hear something from her Michael. She would either be here at the villa or at the hospital, so finding her shouldn't be a problem.

Hien hopped out of bed and, after a quick trip to the shower, she pulled on a pair of navy corduroys with little pink flowers and a white button-down shirt. There was a matching corduroy jacket and black penny loafer shoes to complete the ensemble. She brushed her hair, putting it in a braid down her back, out of the way. The thought to wear it long for Michael fleeted through her brain, but her practical side won.

Presentable, she wandered downstairs to see Mil already at the breakfast table. MiVu served tea and toast. "You need more than that to keep up your strength."

"It's all my stomach can handle at the moment. Hien, we need a plan to best use our schedule. I also must speak with Ellsworth to update him on Ernest's condition. He will eventually require a replacement. We must make any transition smooth but not taxing on Ernest. Plus, we mustn't be rushed from here before he can go to the States. I tell you, Hien, it feels like I'm learning to juggle."

"All the more reason to eat something before you start. What type of schedule do we want?" MiVu brought her tea and toast also. Hien realized that was all her stomach could tolerate too.

"What if I begin the morning checking in with the ambassador, and you go to the hospital with Ernest? I'll relieve you for the afternoon so you may get done everything on your list and then meet me there in the evening. We'll come home together."

Hien blew on her tea, mulling the idea. It would give her a chance to contact Mat to see if he learned anything. She nodded. "Yes, that will work. I can be there for the doctor. His English is very good, but I like keeping notes."

While Mil worked on a list—things to discuss with Ambassador Bunker, Hien guessed—she finished her toast and tea and called for the driver.

Within thirty minutes she was back at Pop's room. The nurse arrived five minutes after her. She had the notepad ready.

Pop assured both Hien and the nurse that he felt better. Still there were no changes. Blood pressure, pulse, and temperature remained the same. He was not getting any worse, but should he not be improving somewhere?

Pop informed her he'd had his sponge bath. His damp iron-gray hair was combed.

"Shall we play a card game, or would you like me to read to you?" She reached for the deck of cards, anticipating his answer.

"We can play later. Right now, I'd like you to read Psalm 139. It's another one of King David's. You liked the psalm yesterday, didn't you?"

She nodded and began thumbing through the book to find the section called Psalms. One hundred thirty-nine of them? Was this the last one? No. "Found it. Are you ready?"

Pop leaned back with a smile and closed his eyes. "Ready."

"O lord, thou hast searched me, and known me. Thou knowest my downsitting and mine uprising, thou understandest my thought afar off. Thou compassest my path and my lying down, and art acquainted with all my ways. For there is not a word in my tongue, but, lo, O Lord, thou knowest it altogether." She read about this unseen hand, like a spirit, always there, before and behind and how wonderful the knowledge.

"Whither shall I go from thy spirit? Or whither shall I flee from thy presence? If I ascend up into heaven, thou art there: if I make my bed in hell, behold, thou art there. If I take the wings of the morning, and dwell in the uttermost parts of the sea; Even there shall thy hand lead me, and thy right hand shall hold me." Again, no matter where, the psalmist said the spirit found this man.

"For thou hast possessed my reins: thou hast covered me in my mother's womb. I will praise thee; for I am fearfully and wonderfully made: marvellous are thy works; and that my soul knoweth right well." Even before birth, the psalm writer says he was known to the spirit.

"How precious also are thy thoughts unto me, O God! how great is the sum of them! If I should count them, they are more in number than the sand: when I awake, I am still with thee…"

"Hien, skip down to the twenty-third verse. This says it all."

She slid her finger tracking the page until she found the verse. "Search me, O God, and know my heart: try me, and know my thoughts: And see if there be any wicked way in me, and lead me in the way everlasting."

"That's what I want. For God to search me and know my heart. See if there's anything in there that displeases Him, show me so I can change." Pop's eyes remained closed, but a small tear trickled from the corner.

"Pop, you are one of the kindest men I have ever met. What could your god find bad in you?"

"Kiddo, no one is perfect. All people do things that are wrong. Sometimes it is in their thoughts, and they do not act on them, but if they spend their time dwelling on things that are wrong or selfish or underhanded, then it is as if they actually did it. I have had those thoughts. In fact…" He wiped his eyes and then set his gaze on her. "In fact, I don't think I was supposed to come to Viet Nam. I think Mellie and I were to go into the mission field instead of accepting the appointment to the embassy here."

"Why did you accept?"

Pop picked at the blanket on his bed as if he were picking out his words. "The money was a nice incentive, but I thought if I—we—came and took this position, maybe we could help Mike and Charlie maintain safer postings. I know, sounds a little silly, but I hoped I could pull a few strings here and there to keep them from the real danger. Look where that got me." He shook his head. "And instead of helping those in need, I'm beating my brain against a wall trying to get others to hear me while being polite to people who are steeped in evil machinations, all for diplomacy's sake. Hien, I want you to know something. You're the best gift to come out of this fiasco. You're the one reason I am glad we came."

She stood and planted a kiss on his forehead. "I am glad you came, too, Pop. So glad." This man did not realize he was building a place in her heart. That made his uncertainty of his decision to come to her country quite personal. Where would she be if he had not come? Would Michael have come here? Would they have met? If it were wrong for Pop and Mil to be here, did that make the love she and Michael shared wrong too?

FOUR

Dedicated to the One I Love

B
Y THE TIME MIL GOT THERE, HIEN HAD READ FOUR MORE
psalms, lunch had arrived for Pop, and they'd played three hands
of Spite and Malice. Mil's smile never showed how she had
succumbed to the sadness last night. "Another card game?"

"I think she's a card shark, Mel! I just taught her this, and
she's beat me two out of three." He winked. He did that a lot.

Hien found it enjoyable, though, before meeting the
Wheatens it was not a familiar gesture.

Mil asked for any news.

Hien read to her from the notepad. No one stated the
obvious—no change. No phone calls were mentioned either.

"Now I can leave you in Mil's care. I will return this evening,
Pop." She hugged them both and headed downstairs to where
Mil had left the driver to wait.

Once in the car, Hien's adversity to the lonely villa overwhelmed her intention of waiting for Michael's call. "Please
drive to the Press Corps building." Perhaps Mat might be back
with news from Huế. Besides, she still had the two film canisters
to develop.

"*Bạn có muốn tôi đợi bạn?*"

Hien nodded. "*Vâng làm ơn.*" Yes, she needed him to wait

for her, to help her keep the stop short. Should she develop the film now?

She pushed through the doors to find the place nearly empty. A secretary whose name she had yet to learn filed her nails. The message pad next to her phone lay covered in doodles. Slow day for sure. "Do you know if Mat Morrissey is here today?"

She shook her head and shrugged. Obviously just filling in for the moment.

Hien headed back to her desk and ran into Steve Riley on the way.

"Hien, I heard you were taking more time off. Things okay at home?"

She and Mil had discussed whether to let the press in on Pop's heart attack. He was less visual to the media than Ambassador Bunker. Most would not miss him unless a story got out. Then it would be news.

She peered at her colleague—the one who stood up for her —and weighed what she truthfully could tell him. "It is just that both Michael and Charlie's groups were called up for Tet, so my in-laws have asked for my help." All of which was true. Yet the words felt deceitful.

Steve captured her gaze. "Hien, I know where the minister is. I know about" –his voice dropped to a whisper— "the heart attack."

"Oh." Her cheeks flamed, and her integrity plummeted. "My in-laws do not want the information leaked."

"How bad is it?"

"Steve, I cannot talk about it. I am sorry." And she was.

"Hey, I get it. I mean, it's where we are. But you're like a little sister around here, and I worry about you." He gave her a playful punch on the arm.

"Thank you. One can never have too many big brothers. As long as they really care." She winked, a habit she was picking up from her new family.

"Oh, I do, I do! And when you are ready for an exclusive, we will talk, right?" He winked back.

She chuckled and turned to leave. "Oh, Steve, have you seen Mat?"

"No, haven't seen him since he chased me out of the dark room the other day. What's up?"

"I had a question. He was to check on it…" She trailed off before she had to tell her friend there was another thing she could not share. Instead she hurried off to her desk. Nothing there she required, but she needed to appear busy until Steve moved on. He watched for a moment, but finally went upstairs. She grabbed a canister of new film from its hiding place, stuffed it in her purse, and scurried out to the driver before she ran into anyone else.

The driver apparently spotted her speedy exit and hopped to get her door.

"*Lái về nhà, vui lòng.*" She was ready to go home now.

He drove her through the Mac Dinh Chi street entrance and let her out in front of the villa. The door was unlocked. MiVu ran the vacuum. Glancing up from her work, she asked Hien if she wanted lunch.

Hien checked her watch. One-thirty. She nodded. If nothing else, it gave her something to do. After putting her purse in her bedroom, she came back and found MiVu in the kitchen. She knew they trained the young girl to fix a more American diet for the family—Mil probably ate a sandwich and a bowl of soup—but she prepared excellent Vietnamese dishes. "*Có phở nào còn lại trong tủ lạnh không? Hoặc có thể một vài cuộn mùa xuân sẽ làm.*" The *phở* she made the other day was amazing, and her spring rolls were the best Hien ever tasted. Either would make a great lunch.

It felt good to speak in her mother tongue. Familiar, as though back in her own world. Yet anymore, her English flowed like second nature. She even dreamed in English at times, a sure sign it was part of her. Funny, Michael attempted no Vietnamese words. Oh, he knew what it meant when someone said *beaucoup*, but that was actually a French word the Vietnamese used. Between the French influence still fresh in the country and the fact that many of the soldiers and civilians coming from the States learned to *parle français* a little as an additional language in school, French helped with communication.

Rather than bother MiVu, Hien took a seat at the table and pulled out her note pad. Her intent was to reread her notes, though she could not say why. But it made her think of Pop and his sad confession. She thought him a good man. That he turned to his faith in this hour made sense. Even she found comfort in the beautiful poetry. It gave the impression that there was something beyond this moment, something stronger and greater and wiser.

MiVu served a bowl of phở and one spring roll on a plate with tiny shrimp peeking through the translucent wrapping and hoisin sauce on the side. It appeared lonely, like her. It also looked tasty, and she hesitated no longer in devouring every delectable bite before slurping down the savory soup. The familiar taken to a higher level. That, too, was a comfort. Perhaps the girl would share her recipes.

The phone rang.

MiVu reached it before her. "*Oui*, yes, she here." MiVu held the receiver out to her.

Hien snatched it from the girl's hand quicker than she intended. She owed MiVu an apology. "Hello?"

"Baby, I only have a minute on this trunk line. How's Dad doing?"

Michael. "He is well. He taught me to play a card game, Spit and Malice."

He chuckled. "Spite and Malice. Oh, watch out for him, he's a card shark."

"That is what he called me to your mother. How are you? I miss you so much!"

"I miss you, too, baby. It won't be long. Hey, I—"

"Michael? Michael?" She repeatedly pushed the switch hook and eventually the embassy operator came on the line. Another apology to make. She hung up the phone and ran upstairs. The apology to MiVu would have to wait until she could stop crying.

HER SELF-PITY WAS GROWING OBNOXIOUS. Lots of women had their husbands and sons and brothers here. Very few were as lucky as she. Look where she lived. And her husband would only be away a couple weeks. Others said goodbye to loved ones for a year at a time.

Some said goodbye forever.

No, she must not wallow. She would go downstairs and apologize to MiVu for her rudeness. Plus, she had a moment to return to the Press Corps and develop her photos before she went to the hospital.

The phone rang as she reached the bottom step.

This time she got to it first. "Hello?"

"May I speak with Hien Wheaten?" *Mat.*

"This is she, Mat. I'm so glad you called. Where are you?"

Background noise made the connection difficult, but she caught that he was still in Huế; sounded like "at MACV."

"Listen, Hien, I still have no answers. But something is going on. Can you talk with your father-in-law?"

"He is away from the compound now, but I will mention it when I see him." It was the best she could do.

"Okay. Gotta run. Later." And he was gone.

HER DRIVER PICKED her up by the courtyard. Hien silently rode from the compound until she could take no more. This is stupid. "*Hôm nay bạn thế nào?*" She could at least inquire about his day.

"*Tốt.*" Good. Short. To the point.

What else might she ask? Where all had he driven today? That sounded nosey. Did he have a family? Too personal. Does he enjoy driving? "*Bạn có thích lái xe không?*"

"*Vâng.*" Yes. Without embellishment.

Maybe she should ask his name. She would give him hers. "*Tôi tên là Hien. Tên của bạn là gì?*"

"Minh."

So, her driver, named Minh, was having a good day at a job he likes. It seemed like manual labor pulling that information from him, but now he was less a stranger.

They pulled up to the Press Corps office. He opened the door for her.

As she put her hand in his, she smiled and thanked him. "*Cảm ơn, Minh.*"

"*Bạn được chào đón, bà Wheaten.*"

She felt her smile fade. More words than he uttered the whole ride over, but the formality of his "You are welcome, Mrs. Wheaten" was not lost on her. She told him to pick her up in an hour and scooted inside.

Someone else manned the front desk, more efficiently, Hien noted. The new girl was on the phone, so she slipped past, unnoticed, and hustled to the darkroom. This time no one waited. It was empty. She barricaded herself in without signing up for the spot and got busy.

She had two rolls to develop. Some might be worth selling. That hope kept her going as she popped open the container, placed the film on the spool, and poured the developer into a shallow pan. She put her aggressions into agitating the spool before pouring out the chemicals and rinsing the film. Next the stop bath, wait and rinse. Then the fixer, wait and rinse. She could do it in the dark. At home she had no safe light. But here, the red glow made it less of a challenge. Plus, the tools were not so makeshift as at home.

Once the strip was fixed and wiped with alcohol, she studied the negatives in the light. A few were worth developing. She cut them apart and placed them, emulsion side down, in the enlarger. This equipment was so familiar, the extra test strips were unnecessary. She began processing the paper into photos and soon had six or seven that might be worth selling.

There were a couple shots of Michael taken a day after their wedding. They had gone to the beach. Despite being January, the water was not too cold. Rather than swim, they slipped out of their shoes and wandered next to the surf. At one point, he dropped to his knees and began scooping sand with an old discarded C-ration can. He packed it and then released it in tight cylindrical forms, designing a sandcastle for her. Hien searched for shells and twigs to add. Once completed, she pulled out her ever-ready camera. Michael posed.

Now she cried.

Funny, he was aware she took photographs. He saw her with her camera. That was what she was doing when they met. But he'd never seen her photos. Not one. Nor did he ask to see any.

What did he really know about her? How much did she know about him? How had they gotten to this point?

Their romance was swift. He swept her off her feet with flowers sent to work and limousine rides in embassy cars to dinner and dancing. He made it easy to be swept off her feet.

She fell so in love, she never wondered where she was headed.

That was how she ended up here.

But where was here?

She gathered her photos and negatives and bolted, hoping with all her heart she would spot no one she knew. Her hand reached for the front door when she heard her name.

Nick Jones called.

And he stopped.

He smelled a story from ten miles away.

Once, Hien went to the movies with her brother to see a Disney picture, *The Fox and the Hound.* That movie rushed back as Nick decrease the space between them. She was the fox and this bloodhound reporter wanted to tree her.

"So sorry, Nick. I am in a hurry. My chauffeur is waiting." She shoved her way out and ran for the car.

Minh must have seen her because he had the door opened and closed after her before Nick came close. Her driver might not be the greatest conversationalist, but he came through right then.

She was grateful. The expression on Nick's face as he watched his quarry escape would stay with her awhile. At some point, she knew, she would pay for that.

The urge to giggle came on so sudden, it shocked her. But she could not hold it. The sound started as a funny breath and ended up a geyser of noise. She snorted and hid her face, though she could not stop. Peeking through her fingers, she noted that even Minh cracked a smile.

"*Cảm ơn, Minh.*" She had to thank him. He saved her from an excruciating grilling.

"Please, speak English."

She caught his glance in the rearview mirror. "Okay, why?"

"I need help. My English little. Practice with you."

Hien smiled. "I will help you. You helped me. But occasionally could we speak in Vietnamese? Some days all I ever hear is English or French. I miss hearing our language."

Minh's smile grew.

Ten minutes, and some corrected English later, Minh pulled up at the hospital. Hien thanked him, in both languages, and made arrangements for him to take her and Mil home. She climbed the stairs to Pop's room. He napped while Mil crocheted in the armchair next to the bed.

Mil put her finger to her lips, set her project on the seat and came to the doorway, guiding her into the hall before embracing her. It took a moment before Hien realized she was crying.

"What is wrong?" Hien whispered.

"He's sleeping now, but before," Mil paused, pulled back, and wiped her eyes. "Before he fell asleep, he was so depressed. He spoke about us wasting our time here and how futile this whole thing is. He says he feels useless and chained, that he wants to go home, but I don't think he means Indiana." Mil shoved her handkerchief to her nose and shook her head. "I'm scared for him, Hien."

Hien pulled her back into the embrace but had no words. What could she say? Her own feelings matched those of Mil's. She sensed this when Pop shared about second guessing his post acceptance. Everything in her wanted to fix the problem. But how?

Mil drew away again. "Let me go pull myself together. You will sit with him?"

"Of course."

Mil patted her arm and headed down the hallway.

Hien noticed how her shoulders slumped, the perfect posture buckling to the weight of dark sadness, which only grew heavier. She watched a moment before returning.

Pop's eyes were open. He was aware. "Got her upset, did I?"

She nodded, not yet ready to trust her voice, and moved closer to the bed.

"I'm glad you are there for her. With the boys off doing war stuff and me lying around in here, it's no wonder she's having a moment."

"It is more than a moment. She is concerned for you, and not just the heart attack." The words were out of her mouth before she reconsidered them.

Pop chuckled, dry and mirthless. "I know."

The silence in the room became too heavy for Hien. She broke it with her first thought. "Please, tell me about Indiana."

This time the chuckle had a smile. "Indiana is Mellie's old

stomping ground. I was raised a little west of there, close to Bloomington, Illinois. But it's all the Midwest. Farmland, fields going on forever. Corn, soybean. Good farm country."

"Michael says I will like it, but it will be different."

Pop straightened in the bed, sitting taller. "He's right. It will be different for you. Did he tell you about the farm and the surprise?"

She nodded.

"Then while you are here and Mel is out of the room, I better have you sign this." He pulled a small group of folded papers from his Bible. "Do you have a pen?"

She dug in her purse. "Yes." Victory. It was rare she could find one that fast. She held it aloft.

"Okay, sign on the line here." He pointed to the spot. The papers appeared official. "We can get Michael's signature when he returns. This will make it all legal. I'll keep it in my Bible until then."

She signed where he showed.

He refolded the document, putting it back. "Just remember—"

"Just remember what?" Mil stood in the doorway.

"Look both ways when crossing the street." Pop's wink brought a smile to Mil's face though it was obvious she was not convinced of his truth.

"Right. After living in Saigon, Hien needs a reminder about crossing streets? Next you'll be explaining about jaywalking." She winked back.

"Well, now, that is something to discuss. No one thinks a thing about jaywalking here, but in Indiana, by George, you could get a ticket for it."

"Jaywalking? A ticket? What do you mean?" The confusion made Hien's brain spin.

"Jaywalking is where one crosses the street, but not at the corner, or crosses catty-corner, or not in the provided cross walk.

Small towns are pretty strict about that. You don't want to get caught, that's for sure."

Hien stared at Pop's face, searching. She watched his eyes twinkle and relaxed as the corners of his mouth twitched. Finally, they all laughed together. "You are teasing me."

"Oh, no," Mil added. "It's a real thing, and there have been tickets written for it, but it's nothing for which you need worry."

"There is much to learn about Indiana. I do not know whether to be excited or worried or scared."

Pop patted her hand.

"No need to fear, Hien. We are here for you. Along with Michael, we will make this a wonderful experience." Mil draped her arm about her and gave her a little squeeze.

Just then the doctor arrived. She dug in her purse to grab the note pad and moved out of the way. No changes to blood pressure or pulse rate. O2 stats still required the same level of oxygen. A low-grade fever was noted to watch, but Doctor Baleau stated he was not overly concerned.

"I think we can try moving you to the first floor and adding brief moments of walking by the end of the week."

She watched an unspoken message pass between Mil and Pop with just a glance. She could only guess the message, but doubted it was positive.

The doctor left, so they played two hands of Pinochle before the nurse came to shoo the women homeward. Hien kissed Pop goodnight and made her way downstairs.

It gave her a chance to wonder if she and Michael might get to that point, the point where they communicated with a glance, understanding and being understood all at the same time. How long did it take Mil and Pop? Or had they always done that? She thought of her parents. They had that same communication, but it generally took the form of her mother sending a warning glance that her father was spoiling Hien and needed to stop. Her mother never wanted her to leave Huế. Her father fueled her dreams of seeing the world. That was why she stayed those two years and why she finally left, though it hurt her mother. The thought she might never see *mẹ ơi* again flitted through her imaginings, but she shook it away before she could dwell on it and fuel her tears. Enough sadness enveloped her life without adding more.

Mil arrived downstairs and Minh waited at the curb to return them to the embassy.

The phone rang as Mil unlocked the front door.

Hien ran to answer and then realized Mil hurried for it too. She held back and let her mother-in-law reach it first.

"Mission Coordinator's residence." Mil turned toward her. "Yes! Yes, Michael! We just walked in. How are you?" He must have said something, she paused. "He is doing well. We all are. I love you. Hien is right here. Good to hear your voice, sweetie. Now here's Hien." Mil handed over the receiver.

Her hands shook as she put it to her ear. "Michael?"

"Hey baby. How's my girl?" Despite the static, he was clearer than the last call.

"Lonely and missing you, but I am well. Are you okay? When can you come home?" Her arms ached for him.

"I'm good. Still bored out of my mind. No change of plans yet. If everyone keeps the truce, I should be back pretty quick after Tet. Hey, tell me the truth, how's the old man doing?"

Hien checked to make sure Mil continued upstairs. She lowered her voice anyway. She did not wish to worry Michael nor keep things from him. And she did not want Mil's disapproval for saying too much. "Things are the same. The doctor arrived before we left this evening. He plans to move him downstairs by the end of the week. Everything is still on schedule." All true with no worrisome facts included.

"That's good, baby. Hey, tell Mom I ran into Charlie this morning. He had to pick up supplies in Da Nang, and I saw him for about two minutes. She'll appreciate that." She heard him yawn.

"I will. Are you getting enough sleep, Michael?"

"Yeah, too much. Little else to do. I wait, fly a sortie, wait some more. Easy to nap in the down time. I'd go to the beach for a swim, but it's still a bit cool. But when I'm sleeping, I'm dreaming of you, baby. I miss you."

"I miss you too. I will be here when you return."

"Better go. They get mean when we tie up the line too long. I'll call again soon."

"I love you."

"Yeah, me too." The line went dead.

Hien stared at the receiver in her hand, willing it to again produce Michael's voice. Finally, reality emerged. She hung up and made her way to her bedroom. His T-shirt awaited. She decided to give Mil the message about Charlie in the morning. Instead, she crawled under the covers and punched her pillow. She was in no mood for anything but sleep and sweet dreams of Michael.

She had drifted off when the knock at her door roused her.

Mil peeked in around the jamb. "Hien, I'm sorry. I didn't realize you had already gone to bed."

Hien propped herself up on her elbow. "It is okay. What do you need?"

"I just wondered if you would like to keep the schedule as we had it today."

"That is fine for me. Oh, Michael gave me a message for you. I planned to tell you at breakfast. He saw Charlie this morning."

Mil stepped into the room. "He did? Where? Is he okay? What happened?"

"Mil, it is good. Nothing bad. Charlie needed to pick up supplies in Da Nang, and Michael talked with him for about two minutes, he said. He wanted you to know."

Mil nodded her head. "I see. Yes, okay. I'm glad the boys saw each other." She paused. "Hien, you might not know this, but when they were growing up, we moved a lot because of Ernest's job. They wound up being each other's best friend. Oh, I know that brothers fight and carry on. Mine did their share of that, but they are close, even when they want to be independent and individual. I mean, Charlie attended the Naval Academy in Annapolis, so Michael chose the Air Force Academy. Yet both ended up flying. Neither would do the army thing like their father." Mil sat on the edge of the bed. "They are good boys, Hien, well, men, young men. I guess they will always be my babies." She smiled and wiped her eyes.

Hien sat and squeezed Mil's hand. "I hope I can be as good a mother as you."

Mil squeezed back. "You will, Hien. I know you will. And, I'll tell you a secret. Ernest and I have dreamed of being grandparents. We cannot wait to hold your beautiful babies. Now, get some sleep. Until the morning, sweet dreams." Mil kissed her fingers then placed them on Hien's forehead before exiting the room, pulling the door closed behind her.

Babies. It was still too soon to start planning for that, but a little dreaming about them, along with being back in Michael's arms, would be the very definition of sweet dreams. Hien closed her eyes and cuddled her pillow.

FIVE

The Letter

THE REST OF THE WEEK FELL INTO A ROUTINE. MIL STAYED at the villa to do what she needed to do. Hien would go to the hospital and record whatever the doctor or nursing staff said about Pop's condition. Nothing ever changed. Even the low-grade fever remained a hair's breadth below 100°. Pop was holding his own, as Mil put it. Even Michael used that expression, only he spoke of his own attitude about being away and of how things progressed in Da Nang. He phoned once a day, which was better than not hearing from him, but it also left Hien crushed with an aching loneliness.

Friday arrived. Mil decided to go to the hospital with Hien in the morning. She planned to be there when they moved Pop. Hien offered to trade times, but was glad Mil said he needed both of them.

The doctor had yet to stop by when they arrived. There was a possibility he might veto the move until next week. If Pop needed to wait, they would wait. But it would be a blow. Pop needed to believe he would get better. Which explained the nervous energy in the air as Mil paced and Pop picked at his breakfast. Even Hien wanted to speed walk the hallway until fatigue forced her into an exhaustive peace. Instead, she stared out the window, framing photographs in her mind.

"Good morning, Wheaten family." The smiling doctor beamed from the doorway. It was as if he ushered hope into the room.

"Doctor, are we still on track to have Ernest moved downstairs?"

Hien nodded, thankful that Mil asked the words bouncing inside her own head.

The doctor pulled his glasses from his forehead onto his nose and scanned the clipboard notes. "What does our patient think?"

Pop grumbled. "Our patient thinks he needs out of this joint, and the sooner the better. Our patient is a wee bit out of patience."

Dr. Baleau chuckled. "I can imagine. However, since I cannot release you for home, I will give you the next best thing, a change of venue. Oui, Mrs. Wheaten, we are moving our patient to the ground floor, so he may take advantage of our courtyard for some brief and easy activity."

"Wonderful. What do we need to do?"

The doctor glanced about. Handmade cards and drawings were taped on the closet doors. A deck of cards sat on the night-stand. "It appears you have little to pack, but that is all. I will put in the order to move. An orderly should arrive in an hour or so to move you, Minister Wheaten, to your new room. Then you two Mrs. Wheatens may follow with his personal things." He paused and smiled. "We are not out of the woods, as you Americans say, but we are closer to the clearing. It depends on how your strength returns. You might say goodbye to this place in a couple of weeks. Now let me get this paperwork processed so I can get you moving." After shaking hands with both Pop and Mil, Dr. Baleau left.

Without another word, Mil and Hien carefully removed the "gifts" from Lai's preschool students. She brought them last evening. The children's artwork brightened the room. With Pop's stay in the next room being longer, the artwork would need to work its magic there as well.

Five minutes later, all of Pop's personal items were packed and ready to go. Hien's glance roved the room. Now what?

"Did you pack those cards, Mel? I'm feeling lucky." Pop chuckled as he got the last of his breakfast things onto the tray. "Would you set this out for me, Hien?"

"But of course." She grabbed the tray and took it into the hall. A matron who pushed a cart down the hall agreed to get the breakfast tray where it belonged. After handing it off, Hien returned to the room.

Mil had Pop leaning over the bed table while she fluffed his pillows. She helped him lean back, raised the head of his bed with the crank and then took a tissue to wipe the bed table. "Looks like we're ready."

"Well pull up your chairs and be prepared to get whupped." Pop winked, and the games began.

After his second win, Pop chortled. "I told you I felt lucky." After the fifth win, the orderly arrived, putting Hien and Mil out of their misery.

Mil's whispered "about time" was as much for Pop being moved as it was for having a Pinochle reprieve.

The orderly explained, in Vietnamese to Hien, that the women must go downstairs. They could meet him at the new room, 135. He would take Pop down in the staff elevator, but he had no permission to take them.

Hien translated to Mil, who was not pleased. Instead, Hien watched her mother-in-law tip her chin a tad higher and head for the stairs. Hien followed.

Room 135 was almost directly under Pop's former room. However, this one was larger. The designers had planned it for two people but, probably because of Pop's status, it was empty except for the bed table, two nightstands, and two chairs. Hien checked out the view. The window looked onto the courtyard.

Hedges blocked the view of the city. Now she gazed out on a peaceful garden with a French influence. The orderly, with Pop and his bed in-tow, arrived several minutes after Mil and Hien. They had waited for the elevator and then held it for someone who was in conversation with another someone while holding the elevator door open.

Hien could not help it. Pop appeared about to pop. She stifled her giggle as she imagined a cartoonish face growing like a balloon. Sometimes it became silly in her head.

"I tell you, if I hadn't been laid out flat on my back, I'd have given that guy a knuckle sandwich."

"I'm sure you would have, Ernest." Mil's voice placated. She patted his non-IV'ed hand.

"Well, I would have." Half the bluster disintegrated.

"I know, I believe you. Remember, I've seen you in action." Mil patted his hand once more and gave it a squeeze. "Hien and I will put your pictures on the walls. This room will feel homier. You'll see."

"Sure, you're right. Okay." The bluster was gone, like the last air from a leaky balloon.

It took longer to tape up the children's work. Mil often asked Hien to hold a piece while she stood back to see about the placement. Finally, they finished, and Mil was right. The room felt… What was that word? Homier.

One picture stood out. A child traced his, or her, hand and drew a heart in the middle. There was something tenacious about it, the heart drawn so boldly and strong. Even in a child's hand, it signified endurance, strength. She imagined the child handing Pop the heart, filled with hope and peace. It made Hien think about the Bible passages she read to Pop over the last few days. Those words strengthened his heart, she knew, and gave him those gifts.

"Now that we have you settled, why don't you take a nap, Ernest? Hien, you can go do what you choose. I'll stay here and work on my afghan. Perhaps after lunch you can have your first venture outside." Mil seated herself and pulled out her yarn as if her words settled everything.

"I will go, if you are sure." Hien hesitated, but no one suggested another plan. She kissed Pop on the cheek, waved to Mil, and left the room.

They sent the embassy car home when they got to the hospital that morning, so Hien called for a driver. Minh arrived ten minutes later. Even after ten minutes, Hien still had no decision. Where should she go? So, she returned to the villa.

The ride back allowed Hien time to help Minh with his English. They held a polite conversation about weather. Then Hien pushed and asked about his family.

Minh paused. "I have boy one, girl one. Girl baby. Boy have two year."

"That is wonderful. You have a nice family, one boy and one baby girl. What are their names?"

"Names Chinh Chi and Chau Binh."

In English, his son would be a righteous man with a purpose and his daughter like a peaceful pearl. Hien loved the way her native language gave such a visually emotional element to names. "How lovely. What is your wife's name?"

"My wife she Bian Cuc."

Chrysanthemum woman with secrets. That was a picture. "How long have you been married?"

"Three year."

Three years. How would her life change in three years? Surely, she and Michael would be in Indiana. Would they have children? Would they still love each other?

Minh pulled through the Mac Dinh Chi gate to the walkway. "Thank you for speak English with me."

"Không có chi." She was happy to. It made the ride far more pleasant. Minh seemed like a nice person.

She made arrangements for him to pick her up again at four o'clock and waved before unlocking the villa door.

He returned the wave, more of a salute.

It was a small gesture, but it gave Hien hope that goodness and civility existed in a place where most people only offered caution. Even at work, despite friendly acquaintances, she erred on caution's side. Whether due to professional competition or her new family's status, caution was the maze through which she funneled every word.

That thought led to the return of a strange longing, a longing for a female friend. Part of her hoped she and Lai might become good friends. She never had a sister. Once, when she was eight, she begged her parents for one, to no avail. Now she had a sister, at least sister-in-law, but she hardly knew her.

And whose fault was it?

Not the time to search for blame. Hien raced upstairs to see if she could find Lai's number. She was sure she wrote it in a little booklet she kept in her dresser. Lai would still probably be at school, but maybe she would be free for lunch. The school was close enough that Hien could walk to meet her. She flipped through the pages until she found it. There were two; one for the little apartment where Lai, and Charlie, when possible, lived, and one for the school.

Downstairs, Hien dialed the school and asked what time Mrs. Wheaten might have lunch. They informed her the teacher would eat with her children in twenty minutes. So much for that idea. She offered her thanks and replaced the receiver.

Disappointment trickled in, trying to drown the earlier bit of elation. But the truth was Lai had no idea she wanted to meet for lunch. The idea just occurred to her. Before she went back to the hospital, she might try calling the apartment. Reaching out and building a relationship with Lai was a good idea. But Hien was sure in her heart that it must start on her end.

Before racing back up the stairs, Hien checked in with MiVu to see if she might have some lunch ready.

She did. A western-style fried sandwich—there was melted cheese between the toasted pieces of bread—with a bowl of soup from one of the cans of American food in the pantry.

Hien knew she needed to get her tongue used to a different diet, so she smiled and thanked MiVu before taking her seat at the table. She had to admit, the aroma was delicious. Trying the sandwich first, she found the bread had been toasted in butter, and the melty cheese wanted to ooze a little. Cheese was not common to her pattern of eating, but it was gooey and yummy and just a tiny bit salty. She wanted to dunk it into the soup, which smelled of tomatoes, like Michael taught her to do with toast and hot chocolate. A quick glance around proved MiVu was nowhere close, so she picked up the sandwich wedge and gave it a quick dip in the soup before biting off another piece. Oh! Her taste buds did a happy dance all over her tongue. What wonderful culinary inventions from the Americans. MiVu must teach her to make this.

Five minutes later, Hien debated whether she should lick the plate and bowl clean when the phone rang. She jumped from her chair so fast, she knocked it over. No matter. It would still be there. First, she must know if Michael called.

Hien grabbed the phone while her heart paused in her chest. "The Mission Coordinator's residence."

"Hien, baby, glad you answered."

Her heart danced. "Michael!"

"How's it going? Any news?"

She took a breath, hoping to lower her voice from a squeak. "We moved your father downstairs today. Pop's new room is the same location, just ground floor. He is supposed to get his first trip to the courtyard this afternoon. Your mother is with him now."

"That's great news, baby! Oh, before I forget, I'm trying to get someone to bring something to you. Should be—" Silence.

"Michael?" She plunged the switch hook button again and again. Nothing but a dial tone.

He had called her. She could hang on to that, even if she was learning to hate the trunk lines that disconnected at the worst times. And he was sending something to her. What? She could not imagine.

When she returned to the dining room, Hien found her chair already back in place and her dishes gone. Her cheeks warmed to think how much worse it could have been if she had tried licking the plate and bowl. A tiny giggle escaped.

"Thank you, MiVu," she called, before heading back upstairs.

The photos she developed the other day were on her nightstand. She sorted them between personal ones and those she could offer for sale. The one of Michael posing with the sandcastle called to her. A moment later she tracked down MiVu to ask for some cellophane tape. With the dispenser in hand, she returned to her room and held out the photo of Michael, testing where it might work best. Finally, she taped it to the mirror over the vanity. She could spot him from anywhere in the room. He grinned good morning and good night. It brought him closer. She wiped a tear from her cheek.

That done, she sorted through the more professional photos, deciding on two with possibilities. One viewed a long line of makeshift shanties on a muddy, rutted road. Two little boys, in only ragged pants, played with a piece of bamboo and rocks. Their hair was flat to their heads, wet from the winter rainwater, and mud splattered their thin bodies and bare feet. Still, they played.

The second photo depicted a man leaning against a tall box, just out of the rain. His shirt was worn and dirty. He held a cigarette near his face as he stared at the world. Hien adjusted the angle of his profile so one could read his eyes, or rather his eye. There was no hope in that eye. There was no hope in his stance. He existed, without care, while she snapped a shot. She sensed his hopelessness.

How awful to be devoid of hope, of caring, of living. How had he come to this? She could only imagine, and once she started, she did not want to anymore.

These were the best of the lot. These were the ones to sell.

She put the others away and placed these two in a large manila envelope before checking her watch. If she called Minh now, she would have time.

Fifteen minutes later, she was back at the Press Corps. She checked at the front desk to see who might be available as Nick Jones rounded the corner.

"Hien, you've been ducking me. We need to talk."

Hien's insides cringed. "Oh, hello, Nick."

"Word has it that your father-in-law had a massive heart attack and is wavering between life and death. What do you say to that?" He blocked any escape. His gaze locked hers, daring her to blink first.

"I am sorry, Nick, but my personal life is that. I do not bring my family to my job. Where did you get such a story?" *Please let the question catch him off-guard.*

"Now, you know I cannot reveal my sources. How about getting me an interview with the minister?"

She sighed. "I will get back to you after I check."

"But you will check, right?"

"Oh, I will check." She nodded as if her head might wobble off her neck until he finally unblocked her path.

"You'll get back to me?"

"I will check."

She could not tell if he believed that she would keep her word, but at least he moved away.

Time ran out to speak with anyone. She needed to return to the hospital before Nick decided to follow her.

Minh saw her coming and opened the door. She did not explain in English. Instead, she used Vietnamese to say she needed to get to Grall right away.

He broke his record.

After Hien caught her breath, she thanked him and hurried to Pop's room.

Mil must have noticed the expression on Hien's face, because she met her at the doorway.

Hien pulled her aside. "Mil, can we get a guard for Pop's room? I think he will need one to keep journalists away."

To Hien's surprise and relief, Mil did not act upset. She tapped her chin a moment and then went to the nurses' station. Seconds later she was using the phone. The call was brief, and Mil returned with a smile. "All taken care of."

"What did you do?"

"I called Ellsworth. He will make arrangements."

An hour later, a marine knocked at the doorframe and introduced himself. Private First-Class Jonathan Zorich stationed himself outside the room's entrance. Hien relaxed. Nick might not like the answer, but she checked.

Mil made a list of approved visitors and named the official medical personnel allowed to see Pop before stepping out of the room to go over it with the PFC. By then, Pop was awake, so Hien brought him up to date.

"Nick means well, but he is like a dog after a bone when he gets an idea there is a story. It is a little overwhelming."

Pop squeezed her hand and gave her a wan smile. "Guess I'm making waves for you at work, huh?"

"Oh, no. This is not your fault. I am so sorry to bring this on you. If I did not go to the Press Corps, they could not do this." Shame flooded through her, though her brain argued. Maybe it was guilt from association as it was her colleagues who tried to invade her family's privacy.

Though she attempted to pull her hand back, Pop held on. "Hien, kiddo, it's not your fault either. It comes with the territory."

"Territory? I do not understand." How was land a concern?

"I mean that because of my job, my position here with the embassy, it's to be expected that news reporters would try to find out what happened and whether I'm fit to keep working." He released her hand only to wipe a tear from her face. "You have done nothing wrong, my child."

My child. And in that moment, she loved him like her own father.

Mil reentered the room, closing the door behind her. "How about a game of Pinochle? Where did we put those cards?"

MIL CALLED for the car to come earlier than usual. Pop was exhausted after the move and his first outing to the courtyard—his first and uneventful outing, thank goodness. She also made arrangements with MiVu to have a dinner for the two of them set. The best idea Hien had heard all day. Besides, she still wanted to talk to MiVu about teaching her a few recipes.

Dinner was ready to serve as they walked in the door. Hien could tell. The scent wafting its delicious greeting caused Hien's stomach to rumble in anticipation. It involved chicken, of that she was sure, but other smells harmonized into an unfamiliar medley.

"Chicken Cacciatore over rice. I thought we might appreciate some comfort food today." Mil explained while Hien sat and breathed in the heavenly aroma.

"If this is American comfort food, I will love eating in America."

Mil laughed. "This is Italian-American comfort food. I have a great aunt on my mother's side who came over from Italy and shared her recipes, much to my family's appreciation, I must add." She smiled. "MiVu has learned to read my chicken scratches in my recipe box and does a wonderful job with them."

"I thought they were her recipes."

"They are now. She is brilliant at adding just the right touch. Let's pray." Mil reached a hand across the table.

Hien held hands, as she had the last couple times they ate together. She did not want to make waves. If this made Mil feel better, fine.

Mil said the words, thanking her god.

Hien listened. They were good words, grateful words. Words that Hien could not dispute.

Mil asked for protection for Michael and Charlie, healing for Pop, comfort and peace for Hien and Lai, as well as asking that the food nourish them. She even asked for a blessing on MiVu for her preparations, and for Minh for his driving. Hien agreed with each request.

So why was she uncomfortable?

As Hien took her next-to-last bite, the phone rang. She wanted to jump up, but Mil shook her head. "Let's let MiVu get it. It's her job."

Mere seconds later, MiVu stood in the doorway of the dining room. "For you, ma'am. Embassy office."

"Excuse me." Mil left to take the call.

Hien could not help it. When it was not Michael, disappointment dripped like a leaky faucet.

"I'll be right back. There is someone at the front requesting to see me. Hope it's not one of those reporters."

Hien stood. "Would you like me to accompany you? I might know who it is."

"No, thank you, dear heart. It'd be best if I go alone, in case you do know him." Mil left.

Hien returned to her chair, finishing MiVu's best meal yet. Perhaps this was the time. She scooted back and searched for the maid.

MiVu moved with authority, washing, wiping, and putting away in the kitchen. This girl was in charge, this was her domain.

Hien paused. Maybe if she brought the dirty dishes to her, they could talk and Hien could help clear the table. Yes. she returned to the dining room, gathered up the used utensils and dishes, and headed back.

MiVu's register of surprise was momentary. "Put there." She pointed to the counter next to the sink.

Hien complied before fetching the stemware glasses and

clean utensils. She started to replace the unused spoons in the drawer when MiVu stopped her.

"No, I wash."

"We did not use them."

"I wash."

So, Hien put them with the dirty dishes and summoned her courage. She began with a compliment on dinner. *"Bưa tôi rât ngon miệng."*

"Cảm ơn bạn." MiVu stated her thanks, but never raised her eyes.

It is now or never. *"Bạn sẽ dạy tôi một số công thức nấu ăn của bạn?"* Hien only wanted to learn a few recipes. Not a great imposition.

This time the girl faced Hien, confusion in her gaze. "I no understand."

What did she not understand? Hien clearly spoke in their native tongue. *"Bạn không hiểu điều gì?"*

"Tại sao?" Why?

Hien started to answer, then stopped. It was a fair question. Why did she want MiVu to teach her? She was curious about the food from America, since she would soon move there. She also, being a new bride, wanted to be a good cook for her husband. And then MiVu was an amazing chef.

Hien explained.

MiVu nodded, accepting Hien's reasons.

"Ngày mai sau bữa trưa."

Tomorrow after lunch would be great. Hien smiled her thanks and got out of MiVu's way.

She could hear Mil returning so went to the living room.

"Hien, this pilot is here for you. When he asked for Mrs. Wheaten, the front desk assumed he was here for me. Captain Andrade, this is my daughter-in-law, also Mrs. Wheaten."

Mil stepped aside to reveal the tall man who followed. He was the same guy who flew Hien and Mat to Mang Ca.

His brow furrowed. "Have we met?"

Hien felt her cheeks warm. She glanced at Mil, who cocked an eyebrow.

"Yes, last Monday you took my colleague and me to Huê."

"Oh, yeah, I remember. You came back white as a sheet. Never found out why."

Mil's right eyebrow was no longer cocked. Rather both eyebrows rose.

Hien wondered if she was curious or worried, but at least she did not say anything.

"It was a family matter. I am sorry if it caused you any problems."

"He—heck, no. No problems. I have something from your husband."

"Michael? What did he send?" Then she remembered the phone call.

"Here." He handed her a note and a small package. Hien read the note first.

Baby,

Had some downtime so made this for you. Hope you like it. I need a few things. It's boring and lonely here without you. I know you can't send yourself, but could you please send some other stuff back with Juan? List is on the back. Sure do miss you. Hug my family for me. I will call again soon.

All my love,

Michael

Hien flipped the paper.

jar of peanut butter

loaf of bread

jelly (whatever hasn't been opened)

more work T-shirts

more socks

Hien handed the note to Mil and dashed for the stairs. "I will be back." She mounted the steps two at a time, the way Michael did, and raced to their bedroom.

Mil called from downstairs. "I'll get the food stuff, Hien."

Hien pulled out a drawer, grabbing T-shirts. How many? He needed some for when he returned. She set three aside before moving on to the sock drawer. She lifted out four pair before noticing a picture. It was a snapshot of a blonde, young and pretty, wearing shorts and a sleeveless button-down striped top, tails tied in a bow to reveal her stomach. The photo grew warm in her fingers.

She flipped it.

Writing.

For Mike,

Love always,

Connie

Her hands shook. She dropped it and turned back to the drawer. Were there more photos? No, envelopes. Several.

She took one from the stack. It was addressed to Capt. Michael Wheaten. It had been sent to Viet Nam from Indiana. Breadville, Indiana.

Hien's fingers hesitated to open the flap. This would invade his privacy. She could never undo it. Her chest gripped her heart in a vice. No, she should not do this. No.

Hien pulled out the letter and began to read.

Hey Mike,

Just a line to say I g—

"What's the matter?"

Hien nearly jumped from her skin. Mil's voice behind her brought her back to reality. Shaky hands shoved the letter back into its envelope and pushed the drawer closed. As she gathered the clothing she had tossed on the bed, Mil stooped to retrieve the photo.

"I need to put that back."

"Hien. Look at me, please."

Hien faced Mil who gazed with… pity? No. Compassion? At least it was not judgment.

"Hien, this girl, Connie, is an old family friend. Yes, she and Michael dated, and I'll admit Ernest and I thought for a while they might become engaged, but Michael found you. He chose you. Don't read more into this."

Hien nodded, sniffed, then pulled out the drawer again to grab one of Michael's handkerchiefs. "Okay." Thankfully MiVu had done laundry.

"We need to go. Captain Andrade is waiting."

Hien again nodded before following Mil downstairs.

Mil had started a box with the food requests. Every two weeks the Wheatens received a special delivery of grocery boxes from the U.S. A perk from living at the embassy. It allowed them to not only keep to a more American diet, but it meant there was enough food and crates to send supplies for Michael with the captain. Hien added the clothing before closing it up and handing it to the pilot.

"There's one more thing." The pilot wiggled the toe of his boot onto the carpet and refused eye contact. Were his cheeks growing pink?

"What is it, Captain?"

"He said to give you something." He leaned in brushing a peck on Hien's cheek. "He told me he'd kill me if I didn't deliver it. He also told me I'd better make sure it wasn't on the lips."

She covered the kiss with her hand, her eyes starting to drip, when her brain flashed an idea. She acted before good sense could stop her. With her hands on his shoulders, she bounced on tiptoe to plant a peck on his cheek. "There, now you have one to give to him."

Mil hooted. She caught the pilot on his other side and mirrored the action. "Keep these kisses straight. This is from Michael's mother." She gave him a good-natured wink while the captain flushed from his hairline to jaw. Even his ears pinked, causing the women to giggle all the more. He picked up the box and excused himself.

"Hien, that was perfect." Mil flopped on the sofa, a big smile lighting her face. Hien had not seen Mil smile like that since before Pop's heart attack. "Have you opened your gift?"

It was still on the coffee table where Hien left it. She lifted it. Whatever it was, Michael had "wrapped" it in more notebook paper and twisted the ends closed. Hien unwrapped the package and drew out a shell. An elongated cone shape, it spiraled in shades of cream to tan to brown. At the largest part, a hole was drilled, and a strip of leather strung through to make a necklace. Hien turned it over, admiring its beauty from every angle.

"Here, let me put it on you." Mil stood next to her.

Hien handed it to her before moving her loose-falling chignon out of the way.

Mil tied the ends and Hien checked the mirror.

"See, Hien, he loves you. You are the one he chose."

Hien stared at the girl reflected while her left hand caressed the shell. Michael's other gift, her diamond wedding ring, flashed a reminder. *I am the one he chose.*

SIX

Say a Little Prayer

"Thank you for inviting me over." Hien relaxed, enjoying a simple conversation in Vietnamese, and allowed her gaze to wander the tiny studio apartment. Minimalist. That was the only word to describe what she viewed. The bed, she guessed, was a Murphy bed tucked into the wardrobe on the east side of the room. A kitchenette took up the west end. Bathroom and closet doors rose side-by-side across from the entrance. A small bar extended from the west wall as a part of the kitchen. One might sit at the counter and watch the resident cook. The only furniture for seating were two bar stools. She occupied one.

Lai stood in the tiny galley making tea and put together a tray of cookies. "Thank you for calling me. I wrap myself in work, and when I come home, it is so empty without Charlie. I only want to sleep until I can be with my students."

Hien nodded. How well she understood. "Sometimes I miss Michael so much I imagine curling up with his clothes and sleeping until he comes home." The kettle whistled, bringing her back to the present. "I wondered if you might care to talk. I have no sister. You are the closest I have. I do not know what sisters do."

Lai nodded. "My sister is twelve. What does she understand

89

about being young and in love? She is not sure boys should exist."

They both chuckled. "Well, if anyone understands, it would be you and me. Let us change the subject before we depress ourselves. Tell me about your students. The pictures you brought for Pop are so sweet."

Lai shrugged. "Children that age love art. If their art has a purpose, such as bringing a smile to someone, even better. They were quite pleased with themselves."

"Pop enjoys looking at them. It brightens his hospital room."

Lai set the tray of tea and cookies on the counter and took the other stool. "I wonder something. I hope you will not mind my asking. Why do you call them Pop and Mil?"

"That was Pop's suggestion. Pop is American slang for a father. Mil is short for mother-in-law." Hien stared at the floor, twisting her ring, as she finished. She was positive her explanation sounded silly. "What do you call them?"

Lai poured the tea. "Colonel and Mrs. Wheaten. We live here so I am not around them much. You live with them, so I think your names make sense. I might try them."

"That should surprise them. I am sure they will like it." She tried a macaroon.

"That is a lovely necklace. May I see it?"

Hien moved closer, lifting the shell from where it lay, just above her cleavage.

Lai admired it. "Where did you get it?"

"Michael sent it to me on Friday." Friday. The day before yesterday. Tomorrow he will have been gone a whole week. If all goes well, he returns in two weeks. *Please let all go well.*

"He sent it to you?"

"There is a cargo pilot who flies from Saigon. Michael convinced him to bring this and a list of things for me to send back to him—some clothes and food." Lai's expression made her pause. "Haven't you spoken with Charlie?"

Lai shook her head. "Not much chance of that while he is aboard ship."

Hien hesitated. She did not want to hurt Lai by sharing that she could receive phone calls. But there was something she could share. "There are trunk lines at Da Nang. Michael called and mentioned that he saw Charlie there one day. They spoke for a few minutes. He wanted me to tell Mil. I doubt he knew you had not spoken. It also would have been when you are teaching, so even if Charlie could use a trunk line while at the base, he could not have reached you." She covered Lai's hand with her own. "I am sorry. You must be desperate to hear his voice."

Lai nodded and took a sip of tea. "I count the days until he comes home. Other wives go much longer without a word, I know, and I should be grateful. But those are other wives, and he is my Charlie. I want him home."

Hien understood.

AN HOUR LATER, Hien made her goodbyes and left with the promise of meeting again next Sunday. It was a good start. She liked Lai more than she realized.

Rather than bother Minh, she walked the few blocks to Lai's apartment, but now the wind had increased, and rain pelted. Hien put up her umbrella and pressed on to Mac Dinh Chi Street. The pedestrian entrance to the embassy, located at the front on Thong Nhut Boulevard, was closed on Sundays. Today she must go through the vehicle entrance.

Ten minutes of walking against the wind brought her to the gate. She showed her ID, and they gave her access.

Looking up, she spotted Minh and started to wave but stopped herself. He had not noticed her. Instead, he appeared in deep conversation with someone on the other side of the wrought iron at the opposite end.

All at once, he glanced her way.

She smiled, but he hurried off. Strange. Hien shook her head and continued treading the short driveway to the villa.

Once inside, she placed the umbrella in the stand by the door before heading upstairs to get dry. Because she'd been slow putting it up, she now sported wet hair and soaked clothing. She stripped to her bra and panties, toweled down and then turned on the radio for music while she found drier attire. The Monkees were on the final chorus of "I'm A Believer" when the DJ interrupted with an announcement.

Hien paid little attention, the sound only background noise. Then the voice said, "Khe Sanh" and she became alert, intent.

"What about Khe Sanh?" She picked up the radio, willing it to release more information. "… in a surprise maneuver. Villagers from Khe Sanh are now safe at Khe Sanh Combat Base. The NVA move was expected and has been counteracted. We will broadcast more as we receive it. In the meantime, we return you to your regular programming." The Turtles began where the Monkees left off, singing "Happy Together." Hien was neither happy nor together with anyone she loved.

What just happened?

She put the radio on the nightstand and dressed. Her maroon corduroy jumper with her pink paisley blouse would be good enough. She towel-dried her hair, brushed it free of any tangles, then pulled it back into a bun at her nape. A touch of Slickers before grabbing her purse, and she flew down the stairs.

MiVu was busy in the living room, dusting and keeping everything in order. The perfect time to ask for another cooking lesson. Too bad she had listened to the radio. She called for Minh.

He arrived within a couple minutes. He showed no signs of having seen Hien earlier, so she did not broach it. His private business was just that. Besides, her mind was too intent on learning about Khe Sanh to want to chat over an English lesson.

Minh let her off in front of the Press Corps building. She tried to plan the best way to gain information without having to trade on Pop's condition. Steve might help her, but she had asked much of him already. Mat was still gone. To ask Nick would be too costly.

Not many people milled about. A few correspondents might be upstairs. But everyone? The place was about bare. She paused. Where could she find someone? Better try the phone bank. She climbed to the second floor. More people huddled in chairs, receivers cradled to their ears, but still few. She listened. Those speaking with affiliates in the States used hushed tones. Eavesdropping was unethical. No matter the innocent reason.

She listened harder.

"… and Niagara II was launched this morning, Sunday, January twenty-first, coincidentally at the same time as the NVA began its artillery barrage on KSCB. The Marine Direct Air Support Center, located on the base, is coordinating the air attacks, and looks to be the biggest concentration of aerial firepower this world has ever seen. The Air Force and Marines are going at this in a concerted effort, both ground and air. It is possible Westy was right. This is where the VC and NVA planned to hit. The US is ready to stop them." The speaker scanned the room.

He scowled and scrunched closer to the phone.

She moved.

Hien had what she came for. It iced her insides more than her winter monsoon drenching. It froze her heart mid-beat. It stole her breath.

MINH HELD the door for her and asked no questions. Perhaps her expression told him it was not the day for English practice. Whatever the reason, he allowed her to travel in silence to the hospital. When she thanked him for the ride, Hien hoped he understood she was grateful for his gift of quiet time to pull herself together.

Now the question became should she tell Mil what she learned? The gearing up for escalation at Khe Sanh was why Michael was sent to Da Nang, to be ready and available on short notice. With that much air power concentrated on the area, and with the NVA's sudden attack on the village and base, Michael certainly flew into danger. It frightened her to hold this information alone, inside, without someone to share her fears. Yet Mil was Michael's mother. Not only would she understand Hien's fear, she would feel it. She almost cried out to Pop's God.

Almost.

PFC Zorich waited outside Pop's room. He gave her a nod and opened the door for her.

Hien smashed a smile on her face. "Would anyone like to play cards?"

Pop sat in bed, reading through mail. Mil still worked the ever-present crochet hook on a length of navy-blue yarn. It looked to become the longest scarf in history. Or afghan—what was an afghan, anyway?

"Great idea, Hien." He gathered up his papers.

Mil smiled as she put her crocheting back into her bag. "Tell us about your lunch with Lai. How is she doing?" Picking up the deck from the bedside table, she began to shuffle.

"It was…" Hien searched for the correct word. "Peaceful. We chatted about things in our language without having to think to translate. Her apartment is small, very much like mine was before we, Michael and I, married. We talked about being newly wed to Americans and… our hopes." She shrugged. That was the best she could do. "I want to do it again. Her work schedule makes it difficult, so Sundays are the only opportunity."

Mil dealt. "Well, I was pleased you two got together. I think that is good. You are family. You need to know each other."

Pop picked up his cards. "I agree. Now let's play some serious Pinochle!"

The women laughed, Pop winked.

It was not time to share about Khe Sanh. What could she share? Instead, she would play the hand she was dealt.

Two hours later, Hien and Mil called for Minh to take them back to the villa. MiVu had left dinner in the oven. There was little to talk about, so they ate in silence until the phone rang. Hien's heart squeezed in her chest so hard she feared she might have a coronary attack like Pop.

Mil answered, giving her a chance to breathe.

"Hien, dear, it's for you."

Perhaps it was Michael. She shoved back in her chair, more careful this time to not let it fall, and hurried to the phone.

Mil held out the receiver and shook her head.

She closed her eyes and breathed in deep. "Yes, this is Hien Wheaten. May I help you?"

"Hien, Mat Morrissey. I'm still up here in Huê."

"Oh, Mat. What have you learned?"

"I suppose you heard about Khe Sanh?"

She paused and glanced about. "Yes."

"Can't talk, right?"

"Yes," Good, he understood.

"Well, several journalists and photographers headed out there as soon as news leaked. I'm staying, though. My gut says to stay put. But I talked with your brother."

A shiver went through her. "You did? What did he say?"

"He said for you not to worry. Your mother is playing it safe. She doesn't want you to have any trouble. He left his dog with her to give her some protection because he is part of the skeleton crew staying at Mang Ca during Tet. It is supposed to be a shorter cease-fire, so everyone there is on alert. But he says don't worry."

As if saying not to worry would stop her. "Thank you, Mat. I am grateful." More grateful than she could express. "You mentioned that other place. Any word from there?"

"Not much. It doesn't jibe with the positive spin the admin and friends want to put on things. There's a tight clampdown."

"Please, if you learn anything from either place, would you tell me?"

Mat agreed.

After letting him know she would pass the information on to Pop, she thanked him again and said goodbye.

Not that Pop could do anything from his hospital bed. But if she did not say that to Mat, she would have to explain about the heart attack and Pop's condition. She did not spell out how she would pass the information on to Pop, or how much of it she would share. She had his health to consider. Her head had become compartmentalized with information, filled with boxes delineating who could know what.

"Everything okay, dear?" Mil surprised her.

"Oh! Yes, everything is good. That was Mat. From work. He spoke with my brother and my family is well."

Mil accepted that. One more thing that was good. Or well. Or fine. Or maybe just out of her control.

HIEN CITED a headache as her excuse and spent the rest of the evening in her room listening to the radio. No more information on Khe Sanh was forthcoming, and by nine o'clock she truly had a headache, so she prepared for bed.

Sleep claimed her with vivid dreams of Tet at home in Huế. All around were children and venders selling sugary rice candies and treats. She wandered to the banks of the Huong—the Perfume River—and formed her little paper boat with a candle before setting it afloat among the rest. She knew her wish, the one she wished with all her heart, to be in the arms of her husband. Then there were fireworks—glorious, booming fireworks, lighting the sky with bright blazing jewels and glitter in colors no artist could paint. They grew in size, getting louder and louder.

Soon it was no longer fireworks. It was something more dangerous, more deadly.

Bombs.

Missiles exploded. The city toppled. This was Huế. How could it happen?

Planes buzzed dropping their destructive power. The Imperial Palace, with its ornate bronze guardians, flattened into debris. Then the University where she had attended, where her father taught, rubble. Historic, beloved sites covering the Citadel, gone.

Aircraft continued to fly over, but now ground fire shattered the sky. Sparks shooting up from where Mang Ca's armament fought the bombers. All at once there was a plane, one solo jet. She knew in her heart it was Michael. He was not there to destroy her city, he would protect it. But Mang Ca's guns did not see the difference. They fired and fired. They hit Michael. *Jump, Michael! Jump, I am here for you!*

He did not jump.

The jet crashed, bursting into a colossal ball of flame.

Hien bolted upright, her breath caught in her chest. Lightning cracked the sky outside her window into jagged puzzle pieces. Thunder boomed like cymbals.

She rubbed shaky hands over her eyes and realized she was crying, possibly out loud. She swiped the tears from her face and tiptoed to the door, peeking into the hall. All lights were out, no one stirred—Mil did not hear her. Good. It was scary enough to dream it; she did not want to scare Mil or relive it by sharing.

Hien slipped into her robe and slippers and padded downstairs to the kitchen. A cup of tea would help. Besides, there would be no more sleeping tonight, or rather this morning. The clock read 3:42.

FEAR SUBSIDED to an undercurrent of foreboding, a musical underscore to the dramatic movie of their lives, by the time Mil came down at seven. Hien downed three cups of tea, showered, dressed, and convinced MiVu to let her help with breakfast. Today's lesson—Eggs Benedict. Even stoic MiVu seemed pleased with the outcome.

Hien and Mil kept to their routine—she took the morning with Pop, so Mil might take the afternoon. Minh drove her to the hospital. They practiced English via their usual conversation. This was her new normal. Everything was just that, normal.

Except it was not normal.

The dream changed how she viewed life. Not that she lived in fear, more like in apprehension, a waiting for what she feared could happen to happen. It left her feeling hollow.

Something had been stolen. Hope. That was what was missing. The nightmare drained her of hope. Where did she find more? Could she find more?

The rain subsided by the time Minh dropped her off. At least Hien could take Pop for a walk in the courtyard. She would need to remember to bring a towel to dry the bench in case he needed to sit. Activity, doing things—routine things —helped.

PFC Zorich again stood duty at Pop's door. Hien learned there was a rotation of three MSGs assigned to guard Pop at the hospital, but she always timed it to arrive for Private Zorich's turn.

She spoke a brief greeting.

He offered a brief nod.

All very brief. Then she was in the room.

Pop lay back against his pillows, blankly staring out at the cloudy day. His expression said he only stared into space, his thoughts far away. He appeared as hopeless as she felt.

"Hello, Pop."

He started. "Why, hello, Hien. How are you this dreary day?" He smiled a practiced smile that did not show in his eyes.

She hugged him. "I am well. How are you?"

"I don't know, kiddo. Could be it's this monotonous rainy weather that keeps the sky crying, but whatever the reason, the malaise is thick today." He did not hide his feelings. It was the most transparent he had been with her since talking about his mistaken decision to come to Viet Nam.

Hien's heart broke for him. "The rain stopped when I arrived. It is merely cloudy. Maybe a walk outside will help. I can get a towel."

"Okay, if that's what you want. It doesn't matter."

They both needed hope.

"I will bring your Bible."

He nodded.

Hien helped him into his slippers before holding the robe out for him. He behaved as if content for her do the work. She assisted him to a chair, picked up his book and a couple towels before letting Private Zorich in on the plan.

The marine security guard held the door as Pop shuffled out, leaning on Hien's arm. Private Zorich then took point to the next door which led to the courtyard. After checking for other persons in the garden, he held that door too.

The rain remained in check, though everything from the statues to the seats to the foliage glistened with droplets. Pop's slippers would be drenched if he did not pick up his feet.

"I need to sit." Pop steered her off toward a molded-cement bench with a puddle in the middle.

"Let me wipe that for you." Hien put a towel to use. "Now it is dry." She helped him get situated then joined him. "Pop, I know it feels gloomy. Is there something I may read to you?"

Pop remained silent.

"Please, Pop. I..." She was supposed to be there to assist him, but she needed help herself. "Please. I am running out of hope."

She watched as one tear, then another, dropped from his face. All at once, he sat more erect and swiped at his eyes. "Yes. Yes, there is a passage. Many years ago a man named Saul thought Christians were the enemy of God. He even got authority to go to various cities, break into homes, and drag families out into the streets. He would arrest them, put them in prison or worse, have them killed."

"That is awful!"

"Yes, it is. It was not safe to be a follower of Jesus. But Saul met Jesus in a vision. It is a wonderful story you can read in the Book of Acts. But the best thing is that he also became a follower and made several long journeys to various countries to tell of Jesus, and help start churches. He taught lots of people and was much loved. Part way through his first trip he changed his name from Saul to Paul—it means the same, only Paul was the Greek version and didn't bring up the scary memories. He wrote letters to the churches he'd started, and that is where we get many of the books of the New Testament. They are Paul's letters."

Hien hung onto Pop's every word. As he spoke, he grew stronger. If talking about Paul's letters helped, what must his words say?

"Toward the end of Paul's life, they locked him in prison. He wrote the book of Philippians while in chains. Would you read that first chapter to me?"

"Yes, Pop." Hien opened the Bible and scanned the table of contents, running her finger down the list until she found the word Philippians and the corresponding page number. Soon she was ready. "'Paul and Tim-oth-e-us, the servants of Jesus Christ, to all the saints in Christ Jesus which are at… '"

"Philippi."

"'Philippi, with the bishops and deacons: Grace be unto you, and peace, from God our Father, and from the Lord Jesus Christ. She continued until the passage became strange. "For

God is my record, how greatly I long after you all in the bowels of Jesus?'"

"It means in his heart of hearts."

"Oh, I see." She continued reading. "'But I would ye should understand, brethren, that the things which happened unto me have fallen out rather unto the furtherance of the gospel; So that my bonds in Christ are manifest in all the palace, and in all other places;'" She shook her head. "I do not understand this."

Pop patted her hand. "Remember I said he was writing this from prison? Well, back then they would chain a guard to him. So, he would talk to the guard and share about his faith and the guard would become a follower of Jesus. So they would find another guard. Paul would talk to that guard and another person would change his life for Jesus. He became the talk of the palace. And though he was in chains, he still did what God called him to do—share about Jesus and how He loved the world so much that He died for everyone and then conquered death and rose from the dead."

Pop believed this. Hien could see he truly believed this man Jesus died. She could believe that the man died. But that his death fixed every wrong, and that he became alive again? That was where she had trouble.

"Okay." She read how others became bolder because they saw this man Paul talking to guards. "'I therein do rejoice, yea, and will rejoice. For I know that this shall turn to my salvation through your prayer, and the supply of the Spirit of Jesus Christ.'"

Why Pop wanted her to read this was making sense. They chained this man in prison, yet he rejoiced. If he could rejoice in his circumstance, then maybe she could find reason to hope.

Pop sat with his head tipped back and his eyes closed. "Go on, kiddo. I need to hear this."

"'According to my earnest expectation and my hope, that in nothing I shall be ashamed, but that with all boldness, as always, so now also Christ shall be magnified in my body, whether it be by life, or by death.'"

Pop's voice joined with hers. "'For to me to live is Christ, and to die is gain.'"

She glanced over at him. He no longer appeared depressed. In fact, he appeared more at peace than she had seen in days, so she kept reading. Was this Paul saying that he couldn't make up his mind about what he wanted more, whether to keep telling others about Jesus or die? "'...that whether I come and see you, or else be absent, I may hear of your affairs, that ye stand fast in one spirit, with one mind striving together for the faith of the gospel; And in nothing terrified by your adversaries: which is to them an evident token of perdition, but to you of salvation, and that of God. For unto you it is given in the behalf of Christ, not only to believe on him, but also to suffer for his sake; Having the same conflict which ye saw in me, and now hear to be in me.'"

Again, this was not clear. But just as she opened her mouth to ask Pop, Private Zorich came to attention. Hien glanced past him and noticed two men headed their way. Both looked familiar. One was Ambassador Bunker.

"Sir!"

The other man addressed the MSG. "At ease, Private."

Private Zorich relaxed a little, as least he was not so rigid, and moved where he could still watch.

Pop stood and shook their hands. "Ellsworth, George, good to see you both. You don't mind if I sit, do you? Oh, this is my daughter-in-law, Hien. Hien, I think you remember Ambassador Bunker, and this is Colonel George Jacobson."

Hien shook hands. "Very nice to meet you." Both she and Pop sat while the men stood.

"Ernie, we're not here to wear you out, but we need to touch base. George, here, has agreed to step in as the temporary mission coordinator. And if you can't return, he would be up to speed, the transition that much easier."

Pop's brow furrowed. "How would you work that? Mellie and Hien are still living in the villa."

Colonel Jacobson nodded. "Don't even worry about that. They are fine. Aren't those old servants' quarters attached off the kitchen door? I can stay there so I'm close but out of their way. Also, if they don't mind, and when it works for them, I can use your office to keep things rolling."

Pop mulled the information. "I think that would work. Yes, that will work. Let me know if you have questions. I can explain my pigeon scratches to you. Mellie put our calendar on hold, you should be fine for now."

The men made their goodbyes and left. Hien peeked a glance at Pop. He appeared more relaxed. She could imagine that having the colonel fill in for him took a weight off his shoulders.

"One concern done. I still have a couple more but glad that one is off the table."

"What others do you have, Pop?"

He turned his head. His gaze captured her soul. "I am concerned for you, Hien. I will not always be here. You must make a decision one of these days, before it is too late."

"What decision?"

"You must decide if you will trust Jesus for your life or just consider him some historic figure."

Hien did not know what to say. Her silence said something to Pop, though.

"You only need to pray. Tell God that you are sorry for any wrongs you have done and then tell Jesus that you give Him your heart, ask Him to be your Lord and Savior."

"That is it?"

"That is the start. From then on you trust Him. No matter how things look, like this gloomy sky, you relentlessly trust Him to do what is best. I guess I am saying this for both of us, because I need to remember too. Even if it looks bad and feels hard, trust Him to work it all out—for your good and His glory."

Hien felt the pull in her heart. There was something to what Pop explained. Still, she was not ready. Not yet, at least. "I promise to think about this, Pop."

"That's all I ask. I will be praying."

She knew he would.

SEVEN

Heroes And Villains

Though the sky remained gloomy, the week passed with a better outlook. Michael called Wednesday to say he was safe. He could not phone every day. But, like everyone else, he said not to worry. He would call when possible.

The cooking lessons continued, with Hien learning the basics of roasted chicken and rice and a special dessert using cream cheese, graham cracker crumbs, and a can of cherries. It resembled a pie, but was called a cake; strange, all those things together, but the result was delicious. She snuck a tiny piece into Pop to show him what she had learned.

Pop's outlook improved. It was like he needed to remember how to find hope, and once he talked to her that Monday morning, something clicked back into place. He again found his hope.

And another thing. Lai began coming after work to see Pop. They grew closer, more like a family. Now the four of them played pinochle. Lai shared the funny little jokes her students enjoyed. The laughter did them good.

The evenings occasionally saw Colonel Jacobson working in the office. He tried not to be an intrusion, but the work required his attention. Once or twice he accepted Mil's invitation to stay for dinner. He told stories of his life and entertained with a few magic tricks—he had been a professional magician before he joined the army in World War II.

Her favorite thing was when he recited poetry. He'd memorized a poem for any topic.

One time he excused himself, apologizing that he needed to "hole up in the office until the wee hours" to take care of calls to the States. After that late night, he was gone for two days.

Sunday arrived and Hien visited at Lai's again. It was more open, easy. The relationship grew as did her sisterly feelings for the girl.

"Your students will be out of school for Tet, Tuesday and Wednesday, am I correct?" Hien waited for Lai's nod. "You could stay at the villa with Mil and me. We can celebrate together."

Lai smiled. "That would be fun. My parents said something about me staying there. Let me ask. If they are counting on me, I should be with them. We need to honor the family together." Though Lai was only half Vietnamese and her family Catholic, they still followed the customs of Tet. They would require her to be with them.

"It was a thought. I want to teach Mil about our traditions. She has never celebrated Tet."

"That reminds me. I made a treat." Lai reached into her tiny refrigerator and pulled out a box wrapped in red paper. "I made some *bánh xoai* and *Ô Mai* for you and Mil. It probably is not the best food for Pop, but you can enjoy it."

A tingle sparked through Hien. Bánh xoai, or rather Mango Cake was her favorite Tet treat. She regretted not learning how to make it from her mother and planned to have MiVu teach her. The candied fruits and ginger, Ô Mai, were delicious and delicate. Hien was sure MiVu would have a tray of *Mut* ready for guests—a selection of dried fruits and nuts—and Ô Mai would nicely go with it. "Thank you, Lai. I cannot wait to try them."

The girls hugged, and Hien pulled out her umbrella for her short walk back to the compound. "Please let us know about

Tet, if you can stay. You are most welcome, but I understand about your family. That is important."

"I will. Hug Pop for me."

Hien nodded and left. Lai's door closed behind her before a clap of thunder drowned out other sounds. Hien shivered, pulled up her raincoat collar, and continued down the street. Soon she shivered at the gate, fumbling for her ID. The guard, though he recognized her, waited for her to flash it. Hien understood the precaution, but wet as she was, it irritated. As she plucked the card out of her purse, she glanced up and noticed Minh on the far side of the fence, his back to her. He leaned in at the end of the wrought iron bars in a way that reminded Hien of something, something she couldn't pull from her brain, but it was there.

The guard waved her through. She dismissed the image and hurried inside the villa. The phone rang as she entered. No one else was home.

"The Mission Coordinator's Residence."

"Hien, is that you?"

Mat. It had been awhile since she heard from him. Something about his voice brought that image of Minh back. It also triggered the other memory from Mat's photos.

"Yes, are you okay? How is my family?"

"I'm fine. So's your family, at least last time I spoke with your brother. He said to tell you hello."

That helped her relax, a little. The other image still sent nervous pings.

"Tell him hello from me, and that I love him and wish him a wonderful Tet."

"That's kinda why I called. This Tet thing. The closer we get to it, the more my gut churns and tells me something big is in the air. I know it, and your brother feels the same. Are you able to talk to your father-in-law? Word has it that someone else is in his position."

Hien sighed. She still could not explain. "All I can say is I will mention it to my father-in-law. No other information is available."

She heard his grunt through the phone. "Mat, please. I would tell you everything if it were in my power, but it is not. Just realize, even if I cannot explain, I will not lie to you."

There was a long pause. "I know that, Hien. You've never been one to lie. Okay, I'll trust you with this. My gut says Huế is about to be hit. Probably during the Tet truce. A bunch of the ARVN guys at Mang Ca are already gone for the holiday. The skeleton crew is thin. Your brother is part of it. If the brass doesn't beef up the site here and at MACV, I'm afraid Huế is a sitting duck."

"Are you safe?" It scared her that her family might be in danger, but they were Vietnamese. They could blend in if need be. Mat was so obviously American, he didn't stand a chance, if what he claimed was true.

"I'm fine. Don't worry. I will keep you posted. I flew down to Da Nang to call in some info and ran into your husband. He also said to tell you he's fine—"

"You saw Michael?" She could not help the squeal in her voice but was sorry to have interrupted him. Just hearing about Michael was important.

"Yes. No worries. He's doing great. And I can fly back and forth without a problem. For now. Trust me, I enjoy breathing. So I'll behave. Please be sure to talk with your father-in-law, okay?"

"Okay. Mat, thank you. For everything."

"No worries, kid. Gotta go." And with that, the line went dead.

Hien did not try to plunge the little black buttons. She knew when he said "gotta go" he was through. Still, she had no opportunity to share what she noticed. If his gut caused him fear for Huế, what would that tell him about what she saw at the embassy gate?

BACK UP IN HER ROOM, Hien searched through Michael's drawers. She would not get nosey with that photo and letter. She would not entertain such thoughts. Absolutely not. She wavered on the precipice of temptation when she saw what she looked for, tucked beneath the very letters she hoped to avoid. She tugged it out and slammed the drawer shut, a tad harder than planned.

Michael's Bible.

It appeared brand new, especially when compared to Pop's notations in the margins and underlining throughout. She cracked it open. *To Michael, with love on your graduation. Psalm 119:105, Mom and Dad, June 15, 1962*

Hien turned to Psalm 119:105. She now knew how to find that.

"Thy word is a lamp unto my feet, and a light unto my path."

Did he believe that? She had no idea. It bothered her, too, that she did not know what her husband believed. Did he believe anything? When Pop explained things, it made sense. But it was not what her family understood. If Michael believed in this God who loved so much that he came and died, maybe she could believe too. *Died and rose again.* Pop's voice corrected her. Many men through history died for others. There were soldiers all over Viet Nam, on both sides of the war, who were dying for a cause or loved ones they wanted to protect. But none of them would return to life in three days to keep fighting.

Yet Pop believed this. He embraced this with his whole being. And Pop was as dear to her as her own father.

The phone rang.

Hien ran for it, even though she was alone in the villa.

"Mission Coordinator's Residence."

"Hey, baby."

Michael! "Oh, I am so glad you called. How are you?"

"The same, fine. Just fine and dandy." He did not sound fine or dandy.

"Do you need anything? I can fix another package for you."

Pause. "Nah, nothing like that. It's just… I miss you and wanted to hear your voice. Our one-month anniversary is coming up on Thursday. We've been apart more than together. It's hitting me, that's all."

Hien was aware but had not wanted to sound selfish. But, it warmed her that Michael remembered too. "I understand. But it is only a short time. You will come back, and we will leave for Indiana. Soon we will be together. We will forget this loneliness."

"I needed that. Love you, baby."

"I love you too." She hesitated, then plunged. "Pop has been teaching me about your faith."

"Oh, honey, don't get involved in all that. Don't let them turn you into a fanatic. God's okay and all, but they can take it to an extreme. Especially Dad. Just hang in there. I'll rescue you when I get back."

That was not what she expected. It did explain the condition of his Bible.

"Hey, babe, I gotta go. I only had a few minutes and wanted to remind you to have your passport ready. Love you. See you soon."

"I love—." *Click.* Oh, how she was learning to hate the telephone.

MONDAY SPED PAST. Hien told Pop she'd discovered Michael's Bible but not about the pristine condition. She feared that would upset him, and she would not hurt Pop for the world. He advised her to begin reading in the book of Luke.

After another cooking lesson with MiVu, she followed his advice, though it seemed strange to start more than halfway through. She read a couple chapters of the book before bed that night and read again before breakfast. The more she read, the more she wanted to read. It fed a hunger in her. She could not name what it was, it just was. Tuesday morning, when she tried to explain that to Pop, he smiled and nodded.

Tuesday, she also remembered to call about getting a passport. She realized Michael assumed she owned one, but she never had a reason to apply. And she assumed it was a simple thing. Now all she could do was leave a message, since no one wanted to work during Tet.

The rest of the day ran true to form, only the streets were clogged with revelers celebrating and street vendors hawking tasty treats while fireworks could be heard all over, some in the distance, some quite close. The ride home from the hospital took twenty minutes longer than usual, but Minh stayed calm throughout the whole time, safely getting them to the villa. "Hope you have a nice evening with your family, Minh."

"Thank you." He paused, like he had more to say, but stopped.

Hien slid out of the car and turned to wave.

The front passenger window lowered. *"Bạn sẽ ở lại vào buổi tối?"*

She smiled. "English, remember? Yes, we'll be staying in. Goodnight."

He nodded, rolled it up, and pulled away. His courtesy made her embarrassed at the ideas she harbored.

They opened the door to delicious wafts, whisking all thoughts of anything but food from her mind.

"MiVu, it smells wonderful in here!" Mil headed straight for the kitchen.

Hien followed close on her heels. "Is the *Banh Tet* ready?" Rice cake made with sticky rice, pork, and mung beans and wrapped in banana leaves was the last project she worked on before meeting Mil at the hospital.

MiVu pointed to a tray where the neat little packages waited to be unwrapped.

"Oh, your cooking lesson for today. Well, we need to try it." Mil smiled and carried the Banh Tet to the table. Hien and MiVu trailed with other dishes.

A brief tap at the back door, and Colonel Jacobson peeked around the jamb. "So, how is my timing?"

"Perfect, George. Come and join us." Mil waved him in with her invitation. "You can taste one of Hien's latest culinary products."

She felt warmth that had nothing to do with the kitchen creep up her cheeks. "It is MiVu's recipe, but I will take the blame if it did not turn out."

The colonel chuckled, but Mil shook her head. "None of that. I know it will be wonderful. You are an excellent student. MiVu is a wonderful teacher. Bows all around."

MiVu ducked back into the kitchen.

Hien, Mil and Colonel Jacobson took their seats as MiVu brought in the *Canh Bong Thap Cam*, a soup of carrots, peas, shrimp, and dried pig skin. Mil invited MiVu to join them, but the girl declined. "Thank you, no. My family he wait for me."

Of course. Hien hoped she would, but Tet bonds family. "Thank you for staying so late and serving our meal."

The colonel stood. "I can see you home. It's dark, and there's a lot of people out there. Besides, it's rainy."

"No, I will be fine."

Mil stood too. "I'll call for a driver. That might get you there sooner."

MiVu agreed. Mil called for Minh. Five minutes later, MiVu was on her way. After a brief prayer, they tucked into the amazing spread.

"Hope you don't mind, I've got to take a phone call from D.C. around three a.m. I'll hole up in the office, catch up on some work, if that's okay."

He asked as a courtesy. The job required him to receive the call. That was what he must do.

"That's fine, George. To be honest, I sleep better knowing you are here. It's silly, I know. We've got the guards and all." Mil almost chuckled. Not a true laugh. Only a noise concealing what she dare not voice.

Hien understood without Mil saying it. She was afraid. She was lonely and scared and doing everything she knew to hold her world together. The fear that liked to claw at her at the most inopportune times also tore at Mil. Hien recognized it.

"I promise to be quiet."

"It's fine." Mil did not glance from her soup.

Tension and silence filled the room. The colonel started to recite.

"There once was a maid who made soup. Whose noodles all seemed to droop. So she pondered the fix. Reconstructed her mix. And now rolls them into big loops."

Mil nearly choked. "Oh, George, that was bad." She dabbed her face with her napkin.

Hien held hers to her mouth. The poem was funny-bad, but watching Mil and the colonel react, that was the best part. Soon they were talking and laughing. A good time. The way Tet should be.

Finally, Hien excused herself and began clearing the table. She brought out the gifts from Lai, leaving them for the colonel and Mil, and washed dishes. She could have stacked them in the sink, MiVu would handle it in the morning. But this would be her thank you for the cooking lessons.

She restored the kitchen to MiVu's preference in under fifteen minutes. By then, Mil sat alone at the table. Hien joined her.

"This differs from your usual Tet celebration, doesn't it, Hien?"

"Yes." She did not know how to explain the differences without making Mil sad.

"Hien, are you happy?"

The question took her by surprise. Was she? "I am happy to be part of this family. I am very happy to be married to Michael. I am excited to go to Indiana. Yes, I am happy." Mostly.

"Good. I want you to be. Please know that."

She stood and walked around to Mil, embracing her and leaning her cheek on Mil's crown. "I do." She kissed Mil on top of the head. "I think I am ready for bed now. There is no reason to stay up. My New Year wishes are in my heart. I need not send them out in a paper boat."

Mil nodded. "Then sweet dreams, dear girl. I will see you in the morning." Mil patted her hand. "I might as well go up too. I received a new paperback in the mail today, *The Cat Who Ate Danish Modern*—isn't that a title?—so I shall read for a while."

Hien thought of the book on her nightstand. It was what called to her to retire early. "Good night."

After donning Michael's T-shirt and climbing into bed, she plumped the pillows behind her. The marker noting where she left off brought her to Luke, chapter four. She kept a pad and pencil next to her lamp, noting what confused her. Pop had a knack for explaining, like he did with those names in chapter three.

For more than an hour, she read and made notes. So much was difficult to grasp. When she got halfway into chapter six, parts looked familiar. There were lots of "blessed" things, similar to what she read to Pop from the book of Matthew. Somewhere around chapter eight she caught herself yawning and stopped for the night. She had ten pages of things to discuss with Pop. Oh, he would be excited. She could picture his expression. Even after she turned out the light and snuggled down with her eyes closed, his smiling face beamed at her.

~

THUNDER ROARED, jarring her from dreamlessness. Hien opened her eyes. The room remained dark, even before the next rumble. Why was there no lightning?

She glanced at the bedside clock. 2:47.

A sudden boom shook the foundation and echoed in its roar.

That was not thunder.

She slipped into her bathrobe without bothering with her slippers and cracked open her door.

Mil was at the end of the hall, wrapping her robe about her.

She stepped out and turned.

Someone mounted the steps in giant leaps.

A scream stuck in her throat as a hand grabbed her arm.

"Shh! It's me. There's shooting outside." Colonel Jacobson ushered her toward Mil. "Mel, let's get in your room. Do you have a line to the embassy office?" His whisper rasped in Hien's ear, but Mil understood.

She nodded and went back into her bedroom, leaving the door open for them to follow.

"Keep your lights off. Stay away from the windows."

Mil dialed the number and handed the receiver to Colonel Jacobson.

Little *pop-pops* sounded from outside, each one making Hien jump. She glanced at the colonel and Mil, who focused on the phone conversation. If she hurried…

Hien scurried to her room, slipped into her slippers and took Michael's Bible and her camera. Someone grabbed her arm again. This time, a hoarse, high-pitched squeak squeezed out of her throat and cut the silence.

"Get back there!" Colonel Jacobson pushed her to Mil's bedroom. "Don't leave here again unless I tell you."

He locked the door and moved the wardrobe in front of it with Mil's and Hien's help.

"What did the office say?" Hien did not recognize the whispery screech of her own voice.

"Spoke to Alan Wendt. He said it was good to know we're here. They'll get us support as soon as they can."

"So we're on our own." Mil's voice didn't squeak or screech or crack. It struck Hien that it remained calm as the colonel nodded. "Okay, George, what's the plan?"

"We'll hunker down here. There's glass on two sides which means, for now, we keep clear. Once I know our guys are out there, I'll attempt to get some weapons." He glanced at something in his hand. "I don't think this M26 grenade is enough." The colonel paused and shook his head as cold prickles worked up Hien's spine. He continued, "If there're sounds from downstairs, you ladies are to immediately lock yourselves in the bathroom, scrunch into the tub, and stay put. Is that understood?" He stared at Hien.

She did not trust her voice. Instead she nodded and clasped the Bible and camera to her chest. A peek at the illuminated dial on the bedside clock revealed it was 2:58. Another huge explosion rocked the foundation.

Mil enveloped Hien and pulled her close. "It'll be all right, Hien. You'll see."

She could not tell if it was Mil's heart or her own that pounded so hard, probably both.

Mil must have realized what she clutched in her arms. "Climb on my bed and pull up the covers. I'll get you a flashlight. You can read to us."

Trembling, Hien kicked off her slippers and slipped beneath the sheet, pulling it and the blanket over her head. Mil crawled in, too, and handed her the small light. Hien opened the Bible. "I do not know where to start."

"Try Psalm twenty-seven."

Hien fumbled a moment as pages tried to stick together, but she located the psalm. "'The Lord is my light and my salvation; whom shall I fear? The Lord is the strength of my life, of whom shall I be afraid?'" Hien paused and glanced at Mil.

Mil nodded. "It helps me, too."

Hien forged on, allowing the words to wash over her. Her heart pounded less. When she finished one psalm, Mil suggested another. Still no sounds came from other places in the house, though the *pop-pops*, *ratta-tat-tats* and occasional explosions continued in the compound.

Nothing changed, time froze. Hien peeked out at the clock. Now it showed 4:39. She had read for over an hour. The colonel sat with his back to the wall, across from the bedroom doors, silent and stone still. Had the office forgotten them?

Mil suggested Psalm ninety-one again.

She figured Mil liked that one. She did too. "'He that dwelleth in the secret place of the most High shall abide under the shadow of the Almighty.'"

Twenty minutes afterward, she grabbed Mil's hand. "Can you hear it?" She switched off the flashlight and threw back the covers.

The colonel moved to his hands and knees, crawling to the window. "They're trying to land a copter on the embassy's helipad." Then seconds later, "No, no!" He sank to sitting. "Too much ground fire. They couldn't touch down."

His words crushed the room. The shared silence in the midst of the peripheral gun noises enveloped Hien.

"Daylight. That's what the Marines need. We'll hold out for daylight."

The colonel was right. Hien trusted him. She nodded, slipping under the covers with the flashlight to continue reading. If she could just keep her mind on the words...

An hour later, whirling sounds of wind and the rhythm of helicopter blades filtered through from outside. She peeked again.

"It's a medivac. Looks like they're trying to get someone out. If this works, they'll return." Lighter shades of gray filled the suite. Hien realized she could more clearly see the colonel. Dawn was on its way. *Please bring help.*

Every few minutes she peeked from the covers and took

note. Bit by bit, things became sharper. Her hope of rescue grew with each item that came into view. Once she could recognize the furnishings on the far side of the room, she noticed a change in the sounds. The *pop-pops* and *rata-tat-tats* were closer. Louder. Her heart thumped louder. And faster.

Crash.

Downstairs.

Hien's heart jumped to her throat.

Colonel Jacobson hopped up and fiddled with the French doors leading to the balcony. "I'll slip out. Get on the floor, under the bed."

Mil dropped to the carpet from her side, Hien the other. She peered from beneath and saw the French door left ajar. Suddenly feet entered from the balcony. The door closed.

"Mel, Hien, into the bathroom. Lock yourselves in. Put towels at the base. They're going to use gas, sent only one mask. Get in that bathtub and stay silent!"

The colonel's harsh whisper renewed the chills up her spine. Hien crawled from under the bed after Mil, following her into the lavatory.

Hien locked the door while Mil rolled up the bathmat and pressed it to the bottom.

By the flashlight's illumination, Mil wet two washcloths and handed one to Hien. "Hold it to your face, just in case."

Hien nodded and obeyed. They both stepped into the bathtub and scrunched. Hien turned off the light, plunging the space into total darkness.

The house was so quiet. Hien realized she was not breathing and reminded herself to do so. The throbbing in her ears deafened, she was sure anyone near could hear it. *Oh, God, Pop and Mil say you can hear me and that you love us. The words in the book say you can protect us. Please, be my God, too, and protect us. Please.*

There was a quick burst of fire and a solo shot from inside

the house. Mil grabbed her hand. Hien shoved the washcloth into her mouth to block her screams.

A couple minutes, or more like an eternity later, someone pounded on the door. "Mel, Hien, it's me. Don't open up yet. It's over, but there's still some gas. Just rest there. I'll wait here and let you know when it's fine to come out." The colonel remained their protector. What would they have done without him?

Mil squeezed Hien's hand. "Thank God. Thank God." She repeated the words, over and over. Hien joined her. "Thank God. Thank God." She meant every word.

They still said it when the colonel knocked, saying they might come out.

Hien climbed out first, flipped on the flashlight and then helped Mil step out. As she watched Mil waver on wobbly legs, she realized her own were not that steady. They both trembled to the door. Mil turned the lock; Hien pulled it open. The colonel, gas mask pushed up on his forehead with the morning light glowing behind him, was prepared for their ungainly gait and caught them both in a hug.

"What happened, George?"

There was a hesitation. "The need to get you from here outweighs taking you past things I don't want you to see." Another pause. "A sapper got into the house. Only one, trying to hide. He spotted me and shot." This pause was longer yet. "I had to kill him. He is still on the stairs."

Hien felt herself staring. This man ate meals with them and laughed, and joked, and recited poetry. This man killed to rescue them.

He took a life.

"Are you okay, sir?"

"I am alive. So are you. We will be fine. But we must get downstairs. Pack an overnight bag, both of you. You won't be here tonight."

Mil nodded and pulled away.

"My things are in my room." Hien stared at the door.

The colonel understood. "I'll walk with you. You are safe."

Hien nodded. She inhaled and blew it out. "Let us go." The first step through the doorway was the hardest, but as she kept putting one foot in front of the other, she made it. All was as she left it, a few hours ago—a lifetime ago.

"Do you want me to wait here?"

Hien shook her head. "No, thank you. I will return to Mil when I am done."

"Okey doke." He stepped out and then glanced at her. "I didn't have a choice, you know."

She gazed at him. No flinching, no glancing away. "I know."

He patted the door jamb, nodded, and left.

HIEN RETURNED to Mil's room, overnight bag in hand. She kept her eyes averted from the stairs, sure that was what the colonel wanted.

Mil was ready too. Colonel Jacobson took them as far as the steps and stopped, blocking their view. "Give me your bags. I want you to hold the handrail and keep focused on the wall. I will get you past."

The women did as he said, though out of the corner of her eye, Hien could see a body draped across several of the bottom treads. His face was not visible, but the red stain which surrounded him was hard to miss. She had photographed many things in her work, including a few dead bodies. But this was in her home. Her stomach roiled, she fought to keep from vomiting.

The colonel led them through the living room to the front door. It was broken. Wood splinters and glass shards carpeted the tile entry. Mil took hold of her hand.

Once outside, Marines gathered, searched, cleaned-up everywhere. Lifeless bodies lay strewn on the grass, now stained red.

Two soldiers stood over one of them. "Hey look, this one here has an embassy pass. Looks like he worked here."

The voices drew her attention. She turned as they rolled the body face up. "A driver. Nguyen Minh."

Her legs became rubber. Air stopped flowing into her lungs. She sank to her knees as the world spun, or was it her head spinning? "Minh."

A black curtain dropped.

EIGHT

Cry Like a Baby

"Open your eyes."

Hien did her best to obey, but her lids fought the light.

"She's coming around. Give her a little air."

Finally, she got her world to focus. A Marine leaned over her, and she realized she lay on the grass. That realization catapulted her to her a sitting position, as if an electric charge shot through her. The ground swayed, or was it she? Bond-like hands clamped her arms. The swaying stilled.

"Hien, you worried me. How do you feel?"

It all rushed back, the fear, the night, the noises. Then —"Minh."

"Ma'am?"

"Minh, our driver." She pointed to where she'd seen the Marines and the body. They were still there. "He's dead."

"Oh…" Mil grew pale. Hien recognized the same turmoil in her mother-in-law's eyes that churned inside her.

Somehow their hands found and held tight to each other.

"I think it would be a good idea to have you checked at the med station." The marine who first leaned over her must have medical background.

"Doctor, we need to get to Grall hospital anyway. Is it

possible to catch a ride?" Mil squeezed her hand and let go before stooping to gather up the overnight bags and purses scattered on the ground.

"I'll check on that, ma'am. There're still areas of fighting throughout the city." He called over a private, gave him instructions, and sent him to find out about the possibility of a vehicle and driver.

The private was resourceful. He returned within five minutes, declaring success. He was also the driver.

By then, Hien managed to get to her feet.

Colonel Jacobson, once he knew they were safe and heading for the hospital, promised to catch up with them there. He turned back to the aftermath, continuing his duties.

Mil sat still throughout the drive, still except for her middle finger on her right hand, which tapped out a quiet beat.

Hien's crazy brain labeled it a Morse code prayer. No matter what she labeled it, though, it was clear Mil's concern was for Pop. What had he heard? Would he be worried? What about his heart condition? Mil did not have to speak her concerns. She wordlessly tapped them.

They took a longer than usual route through unfamiliar streets to arrive at the hospital. Hien sent Mil in ahead.

Mil showed a concerned glance over her shoulder, but Hien motioned her to go.

Once Mil was out of sight, though, she gave the PFC her most needy-female look. "I am sorry to bother, but would you help me?" Truthfully, she was still wobbly. A part of her wanted to tough it out like a good soldier's wife, but the other part reminded her she had just come through a battle, seen someone she thought a friend lying dead, and had known very little sleep for over twenty-four hours, not to mention the fact she had passed out. She could forgive herself this once.

"Yes, ma'am. Stay right there." It was as if he suddenly remembered she needed medical attention. He grabbed every bag in his left hand and helped her from the jeep with his right. "You just hang on to my arm. I'll get you help."

"Get me to my father-in-law's room, please. That is enough."

"Whatever you say, ma'am, if you are sure." He seemed so sincere and young, that Hien could not help but smile.

"I am sure." The thought occurred to her she was glad Pop was on the first floor. Less time as a spectacle. Besides, she could picture herself tripping on the stairs and knew that rolling down them might bruise more than her ego.

The fear of what she might see at his room slowed her steps. No Marines guarded his door. Mil was nowhere in sight, but as she drew closer, she could hear both Pop's and Mil's voices. Her load of worry lightened. Hien released the PFC's arm and hustled into the room.

Pop glanced up first. "Thank God you are both all right!"

"Ernest, I am so glad you are okay!" Mil only had eyes for her husband as she sat on the edge of his bed and stroked his cheek.

He appeared pale, more so than usual. He reclined more in the bed. "Better start talking. No one tells me a blamed thing. I only get snippets from conversations in the hall."

The PFC entered the room, still carrying the overnight bags and Hien's purse.

"Over there, please." Hien pointed to the corner by the window. "Thank you so much, private."

"My pleasure." He touched his cap and started to withdraw, then stopped. "I sure hope y'all feel better fast and are back into your place real soon." Then he stepped into the hallway.

Pop was the first to speak. His voice carried a low rumble. "What in blazes is he talking about?"

"Now Ernest, don't get yourself upset. We will tell you, but you must promise to remain calm."

"Well, somebody better start talking or all bets concerning my calm are off."

Hien stepped to the bed. "Pop, we were safe all night.

Colonel Jacobson took very good care of us. He was in your office and realized what was happening. He kept us from harm."

Mil patted his hand. "Yes, dear, you owe George a huge thank you. We all do."

"Why did you move from the villa?" He sounded calmer, but his questions continued.

Hien searched Mil's face for guidance on what to say. Just thinking of the debris they passed brought up a stomach full of raw emotion.

"There was some damage to the front door and living room window from the Marines trying to capture the sappers." Mil's voice flowed as smooth as honey.

Pop was not fooled. "Sappers? There were sappers tunneling onto the grounds?"

"That's what George called them. I honestly do not know what the word means and wouldn't have used it, correct or not, if I knew it would upset you."

He cleared his throat. "A sapper, my dear, is a soldier who is employed in the building of fortifications, trenches, or tunnels that assist in the approach of an enemy's position or the undermining of said position. So, you are telling me that enemy soldiers tunneled onto the compound?"

"Frankly, sweetheart, I'm not exactly sure what happened. All we know"—she glanced at Hien—"is that somehow some enemy sappers, for lack of a better word, got inside the compound. The Marines could not land a helicopter until daylight, but when it was, they did, and things wrapped up quickly. George escorted us out, and we asked for a ride here. I understand there are still some skirmishes in other places in the city, but the Marines we spoke with believed the mop up, as they put it, will be complete in a matter of hours."

Hien scrutinized Pop's face. Would that be enough information? Was it too much?

Pop relaxed. "Okay. I guess." He tipped his head back and closed his eyes. "Don't know what I'd do it something happened to you, Mellie. I need to rest awhile. Haven't slept since the first whispers." He was asleep the second the words left his mouth.

Mil stayed next to him on the bed, caressing his face, until a snore convinced her he was out.

Hien was the voyeur. She stepped into the hall. At once the walls moved. She grappled for the nearby chair. Their driver managed to get her into it. Putting her head down, she took slow, deep breaths. If she opened her eyes, the room swam. If she closed them, she saw Minh. She wanted to vomit, but nothing was in her stomach. She wanted to run, but how does one outrun one's self?

A touch made Hien glance up. Mil's concerned face hovered. The private must have gotten her attention.

"I want someone to see to you. Will you be okay while I talk to the nurses at the desk?"

Hien nodded. She lowered her head.

A few moments later, Mil returned with a cup of water and a nurse, who performed a cursory exam and pronounced her findings. "She need food. Protein."

Hien cringed. No, she did not need food. But to placate, she smiled while Mil thanked the nurse who hurried back to her regular charges.

Mil sat next to Hien. "I can see what I can find. I think there is a cafeteria area, but from what I was hearing, I'm not sure if it will be open. What I overheard sounded like a mix of several languages. The gist was employees aren't arriving for shifts because of the attacks. Those here are afraid to go home."

"Do not worry. If I can rest here…"

"Of course. You rest as long as you need. You can lean against me."

The thought invited. A couple weeks ago it would have been too familiar. Hien let a small sigh escape as she placed her head against Mil's shoulder. She closed her eyes.

The picture of Minh on the grass, bloody and lifeless, floated through her mind. Her eyes popped open.

Mil must have sensed what happened. She wrapped her arm around Hien, pulling her closer.

I have made you. I will sustain you. I will carry you, I will rescue you.

Hien heard the words as if someone spoke them in her ear. Only it was not Mil's voice. No one else was near. She remembered reading those very words under the covers during the battle. Again, she closed her eyes.

Do not fear. I will help you.

This time she did not question. She accepted the promise and drifted off to sleep.

CREAKY NOISES ENTERED Hien's consciousness. She cracked one eye open. Wheels rolled along, crying out for oil, as an orderly moved a gurney down the hall. She tried to sit up, but something weighed her down. Mil's head rested on hers. Slowly, with great care, Hien began to extricate herself. She stood and stretched. Wandering by the nurses' station, she spotted a clock.

She had dozed for several hours. Did she recognize any of the staff from the morning? A couple people looked familiar. Some had braved the fighting to do their duty.

Next, she headed for Pop's room. Their driver stood by the door. She peeked in. Pop still slept. When had he become so pale, so wan?

Another orderly, pushing another gurney, rumbled past. She stopped him, asking if there was a place to get food. He explained that the cafeteria was open on a limited basis. She might find noodles or eggs.

Back at Pop's room, she stole in to locate her purse and out again before he could wake. Mil still slept in the hall chair. She began her search for the cafeteria.

A solo cook ran the kitchen and counter.

One glimpse revealed he was overworked and overwrought.

Hien requested two orders of eggs to go and told him he could make them anyway he chose. She would wait. No rush.

He seemed to appreciate her attitude and produced the food faster than she expected.

A part of her wanted to ask him about his experiences from last night. Had his neighborhood been in the thick of the fighting? Had he heard of fallen friends? Had he been stuck here since with no clue if his family and loved ones were hurt or even alive? Would he appreciate her asking or take it as an intrusion into his personal life?

Pray for him.

What?

Pray for him.

So she did. Like she had seen Mil and Pop do, she bowed her head and closed her eyes. Only she spoke it in her mind, the way the voice spoke. *I do not understand how to pray for him. But You say pray so I will. I believe You are God. You protected us last night. I ask that You protect this man and his family. Bring him help in his job. Give him peace. Thank You.*

She glanced up. He stared back.

Oh! She bowed her head again. *In Jesus's Name. Amen.*

As she raised her head, a phone rang. The man grabbed it, speaking low. His expression changed from sour to radiant. He hung up the receiver, a smile cracking his face.

Behind her, a voice called out. "I am here, I made it."

She turned to see another man, hustling toward the kitchen, tying his apron around him as he rushed. Just like that, God answered her prayer. She grabbed the eggs and ran to find Mil.

Mil stood in the doorway to Pop's room. Hien wondered, did she watch him sleep? Or were they speaking? But once there, it was clear. Pop was not yet awake.

"I brought you some eggs." She held out the paper container.

Mil took the food and motioned to the hallway chairs.

"And something happened, something good, I think. I would like to tell you—"

"Hien!"

She turned to find Steve Riley striding down the hall toward her. "What are you doing here?"

"Looking for you. I've been to the embassy, and when I didn't see you, I thought to check here."

"You have found me. Mil, may I present my friend, Steve Riley. He is a photojournalist. Steve, this is my mother-in-law, Mrs. Wheaten."

Steve stuck out his hand and Mil juggled the eggs around to free up hers.

"It's nice to meet you, Mrs. Wheaten. Were you at the embassy when it was hit? Or were you here?"

"Steve, I know you. I—" She glanced at Mil "—we will not give you an interview right now. There is too much to sort through. We are taking things a minute at a time. In fact, we do not even have a place to live."

"A place to live? That's easy. The Continental has plenty of rooms."

"And plenty of reporters." It was the unofficial hangout for many of the AP and UPI affiliate journalists. "Besides, how would we get there?" Minh's face floated through her mind.

"George is seeing to all that, Hein. We can stay at the Continental, if we want. George said our driver will take us where we want after he is relieved. He is under orders to remain here for Ernest until he is. The embassy is covering our hotel."

"I have my car. I can get you there."

She again glanced at Mil, who said, "No, thank you. We must stay with our escort."

"Are you positive?"

Mil smiled. "Quite." She nodded with her head towards the

hall where another MSG strode toward Pop's room. "Thank you, anyway."

Hien and Mil finished their eggs and let their driver know they needed to leave.

Steve shrugged and followed them out.

THE JEEP, which was their new mode of transportation, produced sounds all its own. Hien was not sure whether the clutch would hold out for the whole trip as the driver seemed to fight with it every time he changed gears. The gears fought back too. Or at least yelled at the private. It made her wonder how many battles the poor vehicle had seen. But it held together to their destination.

The Hotel Continental.

Though renamed The Continental Palace, it would always be known as The Continental. The ground floor bar also had a nickname—The Continental Shelf—because of the number of journalists who gathered there. It was convenient, especially since *Newsweek* and *Time* magazines kept their Saigon bureaus on the second floor. Hien cringed. Should they move into this dangerous place?

The private stayed with them while they registered. They were given a double room as suites were not available. When the bellboy arrived to take them to the fourth floor, their driver went up too. He checked the room, then gave Mil a number to call and left.

It felt good to be somewhere secluded.

Mil opened her bags on the bed closest to the windows, which overlooked the street. "Do you mind if I shower?"

Hien shook her head. "No, not at all. Go ahead." She put her bag in the closet without opening it and then lay down. Just as she closed her eyes, thoughts of Michael began to call. She realized he had no idea what happened, or maybe he had some scary snippets of information. He had no way of knowing if she were alive. He did not know that his mother was safe, that they were now living in a hotel because of a dead body and a bunch of glass shards and a pool of blood that needed to be removed from their home.

He could not reach her.

No one knew how to contact her.

She sat, trembling. Who might need to find her? Michael, of course. Mat—he could get word to her family, if she could connect with him. The people at the passport office. She had left her message using the mission coordinator's contact information. She should call them.

Dialing zero, she asked the hotel operator to connect her with the passport office. The line rang and rang. Dejected, she hung up the phone. How silly to think any government agency might answer today, or even all week, between the Tet celebration and the attack all over the city. Why worry about a passport now? The walls closed in. Thoughts jumbled.

She crumpled to the floor. Her body shook with stifled cries. Her bun, already loose, released a wall of hair that began to soak up her tears and stick to her face. She swiped at the strands on her cheek. It only dragged them across her eyes and nose. The absurdity of the hairy mess brought up a heated anger, searing but without logic or reason. She grabbed her bag from the closet, flung it onto the bed. She shoved her hand into each pocket and section, over and over. Surely there was a rubber band in there somewhere. She breathed harder.

Thwarted at an easy find, she dumped the bag. No hair ties.

Fury rose from her toes, pure and fiery. A desire to hit, to scream, to break something boiled. She fed the heat with fresh emotion as the fury climbed higher, through her core, nearly choking her, searching for an exit.

It found one, her right arm.

Her right hand still held the bag.

Fury flung it across the room. *Crash!* The mirrored closet

door shattered into millions of tiny reflective shards, a shower of glittering fractures all over the carpet.

An emotional stranger stared at her from a piece of the mirrored door. She covered her mouth and sucked in a breath. *What have I done?*

Mil emerged from the bathroom, a towel wrapped about her body and a second wound as a turban.

"Stop! Do not come in here. There is glass." Hien dropped to the floor and began picking up the shards. Her foolish outburst brought a new heat that warmed her neck and cheeks.

"What happened?"

"I, the bag, oh… I threw a tantrum." The heat building in her face at that confession burned off the last of the fury and self-pity, leaving her as stupefied at her actions as anyone. "One minute I was sobbing over not being able to contact the passport office. The next I was furious over my hair getting in the way and not finding anything to hold it back. Mil, I think I am losing my mind." She looked to the older woman, hope for the perfect answer rising in her heart. Mil would know what to say.

"Darling girl, what do you think I was doing in the shower? It's the best place to let go, nothing gets broken, and your tears all wash down the drain." Mil met her gaze with a smile.

"I should have waited my turn." Hien could feel her own smile tickle the corners of her mouth.

Mil chuckled. "Perhaps you should have. Let me get something on my feet, and I'll help. Better yet, let's just call room service to clean it. You will cut yourself." She slipped back into the bathroom a moment and reemerged in her slippers. Pulling her make-shift turban from her hair, she dropped it on the bed and called the concierge. "We need a glass clean-up in room 403." Pause. "Yes, thank you." With that, she hung up. "Someone will be here shortly. In the meantime, I'll get dressed. You take your shower and we'll go down for a proper meal."

Hien did not argue. The plan seemed perfect to her.

As long as they avoided reporters.

∾

THE HOTEL's less-famous restaurant was adjacent to its infamous bar. Hien and Mil sat near the back. They didn't notice much curiosity in their direction. Things worked in their favor until the entrees arrived.

"Yum, chicken cordon bleu. Wise choice."

Hien jumped at the sound of the male voice. "Steve, what are you doing here?"

He pulled up a chair and joined them. "Been over at the bar waiting for you to emerge. Did you get settled?" He picked up a triangle of toasted bread from Hien's plate and popped it in his mouth.

"As much as possible, I guess." She shrugged while Mil took another bite of her meal. "Steve, what do you want?"

"You said you needed a place to live. I got you a place. Now how about an interview?"

Hien held her hands to her face, trying to regain her composure. He was her friend, and he had helped her. More than once. She blew out a breath. "If I were to give anyone an interview, it would be you. Even though Colonel Jacobson secured us our room. You only mentioned it. But right now, too much is happening." A thought crossed her mind, along with a memory of a snippet she once heard about her resourceful colleague. Maybe, if it were true, he might help again. "I wonder, will you make a bargain?" Hien glanced at Mil who gave a brief nod.

"Sure. What can I do?" He sat straighter.

"I need a passport. I have called, left messages when they answer. But now they do not even do that." She leaned back. What could he do?

"A passport, huh? Before Tet, it would've been a snap. I doubt anyone is in the office these days. Once someone is there, I'll help you."

Hien laced her fingers in front of her plate, took a breath, and smiled. "Well, if you do that, I will give you an interview."

Pointedly, she waggled her index finger at him as he started to get excited. "But, but, but, not one word of an interview until I have my passport in my hand. Do you understand?"

"That could be days, weeks even."

Her finger waved under his nose.

He sighed. "I get it. Okay, you've got a deal. I'll contact you once I have a handle on things."

Mil cleared her throat. "And, Stephen... May I call you Stephen?"

Steve nodded.

"Stephen. I'll sweeten the deal if you can do something for me, or actually both of us."

His eyes narrowed. "What would that be, ma'am?"

"Stephen, we find ourselves limited because of circumstances. It is important that we be able to accomplish things. If you are willing to run errands as needed, I'll give you exclusive rights to meet us at the hospital. I don't know if my husband will be up for interviews, but you'll have access to Hien and me and we'll share limited information. May we count on you?"

Steve's eyes lit up and his smile nearly broke his face in two. "Yes, ma'am, you may."

"Very well if we may finish our meal..."

Realization bloomed, and he stood.

"Oh, you do not have to leave. Feel free to order something of your own and join us. Please." Mil's eyes twinkled, and Hien could see she enjoyed his discomfort. Nothing mean, just a polite reminder.

"Uh, yes, thank you, ma'am. I'll do that. Thank you." He waved his hand for the waiter and soon had his own meal before him. No more picking from Hien's plate.

Twenty minutes later, he followed them back to the hospital.

IT WAS NEARLY six-thirty when they returned to Pop's room. PFC Zorich stood outside his door, his uniform not as crisp as usual. His brown eyes appeared tired, weary, but his posture never sagged. Mil patted his arm as she stepped into check on Pop.

Hien stopped to say hello. "I did not know if we would see you today." Or again.

"I was at the embassy. The consulate side. Once everything was secured, they told me to return here." He paused a moment then quietly added. "Don't worry. The compound is protected. I will remain here on guard. You are safe."

She was taken aback. These guys did their duty, gave all if needed. They stood so tall and strong and reliable. The gentle words touched deep. All she could say was "Thank you."

Mil came back out. "He's still asleep. He should be awake by now. I'm going to ask some questions at the nurse's desk."

Hien nodded and, after a glance in at Pop, followed Mil.

The staff looked weary, each having aged over the last twenty-four hours. They'd worked longer periods owing to colleagues unable to get to work. Add to that the increase of patients due to the various ongoing battles and they must feel overwhelmed.

Mil got the attention of the French-speaking nurse assigned to Pop. Hien realized she should help translate.

"Excuse me, we've just returned. My husband is still sleeping. He did that before we left. Do you know if he slept this entire time?"

The nurse seemed to decipher the words in her brain. "Un moment." She murmured with a couple other staff members at the desk, and returned. "He sleep. No awake."

"Then could you check on him to make sure he is okay?" Mil's concern made her voice quaver.

The nurse nodded and led the way to Pop's room. She began by taking his pulse. Becoming more intent, she jiggled his shoulder, then opened his eye to assess pupil dilation. Her whole body took on a different stance, more business, more importance. She pulled the red cord behind the bed before stepping to the door, calling for assistance. "You go to hall. Wait in hall." The nurse pushed Mil and Hien out while several medical staff members rushed in with a cart.

Hien's feet froze in place, numbness creeping up her legs and torso and clawing at her heart with growing icy fingers. Her mind, however, raced with possibilities, none of which were good. She glanced at Mil.

The same freeze caught her. She stood rooted to the spot where the nurse had shoved her, her body immobile, but her eyes somehow twice their normal size.

Something was wrong with Pop.

PFC Zorich checked those who rushed into the room—he prepped himself to know the faces of those on the approved list and did not slow them from their jobs, yet still did his. Once the medical parade made it through the door, he turned his attention to Mil and Hien, assisting them to chairs. "It will be all right. They do good work here. Just give them room and time. Rest here."

Mil nodded.

Hien tried to say "thank you," but it came out more of a squeak.

The PFC did not wait but returned to his post.

Minutes later, Dr. Baleau arrived, walking past them without recognition, charging straight into Pop's room.

Mil reached out and grasped Hien's hand.

She felt more than heard Mil's prayers and began praying too.

HIEN STARTLED. Someone touched her shoulder. She glanced up to see a nurse.

"Phone call for Hien Wheaten? Is that you?"

"Yes, I am she. Where can I take it?"

The nurse motioned for her to follow. She punched a button on the phone base where a red light blinked. The light went out, and she handed the headset to Hien.

"This is Hien Wheaten."

"Thank God! Oh, baby, I've been so worried!"

"Michael! Are you all right?" The air in her lungs built up speed.

"I'm calling to ask you that. What happened?"

What should she tell him? There was so much. "Mil and I are all fine. There was damage to the villa, so we moved to the Hotel Continental. We are here to see Pop. They say there is fighting everywhere. Are you safe?"

"Gotta go. Yes, I'm safe. Love—"

Stupid trunk lines. But he called. For that she thanked God and hurried to tell Mil that Michael was safe.

Mil gripped her hand, a tear etching its way down her cheek.

"Mrs. Wheaten?"

She spun around.

Dr. Baleau stood behind her.

Mil rose.

"No, sit. Please." He took a seat next to Mil. "He is stable for the moment."

Mil let out a breath as if she had held it for a while.

"What happened, Doctor?"

"We are not sure. And though he is stable, he is in a coma."

Mil's grip on Hien's hand intensified. Bone-crushingly so.

"What does that mean, for his prognosis?"

"Again, we are not sure. We have accomplished the first step to stabilize him. Now we need him to improve and wake up. Recent studies have shown that even in a coma, patients can hear things. I recommend you continue to have conversations around him, uplifting, and positive exchanges. Normally he would be on a different floor, but I do not want to move him in this condition."

"May we see him?" Hien still did not recognize her voice.

"Yes, but be prepared. There are more cords and monitors. Do not be concerned. It helps us help him. Just remember, warm, lighthearted conversations." He stood.

"Doctor, you realize what we have already dealt with today. Frankly, I do not know if we, um, I will sleep tonight. What if he senses our stress from what we don't say? Even when we keep the conversation light? What if he can feel our anxiety?" Mil's voice quivered.

"Mrs. Wheaten, I understand. I would be happy to write you a prescription for a sedative, but the bottom line is, you now know what you need to do. This is what he needs. All you can do is your best. That and pray. The rest is up to Colonel Wheaten." He held out his hand.

Mil released Hien's and clasped his in both of hers.

"I will be back soon. You will most probably tire of me as I intend to check in as often as I can. However, I have several other new patients due to the ongoing skirmishes, so…"

"Thank you, Doctor. We understand."

Hien tried clearing her throat. "Yes, thank you."

Dr. Baleau headed down the hall, stopping at the nurses station where he murmured something, tapped the desk at the response and then rounded the corner.

Mil stood. "Shall we?"

Hien nodded and followed her past PFC Zorich into Pop's room.

THEY STAYED until the nurse came to tell them visiting hours were over. Then Hien realized they didn't know how long before their ride could arrive or where to meet him. They had been focused on other details.

When they entered the foyer of the hospital, there sat Steve, head leaned back against the chair, snoring. His horn-rimmed glasses were shoved up on his forehead, nearly onto his white-blond crew cut. His long legs stretched like barricades, crossed at the ankles, and revealed mismatched socks that had lost their elastic hold.

A part of Hien hated to wake him.

But only a part.

She shook his shoulder, not too hard.

He shrugged her off.

She tried again, less worried about being gentle.

He brushed her hand away and attempted to curl up in the chair.

"Steve, you can go now."

He cracked an eyelid open. Recognition dawned in that eye. He turned his head. Hein knew the second he spotted Mil. He jumped from the chair, tipping it over, and knocking his glasses to the floor.

"Oh, Steve, oh! I am sorry." Hien stooped to retrieve the eye-wear only to discover they were in two pieces—they split at the bridge. She scooped them up, handing them to him. "Can you see without them?"

"I guess we're about to find out." He tried to fit the pieces together, but they only fell apart in his hands. "I'll travel slow."

With that announcement, the driver arrived.

Steve followed them to the hotel in his beater of a Renault. He was stopped at one point, but because Hien and Mil noticed, the driver took them back where Mil vouched for him.

Finally, they reached the Continental. They planned to meet Steve at the hospital the next day and went to their room.

Hien saw the pill bottle the doctor had slipped to Mil clutched in her hand. A part of her hoped Mil might share. The other part wanted to stop Mil from using any. By the time they crawled in bed, neither part won. Hien feared that no matter which part won or lost, in the end, Mil could be the bigger loser.

NINE

Shades of Gray

As the rest of the week ground on, they developed a routine. They woke at the same time, showered and dressed before going to breakfast where they both scooted the food around their plates, no matter what they ordered. Who could eat when one's stomach was in perpetual motion?

Then the private took them to the hospital, where they stayed until the nurses kicked them out. Afterwards, their driver returned them to the Continental to sleep and start all over.

On Friday, February second, Lai arrived to stay. Her presence helped. Together they spelled each other on food runs. They kept funny, silly conversations going in the room and they found a new normal in a crazy, surreal situation that was anything but normal.

Real would be letting her fear and anger loose. Instead, Hien stuffed it inside, just like her mother taught her. She would be stoic and slap a stupid grin on her face. There was more at stake than Pop's health. However, if this continued something else could be at stake. Her sanity.

Each day, other than Saturday or Sunday, Hien continued to call the passport office. Friday, she heard a human voice who told her to leave a message. This time she left every bit of her contact information, including the hospital number, though it was of no consequence to the human voice. She wanted to reach through the phone line, tear the person apart and then scream at the pieces.

One thing she noticed. No one opened Pop's Bible. No one read to him. She kept thinking she should. But then she would get involved in a conversation with Mil and Lai and forget. At the hotel, she only cried in the shower or stared out the window when sleep eluded. When she viewed the scarred city, she felt a tug to pray, but she was not sure what to say. Who needed prayer the most? Michael and Charlie? Her mother and brother? Pop and Mil? Lai? What about herself? Was she losing her mind? The more she reflected, the more tendrils the vine of fear seemed to shoot out enveloping her soul.

Colonel Jacobson stopped by Saturday. He volunteered to take Hien and Mil to the villa for more clothing and needed items. Hien confessed to Mil that she was tired of washing her undergarments in the bathroom sink. Mil agreed, so both appreciated the colonel's offer.

Returning was hard. Hien's heart pounded as they drove onto the compound. She did not recognize the guard at the gate. Would he question her presence there?

The living room windows were boarded. The front door displayed scars from the forced entry. Hien could not swallow for the too-large lump in her throat. The shards and splinters were swept away. The carpet ripped from the first floor.

And the staircase.

Where the body bled.

Died.

No dark stains marked the spot, for which Hien was grateful. And sad too. A life passed, swept away like the shards and splinters, and nothing marked its passing. Then she remembered, that life would have taken hers, given the opportunity, without a passing thought. She shivered and forced herself to climb the stairs.

In her room, she gathered a larger suitcase and filled it with the clothes and items she missed at the hotel, including the photo of Michael from her vanity mirror, her little phone directory, her notebook from her nightstand. As she snapped the lid closed, she remembered her small jewelry box, adding that. She set the luggage on the floor and scanned the small suite. It was hers and Michael's first home together, though they did not spend much time in it. However, the time they had was sweet.

Mostly.

That was what she would remember. She wiped an escaping tear.

Would she ever hold Michael in this bed again? Would he kiss her in front of the closet again?

"No, I will not accept that. I look forward to again sharing you, dear room, with my husband." Yet, though spoken aloud, she still could not completely believe it.

She dragged her suitcase into the hall where Colonel Jacobson waited. Mil arrived a second later. He took both their bags and led the way.

Down and out.

Funny, that is also how she felt.

The colonel dropped Hien and Mil by the hospital entrance with the promise of delivering the luggage to the Hotel Continental for them.

Then they returned to the new routine, the new normal. Their new life existed between what was and what was to come. No recognition of truth or now.

Change filled the air. It left its scent in the atmosphere of their lives. But instead of dissipating, it grew stronger with each day. The one time Hien tried to speak of it, Mil called it "waiting for the other shoe to drop." That word picture resonated with Hien's feelings and built on the gut-tingling anticipation of the "what next" roller-coaster free-wheeling inside her.

Sunday and the start of Monday it remained the same.

However, that afternoon she heard a familiar voice outside Pop's door. "Tell Hien that Steve has good news."

PFC Zorich maintained his post.

She slipped out of the room. "Shush! You cannot be that loud here, Steve."

His sheepish smile told her he planned this.

She turned to the private. "It is all right. He is a friend." Then she grabbed Steve by the arm, directing him to a pair of chairs. "You have my attention. What is your good news?"

"I know a guy. Well, I know a guy who knows a guy."

"I know many people. So what?"

"This guy that my friend knows is a… fixer. They call him Uncle Lanh."

Lanh, meaning smart, quick minded, or street wise. Hien could imagine someone with that name being a "fixer."

She crossed her arms and nodded. "Go on."

"Anyway, for a price, he will help you get your passport."

"A price? How much are his services?"

Steve cleared his throat. "Two hundred dollars."

Hien stood. "TWO HUNDRED DOLLARS???"

Now Steve shushed her quiet and pulled her back to her seat. "Uncle Lanh needs something to grease the wheels, so to speak. Don't you have two hundred dollars?"

She had two hundred dollars. It was all she had. Every cent she saved since moving to Saigon. Once she met Michael, it was easier to save, as he did the spending. What if they needed something in Indiana? What if the farm cost more money? Michael said the house needed work.

But without the passport, there was no Indiana.

"All right. What do I have to do?"

Steve laid out the plan. He would need to give the cash to Uncle Lanh up front. That was important. When Hien balked at the idea, he promised that if this fell through, he would replace the payment. They decided Hien would give him her money when he followed them home that night. Once the money was paid, Uncle Lanh would tell them when to meet him at the passport office.

The scent of change grew stronger.

That evening, Steve waited in the hotel lobby while Hien ran to the room. Her stomach flipped at how close she came to leaving her little jewelry box. Aside from Michael's necklace and her wedding rings, she only wore small gold earrings, if she wore jewelry. But the box held a secret, a place where she kept her extra cash. Exactly two hundred dollars was hidden in the compartment. Hien removed it and, after a moment of hesitation, hurried to Steve before she could change her mind.

"You are sure this will work?"

He did not appear sure. "It's all I've got, Hien. I promise, if it doesn't, I'll repay you."

With that, she placed the bills in his hand. Hard earned American dollars. She learned they went further in the economy and then when she and Michael decided to go to Indiana, it made even better sense.

Now, it might be all for nothing.

"It's gonna work. I'll let you know what he says." And he left, taking her savings with him.

Tuesday evening, Steve waited for them in the lobby as they arrived from Grall. He motioned for Hien to hold back.

She told Mil she would be up in a minute.

Mil nodded. This new life took a toll. Away from the hospital, her mother-in-law spoke little. The growing despondency made Hien more closely watch her. Maybe Steve brought good news she could share with Mil—with no mention of the money. But something positive would not hurt.

Once Mil entered the elevator, and the doors closed, she returned to him.

"Any word?"

He took her by the arm, guiding her to a more secluded spot. His gaze scanned the area, his voice dropped to a whisper. "We've got an appointment tomorrow morning at eleven. Answer only when asked something. Don't appear surprised at what happens or is said. I'll go with you too." He paused. "We might have to say we're getting married."

"Married!"

"Shh-shh. Not so loud. That is only for a last resort. To suggest we are getting married in the States, and you need your passport to get there. Don't worry, Uncle Lanh and I worked it out. Just keep your poker face."

"Poker face?"

"Yeah, it means, don't show surprise or disagreement. Only talk when you have to and make your answers short. No added details."

Hien stared at her friend. She knew he was trying to help. And ordinarily she could trust him. But to deceive?

She must have that passport. "Fine. I will do as you say. But I cannot lie. I hate not being able to explain things. I do it because it is needed. I did not lie, though. Now you ask this. Please, I do not want to lie."

"I understand. We'll do our best to keep that from happening. When the driver comes to take your mother-in-law to the hospital, just wait here in the lobby. I'll come get you. We'll meet Uncle Lanh."

She nodded and started for the elevators. He was her only help. She turned. "Thank you, Steve."

He waved and left.

She took the elevator to the fourth floor, wondering what to say to Mil.

THE NEXT MORNING ran just as Steve said. He was waiting when the driver picked up Mil for the hospital. She appeared less despondent, though all Hien had shared was that Steve knew someone who might help with her passport. They were to meet him at eleven. Mil asked no questions but accepted the information as good news and left alone.

After a ten-minute ride, he parked a block from the passport office and assisted Hien from the car. She smiled. That door was stubborn like her friend.

As they neared the entrance to the building, a man with an overnight bag approached. He wore a threadbare pinstriped suit and fedora. It reminded Hien of an old gangster movie she saw as a teen.

He tipped his hat. "You are Mrs. Wheaten?" His accent revealed he hailed from a northern province.

Hien glanced at Steve and then back. "Yes?"

"Come."

They followed Uncle Lanh inside to a small office at the rear. He held the door and ushered them into the cramped quarters.

A man, about thirty years of age Hien guessed, sat behind the desk. His back was to the dirty window that overlooked what she presumed to be an alley, as she could see a sort of shadow through the grimy windows belonging to the building across the way. The man let them stand there without acknowledgment for nearly five minutes before raising his head.

"Yes?" He spoke in Vietnamese.

Steve answered in English. "We're here for a passport. For her."

The man turned his attention to Hien still speaking in Vietnamese. "What is your name?"

"Hien Wheaten."

"Where are your papers?"

Hien pulled out her documentation—her embassy ID, her birth certificate, and her marriage license. She couldn't help the slight twitch of a grin as she handed over that document. Then she remembered her poker face.

"You are married to an American?"

"Yes."

"You want to go to America."

"Yes." She started to breathe.

"Okay." He switched to broken English. "Come back ten month. I have for you. Maybe."

"Ten—"

Steve grabbed her arm.

Hien shut her mouth, though her brain continued to scream.

Steve patted her shoulder.

But she shrugged, wanting to, like Pop would say, give him a knuckle sandwich.

Uncle Lanh stepped forward. He remained silent, setting the overnight bag on the desk.

The passport official glanced at the bag and then gazed up as though Leonardo Di Vinci were painting the ceiling above him and he could not be drawn away.

After unlatching the bag, Uncle Lanh removed items and placed them on the desk. So many things came from the bag, Hien began to think it had magic powers. Bottles of various liquors, boxes of cigarettes, even small baggies of what appeared to be flour were placed on the desktop with many more things.

Then Uncle Lanh stopped. He closed and removed the case and then stepped back without ever saying a word.

The official continued to stare at the ceiling, though he opened a desk drawer. With one swipe of his hand, he pulled everything, but the liquor bottles into it. Then he raised each bottle, one at a time, his gaze never leaving the vision above him, and set them with the rest of Uncle Lanh's offering. Hien could not comprehend how he did it without dropping or breaking a thing. But he did.

When finished, he shoved the drawer closed.

As if the transaction never happened.

"You want passport. I need you photo. Come."

Hien followed him to the corner of the room.

He pulled down a screen and had her stand in front of it. Then he pulled out a Polaroid camera from a different drawer and took her picture. After returning to the desk, he opened a third drawer and removed a blank passport, affixed the photo, stamped the front page, and added her name before closing it. Gathering up her personal papers, he handed the stack back to Hien. "Here you passport. Have good trip."

Hien's hands shook as she reached for the booklet. She owned a passport. She could never explain how it happened, but she had a passport. "Thank you."

Steve grabbed her arm and hustled her out the door.

Once outside the building she pulled out the precious booklet and checked it again. It was real. She wanted to scream and dance.

"You want to leave now." Uncle Lanh spoke as though he read her thoughts. "Return to your life. Tell no one."

"Thank you, Uncle."

"You paid. Now you go."

Steve and Hien followed his instructions. They left. They did not look back.

Passport and papers stayed tucked in her purse once they reached the hospital. It was now Hien's turn to keep her promise. Steve parked the car and got the door for her.

"I need to let Mil know everything is okay and then we can talk. I will tell you all I am able."

They turned down the hall to Pop's room. Hien slowed at seeing so many people gathered. She recognized Colonel Jacobson and Ambassador Bunker, and of course, Mil and Lai, but more military personnel milled about besides PFC Zorich.

Hien's feet paused like a slow-motion video. Every movement, every expression stalled into tiny increments of time. A man in a dress-white uniform stood by Lai who covered her face with her hands. Mil sat next to her, and when she sluggishly gazed in Hien's direction, the fathomless grief etching her face poured over Hien, pulling her under, stealing her breath. She was drowning without a spoken word.

But she knew.

Someone was dead.

"Hien?" Colonel Jacobson's voice. He came to her, guided her to a chair, knelt in front of her.

"No. No, no, no, no, no." Hien shook her head, squeezed her eyes closed. Her right hand twisted her wedding rings around and around her finger while her lungs fought for oxygen. It could not be. No. Not her Michael.

Something broke through. The man in the dress-white uniform was Navy, not air force. Michael was Air Force—dress blues. It could not be Michael.

It was Charlie.

Sudden relief turned to guilt and then grief for her new sister. The pain she must feel.

And Mil. Charlie was her son too.

As Hien opened her eyes, she noticed black shoes next to Colonel Jacobson. Spotless and shiny. She raised her head. The shoes belonged to a man in a dress-blue uniform.

Dress blue.

Air Force.

Her head began to shake again.

"Mrs. Wheaten, I regret to inform you that your husband, Lieutenant Michael Wheaten, was shot down. His plane crashed without him ejecting from it. My deepest condolences."

At that moment, realization dawned.

It was not just Michael or Charlie.

It was Michael and Charlie.

It was both of them.

Hien glanced at Lai and Mil. It was true.

With no warning, the light above Pop's door began to flash.

A buzzing came from the nurses' desk. "*Chambre 135 Code Bleu.*" Code blue room 135.

Medical staff pushed past into Pop's room. Dr. Baleau followed.

Now all stared at the closed door. Seconds stretched into hours. No one moved. No one breathed. It was waiting for the tiger to make the kill swipe, for the impact of the car as you stood paralyzed.

It was waiting for the other shoe to drop.

And then it did.

TEN

The Green Green Grass of Home

March 1, 1968
Arlington National Cemetery
Arlington, Virginia

The icy chill of the metal chairs seeped through the green seat covers and Hien's multiple layers of clothing, making her bottom as numb as her heart. Maybe numb was not the correct word. There were times the pain reminded her she once had a heart until something reached into her chest and ripped it free.

Leaving a gaping hole.

Sucking the air and life from her existence.

So a frozen bum was the least of her problems.

Mil sat beside her. In body. Mil's spirit and passion, her essence, departed with the men of her family.

So much had happened in the three plus weeks since her world crashed into tiny shards. The final blow came when Steve brought Mat to see her. Mat had tried to locate her, without success, until he ran into their colleague, who filled him in on the tragedy.

Or so Steve thought.

Mat had more news. He escaped the horrible mess in Huế. A lucky one on a helicopter not shot out of the sky.

153

Unlike Charlie. Her brother-in-law was evacuating injured Marines to the hospital ship when his helicopter was struck. No one survived that ride. But Mat survived his to come find her.

"I'm so sorry, Hien."

"I know. Everyone is." She had heard the words at least a million times. They had no meaning.

"You don't understand." They spoke in the lobby of the Continental. He guided her to a chair and started again. "I'm sorry to tell you. Your brother and mother…are gone."

She remembered searching his face for a clue. Then she understood. "Gone?"

"Your brother was killed in defense of Mang Ca. He saved several men and stood his ground but didn't survive the first night. The NVA shot your mother. She was caught sheltering some people. She died with those she tried to save. I asked everyone I met about her, from the moment civilians started coming into the compound. I remembered where her apartment was so I could give that information. Last evening, I found someone who saw what happened. I am so sorry but thought you needed to know."

She had no family.

She had nothing left in Viet Nam.

Except for Mil and Lai.

Hien thought about staying in Viet Nam. Mil tried to talk her into it. But, in the end, she knew she must honor her promise to Michael. She would care for his mother. Lai still had her family in Saigon. She and Charlie never wanted to leave there, anyway.

So the decision was made.

Colonel Jacobson helped with that too. Nothing broke through to Mil, but the colonel understood. Hien needed help to go to the States. He made the arrangements, and she now possessed a six-month visa.

The seven men firing three unison shots caused her to jump

as if each barrage tore through her. She sealed her lips to keep the scream inside and reached for Mil's hand.

Mil did not fight it, nor did she respond. She sat there, limp hands in her lap, and allowed Hien to hold her fingers.

Shiny shoes stood in front of her. The image slashed her core. She raised her head to peer into the earnest face of a young man in full dress uniform. Air Force blues. Handing her a folded flag. She released Mil's hand.

"…from a grateful nation."

Accepting the flag, she wiped the tear from her cheek with a gloved hand before it froze on her face. She thought there were no more left.

Then another young man with shiny shoes stood before Mil. She did not respond to his words, but accepted the two flags. The veil on her black hat covered her face well enough that, with additional makeup, the deep purple rings beneath Mil's eyes were concealed. Hien could tell, though, even with the winter coat and heavier clothing, Mil had lost much weight.

A bugler began a song dripping with sadness. The first time Hien heard it, Michael was with her. He told her it was called "Taps." It was melancholy then. It was heart wrenching now. If she still had a heart. Her gloved hands folded over the triangular flag. The tiny bulge on her left hand reminded her that her rings were all she had left of her marriage.

Part of Hien did not want to worry about Mil. She knew enough hurt. She did not want more pain. But Mil was all she had. She was in a strange country with different customs—like wearing black instead of white for mourning—and she needed Mil as much as Mil needed her. But if something did not change… Hien refused to consider the possibilities.

The service completed. Others moved on. It was just the two of them.

"Mil, what do we do now?"

"Go home. I go to Indiana; you return to Viet Nam."

"Mil, I cannot leave you."

"Hien, please hear me. I have nothing. I am empty."

Hien again reached for her hand. "Mil"

Mil pulled back. "Don't call me Mil! My name is not Mil. I am no one's mother-in-law. I have no sons to make me a mother-in-law. If anything I am Mal—Miserable and Lonely. I hurt to the deepest core of me. I am lost. I cannot help you. Go home!"

Hien had not prayed in weeks. Now she thought, *God, help me!*

The words came. "You are my family. I, too, have no one else. But we have each other. Where you go, I will go. Where you stay, I will stay. Your God is my God. We will walk this road together." She took Mil's hand.

Mil did not protest.

Hien took it as a good sign. She stood and helped Mil to her feet. They began their long walk to the car.

The driver opened the doors of their assigned limo and assisted them.

Hien leaned her head against the seat and closed her eyes.

Ready or not, Indiana, here we come.

Indiana

ELEVEN

The Beat Goes On

Monday, March 5, 1968

Breadville, Indiana

Beau smelled the coffee before he saw it. He lowered his newspaper and watched as Margie poured his second cup. He nodded thanks and took a glance about the café before returning to his reading. *The Kokomo Tribune* ran the obituaries for the Wheaten men a few weeks back. Today's issue contained a brief update about the service at Arlington. Aunt Melanie should be home soon.

As if on cue, the café door bells jingled. Beau peeked around the paper to catch Connie Lynn making a beeline for his corner booth. He raised the news a tad higher.

Suddenly, his reading material was shoved from his grip. Connie's smile shone in its place. "Don't you try to hide from me, Beau Salem. The whole town knows you like to hole up in your little hideaway."

"You have my undivided attention, Connie. Provided you keep it short. What's up?"

She slid in the seat opposite him. "Melanie Wheaten just pulled in her drive at the farm." She grinned.

"I've been expecting her. Didn't think it would be this morning, but I was aware. I've already had the utilities and phone service turned on for her. I'll drop by later in the week after she's settled." He attempted to raise *The Trib* again, but Connie kept it smashed to the table beneath her palm. Fortunately, her hands weren't big enough to cover everything. The Pacers' stats looked surprisingly good.

"That's what you know, Smarty Pants. She's not alone."

He raised his head. "What do you mean?"

"She has a girl with her, an oriental girl. Probably Vietnamese." Her gaze searched his face. She hoped for something he wasn't about to give her. A reaction.

"Probably." He had no desire to discuss this. "I'll meet her later. Right now *The Trib* is calling." He snatched the paper from her and wiggled his fingers in goodbye.

"Oh, Beau, your lack of curiosity is appalling." He could hear the huffy attitude in her walk as she strode out the door. Jerry would have his hands full after they got married.

His best friend, Jerry Owen, popped the question to Connie back on Valentine's Day, and she'd said yes. The whole town expected she'd say yes. Those two were meant for each other. He shook out his paper and tried again as the café's bells tinkled.

He didn't even hazard a peek this time. No need to take chances.

However, when someone slid into the booth across from him, he glanced long enough to see whom to acknowledge. "Morning, Jerry. You just missed Connie."

"Morning, Beau. Saw her outside—she tagged me in." He chuckled at his own funny.

"What'll it be, Jer?" Margie put the menu in front of him and poised her order pad at the ready.

"Coffee, black."

She swiped up the menu without a word and headed for the coffee pot.

"Bet she'd given me an earful if you hadn't been sitting there, Beau."

He glanced up. "Why's that?"

"You didn't catch the evil eye she gave me for not ordering more. You'd think she got paid by the item."

"Hmmm." He'd already lost interest. The one thing he appreciated about Jerry, one of the many things that made him his best friend, besides the fact they'd been roommates in college, was that they could silently sit together. Conversation was unnecessary. It was something he treasured and, on a morning like this where he just wanted to read the paper and drink his—he took a sip, it was tepid—his tepid coffee, he counted on Jerry living up to the unspoken rules of their friendship.

Somehow, Beau knew he was about to be disappointed.

"Melanie is back. She's not alone."

He grunted. "I'd heard."

"Looks like we've been nominated to stop by and see what we can learn."

"Nominated?" Beau folded his paper into a neat rectangle and leaned forward, his forearms resting on the front page. "Since when am I running for anything? I will stop by to check on her, them, whatever, after they've settled. If Connie wants to see them so bad, why doesn't she play Welcome Wagon and stop by with one of her pies?"

"That's what I suggested, but I promised I would speak to you. It protects me from later arguments." Margie set a cup before him. He blew into it before taking a sip and choking. "This stuff gets worse and worse. You gotta do something."

"My coffee is worse than Margie's, so until someone answers that help-wanted sign, this is it."

Jerry sipped and made a face. "You better do something soon. This stuff is gonna run off your business."

Beau leaned back against the booth. He'd bought into The Breadville Café as an investment. Now it was taking more of his attention. He thought the girls, Margie and Lulu, could handle the place and he'd just stop in as required, but with Lulu out with a broken leg and her husband not able to help in the kitchen due to caring for her and their kids, he either needed to get behind the counter or hire someone else. Hiring was the better idea. If he had to rely on his own cooking, he'd have long-ago starved. "I'm working on it. Maybe I should pay you to put an ad in *The Breadville Gazette*."

"Next issue comes out tomorrow. You're too late for that one."

"Yeah, about that. When are you gonna change from a weekly to a daily edition?"

Jerry snorted. "When is this town gonna produce enough news to support a daily paper? There's barely enough to print to make good parakeet cage covering."

He sighed. "Yeah. But heaven help me, I love this town."

"Me too." Jerry leaned forward. "Listen, Beau, I'll not get into this if you don't want to. Just need to ask, you okay with Melanie bringing a Vietnamese girl here?"

If anyone else had asked, he'd have politely put them in their place with a glare that said, "None of your business," or "You're an idiot."

But this was Jerry.

Jerry knew.

He was there for Beau's darkest moment. Not only that, Jerry saved his life. He knew the whole story. Jerry was the only one who knew, besides himself and God.

"I'm good. No worries."

Jerry leaned back. "If that changes, I got your back."

He nodded. "Listen, I still have a farm to run. If weather holds, I might start turning things up in a few weeks. Fired up the tractors yesterday. I tucked them in last fall with a lot of care, so they're in good shape. Had to make sure the machinery's ready. Once I'm going, there won't be a free moment." *Yes, I changed the subject.*

Jerry took one last sip of coffee, grimaced and slid out of the booth. "Better get going myself. I've got to put the edition to bed for tomorrow. Catch you later." He waved, paid Margie at the cash register and left.

Beau dropped a buck on the table. Technically he didn't need to pay, but, if nothing else, it set an example. "Margie, I'm heading home. Call me if you need me."

The waitress, who was refreshing someone else's awful coffee, waved. "Okay, Beau. See you later."

He ambled to the parking lot. His old '65 Ford pickup could use a good washing. He might do that today. Nah, it was still too nippy. The big thing was to stay busy. Because he needed to wonder about the other person who came home with Aunt Melanie like he needed another hole in his head.

"Hey, Mom, I'm home." Beau's mother easily startled these days, so he'd taken to calling out the minute he opened the door from the mudroom. He scuffed his boots on the heavy-duty mat before taking them off to pad through the kitchen into the dining room he converted into his mother's new bedroom. Maddie, his red-bone boxer mix, joined him. He scratched her between her ears.

"Ow sings deh?" Her speech remained slurred after the stroke, but her mind was still sharp. Beau understood her, though most people asked her to repeat her words a time or two.

"Things are fine. The coffee is getting worse." He took a seat in the easy chair near her. "I need to hire a new waitress and get 'em trained before I start planting. Talked with Jerry and Connie came by to say Aunt Melanie is home. Looks like she brought someone with her."

"Go see?" She struggled to move in her hospital bed. Her right side was weak at best, non-active at worst.

Beau hopped up to help her. "Hold on to me, Mom." He let her guide the adjustment, adding his strength to her efforts. "Better?"

"Behha."

"Where's Thea? Have you had lunch?" He returned to his chair, trying to conceal his worry. His mother seemed lighter, like she was wasting away. Was his sister, Theodora, feeding her enough?

"Laudy. Yeah, I eee."

The laundry needed doing too. "Can I bring you anything, Mom? Maybe you'd like getting up? Thea and I can get you dressed. We'll go for a ride."

"Nah, ta ma wah."

"It's not too much work. Never. Unless it wears you out. Is that what you mean?"

She smiled with the one side that still smiled and nodded her head. His mother was a dynamo of activity before the stroke, working hard on the farm and volunteering at church. Her days were filled and full and now so… empty. It had been three months. If she'd been found quicker? Immediate help might've made a difference with her progress. As it was, Beau was grateful they could communicate. He knew stories of other stroke victims who couldn't due to aphasia, because the words they expressed had nothing to do with the thought they wished to convey, often causing personal embarrassment.

"All right, feel like doing a puzzle? Or I can read to you?"

"Tee Bee."

"TV? Okay, if that's what you want. I can't believe you've gotten hooked on those soap operas."

She swatted her good arm at him. "Day nee me ta tey da probum, an sis. Ba na un lisses a meh." She laughed.

"Mom, of course they don't listen to you, and you're never gonna fix their problems." He sighed. Her mind was still active and sharp. If only she'd focus on real people. He wheeled the portable television into her room and set it up at the foot of her bed before raising the head so she could see. "What channel?"

"Sis. Ah lub Jin Giade." She flashed her lopsided grin.

Jim Girard hosted a show out of Indianapolis which featured

local talent and news. At least it wasn't a soap opera. Beau turned to channel six, plumped her pillows, and kissed her cheek, before leaving to find his sister.

"Hey kiddo, how's it goin'?" Beau found Thea coming up the basement stairs, arms laden with a wash basket of clean clothes—his clean clothes. "You know I would have done my own. Here, let me take it." He relieved her of the load, tucked it under his arm, and hugged her with his other. "Have you eaten?"

"I'm good. Just wanted to catch up on things. Once I sorted the laundry, it was easy enough to add yours to the mix. So what's the big news from our little burg?" She zeroed in on the spotless counters and began wiping them.

Beau set the basket on the kitchen table and pulled up a chair. "Aunt Melanie is back. Jerry's source couldn't wait to tell me she saw them pull into the drive. Can't imagine why she was out there."

"Them?"

He nodded. "Connie says there is a Vietnamese girl with her. Seemed peeved that I didn't race over. I figure the better idea is to let them get settled. We'll have them over here so Mom can see Mel, if you wouldn't mind making a dinner."

"That's great! I'd love to make something special. We don't eat enough to really cook around here. What sounds good?" She stopped wiping her already clean counters and took a seat at the table with Beau.

"You choose. Get me a grocery list. I'll pick up anything you need. Want to plan for Saturday? Or maybe Sunday after church?"

"Thanks, hon. I will. And let's do it Sunday. I could do a pot roast. It can cook while we're gone. I've got a good one down in the freezer."

He covered her hand with his calloused paw. She was his little sister and, though Thea stayed back to care for Mom, he did his best to care for her. She never complained. But she'd like a life, free of the farm. This he knew. But that would mean losing their mother. That was something she'd never admit aloud. "Sounds great. I will plan to drop by on Wednesday and invite them. We could drive them to church. Mom would like that. Think she'll feel up to going this week? She seemed wiped out after yesterday's trip."

"She'll go. It's hard enough on her when she only goes once a Sunday and not like before. But her mind needs that outing even if her body fights her."

He nodded and stood. "Okay, you get the list together."

"Beau? Thanks. It will be nice." She smiled.

It made Beau wish he'd thought to invite people over more often. He didn't want to pile work on his sister. Instead he'd unintentionally isolated her. He'd need to discover the right balance.

If there was one.

"It's Larry Lujack in the morning on WLS in Chicago." The radio sounded its announcement before Bobbie Gentry started her "Ode to Billie Joe." The song was popular last year so it still got airtime every once in a while.

To Beau it was white noise, just another sound while he hooked up the next set of cows to the milking machine. He almost switched stations to the local talk radio, but he liked Larry Lujack. Besides, the weather reports from WLS were closer to what was going on in his locale than what came from the Indianapolis music stations. He never figured out why—it made no sense—but over time he accepted it.

Once he connected the final cow, Sadie, to the machine, his stomach growled. He hadn't eaten dinner last night. Had Thea saved him anything? He hoped not; he didn't want to put her out. Besides, other things were on his mind.

The Farm Bureau was the reason he'd missed dinner. As president of the local chapter, the meeting took precedence over his meal. Already, before planting started, Pete Warrick wanted to organize schedules for detasseling the corn this summer. This summer. The man was not happy he lost the election. Beau never campaigned, but he had accepted the nomination and win, planning to make things fair for all. He searched for ways where everyone supported each other. To his way of thinking, that was the main purpose of the Farm Bureau. So he listened to each person.

Still Pete felt he wasn't heard.

Thea once said that Pete Warrick reminded her of Barney Fife on *The Andy Griffith Show*. Last night, Beau would have wholeheartedly agreed.

He released the cows one by one. They wandered through the doorway and out to the side pasture, finding bits of new spring grass trying to poke up through the thawing, muddy ground. They all followed suit until Sadie left the barn. Now he could clean his machine and get a bite.

Daylight was doing its best to push the sun over the horizon as he trudged back to the house. He was a morning person, and comfortable with that realization. Scraping his boots before entering the mudroom, he softly called Maddie to him. "Hey, girl, let's be quiet. No need to wake anyone." He held the door and let the dog pad in ahead of him to her food dish.

No need indeed. Thea was up and dressed, making oatmeal in her spotless kitchen. The tea kettle whistled, so he knew Mom was awake. "What are you doing up so early?"

"Mom rang her bell. She'd gotten stuck in an uncomfortable position, so I helped her. Since I was up..." She shrugged and set out bowls for all three of them. "What would you think if we invited Connie and Jerry over on Sunday too?"

"Not too much work for you?" He felt like he left tons of responsibility on her shoulders.

"Of course not. The more the merrier. Besides, Connie could bring one of her pies. Or two." She winked.

"Okay, if you're sure. I'll talk to Jerry when I see him." Beau picked up his mother's bowl and added the brown sugar, cinnamon, and milk, just the way she liked it. "I'll help Mom eat. You relax, have some tea with your own."

Thea's protests followed as he left the room.

"Hey, Mom, how'd you sleep?"

She smiled her half smile. "Goo. Ya?"

"I slept good too. Got your oatmeal here, fixed your way. Do you want to try for yourself a bit?"

She nodded. He cranked the head of her bed up so she could sit. It took some situating, until she was in a position to feed herself. He encouraged any independence. Not that he minded helping, but every tiny victory was worth celebrating.

He put a towel over her chest and the spoon in her hand. "Let me know if you want help. I'll get my own and we can have breakfast together. Be right back."

Again she nodded, so he hurried to the kitchen. Thea had added his favorite ingredients—raisins, butter, and milk—finishing with the spoon sticking out of it, ready to go. "Thanks, sis." He swiped it and rushed back to his mother in time to hear her spoon clank on the floor. By the time they were through, he'd picked it up and cleaned it four more times. Yet his mother smiled and kept trying. Her tenacity and sweet demeanor amazed him. She tempered his life.

They chatted, their normal morning chatter, and then he excused himself. The animals needed their breakfast. Their stalls needed cleaning. He kissed his mom on the forehead and took her bowl with his back to the kitchen.

"Thanks for the oatmeal, sis." He kissed her cheek and headed for the barn—the barn where Larry Lujack waited with his "Animals Stories," and where work was as natural to him as breathing. The barn housed his other girls—the cows. Then to the hen house to feed the hens and gather their eggs before slopping the sow and her babies.

It dawned on him, other than Larry Lujack keeping him company, he was surrounded by females.

And none of them would be considered eligible—for him, at least.

Perhaps that was a good thing. At his age, he was looking less and less like the marrying type.

"Hey, Bill, how's your dad doing?" Beau stopped at the counter to shake the man's hand.

"Fair to middlin', Beau, fair to middlin'."

"You tell him I said hi."

"Will do."

"Margie, the usual." He nodded toward his back booth.

"Be right there, Boss." She put her order pad in her pocket and grabbed a mug and the coffee carafe.

He slid into his place and opened the newspaper he'd tucked under his arm. This time it was *The Breadville Gazette*. At least when Jerry showed up, he'd see that Beau was reading *his* paper for a change.

It was the same each Tuesday. Jerry acted like it was the first time Beau saw it and feigned hurt that his best friend didn't read his newspaper every day. No matter that it only published once a week. And on Tuesday, no less. Jerry said it was to ensure that what happened over the weekend could be added Monday. Keeping current, he called it.

Crazy, that's what Beau called it.

The bells on the door chimed their greetings. He spotted Jerry, right on cue.

"Coffee, Margie, if you please?" He slid into the booth opposite. "How'd you like my front-page editorial?"

"Just getting to it. I only got here a minute ahead of you."

"Okay, fine. I'll wait."

"Oh, you want me to read it now?" It was taking all Beau's strength to not start laughing.

"If you don't mind. I mean, haven't anything else to do, right?"

"Right." It must be important. Jerry wasn't usually this intense about an editorial. He read the first sentence—on civil rights. Jerry wanted to rattle some cages.

The bells jingled. Beau glanced up to see a schoolgirl go to the counter. Shouldn't schoolgirls be in school?

Margie pointed over at his booth and the girl headed his way. She was bundled in a green hooded car coat. The fur-trimmed hood was pulled so low it concealed her face. She had a shoulder bag that crossed her body and her hands were gloved though she kept rubbing them together.

As she approached, she pushed her hood back, revealing her face. She was Asian. And older than Beau had thought. "Mr. Owen?" Her voice was definitely older than a schoolgirl's, lower and smooth with a slight accent.

Jerry waved his hand in the air and slid from his seat. "I'm Jerry Owen. How can I help you? Would you like to slide in?" He motioned to the booth.

She shook her head. "No, thank you. Please, sit."

Jerry did.

"My name is Hien Wheaten. I am Michael Wheaten's widow." There was the tiniest pause before she added the last word.

"Oh, yeah. I knew Mike. Hey, I'm sorry for your loss. Guess I didn't hear that Mike got married." Jerry glanced at Beau.

He shrugged. He hadn't heard either. That would explain some things, though. He tried to make like he was minding his own business.

"Your secretary told me I could find you here."

Beau snorted. He worked hard to stop it only to turn it into a coughing fit. Jerry's mom covered the phones for him when he needed to leave the office—she was his secretary. So much for minding his own business.

"Oh, I see." Jerry glared a dagger at him before turning his professional face back to Mrs. Wheaten.

"I worked for Press Corps in South Viet Nam as interpreter. I like to take photos and sometimes they would buy from me. I have two here that I thought you may buy?" She took a manila envelope from her bag.

"I can take a peek. No promises."

"I understand." She handed it to Jerry.

He pulled out the photos, studying each one with care before laying them on the table where Beau could get a glimpse.

The first was a profile shot of a Vietnamese male smoking a cigarette. It was more than just a photo. It told the story of the man's soul. The other showed Vietnamese children at play—ragged clothing on a rutted, muddy road, still smiling. It squeezed his heart.

One thing was obvious—this girl had talent.

"You took these?" Jerry sounded impressed despite his trying to be cool.

"Yes. I did not sell them after I developed them."

"You developed them too?" Jerry's eyebrows raised at that.

"Yes."

Beau could hear the wheels in his friend's brain cranking, 'round and around.

Jerry sighed. "Here's the deal. I'm a small-town paper. I do all my own photography, and I just put out the current edition today. I don't know that I have a story coming up that would use these photos, though right now I wish I did. You are good, I'll say that. Tell you what. I will keep you in mind and perhaps you can help me take photos as the need arises. Would that work?"

She nodded. "Thank you."

He returned the photos to the envelope and handed it to her. "You have a good eye. Thank you for thinking of me."

"Yes, well…" She cleared her throat. "Excuse me for interrupting. Thank you for seeing me." She headed out the door, making the bells tinkle.

A second later, she returned to the counter. Again, she spoke to Margie who pointed her to the back booth.

"I am sorry to bother again. You are Mr. Salem?"

He nodded.

"I saw your sign—help wanted. I can cook. My English is fairly good."

"Your English is great." Actually, it was more correct than his, though her accent was noticeable. "What I need is temporary help. One of my girls broke her leg and is off until the doc says she can come back. We already shortened the hours, not doing a dinner menu. Breakfast and lunch get busy. If you keep the dishes washed in the kitchen and come wait on people when Margie gets swamped, that would be great. Are you interested?"

Her face brightened. "Yes, I am very interested."

"Okay. Hey are you hungry?" He motioned for the waitress.

"Oh, no, that is fine. A glass of water is enough." She would not meet his glance. Instead, she stared at the table.

"Everyone who works here gets a meal. Margie, she would like a breaded tenderloin, mayo, tomato, and lettuce with fries and… What would you like to drink? I don't recommend the coffee."

Jerry scooted to the wall and motioned for her to take a seat. "He means it. You might as well sit." Jerry winked at him. "Tell us all about you, now that you are his employee."

He watched as she raised her head, searching first Jerry's and then his face. Finally, she sat on Jerry's side, hovering on the edge in case she had to jump and run.

"So, hon, what'd you like to drink? Don't let these yahoos make all your choices. Beau did well on the breaded tenderloin, but it's hard to go wrong with that."

"A Coke, please?"

"You got it. I'll be back with it while the meat cooks." Margie hustled behind the counter, returning with the bottle of cola and a glass of ice. She pulled a straw from her pocket and patted the girl on her shoulder before returning behind the counter again.

"Let's start with your name. I know we both caught the Wheaten part. Tell us your first name again." Jerry was enjoying this. Maybe too much. Was he hoping for a problem?

"I am Hien."

Beau and Jerry repeated it at the same time. Kind of musical, like *He* and *Ing* shoved together. More than one syllable but not quite two. "Hien."

Conversation lagged until a thought popped into Beau's head. "How did you get to town?"

"I rode the bicycle. I found it on the farm."

He sat straighter. "You mean you rode all the way from the farm on a bike? That's at least five miles. And in this weather?"

"Yeah, what'd the radio say? A high of forty-nine degrees?" Even Jerry straightened and leaned in.

"I do not know how else. It seemed better than walking." She didn't appear to comprehend what she accomplished.

"How will you get to work?"

She studied their faces. "I can ride the bicycle."

Jerry shook his head and glanced at him.

Beau knew exactly what he was thinking. He had the same thought.

Right then, Margie arrived with the sandwich and a bottle of ketchup. "Dig in."

Hien stared at the plate.

He cleared his throat. "It's a breaded pork tenderloin sandwich. We make the best ones in the state. Trust me, you will love it."

Hien peeled off her gloves and threw a glance his way before picking up the sandwich and trying a nibble. Then her eyes gleamed, and she took a good-sized bite before lowering the sandwich back to the plate, quiet satisfaction in her sigh. "This is very good. I am learning to enjoy American food."

"Oh, this isn't American food. This is Indiana food. I've tried ordering it in other states. They stare at me like I'm crazy. This is pure Hoosier goodness." Jerry was the connoisseur of the breaded tenderloin.

"I have seen that word in places. What is Hoosier?"

"A Hoosier is someone from Indiana. Or something. We're the Hoosier state."

Beau snorted at Jerry's explanation. *And he writes editorials, too, folks.*

"But what does it mean?"

He chuckled. "Well, it depends on who you ask. No one knows for sure, there's always another story. We accept it. We're Hoosiers."

She smiled a little at that. She had a nice smile.

"Listen, when you get finished, I'll give you a ride back."

"That is unnecessary. I have the bicycle."

"No, I insist. It's a long way, and I'm going right past. Jerry, tell her."

Jerry just kept grinning.

Beau threw him a glare. "Jerry, tell her it's not out of my way."

"It's not out of his way."

"See there? You eat. Then I'll drive you home." It was settled. Right? He realized he wasn't exactly breathing while he waited for her answer. *Stupid! She's a million years younger than you.*

She wasn't exactly looking at him, either. Instead she seemed to watch Margie. "Do I need special clothing?"

"Oh, you mean a uniform? Well, that's what the girls wear. Hey, I have an idea. Wait here a minute." He rushed to the pay phone on the wall at the front of the café and dropped a dime in the slot. He dialed his number in record time and, in his head, counted the rings like the operator character on *Laugh In*. One ringy-dingy, two ringy-dingys.

"Hello?"

"Thea, do you still have that uniform from when you used to wait tables here?"

"Beau, I will not work at the café. I've got too much to do."

"No, no, I just wondered if you had it for someone else to borrow."

Her tone changed. "Sure, it's upstairs somewhere."

"Great, would you pull it out? I want to bring someone by the house in a bit. See if it'll fit."

"Okay. Oh, remember to let Jerry know about Sunday."

He'd forgotten. "Yeah, I will. See ya soon."

He hung up and returned to the table.

"I have a plan about the uniform. Don't worry about that now. Hey, aren't you hungry?" She only ate half of the food.

"I would like to take it with me, if I may?"

"No problem. Margie, could we get a carry-out box?"

She brought a cardboard carton for the leftovers.

Beau filled it and stuck it all in a brown paper bag, also supplied by Margie. He left two singles on the table and helped Hien from the booth.

She glanced at the money.

"Jerry and I drank a lot of coffee."

She didn't appear to believe him.

No matter. He tucked the newspaper under his arm, picked up the sack and ushered Hien out the door. Something told him as he exited that he was leaving his old life behind. He shook his head at the thought. She's just a kid. He was only helping her so she could help him with the café.

That was all.

TWELVE

Young Girl

Beau did not believe what he saw. How had that bike held together to get Hien to town? The fenders were nearly rusted through and the tires low on air. He picked it up and laid it in the bed of his truck before helping her into the passenger seat. She was so short, for a second he was afraid he might have to lift her. But she hopped in with a bit of support from his hand.

He closed her door and walked around to his. Climbing in, an electric charge shot through him. He had a rider in his truck —one of the opposite sex. Who was not a relative.

Definitely not a relative.

"Do you mind if I turn on the radio?"

She shook her head, so he twisted the knob. It was set for WLS. Otis Redding crooned about wasting time while "(Sitting on) the Dock of the Bay."

"I called my sister before we left. I remembered she has a uniform she isn't using and asked if you might borrow it. She agreed. I can take you there to get it if that's okay."

"Thank you." She kept her hands folded in her lap, her focus straight ahead. The thought crossed his mind that she was silent. Then he reminded himself that she had just become a widow, was living in a strange country, and rode in a truck with a complete stranger.

Guarded might be the better word.

The radio continued to play. He restrained himself from singing along. She'd been through enough without having to put up with his lack of tone.

Ten minutes later, the Lemon Pipers warmed up their "Green Tambourine" as he pulled into the drive. Beau switched it off, proud he'd not embarrassed himself by joining.

Hien had yet to move a muscle.

He hopped out and hurried to get her door. She seemed to size up this part of his farm. Did she compare it to the Wheaten place? If so, his was bigger. And in better shape. Not that he'd ignored their place when Uncle Ernie and Aunt Melanie asked him to keep an eye on it. But he didn't do a lot of renovations either. But he had brought the livestock home to make it easier to care for while he cared for his own. When Aunt Melanie wanted them, he'd personally return everyone.

And he had made some improvements. A few. When he heard Uncle Ernie and Mike weren't coming back, he knew Aunt Melanie couldn't handle it alone. She'd most likely want to sell. Any upgrade would get a better price. But they were minor compared to what he could have done.

Should have done.

She took his hand long enough to jump from the truck—a true jump. Then she smoothed out her coat and waited to follow him into the house.

Maddie wandered over and began to sniff.

"She's friendly."

To Beau's surprise, Hien smiled and petted the dog.

All at once he couldn't decide. Should he take her in the front door, as company? Or the back, as family? Would she understand that concept?

Backdoor won—his front drive area was still muddy. He scraped his feet and held the storm door for her.

She observed his example, and with her hand on the door-knob, watched him until he nodded before opening the mudroom door.

He followed her inside and slipped out of his boots, leaving them on the mat near the kitchen door, and paused to see if she would do the same.

She did. Her sneakers were mud-splashed.

He held the kitchen door for her and whispered, "My mother is recovering from a stroke and startles easy, so I try to be careful."

Something in her gaze softened, and she nodded.

Thea entered from the dining room now Mom's bedroom. "Hey, you made it." She walked over and stuck out her hand. "I'm Thea, this guy's sister. Nice to meet you." She spoke with extra clarity—nothing abnormal, but clearer and slower than a Thea usual.

Hien took the outstretched hand. "I am Hien Wheaten. Michael was my husband."

Thea's eyes grew wide, and she pulled the girl into a hug. "Oh, I am so sorry. So deeply sorry. We all loved Mike around here. All the Wheatens, in fact. Those three guys are so missed." When she released her, Hien appeared shaken.

"You okay?" Beau guided her to a chair.

Hien covered her mouth and nodded. He could see she blinked away tears. Finally, her hands were again folded, in her lap. "Thank you." She swallowed. "It is good to know."

The pain in her eyes was a gut punch.

"So, Thea, did you find that uniform?"

"Oh, yeah, I put it… Where did I put it? Mom's room. Just a minute." Thea scampered out.

Beau took off his mackinaw and slipped it on the back of a chair before removing his hat and adding it to the table. He suddenly needed to fix his hair and ran his fingers over his head until he sensed her gaze. Followed by a desire to disappear into the floor. He coughed. "Would you like me to take your jacket?"

"Okay." She stood, slipped her gloves into her pockets, and unzipped before shrugging it off and handing it to Beau.

Now he felt more stupid than ever. This girl was tiny. Not that his sister was huge, by any stretch of the imagination. But Thea had at least six inches in height—could be more—and probably a good thirty pounds on her. That uniform would hang like a sack.

He put her coat over his as Thea returned to the kitchen. "Here… Oh, this'll never work."

Hien's eyes gleamed with understanding. "Perhaps if I fix the hem and we pin it?"

"It'll take more than that, I'm afraid. Let me grab my sewing kit. Better yet, Hien, why don't you follow me upstairs and I'll use my sewing machine. We'll get this fixed." Thea motioned to their guest who followed her.

So did Beau's gaze. He had no idea she was that tiny. All of five foot, maybe, she looked to be an Asian version of that super skinny model Thea and Connie talked about—Stick? No, Twig. Kinda. Except she didn't go in for that eye makeup stuff. She had lovely eyes. Without all the goop. And a voice like honey. He shook his head. He was too old for those thoughts.

Not that he was supposed to know, but he'd figured out that Thea planned a celebration for his birthday in a couple weeks, his thirty-fifth. Just thinking the number made him feel old, way too old to contemplate a girl that young. How young was she anyway?

He wandered into his mother's room. She was trying to work a puzzle. The doctor said that moving the pieces into place would help with her dexterity. Instead, it frustrated her.

"Te-ha sa you bough ho compy."

"Yeah, I brought Mike's widow home. She came by the café and wants a job. Thea is letting her use her old uniform." He moved a piece closer to his mom's hand.

"Mys weeow? He marry? Whass she lie?"

Beau shrugged. "Tiny, I guess is the best word. Quiet. Asian.

Seems nice, intelligent. But of course, a fool is thought to be intelligent—"

She joined him as she could. "when he remains silent."

They chuckled. Not at Hien. Their laugh recalled the millions of times Beau's dad said the same thing. Man, did he wish he were here.

"Wha dey doin?"

"The uniform is too big, so Thea is cutting it to fit, I guess. Or something like that. She took Hien upstairs to her sewing machine."

She laid aside the piece she'd been trying to place and pushed the others away. "He Ing?"

"Yup, Hien. That's her name. Hien Wheaten."

"Yo taw a Melli yea?"

Beau moved the puzzle board out of the way. "Not yet, I haven't talked to Aunt Melanie. I figure I will when I take Hien home. Guess I'm her ride to work for the time being too. She showed up at the café on an old bike that's one gust away from collapse."

"Has dat go war? Ya biz-ee."

"I know, I'm busy. For now, it will work by me milking the cows and then picking her up. I can have breakfast at the café. It's temporary, Mom. And at least she won't be in trouble for being late if the boss is her ride, right?" He winked at his mother.

She didn't wink back. Actually, she couldn't wink any more, but she could blink her kind of wink at him in response. This time she didn't.

"Why are you worried?"

She moved her hand in his direction and he knew she was reaching for his. A tear traced its way down her cheek. "Too maw"

Beau patted the hand that held his and cleared his throat. "It sounds like too much, I know. Especially with planting coming up and the needs at the café. Plus, the Farm Bureau things and being on the Board of Elders at church. Bet you think I'm burning the candle at both ends. But God has blessed me so richly, Mom. I can't say no when there's a need and He whispers in my ear."

She raised his hand to her lips and kissed it. "I pay."

"Please do Mom. Please keep praying." He kissed her forehead. "Keep Hien in prayer, too. She needs it."

Mom nodded.

"Now, what can I do for you?"

"Tee Bee!"

Oh, those soaps!

A short time later, Beau heard footfalls on the steps. He peeked into the kitchen to see Hien coming downstairs. He called to her so she wouldn't take the wrong turn at the landing and end up alone in the living room.

She followed his voice and took the kitchen side.

"Would you like to meet my mother?"

She nodded, so he led her through to the dining room. She paused at the doorway. Was she nervous?

"It's fine. Mom's awake. She enjoys company, though it can sometimes be hard to understand her. The stroke affected her speech." He held out his hand.

She took it and he brought her to the bedside. "Mom, this is Hien Wheaten. She married Mike. Hien, this is my mother, Valerie Salem."

"Nie ta mee ya." Mom smiled her half smile.

Beau wondered about this idea. Hien appeared almost scared. But then she smiled too.

"It is nice to meet you, Mrs. Salem."

He pulled a chair up close to the bed. "Hien, here, why don't you sit?"

"Thank you." She sat.

"Wha di ya la eegly?"

Hien again had that funny expression. She glanced to him.

Now he understood. Hien figured out the first phrase, but this one had her stumped. No worries, he'd be the translator.

"She would like to know where you learned English. It's okay, Mom knows that sometimes she's hard to understand. I usually get what she means, so if you don't, I can translate."

Hien nodded. "I studied in school. In Viet Nam I went to Catholic school. We were taught English and French as our foreign languages. I continued learning when I attended University. When I moved to Saigon, I worked for Press Corps as translator. I practiced and listened to improve my vocabulary."

"Ya ha pre-ee assen."

"She thinks you have a pretty accent." *I agree, Mom.* His cheeks warmed at the thought and he turned his head.

"Thank you. I try not to have accent, but I guess I must work harder."

"Ya go oonibersy? Ya yang. Ha ode er ya?"

Oh, no. "Mom, you're getting too nosey."

"It is okay. What did she ask?" Hien wasn't the least bit ruffled.

"She said you are young. She asked how old you are. I'm sorry."

Hien and his mom exchanged a glance, and they both chuckled.

"Do not be embarrassed. I am twenty-three. I will be twenty-four this September."

Good ol' Mom, getting answers to questions for him. *Wish she didn't have to embarrass me to do it!* How could she be twenty-three? She could pass for fourteen. She didn't conduct herself like she was fourteen. Nor did she sound fourteen. Talk about looks being deceiving.

No matter. She was too young for him.

Why did that thought keep coming?

Beau stepped back and watched. Hien and his mother

seemed to have made a connection. He listened as they talked, only translating the toughest of phrases. Well, whatever her age, he realized he felt a tad protective of her. What of it? She was nearly family. His father and her mother-in-law were first cousins. So he should be protective of her. And her mother-in-law. His father would want him to look out for them. He always said family was important—and when there's a crisis, that's when family needs to close ranks and bond.

But that didn't change one fact.

She was still too young for him.

$$\sim$$

An hour later, Thea came in with the uniform over her arm. "Hien, would you mind trying it on one last time? I think I've got it."

Hien excused herself and followed her back upstairs.

Beau's mom motioned to him. "Shee seet gil."

"Yep, Mom, I agree. She's a sweet girl. Not many other Asians in Howard County. I doubt if there's any other Vietnamese at all. She might end up lonely, I'm sure there'll be culture shock along the way."

"Ya hep ha."

"I will, Mom. I'll help her. Now you aren't so concerned about me, huh?" He winked and this time she blinked back.

She put her hands together and bowed her head.

"Thanks, Mom. I need all the prayers you can send."

Soon the girls returned, Hien with the uniform over her arm.

"It fits, like I made it for Twiggy." Thea smiled, then noticed the worried expression on her Mom's face. "Yes, the skirt is long enough, Mom. For goodness sake, I wouldn't make it that short. Oh! There's something else." She hurried out, her footfalls on the stairs resounded up and down before she reentered holding out a flat package in her hand. "You'll need one of these to comply with the Health Department. A hair net."

Hien's quizzical look prompted a demonstration.

"See?" Thea opened the packet, "It's this netting. You put it over your hair to keep it all close to your head. You've got a bun now. That will help you. Do your hair the same. You wear the net over it—check out the cover." She showed Hien the model's picture.

"I think I understand. Thank you, Thea, for all your help and the uniform. I am grateful."

"Have a good time at the café. You can tell us all about it on Sunday after church."

"After church?" Hien glanced from Thea to Beau and then to Thea.

"You didn't invite her?"

Ow!

Where'd his sister learn to punch so hard? He rubbed his shoulder.

"Just hadn't had the chance yet. But, since you brought it up, we would be honored, Hien, if you and Aunt Melanie could join us for dinner on Sunday. I understand Thea has planned a lovely meal and her pot roast is famous throughout the entire county." He smiled his best smile for Hien and then turned to his sister. "There. Did I do it right?"

Thea swatted him with the back of her hand. "You goof! My brother is an idiot, but he is correct. I am planning a pot roast. We would love to have you join us."

"I will need to ask Mil. It sounds wonderful. I hope she agrees. Thank you. You have all been kind." She hugged Thea and Beau's mom and then gazed up at Beau.

"Guess we'd better go. Be home soon." He kissed his mom's forehead and his sister's cheek. Leading the way to the kitchen, he helped Hien into her coat before putting on his own jacket and hat.

~

THE WHEATEN FARM was only down the lane, barely more than a stone's throw. But the decrepit bike in back, the muddy roads, and Hien being new to Breadville, made it more than good manners to drive her home. She was silent the whole way, again, though more relaxed. A little.

Beau pulled up in front and turned off the engine. "Think I might go say hello to Aunt Melanie? I don't want to intrude, but I'd love to see her."

"I believe it would be fine."

"She's not my aunt, you know. More like a second or third cousin—I never can keep all that straight. But she and my dad were first cousins, so we're cousins. Only my parents expected us to call them Aunt Melanie and Uncle Ernie. Mike and Charlie called my parents aunt and uncle too."

"I understand. It was respectful."

Her eyes were so dark, like bottomless pits. It took Beau's breath for a second. "Uh, yeah, I think that was the real reason. Let me get your door."

He hopped out and rounded the truck to open it for her.

"Thank you. We can go in this way." She led him to the back porch—which doubled as a mudroom—where she hung up her coat and slipped out of her sneakers.

Though midday, the house was shadowed in a sort of twilight. It took Beau an instant to get his eyes adjusted. Once he did, the sparseness surprised him. He had worried little about the inside, though he patched the roof in a couple places, cleaned out the gutters and trimmed the foliage around the place. He should have gotten Thea or Connie to do some homey things.

"Mil, I am back." Hien walked through the kitchen to what he guessed was the dining room, though no furniture was there to confirm it. "Mil, we have company." Her voice reverberated.

From there he followed her into another empty room. Bare of furnishings and people.

She stopped. "Wait here, please. I will see if she is in her bedroom." She raced up the stairs, her movements echoed through the vacant house. "Beau!"

He charged two steps at a time. At the top, he paused to hear which room. Hien's voice, repeating "Mil, Mil" came from the left. He found them. Aunt Melanie lay with her eyes closed on a make-shift palette on the floor.

Hien knelt beside her. "Help me, Beau. She will not wake."

He stooped next to Hien and checked for a pulse. She had one. A little thready, but still a pulse. He scooped her up. "Let's go."

He heard Hien's footfalls behind him as he dashed downstairs. A part of him needed to let someone know, but the sooner he got her to the hospital the better. "Quick, dial my house."

Hien ran to the phone, he called out the number. She dialed and then held the receiver to his ear.

"Thea, it's an emergency. I'm headed for Howard County hospital. Call ahead. We're on our way. Melanie is unconscious but still breathing. I'll let you know once we learn something." He didn't even say goodbye but raced to the truck in his stocking feet.

When he reached the passenger side, Hien ran from the house, their coats and shoes in her arms. She opened the door and dropped them all on the floorboard. "Let me put her in the middle. She can lean on you once you're in."

Hien nodded. She appeared pale, smaller than ever.

After he had Melanie situated, Hien maneuvered around him to get into the passenger seat and take over holding her mother-in-law.

He slammed her door and raced to his. Spinning gravel, he backed to make a Y turn, and took off out to the lane. He headed for US 31, the main north-south artery. Howard County Community Hospital was closer than St. Joe's over on the westside of Kokomo. Either'd take time. How much time did Melanie have? He knew that Thea and his mom would pray as soon as she made the call. He should start too.

As he silently prayed, a recollection returned, one he'd rather forget. But it caused him to think. "Has she been using anything to help her sleep?"

"Yes, her doctor gave her a prescription for Valium."

An icy tingle shot up his spine. Still, he thanked God for the memory that triggered his question and pressed harder on the accelerator.

Twenty-two minutes later, according to the dashboard clock, he handed Melanie off to the waiting emergency unit. He made a point of telling them of her Valium prescription. Hien went in with the team while he parked the truck.

Elbows on the steering wheel and hands over his face, he prayed harder than ever. "Lord, we know about this danger. Please pull her through. I promise to walk alongside as You say. Also, give Hien hope. She has been through a lot. She needs to see You are here for her. In Jesus's name. Amen."

He locked up and began that long trek to the emergency room doors. Hien was nowhere in sight, but he was sure she was with Melanie wherever she was. He checked in with the desk and they directed him down the hall to a cubical. With the curtain pushed aside he saw Hien couched in a chair in the corner—out of the way of the medical attending team. He moved by her and felt her shake without even touching. Her hands looked so fragile in her lap that he offered his calloused, rough one. It enveloped her delicate fingers. The fear of squeezing too hard nearly made him let go, but he hung on.

"You folks might want to step out. This will not be pretty." The doctor didn't wait for a decision but continued working with his patient. Suddenly, Melanie sat up, vomiting into a tub.

Hien buried her face in his side.

"They have to do this. They've got to get the Valium out of her system."

He could feel her nod against him, but she didn't even peek out for a while. Her shaking slowed but never altogether stopped.

Eventually, Melanie was laid back against the pillows. They hooked her up to an IV. The pole with the tubes of medication flowing flashed to an image he hadn't thought of in many years. More memories surfaced with the sights and sounds of the ER. Beau swallowed hard.

"I hate hospitals." Hien's words dragged him to the present.

He could guess her reasons for hating this place. His own he knew too well. He nodded in agreement.

A young man with a stethoscope around his neck motioned them to the hall. "It's too early to tell, but I think we got to her in time. Any idea if this was on purpose?"

Beau glanced at Hien and caught when understanding coupled with the man's words. Her eyes grew wide, and she made a small gaspy noise. "It was an accident, I am sure of it. She has been under great stress. But she would never take her life."

"Had to ask. We'll get a room ready, monitor her tonight. If she responds well, you should be able to bring her home tomorrow."

Beau stuck out his hand. "Thank you, Doctor. May we sit with her?"

"That should be fine. You might have to leave when they prep her to move. For now, though, you're good." He left, heading in the desk's direction.

Beau held the curtain for Hien and then followed her. She resumed her seat, he stood alongside. Concerned over needless noise, he decided not to attempt conversation. Hien must have accepted that as she didn't start anything either. Instead, it became a silent vigil, waiting for Melanie to make the first sound.

Focusing on hallway noises, bits of passing discussion and even the soft harmony of the two women breathing helped keep unwanted thoughts at bay. Beau played a quiet game in his head, trying to identify who made the footfall squeaks as they traversed the corridor—male or female, young or old, weight, height. He didn't take time to research his guesses, but let his imaginings bar his memories from surfacing.

Melanie moaned and Hien hopped up to check on her. He watched as Hien stroked hair away from her mother-in-law's face, softly crooning her name. Funny, he assumed Hien was saying "Mel," but the more he listened, he could swear she said, "Mil."

As realization dawned, Aunt Melanie crumbled sobbing in Hien's arms.

Hien rocked her back and forth, whispering soothing words. Like a ninety-pound tower of strength.

IT TOOK ANOTHER HOUR, but they finally came for Melanie. Beau ushered Hien to the corridor after they told him the room number. "Let's get a bite to eat. You haven't eaten anything since before noon and it's after six now."

She nodded and started for the outside doors and then stopped, her hands to her face. "Oh, no!"

"What? What's the matter?"

"I left the rest of my sandwich in the truck."

Beau felt the laugh push its way out before he could stop it. "I thought it was something important."

"It is important. I saved that for Mil."

Her expression reminded him of what he saw at their farm. He realized what food meant to her. "I'm sorry. I don't mean to make light. I promise neither you nor Aunt Melanie will go hungry if I have to fix your every meal myself." He took her arm. "Come on. I know a place."

He guided her back to where he'd parked the truck. Once in, he started it and headed further south to a little drive-in—The

Dog n Suds. Now this was worth remembering. On hot summer nights, his dad loaded the family into the car, and they would end up at The Dog n Suds for frosty root beer floats. It was too nippy for a float tonight, but a mug of root beer and a chili dog would hit the spot. He pulled into the parking slot and ordered on the intercom for both of them.

Beau realized she stared at him. What could be the problem?

"Have you ever eaten a hot dog?"

She shook her head. "Sometimes people in my country eat dog, but I have never tried it." She didn't appear to want to now, either.

This time he caught the laugh before it escaped. "It's not made from a dog. Some places call them frankfurters. They are tubes of meat and eaten on a bun. I guess the name comes from how they kinda look like the body of a dachshund, those little wiener dogs?"

She shook her head no but at least didn't appear terrified.

The waitress on skates rolled out with the tray which she hooked on the window. He gave her three dollar bills and then handed a red plastic oval basket to Hien. "Tell me when you want your drink. I can leave it here until you do." He grabbed his chili dog and unwrapped it. Knowing she watched, he modeled how to savor the messy delight.

A moment later she unwrapped hers, sniffed and touched the chili with her tongue. The next instant she bit into the dog, bun and chili with great relish—well, not literal relish. But he could tell she enjoyed her first chili dog. She peeked up at him after the first couple bites, her bottom lip with a smear off to the side, smiling her approval.

"So, you want to try the root beer?" He cocked an eyebrow at her, biting back his laugh.

She nodded. "Please."

He handed her a mug, she took a tentative sip, wrinkled her nose, and glanced at him. "There is no alcohol."

It was beyond his control. He snorted and nearly choked. "No, it's not an alcoholic drink. There's no beer in root beer."

She returned the drink to him. "I dislike the taste of beer, but thought I should be polite and try it."

"Do you like root beer?"

"It is better than beer, but it does not excite me like a chili dog. I am sorry."

"Don't worry about it. Once the weather gets warm, I will treat you to a root beer float. That may change your mind."

The glance she returned didn't seem to buy his assurance, but she returned to eating her new favorite American delicacy. "Thank you for dinner. I do not have any money. You can take it out of my pay, if you still wish me to work for you."

That stopped him mid-thought. "What do you mean? Of course I still want you to work for me. And you start the day after tomorrow because I'm sure tomorrow you will be tied up. Also, until you get furniture at your place, you and Aunt Melanie are moving in with Thea, Mom and me."

"We cannot impose."

"What imposition? You are family and I'm not about to let the hospital send my Aunt Melanie home to that empty house." He hoped that was firm enough without being pushy. Truth was, both Hien and Melanie needed to be under his roof until they got things settled.

She was silent for a minute. Finally she gazed at him. "Thank you. I was concerned about taking Mil home. I do not know how to pay."

"Please, listen. There is no need. Besides being family, we are neighbors. This is what neighbors do. At least, it is here in Hoosier country. Okay?" He was tempted to reach for her hand but settled for a brotherly pat on her arm.

"Okay. Now I hope Mil agrees."

"Why do you call her Mil?" There, he'd finally asked. He couldn't take it back.

"Pop helped me with that. I could not call her mother. I

have—*had*—my own mother. Mil stands for mother-in-law. And it sounds similar to her name, so that is what we all decided."

"Who is Pop?"

She paused. "Michael's father. You call him Uncle Ernie." She grew so quiet, he nearly missed the next part. "I loved him very much."

Though he knew little of Hien, he wasn't surprised she loved her husband. Of course she loved her husband. Or was that what she meant?

He offered her a napkin.

She dabbed her eyes.

He pointed to the corner of his mouth and she quizzically stared back. He pointed at her mouth and her eyes grew. Finally, like a clumsy clod, he took another napkin and tried to wipe the chili from her lip.

She took it from him and completed the job. "Is it all removed?"

He nodded, still unsure of his voice. After clearing his throat he started the engine. The waitress skated over and removed the tray. He rolled up the window. "Are you ready?"

She nodded and folded her hands in her lap.

He knew in that moment, that whenever he closed his eyes and pictured her, it would be with her hands folded in her lap.

THIRTEEN

I Had Too Much to Dream Last Night

MELANIE WAS AWAKE. THE NURSE GAVE THEM TEN MINUTES with her before sending them home for the night. Hien was not pleased, but rules were rules.

Beau stayed long enough to say hi and share the living arrangement plans. She started to resist, but she wasn't up to a fight at that moment. He kissed her on the head and told Hien he'd meet her in the lobby.

The nurse must have monitored the clock. Hien appeared less than ten minutes later.

"She is concerned about what people may think when they hear she has been in the hospital." Hien appeared distressed.

"If asked, we can truthfully say it was something she ate. That is all anyone needs to know. Even Mom and Thea don't know. It's not my story to tell."

She walked beside him to the truck. After they were both in, she turned. "When Pop had the heart attack, it was important that no one worry about his ability to do his job, though he could no longer do it. The doctor advised him to return to the States, to Walter Reed hospital, when he was strong enough to travel. I worked for Press Corps. I have—*had*—friends I trusted. I could mention nothing. It was very hard. They understood. A friend helped Mil and me after the embassy assault. We agreed that, in return, I would give him an interview. And then—Michael, Pop, Charlie… they…" She stopped and took a deep breath. Her voice grew softer. "They all died. I told my friends that I would not lie, but I had to keep secrets. Then it no longer mattered. Maybe if we had not hidden information, we would not be punished."

Her honesty and pain cut through him. "Hien, they did not die because you withheld information."

"You are right. But since then, everything has gone wrong. Mil tried to get her things out of storage. They will not accept her check. The bank froze her account because it was a joined account—"

"Joint. You mean joint account."

"Joint account. For Melanie and Ernest Wheaten. Because Pop is dead, they must close the account until his affairs are in order. The things she sent from Viet Nam are being held at customs. They want to be paid. I would use my money, but I used it to buy my passport."

No wonder the house was bare. This was a simple fix, though. He could pay for the furniture and things from Viet Nam. He had that much easy.

But would they accept his money?

"Don't you receive some kind of widow's benefit? There should be something for you, and I'm sure Melanie has benefits coming." Even if they wouldn't take his money, he'd help them get what they were due.

"I have filled out paperwork. Now I wait. Those who must pay us say wait. Those who want paid do not wish to wait. That is why I need the job."

And that's why I'll help you. "It's late. Let's go home. I bet Thea has something you can wear for bed. Tomorrow I will take you by your place to pack, for you and Aunt Melanie. Sound like a plan?"

She nodded and leaned her head back against the seat.

By the time he'd gone a mile up US 31, she was asleep.

BEAU FLIPPED on the radio in the milking barn and started his girls into their stanchions. Their warm breath and mooing sounds soothed his senses as much as laughing to WLS's *Uncle Larry's Animal Stories*. Maddie lay curled in the corner, waiting to follow the bovines to the pasture. Recognizable chords introduced "Judy in Disguise (with Glasses)." He hummed along. After a commercial, Steppenwolf did their best to get the early listeners' motors running with "Born to Be Wild." He gazed at his ladies going through their morning ritual. Bucolic? Yes. Wild? Not even close. But at least, he was awake.

Once he released Sadie and sent her with the herd, he cleaned up the milking machine. He whistled for Maddie and headed for the house. Despite doing his best to stay quiet, it didn't matter. Thea was already up, working on breakfast. Hien set the table.

"Made pancakes. Want to get the butter and syrup?" Thea threw him a wink as she flipped perfection on her griddle.

"No problem." He pulled the butter from the fridge and got the syrup from the pantry. "If you have enough for Mom to get started, I can cut them and take them to her. She's up, right?"

"I would be happy to do that." Hien looked up from where she was placing the utensils next to the plates.

"Are you sure?" Mom enjoyed their talk yesterday. It was probably a good idea. "Okay." He showed her how small to cut the pancakes and she added the butter and syrup. "Tell her I'll be there in a few minutes."

Once alone in the kitchen, he tested the waters to see what Thea figured out about what happened. Stealing up behind her, he reached to snatch a piece.

She smacked his hand. "Watch it, Bub. You'll get yours when I say."

"How long were you here before Hien?"

"Oh, she was already down here having a great talk with Mom. They are turning into fast friends." She flipped two more pancakes onto her stack and poured two more globs of batter on the griddle.

"Really? Wow. She was so worn out last night, I woke her to get her into the house."

Thea turned, making a point of peering straight at him. "You know they haven't been in the US a week? When they flew over, they arrived only a day before the burial at Arlington. They left for here the day after. The jetlag alone must be horrible. Add to that the culture shock—she doesn't need to be feeling more stress. And the trauma—three deaths so close together. It's unfathomable what they've gone through."

"I'm glad you feel that way. I've invited them to stay here for a while."

The smell of really done pancakes got her attention. She turned back to her job. "How come?"

"Well, I can't go into everything, but they've been hit with even more. Do you know there's not one stick of furniture in that house? They slept on the floor. I'm glad I got the utilities turned on or it would have been on the floor in the cold."

Thea spun like a ballerina, spatula held aloft. "Oh, my goodness! Of course, they will stay with us as long as they need—they are family."

Beau grinned. "That's what I said." He made a quick try to pinch off a piece of pancake, but she swatted him again. "Hey, can't blame me for trying."

She laughed. "Go sit and I'll bring you some."

〜

AFTER EATING he peeked in on his mom. She and Hien were deep in conversation. How patient Hien was with her.

He returned to his girls, got them fed before mucking out

the stalls and then headed to the house for a shower. He eaves-dropped a moment. Mom was trying to explain her favorite soap opera during commercials. He shook his head and climbed the stairs to his bedroom. It would be just like her to get Hien hooked on those stupid stories.

Clean and dressed, he wandered back downstairs. Mom was alone. Thea was running the vacuum. Hien was nowhere. He tried the kitchen. It was empty. Where could she go?

He glanced out the window and spotted her. She sat on the front porch swing. Maddie was curled up on the floor beside her, keeping company. He wandered out. That's when he noticed the tears.

"What's the matter? Why are you crying?" He pulled out a handkerchief and handed it to her.

"Those poor people. Oh, those poor people." She wiped her eyes. "It is awful. I thought I had problems, but it is so awful."

Beau sat next to her on the swing. "What people, Hien? Who do you mean?"

"On the TV. Those people your mother showed me. There was a woman. Her husband cheated on her with her best friend. She needs an operation, or she will die. The doctor is afraid to do it because he has a drinking problem. Then her daughter ran away and was kidnapped. The kidnappers want money. She does not have it. How can this happen to one person?" She burst into a fresh sob.

He tentatively put an arm about her shoulders, and she curled into him. That she trusted him to that extent stymied his thoughts. He collected his words, took a breath, and then plunged. "Hien, you know that's all just actors, right? It's not real. Those are ongoing stories on TV for entertainment."

She sat up, staring at him. "Entertainment?"

He nodded. "I promise. Those people get paid to act. Even the writers are paid to write that stuff. Folks all over tune in daily to learn what will happen next."

She wiped her eyes again, refusing to meet his gaze. "I feel foolish."

"Don't. Some believe these actors are for real. They write letters and pray for them. I guess it's a compliment to the actors that you believed it." He tucked a rogue strand of hair behind her ear. It felt natural until he realized what he did. He cleared his throat, hoping she wasn't offended. "My mom never paid attention to the soaps. She was always so busy with life. Then she had the stroke. She got hooked watching TV. I think it reminds her that, though what happened to her is hard, others have it harder. Even if the ones she sees are actors, there are people who have deep pains and burdens. It also reminds her she can still do something—she prays."

"For actors?"

"No, well, maybe. For issues they face in real life. But she prays for those who suffer illness. Or who are missing their children or are dealing with betrayal. Those people, in real life, have real pain, so she prays for them. The soaps remind her of those who need prayer." Good thing his mom explained it to him yesterday when he let her know he was concerned over her watching that useless stuff. He still hated that she watched those shows, but not so much.

"I do not know what to say." Maddie nudged her knee and Hien gave her a hug.

Beau shrugged. "Nothing to say. Hey, you ready to go to your place? Aunt Melanie will probably come home today. You'll want to get the things you need brought over here, plus she'll need some clean clothes."

"You are right." She stood. "I will get my purse." She went in the house. Maddie followed.

He leaned back in the swing. You never knew where culture shock might rear its head. He closed his eyes and listened. Scripture he'd hidden in his heart bubbled to the surface.

He hath shewed thee, O man, what is good; and what doth the

Lord require of thee, but to do justly, and to love mercy, and to walk humbly with thy God?

Pure religion and undefiled before God and the Father is this, To visit the fatherless and widows in their affliction, and to keep himself unspotted from the world.

Delight thyself also in the Lord: and he shall give thee the desires of thine heart.

He understood why the first two verses spoke to him. They guided him in his walk. But that third verse? He loved the Lord Who not only saved him spiritually, but physically too. He delighted in doing for the Lord, in putting the kingdom of God first in his thoughts and heart. He also believed God would put what He desired into his heart, that they would share the same desire—at least that was his prayer.

Only lately…

He shook his head and opened his eyes. The view of the farm from here, even without growing crops or covered in a white blanket of snow, still brought waves of gratitude. No rolling hills as in other parts of the Midwest. But the possibilities were limitless. He could envision this land, bursting with corn and soybeans, and how that would bring sustenance to others, either through temporary jobs during harvest or just availability of food for purchase.

From the pasture where his girls grazed to the catfish-filled creek filled that cut through his land to the stand of sycamores that bordered the fields soon to be plowed and planted, God blessed this farm. So well that he could invest in businesses in town, keeping more people employed. The more he gave, the more God gave him to share. He couldn't out-give God. Not that he tried. It was just that when God showed him a need, he did his best to do whatever God put on his heart.

So what was God saying about Hien?

～

They made a run to the Wheaten farm, packed a few changes of clothes and brought them back. Then they took off for Howard County Community Hospital. The doctor was finishing his visit to Aunt Melanie's room.

"I see you have family here, so if you want to get ready, I'll make arrangements at the desk for your release. They can drive you home. Now remember, you still need to rest. Easy does it for the next couple of days. The nurse will have my written instructions. Take care."

Aunt Melanie nodded. "Thank you, doctor."

He left.

Hien hugged her mother-in-law.

Though Aunt Mel returned the hug, she didn't make eye contact. And her face pinked a bit.

Hien didn't notice. "I am so glad you can leave here today. This is good."

"Yes, dear heart. I guess it is. Hi there, Beau."

He came and held her hand. "Hi there, yourself. We've got things moved to our house. That's where you'll rest, for now. Hien brought you some clean clothes. Would you like a shower while the nurse gets your paperwork ready?"

"Sure." She started to swing her legs out of bed and glanced up at Beau.

"Ah, how about I take a walk while you ladies get this shower thing done?" He grinned, giving a finger wave before returning to the hall.

At the cafeteria, he bought a cup of coffee and found a corner where he could drink it. Someone left a newspaper, *The Kokomo Tribune*, so he thumbed through it. He'd downed the last drop and was about to leave *The Trib* for the next person when he noticed an ad. It was for an auction this Saturday. Hmmm, should he go? There was nothing he needed, but the little voice in his heart convinced him to read the ad again. "Open for viewing at 10:00 a.m. Bidding to start at 11:00 a.m." Jerry might go with him.

Figuring Hien and Melanie to be done, he refolded the paper, tossed his disposable cup and returned to the room. The nurse arrived with the wheelchair. He gathered up the bag of clothing, striking out ahead to pull the truck to the entrance.

This time Aunt Melanie suggested Hien sit in the middle. Because she was smaller.

Thanks, Aunt Melanie.

Like not thinking of pink elephants. All your brain conjured were images of pink elephants. But instead of pink elephants, his brain focused on the tiny, soft-spoken woman with the kind heart seated so close he felt her breathe.

He didn't need this. The ride home was torture.

Once there, he helped everyone from the truck and carried the luggage. Aunt Melanie seemed steady on her feet, even when Maddie made a swift entrance to the house right past her ankle. Hien walked at her side, just in case. He brought them through the kitchen. Thea was putting the finishing touches on lunch. Hien stayed to help while he led Aunt Melanie, after quick greetings with Thea, in to see his mom.

The old friends hugged, and emotion ran high, so he excused himself to take the cases upstairs. Hein and Melanie could share Mom's old room. He left the baggage on the bed and returned to the kitchen.

"Might we eat with your mother?" Hien's request was so simple. Why had no one thought of that?

"Sure. We have TV trays in the closet, Beau. Can you get them?" Thea still manned the stove.

He was at the closet before she finished speaking. Mom had a bed tray, so he grabbed four and slipped in to set them up. "Don't mind me. We thought we'd eat together. I'll bring in some chairs, too."

The women smiled at him. Mom said something he couldn't hear.

"Yes, he is a wonderful young man. You did a great job, Val."

"Ee Ing sa goo, seet. She lub oo sa mush."

Tears glistened in both women's eyes.

Aunt Mel squeezed his mom's hand. "Yes, Hien is very sweet. I love her very much too. I don't know what I would do without her."

Beau cleared his throat. "I'll get the food." He dashed to the kitchen, glad to be away. "About ready?"

Thea put two plates in his hands and waved him forth. "Go, for Mom and Aunt Mel."

Hien followed with the drinks—glasses of milk—and utensils.

Maybe being together, they wouldn't get so emotional. He hated that. He wanted to fix things. But sometimes things couldn't be fixed. That was his thorn. However, he'd had enough emotion the last twenty-four hours to keep him a good long time. He needed a break, or at least a laugh.

He eyed the plates as he set them on the trays. Thea's recipe for roasted chicken with vegetables was one of her best. The aroma wafting from the kitchen made him hungrier.

Beau put Maddie out. Chicken was her downfall.

Hien and Beau gathered their plates and things. Thea dipped up her own, and the three of them returned together.

"Bu, gase."

"Okay, Mom, I'll say grace." He caught Hien watching the women bow their heads before following suit. "Lord, thank you for this day. Thank you for bringing us all here. Please, bless this food to the strength and nourishment of our bodies. Bless the hands that prepared it and bless our time together. We love you, Lord. In Jesus Name, Amen."

Amens echoed, and they dug in. Beau stole another glance at Hien to see what she would think. Had she eaten chicken? They ate poultry in Korea. It was likely they did in Viet Nam. But what about mashed potatoes, or roasted carrots and onions?

She must have felt his gaze. She glanced up and smiled.

He smiled back and refocused on his food. Thirty-five was much too old to play these games. Aside from her age, she had only been a widow less than a month. The glistening diamond on her left hand glared that reminder. Just in case he forgot.

He disgusted himself.

~

AFTER LUNCH, Hien went to the kitchen to help Thea with dishes, leaving him an opportunity to talk with Aunt Mel. He suggested they go to the front porch, and she agreed. Maddie padded out with them. But she caught sight of a squirrel and took off.

"Are you warm enough? I can get you a jacket." She only wore a light-blue turtle-neck sweater and navy slacks.

She shook her head. "No, kiddo, I'm fine. The nippiness feels good. I need it. So what shall we talk about?"

He motioned for her to sit in the swing and then shoved his hands in his pockets, struggling for the best approach while leaning against the porch railing. "When we found you yesterday, I couldn't help but notice the lack of furniture. I made Hien explain. I've two ideas."

She started the swing moving and stared out into the distance. "What is your first idea?"

"You let me pay your storage fees and get your things delivered. I can also pay the custom fees for the rest."

"And your second?"

He knew she wouldn't go for his first one. "I can front the money and bill Uncle Ernie's estate. That way you'll have your stuff. You pay me back after they settle things."

She still hadn't looked at him. "I'm trapped by all this. So much gone and now trapped. I haven't any fight left." She turned to him. "You win, kiddo. I choose your second idea. I cannot let you pay for us. I'll give you the information and let you handle it if you don't mind. I'm too worn. Maybe next week I can get in to see my lawyer, light a fire under him. Maybe next week I'll have more energy, be more myself."

"That's the second time you've called me kiddo. That's an Uncle Ernie thing. I've never heard you call anyone that."

"All those years together, it must've rubbed off. I miss him, you know."

"Yeah, I understand that. Caught myself using that term, then I remember him."

She patted the swing next to her. "Come, sit with me. We can swing and enjoy the air."

He sat. Aunt Melanie always was one of his favorite people. She was pretty and smart and sophisticated. Now, he saw how this aged her. Fine lines had developed near her crystal blue eyes and the corners of her normally smiling mouth. Slight jowls added to her facial features. Her blonde hair, cut chin length and tucked behind her ears, lacked luster.

"What have you mentioned concerning last night?"

"Nothing. Well, I told Thea and Mom that it was something you ate."

She smiled a smile that didn't reach her eyes. "Clever way not to lie."

"You must understand, it's not my story. I won't be talking about it. Besides, I understand."

She stared at him, her expression calling him a liar.

"Aunt Melanie. I do not lie. Believe me, I understand. To an extent. It's nothing I've shared, but—"

"Don't. You don't have to tell me. I believe you."

"Good, because I don't think I'm ready to speak about it to another person. One day, maybe."

She patted his knee and stared off in the distance. "One day."

The gentle rocking of the swing seemed to echo her.

LATER THAT AFTERNOON, Melanie gave him the information. He made some calls and since the storage company was fairly local, he got a commitment to have the furniture delivered next Monday. It would take longer on the items coming from Viet Nam. He wasn't sure how much longer, but at least he'd gotten things moving.

Thea started to plan a full supper, but Melanie suggested making chicken salad sandwiches from the leftover meat.

Beau ran into town to check on the café, then stopped by the IGA for ice cream. Afterward, while Thea dipped up the sweet treat for everyone, he wheeled the television into Mom's room and checked the *TV Guide*. Everyone voted and CBS won over NBC. He'd hoped for *The Virginian*, on channel six, but the women wanted *Lost in Space* followed by *The Beverly Hillbillies* and *Green Acres* on channel ten. Mom liked *He & She*, though it did nothing for him. Besides, it was on late enough that he could excuse himself and head for bed.

He had to admit, he'd hoped for a laugh and the downright silliness of *The Beverly Hillbillies* brought a chuckle. He liked the Jed Clampett character. He had intelligence, no matter if he was simplistic and uneducated. The Jethro Bodine character bothered him. Throughout his military experience, and even when he was at Purdue, there always seemed to be someone who expected him to be dumb, because he grew up on a farm. The memory still irritated. He needed to let it go. Those that knew him, those he cared about, never considered him a stupid man.

Though there were memories that made him feel stupid. Maybe that was the real reason it got to him.

After watching Ava Gabor win the day on *Green Acres*, he kissed his mother, his aunt and his sister goodnight. That left a ticklish moment with Hien. He ended up sort of patting her shoulder and kind of hugging her. *Man, that was awkward.*

It was great to tumble into bed. They'd had two busy days, and morning always came early. He took out his Bible and read awhile before dousing the light and rolling over. Sleep eluded for nearly an hour.

Then she walked in.

Her hair hung to her waist, not pulled back with a thong. Her conical hat had slipped down her back, her face was clearer than it had been in over a decade.

Nam Sun.

He had loved her. He wanted, needed to hold her. His brain told him she was gone. His heart said, "Here she is." She strolled toward him, her arms outstretched to him. She'd returned. He reached for her.

The world exploded.

He sat in the road.

Correction, he sat on the floor. The floor of his Indiana bedroom. Korea was far away. She was even farther. He held his hand in front of his face and through the moonlight seeping in between the curtains he could tell, it shook. Why not? The rest of him did. His heart pounded. Breathing labored. Tears streamed down his face.

The last time he'd dreamed this way he was in college.

God, why now?

He knew why now. But he couldn't think about it.

Beau glanced at the clock. Great, he needed to be up in fifty-six minutes.

He threw on his clothes and tiptoed downstairs. Might as well start the day.

THE BREADVILLE CAFÉ's bells tinkled announcing another person. Beau peeked over his newspaper long enough to spot Jerry. Seconds later his friend slid into the booth across from him.

"Wow, you look terrible. Rough night?"

Jerry was aware of Beau's rough nights from firsthand experience. The last time he'd had this kind of rough night, they were roommates. Jerry understood.

"Kinda snuck up on me. Been awhile. Years."

"She's not Nam Sun."

Beau took a sip of coffee. It tasted better today. "I know. We've just had a couple crazy days."

"Yeah, I was wondering about that. Thought for sure she'd be working yesterday. Then both of you were gone." He was fishing. He couldn't help it. It was in the ink pretending to be blood flowing through his veins.

"Made more sense to start today. Thea practically had to make her a uniform." He caught Margie's attention and lifted his mug.

Jerry glanced around. "So, where is she?"

"In the kitchen. She's on dishes duty with some potato peeling on the side."

Margie brought the pot and gave Beau a refill. "What'll it be, Jer?"

"Try the coffee. Hien made it." Beau took a sip to punctuate.

"Hey, I'm the first to admit mine is lousy. She does all right. You might want to try it." Margie had a kind heart.

"Okay, you sold me. One coffee."

"And what else?" Her eyebrow cocked and her pencil hovered over her pad.

"Seriously, Margie? Do I ever order anything but coffee?" Jerry shook his head and glanced at Beau for back up.

"Hope springs eternal. Just remember, I gave you the opportunity." She poured him a cup and moved on.

"What did she mean by that?" He tried his drink. "Hey, this is better."

"Hien made some pies. Been getting good feedback on them."

Jerry's mug splashed as it hit the table. "So why didn't anyone say something?"

"You had a chance, but you let it pass." Beau shrugged, wanting to chuckle, but holding it in.

"Hey Margie! Any of that pie left?"

"Sorry, sugar, just sold the last piece."

The expression on Jerry's face made the laugh burst out. Beau grabbed a napkin and wiped his eyes. "Man, I needed that! You are a true friend."

"Well, not so sure about you. Could've given me a heads up. That was cold, dude."

"If you and Connie come for dinner on Sunday after church, I'll make it up to you."

Jerry shrugged and sighed. "Oh, all right. I guess. But it better be good."

"It will be. Thea is cooking, not me."

"Thank heavens for small favors!"

Beau opened the paper to a back page and folded it down before handing it over to Jerry. "Check this out. Want to go with me on Saturday?"

"An auction, huh? What do you hope to find?"

Beau remembered his own questions when he first spotted the ad. "Don't know yet, but I will once I see it."

"Okay, I'm game. It's over in Peru. Want to drive or shall I come pick you up?"

"I'll drive. Pick you up about nine."

Jerry gave a thumbs up and then swiped the business section of *The Trib*. "Here's the rest of your paper."

Beau took it and settled back to read again, grateful for a friend like Jerry

NORMALLY BEAU HEADED for home before the lunch rush hit so he wasn't monopolizing a needed table. But today he didn't want to drive back only to return for Hien at two o'clock. So, instead he wandered out to the sidewalk and looked over his town.

Not that it belonged to him. But it was his hometown. His family had been part of it for generations. Even when his father had met and married a southern girl, he brought her to

Breadville. It was home.

About halfway between Bunker Hill Air Force base and Kokomo, Breadville was in Howard County. Just. All of two hundred residents—that included the pets, Beau was sure—and with an honest to goodness Post Office situated on the Howard County side of the divide (instead of the Miami County side), they were an official town even if they barely qualified as a village. Main Street ran for five blocks and the one and only stop light handled traffic at the very heart where the eastbound artery to US 31 passed through.

It was a good place to live.

Beau shoved his hands in his pockets and began walking. He crossed the street and passed a couple shop doors when someone called his name.

"Hey, Salem!"

He turned. Pete Warrick stood in the barbershop's doorway. "Hi, Pete. What's new?"

"Did you get the detasseling schedule on the calendar yet?"

"Pete, man, I haven't even started planting. Why are you so all-fired up?"

"You know you got to keep that thing set up to a year in advance. We're all counting on getting the help. Last minute won't cut it." Fussy. That was the word for it. Fussy.

"I'm aware of my duties. I take my responsibilities seriously." He inhaled and exhaled through his nose. He wasn't going to lose his temper.

"You do? Heard you were running around with some little Asian cutie the past two days."

Beau's breathing slowed. He felt a burn begin in his gut. "Pardon me?"

The Barney Fife lookalike retreated a step closer to the door. "It's all over town." His finger still wagged in the air.

When Beau's fingers curled into a fist, he forced them to flex. "What's all over town? Pete, you have no idea what you are talking about. I suggest you stop running at the mouth before you cross the line."

"Well, I suggest you spend more time on your Farm Bureau duties and less on other things." He spat out "other things," like it was distasteful.

Beau turned and walked to the corner where he crossed the street. *Even a fool is thought to be intelligent when he remains silent. You need to stay silent, Beau.*

The big mouth called after him. "Running away won't change anything. You've got to do your duty for the rest of us or step down from being the president."

He shook his head and blew out a breath before wandering to the hardware store. That was the crux of the matter. Pete wanted the presidency and was trying to goad him into turning it over.

Beau needed a friendlier face. The door jingled as he walked in Crawford's Hardware. "Hey Gus, what's new?"

"Not much. You?"

Gus had no other customers. That gave them time to chat. Gus was concerned as his wife had been down with a cough for a couple weeks.

Beau prayed with him. They chatted more before Beau decided he'd better move on. "I'll see you Sunday."

He needed that, to talk with a brother in Christ, pray for a need. It wiped away the negative attitudes and he left refreshed.

A thought came to him. *Maybe you should pray for Pete.*

Beau started to argue and then decided he wasn't that stupid. It was much simpler to obey.

So he did.

FOURTEEN

Gimme a Little Sign

BEAU CHECKED HIS WATCH. 1:35. HE COULD WANDER BACK to the café, grab another coffee before Hien got off work.

Jingling bells announced him as he greeted a couple guys at the counter. "Hey Jonesy, missed you Sunday. Everything okay?"

"Wife twisted her ankle, so we stayed home. I ended up fixing dinner." He chuckled. "That's why I'm here. Can't stand my own cooking."

"Wow, I'll be keeping you both in prayer. Don't need you poisoning anyone." Beau playfully punched his arm.

"I appreciate that. So will Bonnie. She's doing better now, but still has to take it easy."

"Margie, do we have anything with a lot of leftovers?"

She glanced up from wiping a table. "Sure, there's plenty macaroni and cheese. Want me to serve some up?"

"Yeah, make a doggy bag for Jonesy here and stick it on my tab."

Jonesy started to protest.

"Hey, can't have you giving your family ptomaine poisoning, can we? Besides, we've too much. You take it." Beau patted his shoulder on his way to his corner booth.

She brought out a brown paper sack and set it in front of Jonesy, whose "thank you" floated back to Beau.

His newspaper was where he had left it. He returned to his reading.

Margie arrived with the coffee carafe and poured him a cup. "The new girl is pretty good. She jumped in with a smile. Only thing, she struggles some with vocabulary."

"Like what?"

"She didn't understand what a Manhattan was."

"Most people outside of central Indiana don't know what we mean by a Manhattan. She knows now, right?"

Margie nodded. "Plus a couple teens came in during their lunch break. They started making comments about her being small and oriental."

The burn returned, churning in his gut. "What happened?"

"Well, one of them said, 'Groovy' and the other said 'Can you dig it?' and she was lost. Told them she did not dig grooves. But she could make them a grilled cheese sandwich and would that be okay—you should have seen their faces. By the time they left, they loved her. Even gave a tip. And you know those kids don't have extra money for that."

Beau's heart rate settled. He smiled and took a sip of the coffee. "By the way, let's have Hien keep making this stuff. She's good with it. And Margie, thanks for looking out for her."

"Hey, she's a sweetie. No problem." Margie started to take her coffee pot and return to the counter, but Beau got her attention.

"Would you do something for me?"

"Anything for you, boss."

He handed her a quarter. "Go play B14. You can pick the other two songs."

She tossed the coin and caught it in her fist. "Sure" After putting the carafe back, she went the jukebox, dropped in the coin and punched the buttons.

Carl Wilson's distinctive tenor began Beau's favorite song, filling the café with "Good Vibrations."

"When are you gonna let them take that record off there?" Margie now wiped the counter at his end of the cafe.

"Never. Besides, I bet I can name what you picked. 'Groovin' and 'Happy Together'. Am I right?"

"Just shut up and listen." She called over her shoulder. "Hien, you need to get this guy out of here. He's bothering me."

Hien peeked out from the kitchen, drying her hands on her apron skirt. "Is it time?"

"It's fine. You did great. See you in the morning." Margie put her arm about the girl's shoulders and gave her a quick squeeze.

Hien beamed. "Thank you. This was busy, but fun. I will see you tomorrow."

Beau stood and met her at the register just as The Beach Boys' song ended and The Young Rascals started. "Hey, hey, see? I told you." He winked at Margie who tossed a rag at him. He tossed it back and walked Hien to the truck.

THE NEXT MORNING, they repeated the schedule. Hien was ready to go as soon as Beau finished milking. He returned to feed the animals and grab a shower before getting a quick bite and heading back to the café. For the time being, this worked. But there were glitches ahead. None of which could be avoided.

For one, after the furniture arrived, Hien would be at the Wheaten farm. Another problem was that he needed to start plowing and planting. Soon. He wouldn't be available to play chauffeur. Not that he minded. It gave him a chance to talk with Hien. She was coming out of her shell, or that's how he viewed it. Perhaps she required time to adjust to the changes. Whatever the reason, he anticipated their moments together. Her English was good enough to understand some jokes. The ones she didn't get she picked up with a little explanation. The fun was in how she remembered and applied it later. She had a great sense of humor.

But a sense of humor would not supply her transportation home from work while he rode his tractor in his fields.

That thought continued to bug him as he drove to the auction with Jerry on Saturday. And, of course, Jerry spotted the problem.

"So, you gonna get a chauffeur's license?"

Beau started to say, "What do you mean?" but he knew Jerry knew he knew. "It's only temporary. I haven't figured it all out, but I'm working on it."

"Glad that at least you know you gotta do something."

"I realize it. They do too."

"They?"

"Aunt Mel and Hien."

Jerry stared at him. "So you're gonna drag Melanie into this?"

"I help both of them. They are family. That's what family does."

Jerry snorted. "You'd help anybody with any need if it were in your power. You're that kind of guy. But don't tell me this is equally for Melanie and Hien. I've seen the way you look at her."

Beau stopped. "What do you mean?"

"You think no one is wise to you, but I've watched you. She's not ready for that, my friend."

"*She's* not ready? *I'm* not ready for a relationship. With her or anyone. Besides, I'm old enough to be her… uncle."

That made Jerry laugh. "Right. That age thing? It's in your head. The real problem is she's still too fragile. She needs friends, more women friends would be best." He elbowed Beau.

"I'm not out to save the world. Just helping with what God puts in my little corner." He glanced down at the brochure for the auction. "Hey, this may be the answer."

"What?"

"C'mon."

Beau searched among the displays. Over near the corner of the barn, there it was. This was what he'd come for. There was only one question. What would it cost him?

"You've got to be kidding!" Jerry laughed. "That's gonna be a pretty penny."

"I wonder." Beau ran his hand over the powder blue fender.

"It's still too new."

"I'm going to get this." Beau nodded and whistled low as he inspected the car, noting the circular horse medallion gas cap on the rear. With a two-tone vinyl top, not a convertible, it sported the Rally Pac—the optional tachometer and clock fitted on—as well as vinyl interior with the ponies across the back of the bucket seats. The automatic transmission had a floor mounted shifter, and under the hood Beau noted the V-8 appeared to be in great working order. This was one cherry 1965 Ford Mustang, and though his head said closer to $1000, the voice whispering to his heart said $475. Even he thought he was crazy.

"How does it run?"

The guy from the auction house, a toothpick dangling from the side of his mouth, wandered over. "She purrs. Want to hear?"

"Sure."

The guy turned the key, and she started at once. No clinks or clunks.

"Okay if I take a peek underneath?"

"Knock yourself out." Auction guy had nothing to hide.

Beau slid under. Jerry stooped next to him.

No visible signs of rust and no big oil stains soaking into the barn floor.

Beau slid out and dusted off his backside. "What's the story?"

"It belonged to a guy who didn't come home from Nam. His mom passed away and some of the estate is being sold today. It's the biggest item, but there's other stuff."

Beau nodded. "Thanks." He motioned for Jerry and they walked away.

"Whoa! That car is perfect. Hien could drive it with no problem."

"Can she drive?"

"Okay, so one problem. Maybe. But I can teach her. If I have to."

"What if she doesn't want to accept a gift this large from you?"

Beau realized he hadn't considered that, and it was a strong possibility. He scratched his head and shrugged. "I just know I'm supposed to buy that car. And I'll get a great price. After that, God'll need to handle it."

That shut Jerry up.

"Hey Beau."

Beau and Jerry turned.

"Phil Carpenter. Good to see you, Pro-Fess-Or." Beau shook hands with the tall, dark-haired man.

Jerry did too.

"When did you get back? I thought you were at Penn."

"Just home for a couple days. Dad's got stuff for the auction. Decided to spend time with him. How's…things?"

"You mean Thea? She's fine. You should drop by and see her."

Phil's eyes twinkled a moment, a smile teased the corners of his mouth, but it disappeared almost instantly. "No, that's not a good idea. The visit is too short, anyway."

"She'd love to see you. At least, call her."

Phil shoved his hands in his pockets. "Maybe. Don't tell her you saw me, though, okay? In case I don't get the chance."

"Okay, Phil. Good seeing you."

Jerry echoed the sentiments.

Phil nodded, turned and went in a different direction.

"You gonna tell Thea?" Always the newspaper hound.

Beau threw him a sideways glance. "I'm not getting in the middle. Thea hits hard.

THEY BROWSED A FEW MORE THINGS, then took their seats before the auction started.

An hour passed before the Mustang was on the block. Jerry bid on a couple items, won one, lost the other. Not that he needed anything, but it's boring not taking part.

According to Jerry.

Then the pony car was on the block. The auctioneer started the bidding at $1000. No one put up a paddle. He dropped down to $750. Beau heard crickets chirping. No effort even at $500, so Beau called out "two-fifty."

"We've an offer of two hundred fifty. Do I hear three?" The auctioneer sang out his rhythmic chant and someone raised their paddle. "Three, we have three. Can we make it three fifty?"

Beau lifted his.

"Three fifty, we've three fifty. Do I hear four hundred?"

The someone who bid before, again raised his paddle.

"Four twenty-five, do I hear four twenty-five?"

Beau put up his and glanced over his shoulder at the guy in the red-and-white Case ball cap.

"Now we have four twenty-five, how about four fifty?"

Case-ball-cap-guy raised his again.

Okay, Lord. I heard $475. This is it.

"We now have four fifty. Can we make it four seventy-five?"

Beau lifted his paddle and sent up a prayer.

"We've four seventy-five. Do I hear five hundred? Five hundred?"

The guy shook his head.

"Four seventy-five going once, four seventy-five going twice, sold." The mallet sounded. "For four hundred seventy-five dollars. Congratulations." The auctioneer moved on to the next item up for bid.

"I can't believe I just saw that!" Jerry's eyes and mouth were rounded like O*s*.

Beau's heart thumped, his breath came hard, like he'd run a marathon. "I can't either. Whoa, God is good."

"Yeah, but now He has to convince Hien to accept that He planned this for her."

Beau patted his pocket to make sure he'd brought his checkbook. "I know."

~

BEAU HITCHED the tow bar from the back of his truck to haul the Mustang home. An electric charge still ran through him. He and Jerry relived it the whole return trip.

They stopped at the farm first to unhitch the car before taking Jerry to his place. Then Beau drove to the café to wait for Hien.

The counter was bare of customers. Saturdays were like that. Breakfast was still busy, lunch a lot slower than weekdays. The in-between times were plain dead.

Beau claimed his back booth and his stomach growled. All that excitement had him drumming Beach Boys songs on the tabletop with his fingers. He could eat a... What did he want to eat?

Margie showed up with a mug and the coffee carafe.

"Hey, Margie, how's the day been?"

"Sluggish. Hien did more cleaning than anything else."

"Well, I'll fix that. I'm starving. What looks good today?"

Margie's eyes popped. "Gotta mark this on my calendar, Mr. Boss Man—you eating here at your own establishment?" She pulled out her order pad. "The roast beef is rather good. We can whip you up a Manhattan nice and quick."

"One Manhattan it is. Extra gravy, 'kay?"

"You got it, hon." She tapped her pencil on her pad and took off to make his open-faced roast beef sandwich with a mound of mashed potatoes in the middle, drizzled with beef gravy.

After she left, Beau slid out and walked over to the juke box.

Dropping a quarter in the slot, he first picked "Good Vibrations." That was his given. After studying the new choices, he settled on "A Whiter Shade of Pale" by Procol Harum and "San Francisco" by Scott Mackenzie. There was something soothing about the songs.

Margie returned with his food. He gave thanks.

A few minutes later, Hien came out and sat across from him. "So how is it?"

"Ah-mmm." He grinned.

"I should let you swallow before asking a question." She smiled back.

Beau put down his fork. "Hien, I've been thinking. I have to get the farm ready for planting soon. Then it'll be difficult to get here to pick you up. Plus when Lulu returns, the job is really hers."

"I know. I am grateful you have let me work for now."

"Well, I had an idea. I went to an auction today and bought a car."

She said nothing.

He swallowed and continued. "I was thinking you might use it as you need."

She chewed her lower lip and sighed. "I do not know how to drive."

Jerry was right. "That's no problem. I can teach you. It's easy and the country roads around here are great for learning. Once you are comfortable, I'll take you for your driver's license. You'll be all set."

"So, you will loan me the car until I get one of my own?"

Beau paused. "You can borrow it, or you could buy it from me a little at a time. Whichever you prefer. We'll keep the payments small. If you need to miss a month, we'll work that out."

She mulled it over and nodded. "That is a good plan. I am nervous about driving. Are you sure I can learn?"

"I taught my sister how to drive. I'll teach you." Famous last words? "Let's go home so I can show you my find. I think you're gonna like it."

"Okay." She slid out of the seat, grabbed her jacket, and headed for the door.

Beau dropped a couple bucks on the table and followed. Suddenly his stomach churned. The food? No, nerves. What if he couldn't teach her to drive? What if she hated it? What if this was all his imagination?

Four hundred seventy-five dollars for a pristine 1965 Ford Mustang. And you knew the price before the auction started. Are you sure this is your imagination?

Beau shook his head. Nope, not his imagination. He breathed again.

∽

"Oh, this is very nice." Hien stroked her fingers over the white vinyl upholstery.

"Climb in. It's fine."

Her glance said she wasn't sure she believed him, but she slid into the driver's seat.

"What do you know about driving?" Beau needed an idea where to start.

"Nothing. This is my first time sitting in front of the steering wheel."

So, he had his work cut out for him. "I'll tell you what some of these things are." He began with the foot pedals and the shifter. He figured it was better for her to understand the knobs and purposes before she started it up.

She quickly caught on, repeating his words as he went and quizzing herself as he introduced new parts.

Once she had a good grasp on the features, he suggested a ride. He promised he would drive this first time because she sounded nervous. He held open the passenger door for her and then returned to the driver's seat. One more thing he should show her. "I need to scoot this seat further back. My legs are longer than a wet week. But you'll want to pull it closer so you can reach the pedals. Don't get so close or your knees will bang against the dashboard, but you don't want to stretch your legs, either." He showed where to pull the lever and how to adjust.

She nodded, folded her hands in her lap and stared at his shoes.

"Don't worry about watching my feet. It is something you will learn by feel. I promise not to get you into any dangerous positions. You'll be ready for each step. Okay?"

"Okay."

"Let's see how this baby runs."

Furrows appeared between her brows as if it puzzled her, but she said nothing.

He turned the key, the engine fired right up. Putting it into gear, Beau headed toward the road. Man, the car handled sweet.

"How about a spin around Breadville? You haven't seen most of it."

She agreed.

The whole town was only a quarter-mile square. Most businesses were on Main Street, though the IGA grocery sat on the artery connection to US 31. Beau pointed out the sights—Flo's Beauty Shop, Crawford's Hardware, Flynn's Drug Store, the bank and post office. Miss Lily's Dress Shop and Alterations had a Spring Sale sign in the window.

"Is there a school?"

"Yep, but not in town anymore. We've got a bus that picks the kids up and takes them to the grade school. It's over by Bunker Hill. We're still small, so banding with other communities made sense. The high school kids are bused, also, but in a different direction. Some older kids have cars so sometimes we get a few of the high schoolers for lunch at the café. Heard you met a couple of them already." He grinned.

She smiled down at her hands and nodded. "Yes." Her cheeks pinked.

Beau drove on and watched her as she stared out the window at his town, trying to view it with her stranger eyes. He hoped she saw friendliness, kindness. A good place to live. "Oh, and here's the church. You'll see the inside tomorrow."

"What is it like inside?"

"Like any other small country church, I guess."

"I have never been in a church."

He spun to read her face and ran a stop sign.

His heart pounded as he pulled next to the curb and turned off the motor. "You've never been in a church? I thought you were a believer. Or, I, we all assumed…" He was so stupid.

"I guess I am a believer, as you say. Pop was teaching me about the Bible and Jesus before he died. He said I needed to decide and pray. I decided to believe. I prayed for many things. God helped us when the embassy was attacked, but He did not save Michael or Pop. I do not know what to believe, but I respect and trust Mil's God. Did I correctly answer?"

"You said that with honesty. That makes it correct. Now you need to learn about the God you respect and trust. Church'll be great for that." He smiled encouragement and started the car. "Let's head back. And don't worry. It's all gonna be fine."

At least she returned the smile.

Note to self—no more running stop signs and call the insurance agent.

SUNDAY MORNINGS STARTED EARLIER than other days. Beau had all his regular morning things to do, as well as helping Thea get Mom ready. It was a two-person job. Thea washed and dressed her, but it took both of them to help Mom into her wheelchair. Beau was needed to bring her down the front steps. He purchased "The Tank" with Mom in mind even before she came home from the hospital. In reality, it was a 1966 Lincoln Continental. Equipped with seat belts, those offered her extra help to sit stable in the car. And the inside was roomy with leather seats. That was important. Getting her in and out had to be trouble-free and he didn't mind paying more if it helped Mom. Plus, there was plenty of trunk room for her wheelchair.

Today, though, he was extra glad he'd made that purchase. They had two more passengers.

Melanie didn't want to go with the family, but Mom convinced her. Mom could sell margarine to Mother Nature.

The adventure only started as they left home. Then they pulled up to church, often double parking on the street until he could get Mom in the wheelchair. Thea wheeled her in while he searched for a parking spot, usually a couple blocks away—the lot was not big enough for all the vehicles in attendance, especially ones as enormous as The Tank.

Somehow they managed to not miss much more than the pre-service music, as a rule. Today, Melanie helped Thea while he parked. Hien rode with him, wanting to observe his parallel parking prowess. Normally, he did it in the classic three steps, no sweat. Not this time. That's what he deserved for showing off.

They walked back to the church together. Jerry and Connie waited just inside the front doors. It was their Sunday for greeting regular attendees and guests alike. Beau couldn't help but think his friends were a good choice for that ministry—both were outgoing and friendly.

Connie greeted Hien at the lobby door.

Hien took a step back, bumping into him. Something was off.

Connie practically grabbed Hien's hand to shake it.

Beau could have sworn Hien pulled away. The action was small, so he wasn't sure.

She turned to him, her expression a mixture of fear and hurt. "Excuse me, please. Where is the restroom?"

"Hien?"

She shook her head. "Restroom?" It sounded as if she couldn't say more.

He walked her to the women's door.

She went in.

Connie came up from behind. "Think I should go check on her?"

Beau shrugged. "I don't know. We were fine walking in here. She's been excited and nervous. This is her first church service."

"Ever?"

He nodded. "Uncle Ernie shared the Bible with her before he died."

"Perhaps she got cold feet. I imagine this is overwhelming if you didn't grow up with it." Connie put her hand on the door. "Go save us places. I'll see."

What a relief to leave it in Connie's hands. Pre-service music was winding down, so he entered the sanctuary and found his family, remembering to save seats for Hien and Connie. While he was at it, he might as well set a hymnal down where Jerry could sit since he still greeted latecomers.

Halfway through the opening hymn, "This Is the Day," Jerry slipped in next to him to share the book. He glanced at the pew and cocked an eyebrow.

Beau sang but pointed with his head toward the ladies room.

Jerry nodded and kept singing too.

The choirmaster asked them to turn to "Great Is Thy Faithfulness." The choir added all the harmony, making even the small congregation's offering of praise sound majestic.

Now Beau and Jerry exchanged glances and questioning looks at the narthex.

Thea elbowed Beau and mouthed, "Where's Hien?"

Beau whispered in her ear, "She's in the ladies room with Connie."

She nodded and whispered, "Excuse me." She squeezed past Beau and Jerry and headed toward the lobby.

Beau sighed and joined in the third verse.

By the time the girls made it to the pew, the choir had sung "Rock of Ages," the offertory had played, the collection had been taken and the special had been sung by Sally Ann Meister—"He Touched Me." Beau noticed the song brought tears to his mother's eyes, though his main attention was on the three women squeezing past him. Why did Connie need to squeeze past Jerry, seated on his left? He had no idea. Nor had he an opportunity to learn.

However, one look at Hien's face and he knew she had been crying. She didn't seem upset, though. In fact, she appeared relaxed and friendly with the girls who sat on either side of her. Maybe later he would learn. Maybe.

Maybe he would never know. He involuntarily shrugged, glanced about and shook his head.

That last maybe seemed the most likely.

PASTOR BOB HARRIGAN KNEW SCRIPTURE, for sure, like Beau's dad used to say. Every point he shared he backed up with no less than three separate verses with explanations of the original Greek and Hebrew texts to put things into context. He was personable too. He could tell a story and keep everyone on the edge of their seats while dotting it with just the right amount of humor. All that made him a wonderful speaker.

What made him a wonderful pastor was the fact he was so approachable. He lived his faith and was available to whomever when needs arose. Breadville Community Church was blessed to have such a man lead this group. That's why Beau agreed to serve on the board of elders. Pastor Bob asked him to pray about it and see if God said yes—he didn't just say, "I want you."

Still it made Beau uncomfortable.

Oh, he was happy to do it, helping people came as natural as breathing. It was his gift. But reading though the weekly comments from parishioners often showed a different side, something Beau would've preferred not to see. Some prayer requests seemed more gossipy or even bragging than true concerns. He couldn't help but view a few congregation members different after seeing their requests.

Take, for instance, Miss Sally Ann Meister.

He'd known Sally Ann most of her life. She was about his sister's age. He'd watched her grow up singing in the choir. Such a talented voice. Yet some of her comments seemed to condemn others in the congregation. That bothered him enough. Then she hatched a plan to find herself a spouse. And not just any husband. She had drawn a target on him, even asking for prayer that "a certain person" would return her love. He had no interest, especially after seeing the side of her she didn't display from the front of the church.

Once Thea pointed the big campaign out to him—and it seemed to be just that, a campaign—he avoided her to the best of his ability.

Until now.

"Hi, Beau! Did you like the music?"

He swallowed. Hard. He hadn't seen her sidle up. "It was nice, Sally Ann. Wouldn't you say so, Jer?"

Jerry glanced over and gave him the look—the one that said he wasn't playing today—and shrugged. "Sure, I guess. Nice. Oh, what was that, Pastor Bob?" He wandered in the other direction.

Sally Ann slipped her arm around his. "And who are your friends here, Beau?"

He pulled his arm free with as little effort as possible. "This is my Aunt Melanie and her daughter-in-law, Hien Wheaten. Aunt Mel, Hien, this is Sally Ann Meister."

Aunt Mel gave him a knowing glance. "Sally Ann, how nice to meet you. I thought your song was lovely. God has certainly blessed you."

"Why, thank you." Sally Ann blushed. "I do so love singing for the Lord."

"Excuse me, I need to get the car." As he slipped away, he

heard Aunt Mel ask Sally Ann more questions. It would only bolster her confidence, as if she needed any more confidence.

However, it felt good to escape that woman's clutches one more time. Hien had stayed behind with Thea and Connie—they'd bonded into a female three musketeers club or something. Beau still wondered what had kept them so long, but figured if he was supposed to know, someone would tell him.

Minutes later he pulled up to the curb. While helping Mom into her seat and buckling her in, that jingle rang in his head, the one to the tune of "Buckle Down, Winsocki." He sang it to his mom. "Buckle up for safety."

She chuckled, trying to sing the last part with him. At least she was in tune. She ruffled his hair on the final note.

The rest of his passengers took their seats. Jerry and Connie agreed to meet them at the house.

He hadn't driven two blocks before Thea started. "So, Sally Ann has you back in her sights. What'cha gonna do, big brother?"

"Not a clue. Why does she do that? I'm not interested in her."

"Oh, but she is interested in you." That was Aunt Mel's voice.

Mom patted his arm.

He glanced at her. She had that sympathetic puppy expression.

"I'm in a car full of women. One of you should have an answer."

Tittering teased from the back seat. He peeked in the rearview mirror. At least Hien only smiled.

"You could be honest. Tell her you are not attracted to her. You wish her all the best, but there is no future with you." Hien's answer sounded good.

"And that wouldn't hurt her?" He glimpsed in the mirror again.

"Oh, it will hurt. Think of it this way. A surgeon's cut heals better than something jagged that gets infected." That was Melanie's voice.

"You could pray for her." That was Thea's voice.

"Yeah, I could do that." He mulled that over in his head. He needed alone time before he went any further with this. "How about we change the subject?"

"To what?"

"I don't know. Must I think up all the topics?" Beau resisted the urge to peek at the backseat passengers in his mirror again.

"I know." Thea's voice rang out. "Somebody has a birthday coming up. Somebody's getting old." She put too much emphasis on "old."

There was no way to win.

FIFTEEN

Reflections

"Please pass the carrots. Thea, you are the best." Jerry was lavish with his praise. Though truth be told, Beau's baby sister was one of the finest, if not the best cook in the county.

"Thank you, Jerry. It's nice to be appreciated." Thea's steely glance Beau's way made him squirm.

"Hey, I've always said you were good."

"Maybe to others, but rarely to me, big brother."

"Then let me fix that fault. Thea, you are the most exceptional culinary artist I know. Now, how's that?" Beau offered his most winning smile.

"Too little, too late."

Those seated around the table laughed.

She planted a kiss on his cheek. "Okay, I accept your apology."

"Wait, did I apologize?" He winked at her.

"Oh!" She tossed her napkin at him. "You're on dishes duty."

Even Mom chuckled at that. She didn't talk much with so many present. And she would soon need her bed. Beau and Jerry had brought the old dining room table in from storage and enough chairs to fill in what they needed. She remained in her wheelchair and church clothes for company's sake. Beau could see, though, she wouldn't last much longer.

"Tell you what, sweet sister, if you'll help me clear the dinner table, Jerry and I'll get it out of the way. Then you can assist Mom while we men do the dishes. We'll even serve dessert. What do you think?"

"Deal." Thea stuck out her hand to make it official.

Beau shook it. "We got this."

"Hey! I'm still working on my carrots here. What did you just volunteer me for?" Jerry would eat Thea's cooking all day and night if he could. Years ago, in high school days, they had dated but realized they were only meant to be friends. But he might've married her for her cooking if he could have gotten her to agree.

"Shovel'm in, dude. Your time is up." Beau stood and began to pick up dishes.

Jerry followed Beau's advice and shoveled before handing over his plate.

Ten minutes later, the table was cleared and back out in storage. They piled the dishes in the sink while people dispersed around the house and grounds. Thea got Mom into bed. Jerry disappeared on a walk with Connie, making it up to her about all his raves regarding Thea's cooking, and getting out of dishes duty.

Hien wandered in. "Would you like help?"

"Oh, that's okay. You don't have to."

"So, you can help others, but you do not want to receive any?"

"Grab a towel and start drying." He winked at her.

She did. "You know who often used to wink at me? Pop. Well, the whole family, but I mostly think of Pop when someone winks. I came to love that. It felt friendly and playful."

"I remember him doing that. My dad did it a lot too. They were close, though Aunt Melanie was the blood relative. Could be it's a Midwestern thing. Dunno, but I think of my dad and

Uncle Ernie when the winks start flying. Uncle Ernie was quite a guy. Funny, smart…"

"And kind." She added.

"Yes, that he was."

They worked in silence.

Beau's brain battled until he got up enough courage to nonchalantly ask. "So, Hien, what happened this morning? Were you sick?"

She said nothing.

He could kick himself.

Then she spoke. "One day Michael sent a package and note with a pilot. It was a gift and request that I fix him a box. He had a list. Some things to eat, some clothing. Mil gathered up the food while I got the rest. When I opened his drawer, I found a stack of letters and a photo banded together. It was from Connie. Mil convinced me not to read them. She said that he had chosen me and not to worry. I tucked the memory away until this morning. I did not expect to meet her at church."

"Oh." He couldn't imagine. Well, he could imagine, just not understand.

"I also did not expect her to be so nice. We talked. She guessed the problem. I told her I had seen the photo. She said Michael wrote saying we were to be married. She had not heard it had happened. Plus, she was already dating Jerry. She and Michael broke things off soon after he arrived overseas but remained friends. People thought they would be together. They did not question it until he was sent to Viet Nam."

Beau dropped the dishrag in the water, wiped his hands on the towel at his belt and turned to Hien. "That must have been difficult. I bet you get hit with stuff that suddenly brings back memories."

She nodded and put a plate in the cabinet.

"Hien, if you ever want to talk, I will be glad to listen."

"You are a good friend, Beau. Without you, Mil would be gone. Thank you."

He fished for the dishrag and another pan. "I did nothing that anyone else wouldn't have done."

"I do not believe that. But we should change the subject. You have become uncomfortable."

You nailed that one, kiddo. "Good idea. Tell me what you thought of church."

She relaxed with the change. "I liked it. Who was the man who spoke? What was his name?"

"That was Bob Harrigan. He is our pastor, preacher, minister, however you want to say it. We just call him Pastor Bob."

"Does he always do the talking?" She dried the last dish and put it away.

"An occasional guest might speak, but he does most of the preaching."

"Where did he learn about the Bible?"

Beau pulled the plug in the sink and laid the dishrag over the faucet. "Well, he is ordained. He had a special service where people in the church administration decided he had the training, and understanding and commission from God, to become a pastor—or minister—of the gospel. You understand what gospel means, right?"

"Pop said it meant good news. He said it referred to the good news that Jesus is the one promised in the Old Testament."

"Yup, you got it. Pastor Bob attended school to learn how to be a pastor. But that's not enough. He did that many years ago, but he still reads the Bible and prays about what he reads. He prays about what to share with us. God puts it on his heart and helps him to understand what to say."

"God puts it on his heart?"

Beau guided Hien to a chair and pulled up another next to her. "You know how something comes to you? Not just a thought or emotion. But a sure thing? If you are a child of God and you spend time with Him, He will do that for you."

"God has done this for you?" Her eyes were open, clear. No scorn, only a wish to know.

"Yes, many times."

"Then you read your Bible and pray?"

"I do."

She grew quiet, her gaze focused on something outside the window. Finally, she turned back. "I started to read the Book of Luke in Viet Nam. Pop told me to write my questions and he would answer them. Then he died, and I stopped. Would you be willing to explain things to me?"

"Absolutely." He needed to calm himself. If unchecked he would… He didn't know what he would do, but it needed to be checked, of that he was sure. He took a breath. "Tomorrow after work? I've already talked with Jerry. We'll get your furniture moved into the house when it arrives and hopefully be done by the time you get home. If things are settled enough, we might have your first driving lesson and then talk about your questions."

"Thank you." She glanced about. "Should we prepare the dessert?"

"Yeah. Connie brought her famous French silk chocolate pie. Trust me, you will love it."

He brought the pies out while she got dessert plates and forks. They served the others and themselves. Somehow in all that, Hien wandered out with Connie and Thea.

Beau stood in the background, watching the girls talk and laugh together. Hien was finding her spot in the community, or at least this little group. There was still the rest of Breadville. With people like Pete Warrick, that might prove more difficult. He sent up a quick prayer. *Lord, help her find her place in Your love.*

MONDAY DAWNED WITH INTERMITTENT SHOWERS. Even if he found time, after moving furniture into the Wheaten house, the roads weren't ready for a beginning driver. But what about Bible study? That thought excited Beau. He would see the gospel message through a searcher's eyes. Though she said she was a believer, he wasn't sure she understood. Maybe it was more like accepted. There was much she didn't know. He had prayed last night that God would guide him however Hein needed so she'd believe.

After milking, he took Hien to the café and dropped her off before racing back to the farm to get his animals fed and the barn cleaned. Thea made him a pancake sandwich—two pancakes with sausage, egg and maple syrup in the middle. Somehow she seamed the edge, so he had a fighting chance of not losing the insides while working and inhaling the food, all at the same time.

He was coming in when the phone rang. It was the moving company. The furniture was en route and would arrive at the Wheaten farm in the next hour. He could grab a shower before he picked up Jerry at his home. Thea called to let Jerry know Beau and Aunt Mel would be there.

He hated waking Aunt Mel. Learning to sleep again without the Valium was difficult. But she was up and packed. Hien packed her own things and left them in the corner. Everyone was set.

The furniture truck pulled into the Wheaten driveway at nine on the button. Jerry and Beau sat on the porch, watching as it turned in.

"Aunt Mel, they're here."

She joined them and the procession began.

The driver and assistant unloaded, setting things on the porch. Jerry and Beau brought the items into the house and put them where Melanie directed. It was a well-oiled machine of a plan. An hour later, the truck was on its way, leaving Jerry and Beau to help lay rugs, set up and position furniture, open crates and do the heavy lifting. Melanie had trouble deciding at times. Eventually, the big stuff was where it needed to go. Boxes got assigned to specific rooms if they hadn't been unpacked.

They were so busy, they didn't pay attention to the weather until a loud clap of thunder boomed, demanding their attention.

Melanie jumped, her hand over her heart.

"Hey, it's okay. Just the storm." Beau put his arm across her shoulders and embraced her. She shuddered. He pulled back to peer at her.

Her eyes grew as wide as saucers. Her emanating fear was palpable.

"Aunt Melanie, what's the matter? Aunt Mel?"

She stared at him, as if she just recognized him and then Jerry. Her hands went to her face and she shook her head.

Beau wrapped her in a hug. "It's okay. You're fine. It's only a rainstorm. You know Indiana weather."

She nodded and pushed away. "Yes, the weather. But it sounded like…"

"A gun?" Jerry volunteered.

"Yes." She straightened and brushed her hair from her face. "But it's not. It's the weather. Let's get finished." She stepped toward the stairs.

"You're sure you're okay?" Her reaction sent worry signals pinging through Beau's brain.

"I'm fine." She smiled as proof.

Beau wasn't convinced but decided discretion was the better form of valor, at least in this instance. He checked his watch. It was two o'clock. "I'd better go to town for Hien before she tries walking home in this."

"Don't worry, I'll hold down the fort." Jerry nodded his head in Melanie's direction.

Beau gave him a thumbs-up and left.

HIEN WAITED JUST inside the cafe entrance. Beau made sure she had an umbrella this morning. She popped it up to run for the truck as he pulled up at the curb in front.

Beau hopped out to get the door for her and got enough frigid water down his neck to suit him for the next hundred years.

Then they took off for Hien's new home.

"Are you excited?" Beau glanced at her, sitting with her hands folded, a big smile on her face.

"Yes. And no. I will miss being with Thea and your mother each day. Your generosity made me welcomed. However, I am looking forward to my own room again. I would like a dark room to develop photos." A smile bloomed as she spoke.

"I hope you can do that. You are talented. I know Jerry's impressed. Don't be surprised if he asks you to take some pictures once you are settled."

Her cheeks pinked at his words and she changed topic. "I must learn about farming too. How to start a garden and feed the animals. When do you plan to bring the animals to the farm?"

"Well, let's start with the gardening. It's nearly time to get things in the ground. We can bring the chickens over in a few weeks. I'll teach you about them. Once you see success, we'll try something else. You don't have a milking machine, but then you've only got two cows. I'll teach you to milk them when you are ready. Your sow is about to have babies. You might save her for last. It'll transition easier."

They continued to discuss all the details that would change or happen now that they'd moved back to their farm. Things would be different. Beau was especially aware that he could not see Hien as easily. She wouldn't be in his home. Still, a stretch of the legs walk shouldn't hurt him.

He decided not to tell her about Melanie's reaction to the thunder. No need for worry.

They pulled in the driveway, parking by the back door. Sweet girl, she held her umbrella for him to share. Not that he would fit, or that she could hold it high enough—his six foot three frame towered above her.

But they raced inside and slipped out of their soppy shoes, leaving them with their drippy jackets in the mudroom before padding in stocking feet into the kitchen.

Jerry and Connie unloaded groceries.

"Connie stopped by with essentials. Glad she thought of it. I wouldn't have." Jerry beamed at his fiancée. She kissed his cheek and kept putting away the supplies.

Melanie came in from another room. "Hien, do you remember when Ernest had his heart attack, and you ran to the office to get his Bible?"

Hien glanced at Beau and back to Melanie. "Yes."

"Did you notice the things he had tucked in it?"

"He had several papers and an envelope."

"So, you noticed the papers?"

"Yes, Mil, I did."

"When did you decide to steal the farm from me, Hien?"

Hien's face grew pale.

Connie gasped. Jerry just stared.

Beau absorbed the reactions but still couldn't understand. Hien steal? That made no sense.

"When, Hien? Was it while you were reading to him? Was it after they all died, and we were getting his things together? When did you steal my farm?"

"I did not steal your farm, Mil. I would not do that."

Melanie held out an envelope and waved it at Hien. "Oh, but you did. You signed this. It is a legal document. I was gathering the paperwork I needed to talk with my lawyer. And there it was, your name on the deed. Did you trick him when he was so ill? How did you do it, Hien? How?"

Hien opened her mouth.

Mil slapped her.

Everyone, but Hien, froze. She gasped and ran out, stocking feet, into the rain.

The slammed door jolted everyone into action. Jerry and Connie went to Melanie.

Beau ran after Hien.

He paused only to pull on his boots and then followed without lacing them.

She stood in the barn, her back to the house. Her arms were wrapped about her and her shoulders shook. The storm drowned out the sounds of her crying until he was close.

"Hien."

She spun around, hands over her face, and landed her forehead against his chest. He felt her sobs, rising from deep within her. She was too broken for him to believe she would even try to steal the farm.

He tipped up her chin. "Hien, tell me what happened."

She struggled to calm herself. Finally, she got the words out. "Pop told Michael he wished to give us this farm. As a wedding gift. We would not have to inherit. It would be ours. He wanted to surprise Mil. He planned to build her a new house. On the land." She stopped to breathe and brushed her forearm under her nose. "When he was in the hospital, Pop asked if Michael had explained. When I answered yes, he told me to sign the paper. He said Michael would sign when he returned." She squeezed her eyes closed, sniffed another breath. "Then they all died. That is all I know." Her arms dropped to her sides and her gaze bore into his soul. "Beau, how can she believe I would steal from her? I love her so much. She is all my family. I have no one else. I would never steal from her." She buried her face in her hands again.

Beau closed his eyes and prayed for help. Understanding dawned. "Hien, Melanie's only been off Valium a few days. She took it because she wasn't sleeping, right?"

Hien nodded.

"I think there are two problems. She's still not sleeping. Right?"

"Yes."

"And there is a thing called withdrawal. When someone stops taking a substance such as Valium, the body doesn't like it.

It can affect emotions and personality. People become irritable, even worse. It is hard to get it out of your system."

Hien searched his gaze. "Will she ever be the same?"

Beau's heart nearly gained control. Her face was so close, so vulnerable. He could envision leaning in and kissing—NO!

He shook the idea out of his head and cleared his throat. "Well, yes and no. She has experiences now that have changed her, but who she is, your mother-in-law who loves you, is still in there. In fact, she might be feeling embarrassed at the moment. I don't want you to catch cold, but I need to talk with her first." He paused to figure out the best way to say the next part. He took a breath and said it. "Hien, I will have to carry you. You're in your stocking feet. Are you okay with that?"

She didn't answer. Instead she wound her arms about his neck and let him scoop her into his.

He nearly over-lifted, she was so light.

She buried her face in his shoulder while he ran for the house.

Beau could run with her in his arms, rain and all, forever.

He set her down, before he had another thought he couldn't overcome, and told her to wait there. Then he crossed into the kitchen, whispering to Connie that Hien was in the mud room and to bring her to the kitchen as soon as he had Melanie in the living room.

She nodded and backed up toward the mudroom door.

"Melanie, let's go into the living room and talk."

She was seated in a chair, Jerry kneeling in front of her. "I don't want to, Beau."

"Melanie, we need to talk. You want this to be private."

She glared up at him, defiant. Then she blinked. With a sigh she stood, trudging to the other room.

Beau followed her and motioned to the sofa he and Jerry had positioned a few hours earlier. She sat; he sat beside her.

"Aunt Mel, I know what happened—"

"You know her lies."

He took her hand. "No, it is your turn to listen. Something you would have done if you were yourself."

She pulled back. "What do you mean?"

"I mean that you are going through withdrawal from the Valium. You haven't slept well. You're irritated about everything and trying to act normal only exacerbates it. Your body aches, your head pounds. Your emotions are on an out-of-control roller coaster while you try to convince everyone else all is well."

She opened her mouth then closed it.

He knew she wanted to deny it all but couldn't.

"How do you know this?" Her voice, hoarse, barely above a whisper, told him he was getting through to her.

Now he needed the strength to be honest.

"When I was in Korea, I met a girl. She was Korean. Her name was Nam Sun. I loved her very much, even thought I'd marry her and bring her home with me." He paused while Nam Sun's smiling face flitted by, the question he never got to ask hung over him. The what-would-never-be knifing him. He hadn't voiced these words aloud in a decade. "She stepped on a landmine and died. I saw the explosion." He felt more than heard Melanie's gasp, but continued. "This was toward the end of my tour. I had seen enough things to never want to sleep again, but watching Nam Sun die… yeah, I had trouble sleeping. Every time I shut my eyes I saw her. Again and again. She reached for me and then…

"When I came home, I attended Purdue. You're aware of that much. I tried to keep busy, coming home weekends to help Dad, taking extra classes so I could drop into bed too exhausted to dream. My junior year I got a new roommate, Jerry. I was still popping Valium and, when I didn't think it was working, I took more. The problem was I would forget. Then I'd take another. Jerry found me one day. He saved my life. Besides you, he is the only person who knows about this. Even Mom doesn't know.

"I was so ashamed. Then the withdrawal came. I was determined not to fall into the Valium trap again. But I couldn't sleep. I was such a jerk. To many people. I pray they don't remember. But this is the bottom line. It took time. Withdrawal takes time. I got through it, with a lot of grace from God and Jerry.

"Aunt Mel, you have us. We have grace for you. But you must believe Hien did not steal your farm. I think you know that. If you are ready, she can come in and explain. When you hear what happened, you'll understand. Are you ready?"

She had remained silent through his story, rarely even glancing at him.

He felt as though he had vomited everything he'd eaten his entire life. At the same time, he was cleansed. Inside. Lighter. An impression in his heart told him he should have done this many years ago—only someone else didn't need it years ago.

Now she does.

But, was it enough?

Melanie sighed and patted his hand. "Go get her. I'll listen."

He walked into the kitchen. "Hien, would you come here? She's ready."

Hien followed him to the living room and stood before Melanie.

"Sit down, Hien. Go ahead."

Hien told her. Every single word.

Melanie listened as she promised.

When it was done, Melanie stood. "You were right, Beau. You said if I listened, I would understand. I do." She turned to Hien. "I'm so sorry, Hien. I was wrong. Leave it to Ernest to do that. So like him." A tear wound its way down her cheek and dripped onto her collar.

He glanced at Hien. She appeared to be breathing again. She raced to Melanie's embrace. Beau could hear the crying, private words whispered between them.

He wanted to flee the room. Should he stay? He agonized over wanting to do the right thing and putting miles between him and all that emotion. It was worse than tripping over a hornet's nest. Just when he'd decided to go to the kitchen, they stepped apart.

Melanie kissed the top of Hien's head and draped her arm across her shoulders. She then turned to Beau. "But that brings us to a problem. And I don't know what to do. No matter Ernest's intentions, according to this document, I no longer own the farm. Hien does. What happens now?"

SIXTEEN

Mercy, Mercy, Mercy

BEAU LEFT FOR HOME TO HAVE DINNER WITH HIS FAMILY. Connie drove Jerry so Beau didn't have to make that trip. The whole way, all Beau could do was ruminate over the blow up between Aunt Mel and Hien and how God so perfectly intervened. Scripture proved that bad things happened to everybody, even those who put their faith in God, but that He would not only work it out for their good and His glory, He would use that pain to transform the lives of others—comforting with the comfort received. Until today, this was head knowledge. Now he understood at a new level. And he felt cleaner having vocalized his story. He was cleaner. Not everyone would understand, but Aunt Melanie did.

The weather kept Hien and him from driving practice. The situation blocked them from Bible study. But watching them talk it out, once all the crying was over, was better than the best preaching.

Hien claimed the farm belonged to Melanie, no matter what the paperwork said.

Melanie apologized. Profusely.

They hugged and promised to never again doubt the other's intentions.

Beau had walked away then, afraid he'd lose his masculine reputation with his reaction. They nearly made him bawl like a baby.

He also knew what he needed to do.

After dinner he sat with his mother and sister. It was time he shared that part of his life with them. He wasn't certain what to expect, but he was pretty sure they wouldn't disown him. He was right. They hugged his neck and told him they loved him. He might have wiped away a tear.

But Beau was so free, it was as if he breathed with an extra lung. He'd never realized what holding all that in had done to him.

TUESDAY STARTED A WHOLE NEW ROUTINE. He still drove Hien to the café, but now he picked her up at her house. Then, to bring her home, he would drive the Mustang. He took them outside of town and let Hien get behind the wheel. They covered the county roads and then headed back to the Wheaten farm for Bible study.

Hien's questions were deep. Beau thanked God he'd been moved to pray before starting each session. The hardest question was the most common one. If God is all powerful, why did he not let Mike and Charlie and Uncle Ernie live? It was the question he'd asked when Nam Sun died. All he could do was share what he found in Scripture, what he embraced.

"Psalm 139:15-16 says 'My substance was not hid from thee, when I was made in secret, and curiously wrought in the lowest parts of the earth. Thine eyes did see my substance, yet being unperfect; and in thy book all my members were written, which in continuance were fashioned, when as yet there was none of them.' I believe that means God knows and set a time for us to live on this planet. What we do with it is in our hands—and whatever we do, we will either reap rewards or consequences or both. Our story is our own story, though what we choose can have effects on others. I don't know that I've got it all right, but it has brought me comfort that God wasn't saying 'No, I won't answer that prayer' but 'It is time to come home now.' I rely on His promise to never leave me. I trust Him, that He loves me and wants only the best for me. So I look to Him and listen for His guidance. I trust that what I don't understand today, He'll help me figure out one day."

Hien seemed far away. She did this each time he tried to explain.

Now it was Friday. She had a response. "So, either God is Who He says He is, and I cannot understand everything, or all of this is a lie."

That caught Beau off-guard. "Yeah, I guess that about sums it up." He waited. Which idea would she embrace?

"I need to consider this. I can go to church with Mil. I can do things her way. But with this question, I need time."

He opened his mouth to say something, but a heart whisper made him stop. *Let her think, you pray.* "Okay. I should go now, anyway. Same time tomorrow?"

"Yes. I will see you in the morning." She walked him to the door.

Again Beau's attention was drawn to her lips. It was the only place he'd notice her using any makeup, and even then it was minimal. The scent of her lip gloss made him hungry to kiss her. Her left hand brushed a stray hair from her face, and he glimpsed a flash. Her wedding rings.

He left, embarrassed and grateful he hadn't lost control.

Saturday brought more rain. The good news was that the soil needed it. The bad news was the soil would be ready to plant soon.

He debated about bringing the Mustang to pick up Hien

after work. She'd had no driving in the rain experience yet. He decided today would be the day for it.

She appeared startled when he pulled to the side of the road for her to change seats. "Are you sure? It is raining."

"It's about time you learn. You will have to drive in all types of weather. In fact, you will need to learn to drive in snow too. But let's just start with rain." He winked at her.

She gave a nervous laugh. "It is your life."

Beau started to rethink. But the decision was made. He wouldn't renege.

Hien adjusted the seat, checked her mirrors, put on her blinker, and depressed the gas pedal. She pulled out onto the road like a champ. It was clear she was growing more confident.

Maybe he should think of taking her into town. "Take a left at the stop sign."

She did.

He guided her through a few more turns until they were among the houses at the city limits. "Pull up in front of that white house with the wrap-around porch." He smiled to himself. She'll enjoy this stop.

"Who lives here?"

"Someone you know. Come on." He climbed from the car and came to her side.

She'd already opened the door, but he held it for her while she exited. The rain was less than a sprinkle for now.

He guided her up the front steps before knocking.

A moment later the door opened. "Hien, Beau! So good to see you. Come in." Connie welcomed them into her parents' home. "What brings you here?"

"Hien brings us here, in her Mustang." Beau grinned. Hien's blush was delightful.

Connie went to the window. "Oh, what a great car. Jerry told me you bought it and for a song. Wow, it looks fun. We should go for a ride and blast Beach Boys music."

"So, why don't we? C'mon, Connie, get your jacket and let's go. If Jerry can slip away, we'll go for a drive."

Hien looked nervous. She had only driven with Beau in the car. Well, she should get used to passengers. He couldn't let her hold back if she was to learn.

It was no work to convince Connie. She called to her mom to say she was leaving before grabbing her jacket and opening the front door.

Beau held the door for them both and then held the car door for them—Connie sat behind Hien in the back.

Hien pulled away from the curb while Beau gave directions to Jerry's office. The girls waited in the car while Beau ran in to get him. They returned in two minutes—Jerry was ready to leave.

By now the rain had ceased, but dark clouds still hung low. Hien relaxed as the talk among the friends brought laughter.

"Let's go to The Casa Grande." Jerry suggested.

"Out on US 31?" That meant going to Kokomo. Beau wondered if that might push Hien too much. Besides, she didn't have a learners permit.

"Yeah, we can go for dinner."

Hien's voice of reason cut through. "I am still in my uniform."

"Oh." It was like a balloon deflated.

"Hey Hien, how did you do for tips today?" Connie must have an idea.

"Good, it was my best day. I made ten dollars."

Even Beau was impressed.

"Okay keep going down 31 until you get to the Markland Mall. I know a little shop where you can get a top and pants with change to spare. I'll help you shop, and the boys can wander until we're done. Then we can eat dinner at The Casa Grande. What d'ya say?"

Beau was sure Hien would decline. She had plans for the money—the darkroom for instance. Plus, she and Melanie were counting pennies just to keep things going. The longer it took Hien to answer, the more sure he was. "Hien, I have a charge card. You can put it on that and pay me as you go. Just add it to the car payment." He winked.

She didn't wink back. "Okay, we will eat at the Casa Grande. I will buy the clothes. Which way is the mall?"

~

THE CASA GRANDE RESTAURANT was one of the nicer places in Kokomo. You didn't have to dress to the nines to enjoy it, but most dressed better. It housed wedding receptions and various celebrations in the back room and was known for its good food.

Hien spotted the frog legs on the menu right off.

Connie told her they were delicious, but that no one would make her try. However, if she liked chicken, she might enjoy them.

Hien decided she had attempted enough new stuff for the day, including the drive to the mall. She'd turned the keys over to Beau in the mall parking lot. After another brief study of the menu, she ordered the roasted chicken breast dinner. It came with a medley of vegetables and mashed potatoes, so everything was familiar. Connie chose the frog legs—said Hien had helped her decide. Jerry ordered the same as Beau—a T-Bone steak with a baked potato.

While they waited for their food, Jerry remembered something. "Don't know if you saw it or not, but Bobby Kennedy is coming to Indianapolis early next month. I think he's testing the waters. Anyway, I was wondering, Hien, if I go, would you tag along to take photos for the newspaper? Perhaps we might have a foursome adventure?"

Beau watched Hien's eyes light up at the prospect of more photojournalism. "I would enjoy that. Do you know when?"

"I gotta check, but I think the notice said the fourth. What do you all say?"

"I'm not positive who has my vote, but I'll listen before deciding. Sure. We should all go. Let's make a time of it. Connie?" Beau thought for certain she'd jump at the chance.

"I need to check the calendar. The wedding is getting closer. I have tons of stuff to do." She glanced over at Jerry. They did that couple's thing of communicating with eye messages and head tilts. "Maybe I'll pick up some things in Indianapolis. Sure."

It was quiet again until Connie started the head tilting again.

Jerry nodded. "Beau, this'll be no great shock. But will you be my best man?"

"Of course. Who else would you ask?"

"Well, I could ask—"

Connie elbowed him. "Now cut that out. There isn't anyone else he would ask. And Hien, would you be a bridesmaid?"

Hien smiled. "I would be honored."

Beau leaned back in his chair. "So you're really doing this? You've set the date?"

Connie and Jerry continued their private couple sign language of lifted eyebrows and tilted heads. Then Connie smiled and shared. "August third at two o'clock."

"Congratulations. I'm thrilled for you both." And Beau was. They were his friends. He was glad for their happiness. He just wished his own happiness boat hadn't sailed so all-fired soon.

Dinner arrived, so they tabled the discussion.

Beau excused himself after putting in his order for dessert. He rarely stayed away from home this long in case Thea or Mom needed him. Fortunately, there was a pay phone by the restrooms. He pressed 0 for the operator and then reversed the charges. It was his second call of the evening, but he wanted to make sure. Besides, he paid the phone bill.

Thea answered. "So how was dinner?"

"Just fine. Hien wasn't ready to try frog legs, though. Did you get one of the Nelson boys to do the milking?"

He heard her sigh. "Yes, Pat came over. Said to tell you he likes it when you ask him."

"Of course he does. He's saving for his first car."

"He told me. In great detail. You realize I can handle the milking."

He knew that, but he couldn't ask her. Besides, leaving Mom alone while she was in the barn that long wasn't a good idea. "You wouldn't want to come between a boy and his car, would you?"

"I've had enough experience with you boys and your toys to last me quite awhile, thank you very much."

Time to change the subject. "We've got an excursion planned to Indianapolis the first week of April. Bobby Kennedy is speaking. Jerry wants to cover it and asked Hien to take photos. We decided to make it a group adventure, and I was thinking, I'll bet Aunt Melanie will spell you if you want to go."

"And be a third wheel, or rather fifth wheel? No thanks."

Beau never considered it that way. He just didn't want his sister left out. "I'm sorry. Thought you would like it."

"It's fine, I enjoy getting out now and again, but when there's two couples and me, nah, not a fun idea."

"Hien and I are not a couple. We only end up spending time together."

She laughed. "Keep telling yourself that, big brother. Hey, better go. Mom's bell is ringing. Later." The line went dead.

That's how rumors get started, he wanted to tell her. Instead he hung up. As he did, something touched his back. He turned to find Sally Ann.

"Oh, hi. Didn't see you there."

"Got a feeling you never really see me, Beau Salem."

He peered closer at her. Had she been drinking? She wasn't all that steady on her feet, and her face was flushed. She wobbled. "Sally Ann, are you all right?"

"Fine, I'm per-feck-ly fine. I am so fine, and you can't even see it. Why can't you see it, Beau?" She cocked her head to the side. It reminded him of what Maddie did when he asked her questions.

"Sally Ann, I don't know what you need from me."

She poked at his chest with her finger. "I need your attention, big boy. That's right. Your attention. What must a girl do to get your attention, Beau Salem? I go to church. I sing pretty. I am pretty. And nice to people. Tell me what to do and I'll do —Oh!" Her hands covered her mouth. She ran for the ladies room.

Beau returned to the table and asked Connie to check on her. What else should he do? He couldn't go in there. Hanging outside the door wasn't a good idea. However, he didn't want to embarrass her. So he left out the part about drinking and said he thought she was ill.

Connie at once left for the ladies room.

Chocolate cake no longer appealed. In fact, he wanted to leave, but they couldn't. Connie was still with Sally Ann. What a mess. How had his life become so chaotic? He hadn't a clue.

But he was certain of one thing. Sally Ann was going to make life uncomfortable for the foreseeable future. That was a sure bet.

SUNDAY MORNING ARRIVED. Beau and Thea went into their routine, pushing the clock because they needed to stop for Aunt Mel and Hien. Somehow they showed up on time. Hien got out at the curb with the others, leaving Beau alone when he parked the car. He found a space less than a block from church, so he counted himself lucky.

Maybe he was too quick. Sally Ann waited for him away from the church. He hadn't seen her when he'd driven past the spot, but here she was when he walked back.

"Beau, I want to say I am sorry and so embarrassed about last evening. I hope you can forgive me." She appeared very contrite. Too contrite? There was just something about Sally Ann that caused Beau to question her motives.

"Don't worry about it."

She wrapped her arm through his and clung to his bicep. "So you forgive me?"

"What is there to forgive? It's fine."

She stopped, a pout protruding. "Beau Salem. How can you be so heartless? I just poured out my sincerest apology and all you can say is it's fine and don't worry about it?"

"I don't know what you want me to say. You did nothing to me that needs forgiving. If you feel you need forgiveness, talk with God. I keep thinking you have a point to make, but you dance around it." He jammed his hands in his pockets. "If you are trying to get me to ask you out, it will not happen, Sally Ann. I don't wish to hurt you, but I don't have those feelings for you. I'm too old, anyway. I don't play games. I don't have time for them. Find someone closer to your own age. Now I apologize if you're hurt. Whether you forgive me is up to you." Where had that come from? But a dam had burst, pushing the flood gates wide open.

Her jaw dropped.

He wanted to lift her chin back into place, but he knew she'd make something of it. So he shrugged and headed for the narthex.

The prelude music had started. He slipped into the sanctuary and found his family. Connie and Jerry were there as well. They saved him a seat.

Next to Hien. Were his friends pushing them together?

Pastor Bob came over and motioned for him. He slid out, and they walked to the back.

"We're having a time of prayer at the end of the sermon. Would you please be available to pray with those who need it? Preferably with the men. I think Connie and my wife can help the women."

Beau nodded. He'd been asked before. In fact, Pastor Bob

was pretty good at listening to where the Holy Spirit led. He returned to his seat and waited for the signal.

The choirmaster had the congregation start with "Crown Him With Many Crowns." Beau sang along, but his head wasn't in the service. Despite apologizing to Sally Ann, guilt ate at him. Knowing he'd hurt her made each off-tonal note more sharp. That wasn't his way. It wasn't his Savior's way. He asked God for forgiveness. Weight lifted, but he knew he needed to apologize to her and this time mean it. He glanced around, but didn't see her, so he continued singing.

After the special, "What a Friend We Have in Jesus," Pastor Bob took the pulpit. His message today was titled "What is Your Story?" Had his pastor been listening to all the conversations he'd had with Hien that week? Somehow he brought it all together with the gospel—Christ's love, the gift of salvation, how we are unique and yet need to be bonded in the love of God. It was one of his best sermons.

When Pastor Bob gave the invitation for prayer, Beau slipped out, ready. He saw the faces of the congregation. Dropping his view so as not to look like he was staring, he silently prayed for those deciding at that very moment. One by one, people knelt at the altar. A man here, a woman there. As Beau moved to pray with a young man new to the congregation, he saw Hien rise from her seat and go to the aisle. Connie knelt beside her.

Something in Beau's heart broke free.

Hien chose to believe.

CONNIE AND JERRY declined the invitation to Sunday dinner. Jerry's mother wanted her turn, so he said. Hien and Aunt Melanie came for a bit. Beau didn't put the big table up again. Instead, they pulled out the TV trays like before. Thea made chicken and dumplings, one of her best recipes, and they enjoyed some time together celebrating Hien's decision. After, Beau took the Wheaten ladies back to their farm.

The trip home seemed empty. It was such a wonderful day. And now, just empty.

Beau needed a nap. He hadn't done that in a long while, but his easy chair in the living room whispered his name. He had been sleeping better since he'd shared with his family. But something about a cloudy Sunday afternoon in March cried out for a little shut-eye. What else could he do?

The telephone woke him an hour later. Thea answered it, so he closed his eyes again until she called him to the phone.

"Beau, it's Pastor Bob." She held out the receiver.

That was unusual. "Be right there."

He got up, yawned, and shook his head to clear the cobwebs before taking it from her.

"Hi, Pastor. How can I help you?"

"Beau, sorry to have to do this, but we need to call an emergency board meeting. I'm asking everyone to come to my house at seven."

Beau checked his wristwatch. "I can make it. What's the problem?"

"We'll discuss it when you get here. See you at seven."

"See ya." Beau hung up. Something was wrong, but he couldn't imagine what. *Pray.* There was urgency in the thought. *Pray.* For whom? Each board member's face flashed through his mind as well as Pastor Bob's and the pastor's wife. Then Sally Ann's floated by. He didn't question it. He prayed for each one.

BEAU CHECKED his watch after he'd knocked. Seven on the dot.

Judy Harrigan, the pastor's wife, opened the door. "Come on in, Beau. Thank you for coming." She took his jacket. "We're meeting in here." She led him to the dining room. Just then there was another knock, so she excused herself.

"Glad you made it, Beau." Pastor Bob held out his hand.

They shook hands. "You sure have me wondering. Are you all right?"

"I'm feeling healthy, if that's what you mean. No, there's a problem, and I'm concerned. It's serious so I need us to deal with it now."

"Okay."

Other board members arrived. Within five minutes, everyone was there, seated around the dining room table. Pastor Bob started.

"Today during the prayer time, several people came forward. You were busy praying and I want to thank you that you let me count on you this way. However, there was an individual who prayed with Judy." He paused, choosing his words. "What's spoken at the altar is sacrosanct. We all know that. But someone made charges against a board member to Judy. When this happens, we must investigate."

Beau sat straighter. He couldn't believe it. Looking at the faces of his fellow members, they couldn't either. He'd known these men many years. He had seen God's love radiate from each one. His mind wouldn't grasp this.

"Perhaps, Judy, you should share what was said."

Judy stood beside her husband. "This person reported that a board member had used drugs and had cohabited with a young woman outside of marriage."

Beau glanced at the other men. None of this made sense. On top of it, he was the only one not married. All'd been married at least ten years. "This is unbelievable. Did she give a name? Her information can't be correct."

"Yes, she did."

"Thank you, Judy. I'll go on with this." Pastor Bob patted her arm. "If I just blurt out the name, it would be wrong. And if I believed one of you had done this, I would speak to you privately. If you confessed, we would have healing. If you did not, I would bring witnesses. That being said, I know this young lady is incorrect. So I called you because a rumor is about to be unleashed. Our brother needs to see we support him."

A chorus of "who?" rang out. Pastor Bob raised his hands.

"First, the information is false. The accusation is false. And we will stand beside you. Beau Salem."

All eyes turned toward him.

He wanted to disappear. Right through the floor.

Tell them. Tell them now.

Beau rose to his feet, slowly, thinking through each word he was about to say. "I don't understand. What is this about? I do not use drugs. I've never cohabited in any wrong sense with a woman." He paused for a breath of courage. "However, twelve years ago there was a situation. I'll explain though I hadn't talked about it in over a decade until recently. In fact, I just told my family." He shared the story of Nam Sun and the Valium. How Jerry found him in time, by the grace of God, and how he'd taken nothing more than aspirin since. "Nam Sun and I wanted to marry, but we never lived together. That would have destroyed her life, and it's not how I was raised. I don't understand. My sister and I live in the house where we grew up so we can take care of Mom. I'm clueless here."

Judy cleared her throat. "I think she was referring to the young lady who came from Viet Nam with your aunt."

"Hien Wheaten? She is Michael Wheaten's widow. You all remember Mike." Now he was incensed. How dare anyone say something like that about Hien? "When they arrived, the bank froze Aunt Melanie's assets until Uncle Ernie's estate is settled. That means she couldn't get her furniture out of storage or pay the customs' fees on the things she'd sent over from Viet Nam. After everything they'd been through. They were in the embassy during the assault. And Melanie lost not only her husband, but both her sons soon after that. Hien has more story, but it takes time to trust. She just gave her life to the Lord this morning at the altar. Even after all that loss."

Pastor Bob raised his hands. "Then we know what this is. It

is an attack. How do we come against an attack? By the Word of the Lord."

What started out as an emergency board meeting ended up a prayer meeting. On the way home, Beau could guess who'd spoken with Judy. If that were the case, he needed a giant hedge of protection. He was on very unfamiliar ground.

Monday Beau spotted a booklet at his place on the kitchen table when he came in from milking. "What's this?"

Thea was making biscuits and gravy. "Found that while cleaning my room Saturday. Just remembered it. Bet it might help Hien get ready for her driving test."

Beau thumbed through it. Sure couldn't hurt. "Thanks, kiddo. I'll give it to her." He swiped a quick bite of a biscuit dipped in gravy before heading out to take Hien to work. Man, his sister was a good cook. Wonder why Phil Carpenter hadn't called?

Hien waited on the porch. She rushed to hop in before he could get her door. It was nippy this time of morning in March. The truck was still warming up.

Beau handed the brochure to her. "It's from Thea. Here's the stuff they will test you on when you go for your driver's license."

"I have to take a test?" She didn't sound too thrilled.

"Yeah, it's the rules. If you read this, since you're driving, it should make better sense. There is a multiple-choice quiz first and then a test where you drive with an assessment person."

"You did not tell me about this before we started."

"No? Didn't realize it was a problem. Hey, don't worry. You've gotten better each time you're behind the wheel. That's half of the test. Read through this. You'll learn the finer points of how to do things. It'll help you answer the questions on the written test. You'll do great."

"Really?" She didn't look like she believed him.

"Really. Trust me. You're gonna do great."

She thumbed through the brochure some more. She was still going through it when he pulled up in front of the café. He came around and opened her door. "See you this afternoon. We'll talk more then."

"Okay. See you then. Tell Thea thank you."

Part of him wanted to give her a peck on the cheek. After last night, though, he was cautious. Besides, how would she react? Instead he said, "I will. Have a good day." He watched her go into the café.

EVERY DAY THAT WEEK, Beau picked her up after work. She drove the Mustang in town, she drove it in the country, she drove it on the highway. She even drove into the city of Kokomo where there was much more traffic, more stop lights and more lanes. Her confidence grew and after that first day, Beau couldn't stump her once with the questions from the brochure.

It was time.

So, Friday Beau had her drive to the Bureau of Motor Vehicles office.

"Where are we?" She was nervous again.

"Settle down. We're at the BMV. You are ready."

"Oh, no I am not. Are you sure? Maybe I can. But what if I fail?"

Beau chuckled.

She scowled.

"Sorry. Not funny, I shouldn't have laughed. Thea would have just hit me. Want to hit me?"

She raised her fist but then dropped it.

"You will do fine. You know the rules inside and out. You're driving great. Now, go get'em."

She took a step forward, paused and glanced back at him.

He motioned her on, so she turned and headed to the

counter. He'd picked a good time, no one else was there. The official gave her a paper to fill out. After that she had to show her ID and visa. She received the written test and completed it in five minutes.

Now was the moment. Beau walked with her and the tester out to the Mustang and waited on the curb until she pulled up again, with tester guy still alive and breathing. Always a good sign.

"Okay, miss, take this inside. They will snap your picture."

Hien's eyes lit up. "I passed?"

The guy laughed. "Yeah, you passed."

She squealed. "I passed. I passed."

Now Beau laughed. "Yeah, but it won't mean a thing if you don't get that paper inside and have your picture taken."

She stopped mid squeal and ran.

Beau waited for her at the door.

She emerged, holding her temporary license.

Look out Breadville, Hien's got wheels.

"THIS CALLS FOR A CELEBRATION. What would you say to a phosphate?"

"What is a foz… fate?"

This would be another first for her. Beau figured she'd enjoy it, though.

"C'mon. You drive and I'll show you."

They returned to the car, and he guided her into the downtown area. They found a spot on North Union, close to the place. Hien parallel parked like an expert. Beau dropped a dime in the parking meter, and they crossed the street.

Fenn's was small with three little round tables and ice cream parlor chairs. It wasn't busy at the moment. But when the high school let out, it'd be mobbed.

"Do you trust me?" Beau decided he should ask before

ordering.

She nodded.

"Make it two cherry phosphates."

The counter man got to work. He grabbed two Coke glasses and filled them with ice, followed by two squirts of cherry syrup in each. Then he cut a lemon in half and squeezed some juice into each glass before filling them full of club soda from the fountain. Last he stirred them with a long teaspoon and added straws to each. "That'll be seventy cents."

Beau gave him a dollar and told him to keep the change. He brought the drinks to the table where Hien waited. "You're gonna like this. I promise."

Hien hesitated only a moment before taking a sip.

Beau knew he'd scored points when her eyes lit up. A big smile spread across her face. She leaned in for more. "Oh, this is very good."

"Told ya you could trust me." He winked and this time she winked back. "Next time we'll try the homemade lemonade—it's the best anywhere."

As Beau finished the last drop, the door opened. Expecting the start of the after-school mob, he didn't glance up until he heard his name.

"So, Beau Salem, you and your little friend are out together. Again. Guess you need to hang out in Kokomo to keep people from talking, huh?"

Beau turned to Hien, who appeared more confused than anything. "Let's go." He stood and held her chair. They started for the door, but their way was blocked.

"Sally Ann, please excuse us."

"Still so polite. Just wait until the church learns what a hypocrite you are."

Beau sighed. "We'd like to leave."

She stepped aside. "By all means, run. Don't let me keep you from whatever it is you plan to do." But she wasn't finished. Sally Ann grabbed Hien's arm as she passed. "You. You aren't fooling anyone. You wanted to get to the States and when your ticket fell through you latched onto this big dumb one. Well, honey, you just wait. You. Just. Wait."

Hien pulled free but remained silent.

Beau held the door for her, and they went out. They crossed the street in silence until they reached the car.

Hien handed him her keys. "Please drive. I don't think I can."

He nodded and drove. They needed to talk. So he maneuvered around to Highland Park. He pulled up near Old Ben, the world's largest steer, now stuffed and mounted for all to admire. It was a pretty, quiet place at this time of the year with the lilac trees in bloom and the tulips and daffodils adding color. There shouldn't be interruptions here.

"Want to get out and walk?"

She shook her head. "I have been on my feet today. I would like to sit. Why did you come here?"

"When I was a kid, my dad brought me here. You see Old Ben there? He's been part of Kokomo a long time. My dad reminded me that no matter how things looked, no matter how big the problem got, there was an end to it. Old Ben's here, but not really. It's just an old stuffed body to help show his claim to greatness. There's a point when our problems become just stuffed claims to fame for the enemy. We must keep doing the right thing and the problem will die. In his day, Old Ben could have done great damage. But now, not so much. He's just a giant stuffed animal. Old stuffed memories won't do us harm."

"That woman will speak lies about you. At church."

"She already has. But God is in control. God knows what is true. We remain in His truth. Jesus said, 'I am the Way, the Truth and the Life.' If Jesus is the Truth, then He cannot lie. I choose to believe His promises."

Hien smiled a Mona Lisa-sized smile. "Then I will too."

Well, that was half the battle. The rest was yet to be seen. Thankfully, the battle was the Lord's.

SEVENTEEN

People Got to Be Free

THE REST OF THE MONTH BROUGHT A NEW ARRANGEMENT, meaning less time with Hien. Now that she could drive to work, Beau lost his excuse to give her a lift. Since she could take Aunt Mel to church, again, no reason to offer a ride. He could have tried the excuse of helping her with Bible study, but Connie invited her to join the one she hosted on Tuesday nights, so he was no longer needed for that, either.

There were a couple after church dinners, the most special occurring on the last Sunday of March. Hien was baptized. Something she wanted to do. Beau's heart nearly thumped out of his chest.

It was also Beau's birthday. To ask Hien and Aunt Mel to dinner had been the compromise, as he'd done his best to talk Thea out of a party. Considering how the rumor mill was working, he didn't want to put others in a difficult position. Besides, he wasn't in a celebratory mood.

That day President Johnson rocked the nation. He would not be running for another term as President of the United States. The announcement shook both political parties. Jerry called that evening after the announcement, wondering about the Indianapolis trip. Was it still on? Looked like Bobby

Kennedy would be a contender for the Democratic nominee bid. This would be big news for his little paper.

Beau felt his friend's excitement through the phone wires. "I'm not sure, Jer, if it's a good idea."

"Why? What's the problem?"

The attitudes and stares he'd received the last couple weeks came to mind. "I know you've heard the rumors. No need to add to them. Life has been tough enough for Hien. I don't want to add to the problem."

"Yeah, I understand. Connie said one girl in her Bible study dropped out after Hien joined. She doesn't want to believe there's a connection, but what do you do about rumors?"

"What does Connie plan to do?"

"Stand by Hien, for one. Me too. We're going to Indianapolis. I think you ought to go. Don't let the rumors rule." Jerry had a way with words.

Beau sighed. "Fine, I'm in. When do we leave?"

"I'll come by around one. Should put us downtown Indy by two thirty, at least before three. Got an idea that area will get full fast."

Beau calculated in his head how much he'd accomplish before having to clean up. "That works. You want to drive? We'll pick up the girls on the way."

"Sure. Better go. See you tomorrow at the café."

The café. Tomorrow would start Hien's last week. He'd kept his routine of checking in each day, but only for a few minutes now that he was planting. He and Hien had little contact. She worked in the back unless it got busy. He only went when it wasn't.

Lulu called, her leg was healing. She improved faster than expected, so would return in a week. And, it was her job first.

Great, now he had to fire Hien. Or let her go. That sounded kinder. Kinder yet would be to step from her life and end the gossip.

One o'clock Thursday, Jerry was true to his word. He pulled up in front of Beau's house and hit the horn of his bolero red 1967 Camaro.

Beau was ready, his hair still slightly damp. He'd changed his routine, getting cleaned up after lunch.

They picked up Connie next, then stopped by the café for Hien, who had permission from her wonderful boss to leave work early. She'd even brought a change of clothing.

They took US 31 south until it turned into Meridian Street —the main thoroughfare through central Indianapolis. A little over an hour into the trip they came to a RAX Roast Beef restaurant. It was far enough north from the center of town, where Beau thought everything would be congested, yet within the city limits of Indy. Hien ran into the restroom to change clothes. The guys bought sandwiches, fries, and drinks to go.

Jerry pulled out his map. "The speech won't be at the Soldiers and Sailors Monument at Monument Circle, like I first thought. The info I got said it would be at Seventeenth and Broadway."

"That's near here." Beau checked the map then scanned the area. Um, they'd be standing out in this group, if this was the neighborhood for the speech. "Maybe we should drive around for a bit, since we're close." He hoped Jerry understood his meaning.

"We can. I guess. But not too long. I imagine it will be a big crowd."

Jerry didn't get his meaning.

They drove until they found the spot near a park, partitioned off and then started cruising up and down the streets. People came from their houses. Beau knew the instant Jerry figured out his concern.

"We may stand out, guys."

"Just what I've been thinking." Beau glanced at Jerry. They were on the same wave length.

"What's the matter?" Connie peered at Jerry.

"We must stay together. Everything should be okay." Beau had read incident after incident in the papers. Race riots broke out everywhere. He didn't want to take the girls where one might erupt. This speech was set in an area of Indianapolis considered "ghetto." Prayer might be the best idea. What was he thinking?—prayer was always the best idea. "We need to pray for the event."

"Sounds like a plan." Jerry parked the car.

They asked for protection for the event, protection for the speaker. They prayed that God would speak through him, whether or not he became the nominee. They asked that seeds of peace be sown and for wisdom and discernment to inhabit all who attended. Finally, they asked that the crowd see each other as brothers and sisters and not as members of any one particular race.

When finished, Jerry started the car. They returned to the neighborhood and found a parking spot.

Beau no longer had that uneasy feeling. The peace he felt gave him confidence to smile and even take Hien by the hand. Only to assist her from the vehicle. Together they made their way to find a good view.

Hien, dressed in a skirt and blouse thing, had her camera on a strap hanging from her neck. It was the first time he'd seen her with it.

As they got closer, it became obvious Hien would not get a shot. She needed to be higher. "Too bad you're dressed like that or you could sit on my shoulders."

"That's a great idea!" Connie took charge. "Jerry, can you help put Hien on Beau's shoulders?"

"Hey, wait a minute. She's wearing a skirt!"

Connie laughed. "You idiot, she's wearing culottes. It's like she's got shorts on under her skirt.

"Oh." So he wasn't up on women's fashions. Sue him.

Jerry patted him on the back—a sympathy pat. "You're the one with the height. She'd have a great view."

Beau stooped and Jerry, with Connie's assistance, helped Hien up onto his shoulders. Then he straightened putting her well above the sight-line of the crowd.

"I will get wonderful shots. Do not drop me."

Beau chuckled. He wouldn't drop her if his life depended on it.

A COUPLE HOURS and many more people later, Mr. Robert F. Kennedy appeared to speak at a podium mounted on the back of a flatbed truck. The crowd roared, waving their signs of encouragement and backing as he came out.

He raised his arms and waited for the quiet. He had a strange expression on his face. Something wasn't right.

"Ladies and Gentlemen, I'm only going to talk to you just for a minute or so this evening, because I have some—some very sad news for all of you—Could you lower those signs, please?—I have some very sad news for all of you, and, I think, sad news for all of our fellow citizens and people who love peace all over the world; and that is that Martin Luther King was shot and was killed tonight in Memphis, Tennessee."

Wails and cries went up from the crowd as a chill settled on Beau.

Connie grabbed him and Jerry.

Beau held Hien's legs ever tighter.

The senator quieted everyone. It took a few seconds, but they listened. He spoke of peace, of Dr. King's mission of peace and equality. He asked the crowd to remember that he understood the pain of losing a loved one by assassination. It was the first time Beau knew of the man to speak publicly of his brother's death.

He continued, "My favorite poem, my—my favorite poet was Aeschylus. And he once wrote: 'Even in our sleep, pain which cannot forget falls drop by drop upon the heart, until, in our own despair, against our will, comes wisdom through the awful grace of God.'"

The wild, amazing, relentless, and awful, or rather awe-filling grace of God—Beau knew it well.

Senator Kennedy requested they all pray. Pray for the country, for peace, and for the King family. He ended with another quote. "And let's dedicate ourselves to what the Greeks wrote so many years ago: to tame the savageness of man and make gentle the life of this world. Let us dedicate ourselves to that, and say a prayer for our country and for our people. Thank you very much."

As Bobby Kennedy left the stage, Jerry helped Hien climb from Beau's shoulders. Tears streamed her face. Beau glanced at Connie and Jerry. They cried too. A drop of something plopped off his chin. He cried with them, with his friends and with the people in the throng. Strangers brought together in this horrible news, bonded in sorrow.

Beau took hold of Hien's hand. It started a chain reaction. Jerry held Connie's, Connie and Hien clasped hands. They stood and prayed together. Others saw them and joined. Before long, there were twenty to thirty people, maybe even fifty, standing together in prayer, praying as Mr. Kennedy had asked, for the King family, for the country, and for peace.

THE RIDE HOME was too quiet. Beau asked if anyone minded and turned on the radio. The WLS announcer in Chicago interrupted the song to say riots had broken out in various parts of the city. They had incoming updates on riots in New York City, Boston, and several more places. Nausea sent bile to the back of his throat. He switched it off. Silence was better.

The next morning, he learned there were riots in over one hundred cities across the United States, with thirty-five dead and over 2,500 injured.

But none in Indianapolis.

Credit was given to Bobby Kennedy's speech.

Beau gave credit to God for answered prayer.

BEAU MADE a special effort to arrive before Hien's last shift at the café was through. He hoped Margie, and the crew, let her know they appreciated her. It would be nice if her regular customers said something kind.

The place was nearly empty, no one at the counters. He grabbed his usual seat.

Margie showed up with a mug and coffee. "Gonna miss that girl, you know that?"

"Margie, is that a tear?"

She swiped the back of her hand across her eyes. "Nope. Just sayin' I'm gonna miss her, that's all."

"I understand." He took a sip of the coffee. "I agree with you." He winked at her.

"Oh, you." She bopped him with her order pad and returned to the counter.

Hien came out, laughing about something, and spotted him at his usual place. She waved and headed his direction.

"What's so funny?"

"Buck said I was about to become a lady of leisure. When I asked what he meant, it made me laugh." She sat across from him. "I will miss working here very much."

"I'm sorry that I can't keep you here. With Lulu coming back, the intake from the place wouldn't pay for another person. But could you occasionally fill in?"

"What do you mean?"

He leaned against the seat. "Well, if someone gets sick or

needs a vacation or an emergency comes up, that sort of thing. Would you be willing to help then?"

"Yes. Oh, I gave Jerry the photos. I was able to set up a dark room. I think he liked them. At least, he paid me for them. He said he would run some in the next issue."

Beau liked the sound of that. "Good. I hope he throws lots of business your way."

She looked puzzled.

"Throw business your way is to give you photo assignment opportunities."

She nodded. "I get it." Placing her hands on the table, she spread her fingers and leaned back. Her diamond glittered. "I think I had better go home. I need to check on Mil. She has been doing much better, but I worry about her being lonely." She stood. "Thank you, Beau, for this opportunity. We needed the money."

"I don't mean to pry, but is it any better?"

She smiled. That soft, Mona-Lisa smile. "Some. A little, I guess. We will make it."

Yes, she would. If he had his way.

PALM SUNDAY ARRIVED. Beau realized it was the first time Hien had heard the Passion Story. Pastor Bob did something a little different this year. He planned a week of services where he spoke as Jesus's disciple, John, relating the experience from a first person perspective. He wanted to make it more personal for each in attendance. By doing his sermons in character, he hoped it would bring people to the garden, to the cross, and to the empty tomb.

Church was still stressful for Beau. It was one thing to start a rumor about him. But bringing Hien into it? That required self-control to not fight back.

The final straw came when his mother, sister, and aunt were

snubbed. It was subtle and, of course, it wasn't everyone. It wasn't even all the women. But one or two incidents stirred an impotent anger. He saw the hurt in their eyes, and there was little he could do. They didn't deserve that sort of treatment.

Pastor Bob and his wife, as well as the other board members and families, made a point of including his loved ones whenever possible. One family stopped coming without trying to find out the truth. They hadn't attended long. Still it was hard to watch. Beau suggested he speak before the congregation and answer all questions. Complete transparency. His friends disagreed. They felt that any stigma from the rumor would only be strengthened if they acknowledged its existence.

Beau wasn't so sure, but he could do nothing unless Pastor Bob agreed. So far, he had not.

Something about the Passion Story, the part that told of how Jesus didn't defend himself, spoke to his soul in a new way this year. If Jesus could take what he did, then Beau could handle the receiving end of a little gossip, even the untruthful kind. God knew the truth. He found solace in that. Jesus had prayed for his followers and their safety. Beau followed Jesus' example.

On Maundy Thursday there was a foot washing service, accompanied by a Communion service and meal. Thea told Beau it was her favorite of the whole year. He understood. It touched him in ways he couldn't communicate. This year Hein experienced it, and that warmed his soul. Thea said it brought her to tears when Hien washed Melanie's feet.

Mom couldn't do anyone else's feet, but three different women asked to wash hers. When Beau heard that, it lifted something off his heart. The members with the closer walk were the ones who went to the Maundy Thursday services. If they embraced Mom that way, maybe those who rebuffed her had the problem. What was he thinking? There was no maybe. Realization of that was followed by an urge to pray for those who blindly snubbed his mother. Beau found that the more he prayed for them, the less they hurt him. That made praying for them easier. Funny how that worked.

Easter Sunday dawned with the freshness of spring. Trees budded, new flowers poked their blooms up through the moist soil. Even the little wild violets sprung up in the dew-drenched lawns alongside yellow dandelions. The season dressed for the King of kings.

Beau could taste the hope in the air. Once at church, the greetings flew.

"He is risen!"

"He is risen indeed!"

It only took a couple times before Hien joined them. Her eyes lit up to share in the tradition. Beau noticed that Aunt Mel and Hien were doing much better too.

His aunt was more her old self, the kind soul whom he had always loved. New life, new growth, a new attitude. A better attitude. He would keep the Kingdom of God first in his thoughts and let God fight the battles until He called him to the fight.

Beau couldn't imagine feeling finer. After church, just before he left to get The Tank, he stopped to talk with Melanie and Hien. Thea was explaining, "We should be ready to eat by noon. Feel free to come straight over, or if you want to change clothes first, there's time."

Mel had a private smile for Hien, who winked back. "I think we'll run by our place first to pick up a surprise."

"Yes," Hien said. "We will be there. You will not have to wait." She giggled and Aunt Melanie tried to hide her grin.

Something was up with those two.

Beau patted his mother's shoulder and left for the car. He'd had to park over three blocks away today since so many others joined the regular attendees. Still a block from The Tank, a lone figure stepped out from behind an oak tree.

Sally Ann.

He needed to see her like he needed another a rock in his shoe. Then he remembered and lifted a quick prayer for her.

"Beau?"

He paused, bracing himself. "Yes?"

"I… ah… Oh, never mind." She turned and walked back toward the church.

That was a mystery, but Beau was grateful no harsh words were spoken. At the car he spotted a piece of paper stuck under the wiper. Opening it, he read the scrawled note.

Beau,

I tried to make you love me and when you didn't, I attempted to get even.

Now, I am all alone. The one joy I had, singing specials, is gone. They've taken that away from me. I wanted to punish you. But I'm the one punished. It's not fair. I hate this. I will not bother you ever again.

Sally Ann

At first glance, he was elated. This was great news! Only then he started to wonder if there were a deeper meaning. He shoved the note in his suit pocket and drove back to the church. Melanie and Hien were still there.

"Thea, please drive. And take Melanie to our house—you don't mind, do you, Aunt Mel? Thea will need help to get Mom inside. I'm sorry, but Hien's gotta help me with something."

Thea nodded. He could count on her, without questions, until later. She threw him the I-trust-you look.

Melanie gave him a funny glance but got into the back seat.

Beau helped his mother into her seatbelt and put her wheelchair in the trunk. He patted the trunk fender and waved to Thea as she pulled away. As soon as they were gone, he turned to Hien. "Let's go. We have to find Sally Ann."

Hien didn't ask anything. She nodded and handed him the keys. "You drive."

Once inside, after he adjusted the seat, she put her hand over his. "Can we pray first?"

Absolutely.

They bowed their heads, and he prayed for Sally Ann.

Hien added a prayer for Beau to be filled with God's wisdom.

Then they were off. The problem was Beau didn't know where to start. At the stop sign, he closed his eyes a moment. An idea came to him. He turned and headed out to Sally Ann's parent's farm on the opposite side of town.

Sally Ann's car was parked in the drive. Beau walked around to open Hien's door, all the while scanning the area. Something told him Sally Ann was not in the house.

The barn door stood ajar, so he started there. Hien followed along. At the doorway, he heard a muffled sound. Not necessarily crying, but soft sniffling. He followed it further into a shadowed corner.

Sally Ann sat on a milking stool, her chin tipped up, staring at the hay loft. A calico kitten lay curled in her lap. She moved her hand over its silky head.

He didn't want to startle her but needed to inform her she wasn't alone.

But she spotted him. "Come to gloat?"

"Why would I do that?"

"Why would you bring your girlfriend along except to rub her in my face?"

Hien's forehead bunched into quizzical lines, but she said nothing.

"Hien had the car. I sent Thea and Mom home in mine."

"Oh. Sorry. Again." She sniffed and ran her knuckle under her nose.

Beau pulled out his handkerchief. "Here." When she hesitated he added, "It's clean."

She turned a You-are-such-an-idiot glance on him but accepted it and wiped her eyes.

"Sally Ann, we need to straighten out a few things."

"Like you're too old for me? But not her?" The glare she threw at Hien was filled with barbs.

"I'm too old for either of you. I do not have a girlfriend.

Hien is family. She and my aunt were hit pretty hard. Would you let any of your family suffer if you had the means to help?"

"You seriously want me to believe you have no feelings for… Hien?" She practically spit her name.

Beau wanted to say he had no feelings for her. But that would be a lie. He wouldn't lie.

Hien raised her hand, and he stopped stammering. "We have not really met. Perhaps you do not realize that my husband died two months ago. We were married for two weeks when he had to leave. We talked on the phone when we could, but I did not see him again. A month later my husband was dead, my brother and mother were dead, my brother-in-law was dead, and my father-in-law was dead. If not for my mother-in-law and her family's kindness, I do not know where I would be."

For the first time, Sally Ann studied Hien.

Beau stared too. Five deaths, all that close? He'd had no clue about her mother and brother. The weight of her words tumbled like bricks on him.

"Coming to the United States was a great gift, but it has not been easy. The greatest gift my in-laws gave me, though, was to share about Jesus. I was afraid I would be all alone. But I am not. He was with me when I was scared and when I hurt so bad I thought I would die from the pain. He was with me, and He is with you, Sally Ann. You already know He is."

Sally Ann nodded. Her voice was softer than a whisper. Beau strained to hear. "You're right. I grew up in the church. I have prayed for someone to love me, to take me away from this." She waved with her arm at everything around her. "I don't want to be plain Sally Ann Meister, the old maid. Why can't I be married, have a family, bring my children to church? I want to be the love of someone's life." She pulled the kitten closer, her cheek resting on its head.

Beau stepped forward. "Sally Ann, you already are. Jesus loves you so much He died for you. That's not what you want right this minute, but if you'll focus on that, on the incredible love He has for you, it can be enough whether you end up with a home of your own or you make a family with other believers."

She wiped her eyes again. "Is that what you do, Beau? Why haven't you found someone yourself?"

"I did." Both Hien and Sally Ann stared at him. "She died a long time ago. Her name was Nam Sun. I guess I just found no one else. Now I'm a certified old bachelor living at home with my mother." He shrugged. "Sally Ann, it hurts when you feel alone. I know. Believe me. But there's peace in knowing you are never alone. And, there are friends to be made. Lots of friends. I am happy to be your friend."

"Me too. I will be your friend." Hien smiled.

"Even though I started those rumors about you?" Sally Ann's eyes filled with fear and her shoulders slumped as if she expected a blow.

"Even though. You actually did me a favor. You pushed me to draw closer to Jesus and take care of some things I've let fester. Why be angry at someone who did me that favor? It may not have been your intention, but you still helped me."

Sally Ann chuckled without mirth. "Can't do anything right, can I?"

Beau twisted the toe of his shoe in the straw. "Perhaps it was like Joseph said. You meant it for bad, but God meant it for good."

"Evil, you mean. No need to soften the word, I get it." She wiped the handkerchief under her nose. "I'll let Judy know the truth. And Beau, I really am sorry." She gazed up at him, her eyes revealing an honesty he hadn't seen. She set the kitten on the floor.

Beau helped her stand. "I know. I forgive you. And thank you for saying you'll talk with Judy. I appreciate it." He wanted to add that it wouldn't hurt to say something nice about Hien, but he let that go.

Hien touched Sally Ann's shoulder. "It will be okay. Just wait and see."

Sally Ann reached up and covered Hien's hand with her own. "Thank you. You are more gracious than I deserve."

"Can we walk you to the porch?" Beau motioned her first.

After a millisecond pause, she nodded and led the way.

They walked together as far as the portico columns. Sally Ann climbed the steps and looked back.

Hien waved. "He is risen!"

This time Sally Ann's smile was genuine. "He is risen indeed!" She waved and went into the house.

AFTER A QUICK STOP by the Wheaten farm, Hien and Beau pulled into the drive at his place. Hien carried in her surprise to a chorus of "About Time!" and "We're starving!"

Beau had brought in the table Saturday evening with Jerry's last-minute help. Now it was laden with ham, scalloped potatoes, green bean casserole, homemade relishes and rolls, candied carrots, and a lime Jell-O salad.

Hien placed her treat in the kitchen—sugar cream pies, better known as Hoosier pies.

Aunt Mel had been teaching Hien the finer points of a Hoosier celebration. Beau chuckled. The idea of a sugar cream pie rounding out the extravagant meal made him hungrier than he could remember.

After two helpings, Beau retrieved an envelope from his desk in the corner of the living room. He'd debated how to do this. Now he was ready. He took a breath. "Aunt Melanie, Hien, it came to me when I received my monthly milk check that I owe you both something. I've been keeping your cows here and getting money for their milk for over eighteen months. I did some figuring. After learning what percent of the milk was from them, I calculated a figure for rent and food. This is what's left. I got it in cash so there won't be a problem with the bank. I also was thinking, if you use this, you can start a joint account that would be separate from the estate and give you a little more breathing room. What do you think?"

Aunt Melanie opened the envelope and her eyes grew wide. "Oh no. We already owe you too much. Hien's car and the furniture and the customs people—by the way, that stuff will be delivered on Wednesday. We're doing fine. Just keep it, Beau."

Beau shook his head. "I can't do it. It's not right. That money is yours. Besides, Hien has been making her payments, as we agreed, and the executor of the estate has my bill. You don't want me to be guilty of stealing, do you?"

His mom laughed, Thea joined in, and soon Hien and Aunt Melanie were chuckling.

Aunt Melanie peeked in the envelope again. She stopped laughing and drew in a breath. "These are hundred-dollar bills, Beau. I can't believe you owe us this much."

"I do. Most likely more because I didn't figure in the eggs we've sold. And I had an idea. Maybe if you, Aunt Mel, would stay with Mom a couple days a week, Thea might get out. I'd be happy to pay. And, Thea, if while you're out, you could some-times teach Hien about their chickens. Or putting in a garden. That could help too. I will start cutting you a monthly check based on the portion of milk coming from your cows. How would you all feel about that?"

Mom gazed at Melanie. "Peez?"

Beau hadn't considered his mother's feelings in all this, only her safety and giving Thea a break. But Mom's expression told him she'd welcome this plan.

Hien and Melanie exchanged a look and then they both nodded.

"We accept. With one proviso." Aunt Mel's pointer finger zeroed in on him. "You Mr. Fix-it-for-everyone, allow me the joy of spending time with your mother with no money involved. We've been friends too long, Val, for me to get paid to enjoy your company." She blew a kiss to Mom. "Oh, one more thing. Don't you overpay us for the milk. Keep it fair, Beau."

He nodded. "Agreed. Now, anyone else care for another piece of pie? Not sure if it's kosher for a Vietnamese to cook Hoosier, but it tastes good enough to be homegrown, so I'm guessing it's allowed." He winked at Hien.

She picked up the pie plate, as if to pass it, then pretended to throw it at him.

Beau jumped out of his chair.

Everyone laughed.

His life was sweet.

EIGHTEEN

Western Union

THE MONTH OF MAY FLEW. BEAU COULDN'T BELIEVE IT WAS time to pull another page off his calendar. True to his word, he had figured in food and keep for the Wheaten cows before writing the women a check to deposit in their new account. Thea had not only shown Hien about raising chickens for eggs, she'd helped her get set up in a small egg business. Not a huge moneymaker, but it paid for the chicken feed the birds needed and saved them from having to spend money on eggs at the IGA.

Sally Ann kept her word too. She spoke to Pastor Bob and Judy and told them she'd made up the whole thing. It took time, but church got friendlier. All that while, his mother never mumbled a cross word concerning her ill-treatment. Now the snubbers behaved as if nothing had happened, and she preferred it that way. Mom was one special lady, for sure.

Though things improved at church, around town, a few people began acting weird. Conversations stopped as he walked into the stores. Once, when he was walking down Main Street, a couple guys he'd considered at least friendly acquaintances crossed over when they saw him approach. Fortunately, he had seen none of that weirdness directed at his household. So, if they wanted to treat him that way, fine. He had no clue what was wrong, but if they kept his family out of it, they could do as they pleased.

The Farm Bureau meetings had been unpleasant because of Pete Warrick. Beau penciled in the detasseling date to satisfy the man. The last two weeks of July. Instead of making it better, the guy searched for other things to complain about. Beau began to think Thea was wrong. At least Barney Fife had a heart and cared about people, even if he was fussy and anal. Pete was just fussy and rude. Not an easy combination for committee work.

A few days into June, the phone rang as Beau padded downstairs for the barn. It was awfully early in the morning for calls. Grabbing it before it woke his mother, he didn't even get out his whispered "Hello."

"Turn on the TV." Jerry's voice was tight, urgent.

"Why? What channel?"

"The channel doesn't matter. It's on all three networks. They shot Bobby Kennedy."

Beau nearly dropped the phone. He grabbed for a chair back before hanging up. The TV was in his mother's room. He wheeled it into the living room and turned it on, setting the volume low.

It was set to the NBC affiliate out of Indianapolis, channel six. Beau sank to the floor in front. Frank McGee interviewed other reporters and witnesses around the Ambassador Hotel. Various stories emerged. Charles Quinn claimed he'd seen the senator having been shot in the head. A guy who drove up onto the hotel lawn when he heard a radio news report, David Roche, said he saw no blood on Mr. Kennedy's head, but that the senator gripped his side. Some claimed the Senator's brother-in-law, Steve Smith, had been a victim, and some claimed they'd spotted Mr. Smith walking unharmed after the shooting. Even the number of people shot varied. One account said just RFK. A different report stated three were shot, this included a woman. Nobody mentioned her identity or how badly she was hurt.

Beau watched a short time before turning off the set and leaving for the barn. The tragedy in California would not change the fact that his girls needed his attention. He turned the radio on out there. Larry Lujack still worked the songs but kept everyone updated on information as it rolled out from the AP and UPI press groups. The musical interludes did nothing to soothe the shock in Beau's gut. Only two months ago he'd listened as Bobby Kennedy asked for prayer because of another assassin's bullet. "Lord, I don't understand."

It wasn't as if Beau had planned to support the guy. He hadn't decided which party he would back, let alone for whom he would cast his vote. But whether he agreed with him politically, he liked what he'd heard in Indianapolis. Mr. Kennedy had turned to prayer. He had asked others to pray. Though famous, he was a human being with a family. No matter where one stood on the political map, this was wrong.

When he finished his chores and had his shower, Beau decided he'd swing by Hien's place and see if she'd go to the café with him. Jerry would be there. A quick call to him made sure Connie would meet them too. The four of them could pray together. It was the right thing to do.

After, when he took Hien home, a Western Union telegram waited for her. She asked Beau to sit on the porch swing while she read it. Afterward, she handed it to him.

We shared credit. STOP

Mid July get LOOK at newsstand. STOP

Letter coming STOP

Steve and Mat

"What does this mean?"

"I do not know. I used to work with Steve Riley and Mat Morrissey at Press Corps. They are both photojournalists. Mat was in Huế. He learned about my mother and brother. Steve was a friend who helped me get my passport. I made a deal with him to give him an interview about the embassy attack for all he did. The thing is, I retched my whole story on him, because right before I was to be interviewed, we got the news about Michael and Charlie and then Pop died. I held nothing back. I am sure I overwhelmed him. Then Mat returned and told me about my family. I cannot imagine what they would write, but for them to work together, that is significant." She pushed out with her toe, keeping the swing going. "I am curious what they will say."

"It sounds like they sold their story to *LOOK* magazine. That's pretty big. Do they have any photos of you to use in it?"

"It is possible. I am not sure." She grew silent and kept swinging.

Beau wondered if she might be concerned about her friends working on something for her.

The next day, June sixth, Beau woke to the news that Robert Francis Kennedy had passed. It felt like this year was kicking the stuffing out of him. And those he loved.

And it wasn't even half over.

VACATION BIBLE SCHOOL started for Breadville Community Church the following Monday. Hien was excited. Connie asked her to help with the three- and four-year-old class, thinking it would help Hien learn some quick Bible stories. The grin on Hien's face, when Beau saw her at the meeting after church the Sunday before only proved it was a good idea. He also liked that he would see her each evening since they assigned him to the sixth-grade boys.

After the first day, her smile dimmed. "How did it go?"

"I am not sure." She shook her head.

"Why? What happened?"

Her voice dropped. "They all needed the bathroom. At the same time."

"Didn't you have a bathroom run figured into the schedule?"

"Yes, we did. In fact, we had just returned from there when

one little girl started to chant 'We need to poop. We need to poop.' Then a couple boys joined in and soon all six children were singing 'We need to poop. We need to poop.'"

Connie walked up as Hien finished her story. She snorted at the last part. In a second, she was laughing so hard tears rolled down her face.

Beau scratched his ear. "It was a little funny, but what's the joke?"

Connie put her hand on Hien's shoulder and her other arm across her own waist, working to get a breath. "I'm sorry. Beau, you'd laugh, too, if you knew what they were really saying."

Hien glanced at her. "What they were really saying?"

Connie nodded and crooked her finger for Beau and Hien to follow. She led them to the three-and-four-year-olds' classroom. Once inside, she went to the toy cabinet and pulled out a yellow stuffed bear wearing a red top and holding a HUNY pot. "Hien, this is Winnie the Pooh."

Hien cocked her head, looking puzzled. "That's what the little girl carried when she chanted."

Connie nodded and put her hand over her mouth.

Suddenly, Beau understood. A snort escaped him, too. He winked at Connie and began to sing, "Winnie the Pooh, Winnie the Pooh."

Connie sang with him. All at once, Hien understood and laughed. "So, not 'we need to poop,' but 'Winnie the Pooh.' Oh, no!"

They laughed together. Judy Harrigan wandered in. Hien shared her story and Judy hugged her. "Welcome to Children's Church."

A week later, as Hien came to pick up Aunt Melanie, she pulled Beau aside to talk on his front porch. Maddie tagged along, curling up by Hien's feet once they were seated. Hien handed Beau a legal-sized envelope.

He glanced at her before opening it.

She nodded. "Go ahead."

So he did. There was one sheet of paper wrapped around another set of folded pages. The first one read:

Hien,

Hope all is well. I'm not much on writing. You can laugh at that coming from me, but pictures say more than words. I stopped in Da Nang and ran into a guy. He worked with your husband. A combination of him being in-country and getting wounded and ending up in the hospital meant he hadn't heard about the crash. Turns out, he had something your husband had asked him to send to you, but by the time he could, he didn't know where to send it. He gave it to me. I'm sending it to you. I didn't read it. Thought you might want it.

Take care,

Mat

"You sure?"

She nodded. "My heart has been troubled since I received word Michael died. It was not only the loss, but something else along with it that made it harder to trust God. This is a gift." Tears rimmed her eyes.

Beau unfolded the paper. It looked to be pages torn from a notebook, worn and crumpled.

Hey Baby,

Got time so thought I'd write. It's too late to call you so this must suffice. I feel awful about what I said to you. Please, keep listening to my folks. They know what they are talking about with God. I should have listened better long ago. I do believe in Him. I'm finding myself spending more time in prayer. Kind of wish I'd had you send my Bible with the rest of those things. But there's a sky pilot here on the base and we've been talking. I'm not sure my dad and he would agree on everything, but he's got the basics. The bottom line is this God stuff is important. I want you to learn all about Him and

His son, Jesus. I want us to go to church on Sundays together, as a family, taking all our kids and bringing them up to know Jesus loves them.

I've not been the best husband. We barely got started, and I pulled that crap on you in front of our friends. I'm sorry about that. I'll make it up to you.

This letter is getting maudlin. Guess because it's nighttime and I'm lonely for you. Anyway, one more thing. I love you so much, but I am aware that I might not make it back. Trust me, I'm counting on making it, but it's hard to run from reality at this time of night. If I don't, Baby, please go to the States with my folks. They will take care of you. You'll have a great life there. Indiana is a good place to live. Don't crawl into a shell. Go out and make friends. Find reasons to laugh. This next part is hard to write. If I don't return, find love again. You are too wonderful. I love you very much. And I am counting the days until I am with you and we can pack up and start our life together in little ol' Breadville. Keep the faith, Baby.

All my love,

Michael

Beau handed it to her. He was lost for words. Why did she share this?

"One of the last times I spoke with Michael, he said for me to stay away from the God stuff. He told me his parents meant well, but not to get mixed up in it. I have hurt so deep inside, worried that he rejected God before he died. I needed to show this to someone. Mil would love his turnaround of faith. But it would hurt her to learn he had said those things to me. I do not want her to have any bad thoughts or memories about Michael. You are the only person I trust enough to share." She gave him a sideways glance and pushed the floor with her toe to keep the swing going.

Beau blew out a breath. "Wow."

"Yes, wow."

"You okay?"

"It was hard to see his handwriting again. But I needed those words. It is a gift from God that I received this letter. I only have one question."

Beau shrugged. "What's that?"

"What is a sky pilot?"

Beau smiled, glad that was it. "It's a nickname for a pastor or priest assigned to a military camp. They don't fly in a plane. They send prayers up to God. That's why they're called that."

She nodded. "I understand now. Thank you." She tucked the papers into her purse and stood. "I must get Mil."

Beau fought the urge to invite them to stay for dinner. He was learning to keep his heart in check and the less time he spent with her, the better.

THE SECOND WEEK of July brought the county fair. Beau had signed up to man the Farm Bureau booth on Tuesday, the late-afternoon-to-evening-close shift. He was swamped this time of year but needed to set an example. The wives and older teens covered during the day, but sometimes it called for a man-to-man discussion. So, Beau put his name on the list. Aaron Nelson promised one of his boys would stop by his place and take care of the evening milking for him, so it was all set.

Tuesday was fairly quiet. He'd encouraged everyone to sign up in pairs so there would be enough and taking a break would be easy. His partner, Les Burkett, had brought his cow, Sandy. He housed her in the big barn with the other animals there for showing or auction. Les hadn't entered her in a category, but with her due to calve any day, he didn't want to leave her home. Besides, he said his wife and kids were going to a birthday party in Russiaville. So, Les was up every twenty minutes doing a quick check on Sandy.

Around seven-thirty, a police officer showed. "I need Les Burkett. I heard he was here."

Beau nodded. "He just stepped away a moment. He should be back any time. Could I help you with something?"

The officer shook his head. "No, but would you get him?"

"Sure." Beau shrugged. "You don't mind monitoring the booth, do you? Here's the Be Right Back sign."

The officer caught it and agreed.

Beau took off for the barn. He found Les with Sandy, who lay on the straw in her stanchion.

"Hey Beau, who's watching the table?"

"There's a police officer who needs to speak to you."

Les said nothing, but the stare he gave asked the big question.

"I don't know what he wants, Les. He wouldn't say. He asked for you."

"Let's go."

The men ran back to the booth where Les introduced himself to the officer.

Beau got busy to give them privacy. If Les wanted to tell him, he'd say so. A minute later, that all changed.

"Beau, Linda and the kids were in a car accident. Kelli has a broken arm and Bruce broke his nose. Linda is banged up but okay. The car isn't drivable, though. I will follow the officer to St. Joe's and check on them. I can get my trailer and Sandy tomorrow. I've got a feeling tonight is the night, and I can't take her with me to the hospital. Can you stay with her in case she delivers? It's her first."

Beau patted Les's arm. "Sure. Don't worry about a thing. Just go to your family. I'll be praying."

"Thanks, Beau. I don't think there's anyone else I could ask to stay here and not spend my time worrying. I'll be back tomorrow as soon as I can get here. I'll aim for five, if everything on the family's end works."

"It's okay. If you have a minute, though, would you call Thea and tell her where I am?"

"Will do. See ya." He waved and raced after the officer.

Beau scanned the fairgrounds. The evening dragged. Tuesday just wasn't a big fair night. That was the reason he'd picked it. But now…

He closed up the booth, put all the brochures away, and locked up before heading to his pickup.

He wasn't dressed for helping to bring a calf into the world. Instead he hoped to appear more businesslike—white short-sleeve dress shirt, navy trousers and wingtip shoes. He grabbed a pair of boots out of his truck and searched for something to cover his clothes. He found an old pair of coveralls he'd slipped in one day after having to change a flat in his church attire. Lesson learned, now appreciated. He kicked off his shoes and stepped into the coveralls, zipped them up and then got his stocking feet into the boots. After that he dashed to the barn. He was sure Sandy wouldn't have gone into labor in the time he'd been gone, but with first timers, you never knew.

She was fine. Still resting. He checked. No baby hooves finding their way into the world. He kicked back on the hay to wait. She'd let him know what she needed.

He glanced at his watch, noticing he'd dozed a moment. Or longer. It was now nine-thirty. Sandy was doing fine. Perhaps agitated, but that was normal. He heard his name and turned.

Hien stood there in a white summer dress covered in big pink flowers. Her hair was pulled back at the sides, but loose down her back. Her camera hung from her neck. She must be on a photo assignment for Jerry. "Hey. How do you like the fair?"

She smiled.

That smile he loved. *Oops, don't go there.*

"It is interesting. I like viewing it through my camera."

"Well, if Sandy here cooperates, you might get something special. She could have her calf tonight."

"Really?" Hien moved closer.

That surprised him. Adults who didn't grow up around cows

were often more timid on their first encounter. Not Hien. She walked up to the cow and began to stroke the short, soft coat.

"Yeah. Sandy isn't mine, but you remember Les and Linda Burkett from church, right? Well, Linda was in an accident tonight and Les left Sandy here to go check on his family. So, I'm spending the evening with her. It's her first calf."

"What happened? Are they okay?"

"A car accident. They're a little banged up—I guess one of the kids broke an arm, and the other has a broken nose. Linda has some cuts and bruises. They will go home from St. Joe's, but since the car isn't drivable, Les needed to get there with his truck —and he couldn't leave Sandy in the trailer while he waited at the emergency room."

"Oh, I see. How long do you think?"

Beau shrugged. "The hospital or the calf?"

She laughed. "Both."

"Who knows? Concerning the hospital, you know what I do. It gets crazy. With the calf, our first clue is when we can see the front feet start to emerge. Then, if everything is normal, it goes pretty fast."

"Oh, I see. Would you like company while you wait?"

If she only knew. "Sure. So, Jerry sent you out for some shots? Hmm."

"The fair runs the whole week. This way we have photos ready. I hope I get ones he can use."

"I'm sure you will. You have a great eye."

She blushed.

He liked it when her cheeks pinked that way. She was too much into his head. Not a good thing.

"Thank you." She got quiet and began to fiddle with her camera.

A thought dawned on him. "There's another reason you're here. You knew where to find me. How?"

"I am sorry. I hope you do not mind."

"Of course not. But how? Why?"

She glanced around and then moved to sit on a bale of hay in the corner of Sandy's little cubicle. "I called your house to speak with you. Thea told me you were here. Jerry talked about my taking photos of the fair when I saw him on Sunday, so I thought that might make a good excuse." She peeked at him, a shyness he'd never seen glimmered in her eyes.

He sat next to her. "What do you want to talk about?"

Her hands, usually folded so still in her lap, now twitched and moved, fingers interlacing and unlacing. "I, we, ah… Mil and I talked. You have helped us so much. It is not fair to always depend on you. With your help, we have enough to eat and can pay our utilities and basic bills. But now we have two new problems. First is tax assessment on the farm. It says we are in ah… ah-rears?"

"Arrears."

She nodded. "Arrears. The second is my visa is about to expire. It is good only through August. Mil cannot sponsor me because she doesn't have the financial means. I am technically the owner of the farm. So, she suggested, and I agree, that we sell half of the farm on the pro-vize-oh?"

"Proviso."

"On the proviso that whoever purchases that half must also sponsor me. We make you the first offer. Would you be willing?" She glanced at him.

His heart melted in his chest. Like ice cream on a July afternoon. Like chocolate on a barbeque. Melted. She could have asked him to stand on the block wall in there and sing every Beach Boys song he knew—and he knew them all—he would have done it without question. Just for that look.

He swallowed. "Hien, is this what you want? I mean, I would be happy to do that."

"Yes. That is what we want. Oh, thank you, Beau." She threw her arms around his neck.

His mind began to swirl.

A voice in his head cut through.

"Wait a minute, though. Before you thank me. There's someone who's wanted to buy your property for a long time. He got beat out when Uncle Ernie bought it and he hasn't been happy about it since. If I buy it from you, and don't give him the chance, well, let's just say he wouldn't think it was very fair."

Hien sat back on the bale. "What should I do?"

"Let me handle it. If he says no, then I'll do it. You don't have to worry. If he says yes, well then, you have a new business partner. He knows a lot about farming, and could make your farm into a good resource for you. Okay?"

She nodded, not quite as happy.

"Hey, don't worry. It's gonna be fine. No matter what he says, you're gonna have a sponsor and the taxes all handled."

He just hoped Pete Warrick said no.

"What is happening?"

Beau glanced where Hien pointed. Tiny hooves protruded from the cow's backside. It was time. The hooves went back in. Then came out followed by a nose. It really was time.

"Step back and get your camera ready." He grabbed an old blanket flung over the cement divider and tied it around her. It might save her dress. Maybe.

"Oh! The baby is coming out." Hien's voice held more than excitement, something akin to awe.

Beau had seen this more times than he could count, but never grew tired of viewing the messy, crazy miracle of life. To hear her, he couldn't help but think she agreed.

Seconds later, a new little life came sloppily onto Sandy's straw bed. The mother began to lick her baby, and within a few more minutes, the little guy was getting his first meal.

Beau and Hien sat and watched. God's design prepared the mother to take care of her baby. They didn't need to talk. Hien snapped another photo here and there, but mostly they just sat. It was… normal miraculous. That was the best description.

He glanced at his watch. One-twenty in the morning? Where had the time gone? Then he peeked over at Hien. If she were seen here when Les got back or when others showed up to start the day, it could ruin her reputation. Enough people spread damaging rumors about her. He couldn't stand the thought of adding ammunition to their fire.

"Hien, you'd better get going."

"Oh, you are leaving?"

"No, I need to stay. I promised Les. But I don't want anyone to get the wrong idea about you."

She tilted her head, squinching her brows. "We have done nothing wrong."

"True, but that won't stop someone from making remarks. I wouldn't want that to happen to you."

"You will call me after you talk to the other person about the farm?"

"I promise." He wanted to hug her but resisted that idea. Instead, he untied the blanket from behind her back.

"Thank you, Beau. Good night."

He chuckled and winked. "Good morning."

She smiled and waved.

Then she was gone.

Wednesday afternoon, Beau sat in his regular spot in the café, soaking in as much caffeine as he could. This time, his paper lay on the seat next to him. He watched the door. Pete agreed to meet him there at two o'clock. It was now one fifty-five.

The bells jingled, but it was only a couple kids, preteens. They spoke with Margie a second. She pointed them in his direction.

"Hi, are you the boss?" The girl appeared braver than the boy who didn't even try to make eye contact.

"I guess, yeah. What can I do for you?"

She showed him the signs her partner carried. "We're part of the Breadville Youth Theatre, and we're getting ready to present the play, *The Old Woman and the Shoe and What Happened to All Those Kids*. May we hang posters around here?"

"*The Old Woman and the Shoe and What Happened to All Those Kids*, huh? That's quite a title. I don't think I recall that play."

"Oh, it's new. That was part of our summer project. We wrote it together. Now we'll present it."

Beau smiled. "Kind of like a premiere?"

Both nodded. "So can we? Hang some, I mean."

"Sure. No problem. How much are tickets?" Beau reached for his wallet.

"Don't know yet. That's another crew's job. We're just in posters. But you if read one you'll get more information."

"Okey doke. Tell you what. Tape one on the door, in the window there," he pointed "and maybe under the cash register? Will that help?"

"Sure. Thanks, mister."

They scurried over toward the door as Pete Warrick entered.

Beau raised his hand, and Pete made his way to the booth.

"Hi, Pete. Appreciate you meeting me here."

"Hey, Salem. So, what is it you want? I'm busy."

"Me too." He would not make this easy.

"Unless you need my help with the Farm Bureau stuff. You're letting people down with your lack of responsibility."

Good thing Beau's hand was not setting on the table or Pete would have seen the determination it took to unclench it. "No, Pete, I didn't ask you here on Farm Bureau business. Listen, I just learned that the Wheatens are willing to sell half of their farm. I remembered you were interested, so I thought I'd let you know."

That changed his attitude. "What are they asking? I knew they couldn't handle farm life."

"They aren't planning to move. They're only selling a half interest. The price is what's owed for taxes."

"Not what I hoped, but sure. Yeah, guess I'm still interested."

Beau stared him straight in the eyes. "There's one more thing. The person who buys the farm must also sponsor Hien Wheaten for citizenship."

"What?" Pete's fist crashed on the table making a boom so loud everyone in the café turned in their direction. "You've got to be kidding. I wouldn't help that commie. I have no idea what Melanie Wheaten was thinking bringing that VC brat to our community, but the sooner she goes back to her hooch the better."

Beau slid out from the booth, standing over Pete, his hands clenching and unclenching at his sides while a white-hot bolt of anger pierced through his brain. He took a breath. "So, let me get this straight. You don't want to take their offer?"

Pete stood. "I wouldn't take it on a dare! All I gotta do is wait. The taxes'll come due, they won't pay. I can get the whole thing at auction, and for a lot less. And I won't have to worry about any Vietnamese cutie destroying my property values."

Beau wanted to hit him. Oh, he needed to hit him. Only the faces of those surrounding him in the restaurant with their wide-eyed stares drilling into him held him back. Somewhere he remembered there were kids in the place. No matter how much he craved to deck Pete, he couldn't. Not here, not now.

But he could do something else. "It won't go to auction, Pete. I gave you first offer, and you refused. This whole café heard you refuse." He glanced at their audience. "Right folks? You all heard Pete Warrick refuse?"

"Yeah, we sure did."

"Sure, that's what he said."

"Yeah, we're your witnesses."

"You heard 'em, Pete. So this is what will happen. I'll accept, and I'll sponsor Hien for citizenship, and you can… You can leave my café." He stared at Pete until the man squirmed.

Pete pushed past Beau and elbowed the kids out of the way as they put up their posters. The one they were taping under the cash register fell loose and floated to a stop in front of the door. It depicted a giant shoe with children hanging off of it. Pete's boot print was stamped on top.

Beau picked up the poster. "Do you mind if I keep this?"

"He ruined it, keep it. We can't put it up now."

Beau went back to his booth thinking where he might hang it in his barn. Just to remind him of today.

Margie brought him a cup of coffee before wrapping him in a big hug and kissing his temple.

"What was that for?"

"Beau Salem, the fact that you can't figure it out only means you are that wonderful. And if you don't do something more than just sponsor Hien, well, I swear I'll…" She rubbed her wrist under her nose.

"You'll do what?"

"I've no idea yet, but something." She stormed off.

But she's too young for me. God help me, she's too young for me.

NINETEEN

The Look of Love

Beau checked out the magazine stand at the drugstore before leaving town. The latest issue of a certain periodical was on sale. He bought a copy and headed for home. Halfway down the road he thought he should give Hien the news in person. Besides, she'd want to see what her friends published.

He made a decision and quick-turned into the Wheaten drive before he passed. Parking under an old sycamore tree, he hopped out with the magazine under his arm and took the front steps two at a time. He called through the screen door. "Hello, anyone here?"

Hien's car sat in the front, so he already knew she was there. Stupid.

"Why, Beau, how nice to see you!" Aunt Mel was home from his house. "Come in. Can I bring you anything? I've got tea in the refrigerator.

"Tea would be great. Actually, I came to see you and Hien together." Well, kind of. It'd be helpful if Aunt Mel stayed. Helpful to him.

"Let me call her and then I'll get your drink. She's upstairs developing photos. Shoo, go on, go sit in the living room." She called up the staircase. "Hien! You have a visitor."

Hadn't he said both? *Aunt Mel, please stop this.*

She disappeared into the kitchen and then he heard footfalls on the stairs.

"Oh, Beau. Hi." Hien sounded glad to see him. Or was she nervous? Her smile tremored.

Aunt Melanie returned. "Here ya go. So, Beau, does this mean you've talked with the other person?"

He took the glass of sweet tea, ice cubes clanking the sides. "Yes, I spoke with him, and he is not interested. So it looks like I will become your new partner."

Both ladies gazed at each other, eyes twinkling, clasping hands. Aunt Melanie shouted, "Yahoo!"

Beau snorted, nearly choking on a sip of tea. "Yahoo? Seriously?"

"Yes, seriously. We have been praying all morning. You are our answer to prayer. Again."

Beau shook his head. No wonder he stayed in control, barely though it was. They prayed.

"I stopped by the drug store. The latest edition of *LOOK* hit the stands. I haven't flipped through, so maybe you aren't in it, but here it is, if you want to check it out." He held it for Hien.

She glanced to Melanie, who motioned for her to get it. With shaky hands, she took it and sat on the couch. The title on the front read, "1968, So Far." The fine print explained that because this had been such an explosive year, full of major events, and only half completed, editors wanted to review the things that marked the year through the eyes of a single individual per event.

Juan Romero, the busboy who cradled RFK's head after the shooting in Los Angeles, was interviewed for the month of June. Ben Branch, the last person Dr. King spoke with before he went out on to the balcony, was highlighted for April.

T.O. Jones, a fired sanitation worker from Memphis was

featured for February. He knew Robert Walker and Echol Cole, his two colleagues who were crushed to death and how it happened.

Other things were noteworthy, such as *The Game of the Century* featuring Lou Alcindor from UCLA. It was the first nationally televised NCAA event. North Korea's seizing of the USS Pueblo (its crew still held captive) was depicted by a sailor's wife. She was interviewed with her name changed to protect him.

Hien was the person through whose eyes they reviewed the Tet Offensive.

She thumbed through to find the page, pointing out both Steve and Mat's bylines. She started to read but then closed it. "I cannot do it. I do not want to relive it." She shoved the magazine to Beau. "I can't. You do it."

"Now?"

She nodded. "I will watch your face."

Beau glanced at Aunt Mel for guidance, but she'd left the room.

He opened it to her page and began reading. Her friends included shots of the destroyed Embassy wall and the front of the Mission Coordinator's Residence. Beau's skin grew icy just staring at the page.

Another photo showed Hien at an apartment house. It appeared she was approaching the front door. The notation under the snapshot said it was her mother's home. Two pictures were obvious shots of someone's personal photos. One was of a Vietnamese man, young and kneeling next to a dog. The other picture showed a woman and a girl posed in traditional attire—the woman, an older version of Hien, while the girl was younger. The caption read that these came from her brother's wallet—the man was her brother and the older woman her mother.

Beau recognized the photo showing the Wheaten family, with the sons in dress uniforms, standing behind their parents—it had been included in a Christmas card. There was also one of

Mike leaning against his plane. Beau figured it was from the military, something they had on file. The final photograph was an ID of Hien. That he was sure came from her Press Corps work.

Most of the story she'd shared. But the details, the depth of pain acknowledged, moved him beyond the printed words. He'd no idea that she and Melanie were barricaded in the Mission Coordinator's master suite for over six hours, or that they'd walked past the bodies of men who'd tried to kill them. He wanted to protect her, shield her from anything evil ever happening again. How'd she rise in the morning? Or function at any meaningful level? Or smile and laugh and care about others? It ripped the air from his lungs to imagine it.

And Hien lived it.

～

THE PHONE RANG as Beau stepped into the house. Thea wasn't in the room, so he answered. "Hello?"

"Salem, is that you?" Pete Warrick. Why was he not surprised?

"Yeah, Pete, it's me." Who were you expecting?

"I just left my lawyer's office. Might be suing you if you make that deal."

Huh? "Sue me? For what?"

"Seems that because your little chink girlfriend isn't a citizen, it might be illegal for her to own that place. If that's the case, I can step right in. You can't buy from her since she won't own it."

"You're out of your mind."

"Oh, am I? Check with your lawyer. Bet he'll say the same thing." Beau could hear the smirk through the phone.

He knew Aunt Mel talked with her lawyer about the farm deed. He would've mentioned something. Beau was sure. But on the off chance…

"I'll do that." He hung up without saying goodbye. His

mother taught him better, but Emily Post had no provision for the Pete Warricks of the world. If he hadn't disconnected, what he said wouldn't have been the word goodbye.

He went to his desk and grabbed the Rolodex card he needed.

Rick Hanks' secretary answered on the first ring. "Richard Hanks, attorney at law. How may I help you?"

"Hi, this is Beau Salem. Think Rick might have a moment? Or, I can make an appointment…"

"Let me see, Mr. Salem." It grew quiet.

Then, "Hey, Beau! What's happening? How the heck are you?"

"Doing fine, Rick. I was wondering, though, if you've a minute to help me with a question."

"I'll have to bill you."

"Go ahead. If you give me the right answer, it would be worth it. And if you don't, I'll need you to fight a problem."

"I was kidding. Shoot."

"I have a friend. She and her husband were to receive a real estate gift as a wedding present. The gifter was her father-in-law. While her husband was away, her father-in-law had her sign the deed with the understanding her husband would sign when he returned. Only the husband didn't return, and the father-in-law died too. Does she legally own the land if she's not an American citizen?"

Rick was silent for a minute. "Hey, I just read something. Are you talking about that girl who married into the Wheaten family over in Viet Nam? I was reading *LOOK Magazine* over lunch and saw that piece. Wow."

"Yeah, that's her. Does she lose the farm too?"

"Nah, not necessarily. He gifted it to her, and old Ernie could gift to anyone he wanted. She'd still have to keep the taxes and stuff current. Why?"

Beau's heartbeat returned to a normal rate. "Oh, there's someone making noise, wanting to start trouble."

"Pete Warrick?"

"Yeah, how'd you know?"

"He called here a bit ago. He neglected to say that the girl was gifted the farm. Instead made it sound like she'd stolen it from the family or that she was trying to use it to get out of taxes or something. He's an idiot. Don't even worry about it."

"Thanks, Rick. Much appreciated." Beau's pulse returned to normal.

"My pleasure, Beau. The bill is in the mail." He chuckled at his own joke and hung up.

THE NEXT MONDAY, Beau had his girls all milked, then hopped in the truck and headed for the Farm Bureau office. Maddie rode along to keep him company. He parked at the side, waiting for the school bus that served as transportation for all the young help. Five minutes later it pulled down the street and he navigated it into the bureau's parking lot. Soon, it would be filled with kids from twelve to twenty, searching for extra cash. It was a hard job and lasted two weeks in his area, but detasseling corn for the seed companies was a rite of passage for the youth of Indiana. Many only did it once. The task was scratchy, muddy, hot, messy, and exhausting. Only the toughest returned for a second year. They got a dollar an hour and a ten cent bonus per hour if they were on time and never missed a day. Beau remembered his forays into the de-tasseling fields.

There wasn't enough money to pay him to do it again—it was for the young.

As the kids arrived, the representative from the seed company had them sign-in. He also kept track of size. The short ones had a harder time, so he tried to keep them in a group. They rode a wagon, allowing them to reach the top of the stalk and pull out the tassel. They couldn't cover as much ground as the taller kids, but they'd still do fairly good.

A detasseling machine had gone through the fields, or at least the ones they'd cover today. The cutter, as they called it, got about seventy percent of the tassels. The teens were expected to grab the rest. They could only miss three in 1,000. Tough, hard work.

Once the school bus pulled out for the first place, Sam Johnson's farm, he could return home and finish his chores. The cutter was due at his field this afternoon. He had three main types of corn growing—sweet corn for eating, field corn for silage, and seed corn, for growing seeds for the coming years. The seed corn was a hybrid developed by pollinating one type of corn with another type. To do that, tassels of the stalks of type A corn needed to be removed so a different type would pollinate. It was easy to tell a seed corn patch as only every fourth row was tall with a tassel. At least it was after detasseling.

Beau recognized many of the kids showing up at the sign-in desk. In most cases, they looked like a parent who'd taken this same adventure with Beau back when their parents and Beau were all teens all those years ago. A few college-age kids always signed up because they could work these couple weeks for their vacation money and not lose a whole summer of fun with a full-time job. That meant there were additional cars parked in the lot.

Maybe that's why he hadn't zeroed in on the blue Mustang. But once he did, the driver grabbed his attention.

"What are you doing here?"

Hien jumped at his voice. "Hi. I want to make extra money."

He took her by the arm and guided her away from the sign-in desk. "Do you have any idea what you are getting yourself into?"

"Do all of these people?"

Beau glanced at the crew. "Yeah, pretty much. Even if they haven't done it before, they know someone who has. Do you?"

She stared at him like he'd grown another nose. "Have you done this before?"

"Yes."

"Then I know someone." She moved towards the sign-in desk.

"Hien, you don't need this. I will help you. Why do you need extra money? I thought we'd worked that all out."

She sighed. "I must pay for something not in our budget. We cannot keep turning to you for money, especially, when I can earn it."

He waited for her to tell him what was outside the budget, but realized she had no intention of doing so.

"Fine. If you're so all-fired set to be miserable." He jammed his hat on tighter and walked back to his Ford.

Maddie was doing her best to get out of the truck, probably needed to relieve herself. He opened the door and his dog, *his* dog, ran across the parking lot to Hien.

Girls always stick together.

It took five minutes to get Maddie in the truck. By then, Hien got relegated to the short people group. At least she'd ride most of the day.

While he steamed, he glanced over toward the building. Two men were in deep conversation. One he knew for sure. The other seemed kinda familiar. The familiar one handed the other guy something. An envelope maybe? Familiar guy hopped in his car and took off. Then Pete Warrick folded what he'd been given and shoved it in his pant pocket. Things with Pete just got weirder.

He waited until the bus pulled out, then headed home to feed his stock and clean out the barn. Once back in the house, he found Thea left him a bowl and a box of Wheaties for breakfast. Not a great start to his week.

He finished his second helping and rinsed his dish as Thea came in. "I can't believe I let her talk me into this."

"What?" Beau turned off the water and dried his hands.

"Connie. She's got me making all of her bridesmaids gowns. I guess I'm lucky there's only two—her sister and Hien. But she's picked this intricate pattern, and Hien is the only one around for the fittings. Her sister lives in Peoria, Illinois, so she won't be here until right before the wedding. Connie bought the material and patterns with the understanding they would pay her back. She told me to collect the money, and that would be my payment for doing this. What is she thinking?"

"She's not." He winked at her.

"Look what she paid for this. I could buy three dresses off the rack for the price of one of these. Yeah, I'll make good money, but it didn't have to be this way."

A thought niggled at his brain. And then the light bulb went on. "Now I get it." He turned on his heel and started for the door.

"You get what?"

He spun around. "That's why Hien is detasseling corn. She said she needed to pay for something outside of her budget. I know she and Melanie are careful with their money right now. But she wouldn't do anything that might embarrass Connie. I'm going to talk to that girl."

"Which girl?"

That stopped him. "Good question."

"It's Connie's wedding. You don't want her to feel bad about wanting to have a nice day. Hien understands this. That's why she's telling no one the reason she's earning the money. You gotta let it go. So do I. They are our friends. We support our friends, right?" She came closer and put a hand on his shoulder. "Right?" Her voice reasoned.

She was. His head accepted that. His heart still broke for Hien, needing to work so hard. She'd been through enough. He sighed. "Yeah, you're right."

"Go get a shower. You'll feel better after."

"When did you get so smart?"

"Always have been. You just hate to think I've grown up." She kissed his cheek. "Now, scram. I've tons to do."

"Yes ma'am." He saluted her and ducked as she threw a towel at him. "I'm going, I'm going!" He raced up the stairs.

His little sister was pretty smart. She understood people. So why was she alone?

And why hadn't Phil Carpenter called her? He should be home for the summer. Didn't professors get summers off? His dad's farm was on the list for the cutter and crew. He could stop, check how the detasseling was going. It was his turn sometime next week if he remembered right.

He brushed his teeth and ran the water for a shave. Normally, this was so automatic, but the thoughts all running through his head had him asking himself questions.

What was Pete doing? The more he thought, he was fairly sure that familiar guy was a mucky-muck for the seed company. Was Pete taking payments under the table?

And Hien. Now that he knew about the dress problem, detasseling made sense. Why did it bother him to see her work so hard?

He studied his reflection in the mirror. A few gray hairs, mingling in his beard and sideburns, stared back. It was as if his father's face had replaced his own. On his father the gray seemed distinguished, an award for godly living. On himself, well, he just saw grizzled.

A Scripture verse came to him.

For if any be a hearer of the Word and not a doer, he is like unto a man beholding his natural face in a mirror; for he beholdeth himself, and then goeth his way and straightway forgetteth what manner of man he was.

Yeah, James knew what he was talking about. It was one thing to sit in church or read his Bible at home, but it was another to realize what God was saying to you each day, all day.

His voice was there. Beau only needed to listen. So. What was God saying about Pete? What was God saying about Hien? As far as Pete was concerned, it was in God's hands, and there wasn't much he could do, but pray.

But with Hien, Beau had to admit, he'd been afraid to ask. He was afraid of… what was he afraid of? What others might say? No. That never worried him. He didn't care what anyone said. About him. But about his family? That was another story. Beau had a lot of conversations with God over that.

Did he fear what people might say about Hien?

No, fear wasn't the word. He grew angry when people were unkind to her but never fearful. Was he worried his anger might get out of hand? Might he hurt Pete for his treatment of Hien?

So what was it? Was he the type to pummel someone as clueless as Pete?

He stared into the mirror. "Who are you, Beauregard James Salem?"

You are a child of the Most High King. You are a disciple of Jesus Christ. You are loved with a passion and blessed beyond reason. You're in love with a wonderful woman. She is a gift to your life. What will you do about it?

"Lord, You will have to show me, because I don't have a clue."

THE REST of the day unfolded. No more surprises. The cutter showed up after lunch. One of Beau's cows gave birth late in the afternoon and Thea fixed sandwiches for supper. No big deal. He wasn't fussy, and besides, it was hot enough that a cooked dinner seemed too heavy.

Thea brought her sewing machine downstairs so she could still be available to Mom after Aunt Mel left. Without Hien to drive her, Melanie walked to their house. Beau gave her a ride home, arriving as Hien parked. She looked tired. Her hair had come loose from the bun at her nape, and there was a scratch across her right cheek, not too deep, but noticeable. She was beautiful.

He kept his mouth shut and waved to her. At least he understood even if she wouldn't accept his help. He prayed for her strength and endurance as he pulled out of the drive.

It would be a long two weeks.

Tuesday, Beau took a trip to Pete Warrick's farm. He had plenty to do, but he needed this in the open. He knocked, knowing full well Pete would most likely be out in the fields. This way, there'd be no surprises.

Pete and his wife never had kids, so it was pretty quiet. Mrs. Warrick answered on the second knock, drying her hands on her apron. "Oh, hello, Beau. How are you?"

"Doing just dandy, Teresa. Was hoping I might speak with Pete if he's around."

She opened the screen door and stepped out on the porch. "He's in the fields getting ready for the cutter. It's our turn today after lunch."

Beau nodded.

"I expect him back to grab a bite in a little while. You could wait out here. I'll bring you a lemonade, if you like?"

"That would be nice, Teresa. Thank you." He sat on one of the Adirondack chairs while she went for his drink.

Twenty minutes later, Beau was on his second glass when Pete came into the yard. "State what you want, Salem, and get off my property."

"Good morning to you, too, Pete."

"I don't have time for chitter-chatter."

Beau stood and walked off the porch to meet Pete. "What I want is for you to stop harassing Hien Wheaten. I want you to stop saying stupid things about her. I want you to stop telling lies about her, and I expect you to comply. Immediately."

"Why would I do that? I couldn't care less about your expectations or your commie girlfriend."

Beau took a breath. *Calm down or you won't get through this.* "Maybe, but she cares about you. She even prays for you, Pete. Were you aware of that?"

"Bah!" He shoved past Beau.

"Pete, I know a lot of things."

"Oh, you do, do you? Like what?"

"Like a lawyer will never take your case. Like why you pushed so hard about detasseling this year."

That made him stop in his tracks.

Beau kept going. "I also learned the real reason you are so ugly to Hien." He'd had a nice conversation with Teresa before Pete showed. "I know about Andy, your nephew. And I'm sorry, Pete. Truly sorry for your loss."

"Those dirty VC killed that boy. He should have come home."

"Pete, that wasn't Hien. She lost far more family over there than you have. Truth be told, she understands better than any of us."

"That stupid war. It's her war, not ours. We don't belong over there. Let them fight it out amongst themselves and leave our boys out of it." He choked and dropped into the Adirondack chair.

"Pete. Hear me. I am sorry for your loss. But you will not bother or speak ill of Hien in public ever again."

"Or what? You gonna tell the rest of the committee about my deal with the seed company?"

Beau shook his head. Blackmail never was the plan. He only wanted him to stop. "Do I need to? Goodbye, Pete. Thank Teresa for me for the lemonade. It was delicious." He turned and climbed into his truck.

THE SUNDAY AFTER DETASSELING, Hien gave Thea a check for the full amount of her outfit. Beau spotted an expression of satisfaction as she did, and he applauded her accomplishment—inwardly, that is.

They all stood outside the church after dismissal. Seeing her made him want to take risks, but it also caused his insides to cringe like a coward. "Hien, maybe we should plan a trip to Indianapolis and submit your sponsorship paperwork. Are you available to go tomorrow?" He hoped he sounded innocuous enough.

"Yes, that is a good idea. August is the final month for my visa. I must get that done. When do you want to leave?" She seemed at ease despite their last conversation.

He missed church to stay home with Mom the Sunday before—she hadn't felt up to going and that concerned him, but she bounced back, and they all made it this week. Perhaps the extra time of not seeing Hien helped. Helped her, that is. It did nothing for him.

They planned for ten-thirty. He would come to her place so they could take her Mustang. He volunteered to drive but figured after her two weeks of working in the fields, climbing in and out of his truck might be too much of an adventure on her sore muscles. They'd grab a bite once they got to downtown and be the first client at the office when it opened after lunch.

He'd missed her. That was the plain and simple truth. He missed talking with her, laughing with her, sharing with her. Did he screw it all up with their detasseling disagreement?

He arrived on time.

She was cute with that silk scarf tied like a headband. Real cute. She handed him the keys.

He held the car door for her. After adjusting the seat—it was a miracle he didn't break his knees off trying to get in—he fired up the engine and they pulled out of the lane.

The problem came as they hit the road. That spark, their spontaneity had vanished. It was as quiet as that first ride, the one to his farm the day they met.

"Would you like the radio?"

She nodded. "If you do."

He turned the dial. The Vogues crooned "Turn Around, Look at Me." It stabbed his heart. His brain wanted to shout the same words. *Turn around, Hien. Look at me. I want to talk with you. I don't know how to start.*

"Pretty song." She spoke, turning his chest into a drum.

"Yeah, it is. Any songs you enjoy?" Lame, but it was a beginning.

"I like the Foundations. 'Baby, Now That I've Found You.'"

Was that an opening? "That's a nice one too. I have to confess, I've always liked the Beach Boys."

She chuckled. "You played 'Good Vibrations' every time you came to the café."

He smiled. She'd noticed. "I also enjoy Herb Alpert and the Tijuana Brass."

"What songs?" Her open gaze gave him courage.

"Well, the instrumentals, of course. 'The Lonely Bull'." Did he just say that? Oh, good grief! Think. "And, uh…" With his heart pounding in his brain, driving and speaking was a bad combination. He pulled to the shoulder, switched off the radio, and wiped his hands over his pantlegs. "And, 'This Guy's in Love with You'." He held his breath, watching her face.

"I like that one, too. Very much."

It was now or never. "Hien, there is another way."

She touched his hand and then retreated her fingers to her lap. "Are you asking?" She avoided his gaze. Her shyness made the pounding increase.

"Yes." He swallowed, hard." Hien, when I lost Nam Sun, I never thought I'd have those feelings again. Your bravery and trust helped me open up about my past. I see how you find the good, chase after what is right. You give me strength to say what I've feared saying. Here goes. I love you, Hien. And this is me asking you to marry me."

She grew so silent, he was sure he misread the signs. Oh, what had he done?

"Beau, I am drawn to you. My heart behaves badly when I am with you. But you need to understand something." She took a breath and fiddled with her rings.

He stopped breathing.

"Michael and I dated but a short while before we were married in January. I loved him, but I did not know him. I might have if he had returned. But he did not return. So, we lived together for two weeks before he shipped out. I never had the opportunity to learn his likes or habits. I did not have time to grow to respect him. This is hard for me to say." Tears welled, her lashes glistened.

"Do you… How do you… What are you saying?"

"I am saying that I know more about you and have more respect for you already than my husband." She swiped at her face and sniffed. "That hurts to admit. Plus, it has only been seven months since I was a new bride. I am not ready to have another wedding that fast." She paused and captured his gaze. "But if I were to marry anyone, it would be you, Beau Salem."

"So. Is your answer no or not now?" How'd he get that question out of his mouth? But her response would make or break his heart.

She turned in her seat, caressing his cheek. "I am saying not right now. Beau, this girl is in love with you." She smiled that gentle smile that stole his breath. "I do not want to rush. Might we start by dating? Get to know each other better? I have never seen you angry. The closest we have come to disagreeing was when I detasselled." The blush on her cheeks proved the difficulty she had expressing this.

"I love you, Hien Wheaten. If that's what you want, I'll wait." He brushed a strand of hair from her cheek.

She stared at her hands again and slid the rings from her finger.

Beau's pulse pounded in his ears. To be so close. Her mouth glistened with that strawberry-scented lip stuff. How could he tell when he couldn't breathe? He leaned in, slow.

She didn't pull back. Instead she drew closer.

His lips met hers in the sweetest kiss he'd ever known. He pulled her to him and deepened it. He'd waited his whole life for this moment.

Breaking it off might be the hardest thing he'd done. His pulse raced as he licked his lip, the taste of her still fresh. "We'd better get moving. I want this business over, so we can start our date."

She giggled, a beautiful sound, and moved into her seat.

For the first time, he officially hated bucket seats.

He guided the car onto the highway and captured her ring-less fingers. If he couldn't kiss her all the way to Indianapolis, he for sure would hold her hand.

THAT SATURDAY, Beau stood up for his best friend as Jerry and Connie exchanged their vows. Throughout the ceremony he imagined the service when he and Hien could make the same promises, sneaking peeks at the prettiest bridesmaid he'd ever seen.

Hien wore a strapless sweetheart gown in soft pink with lots of lacy stuff on top and bunches of shear flowy material on the skirt part. The only reason he knew it was a sweetheart gown, or that it was called an empire waist, was because Thea told him. But whatever the verbiage, Hien was lovely. Thea said it was ballet length, explaining that meant it didn't drag on the floor, but moved gracefully around her. She had her hair down with a rose-colored bow barrette on top of her head.

At the reception held at the Casa Grande, he spotted Connie whispering to her just before it was time to throw the bouquet. Yep, Hien caught it.

Thea hadn't tried for it. Claimed she needed to stay close to Mom. Beau could have done that, but Thea wouldn't let him. It broke Beau's heart until he saw another wedding guest making his way over to her. So Phil Carpenter got an invitation. And Thea didn't run away. Or attack him. That was positive. He only wanted what was best for his sister. Time would tell.

Jerry elbowed him. "Very pretty, huh?"

"Yes, Connie makes a pretty bride."

"I know that, dummy. I'm talking about Hien. You can't keep your eyes off her."

Heat crept up Beau's face. "Didn't think I was that conspicuous."

"Oh, dude, you are *so* obvious." Jerry laughed. "It's about time, you figured it out. Connie told me that Hien confided in her you've started dating."

"You really have got ink for blood, don't you?"

"I'm also married to the best source in town." He grinned.

"Yes, you are." He draped an arm over his friend's shoulders. "And I wish you every happiness. I am happy for you two."

"Yeah. I'm blessed. So, tell me when you set the date, and I'll return the favor. Oh, and since I brought you together, you can name your first born after me." He punctuated his words with a soft punch to Beau's ribs.

Beau doubled enough to pull back and laughed as "The Look of Love" started over the speakers. "You got that. Excuse me, now. I'm going to dance with the most beautiful woman here. They're playing our song."

He crossed the room to Hien who glanced up to catch his gaze. The love in her eyes nearly melted him into the floor. He held out his hand, she placed hers in his. Leading her to the floor, he took a deep breath, then turned her into his arms.

She rested her head against his chest. Even in heels, she couldn't reach his shoulder.

He pulled her closer, knowing she heard each beat of his heart.

Together they moved to the music, beginning a dance that would last the rest of his life.

TWENTY

My Cup Runneth Over

October 13, 2018
Saturday

"And that was our first dance together." Hien tapped the nose of her youngest granddaughter, Jemma.

"Who is that, Bà?" Her little fingers roamed over an old photo of a young woman holding a baby.

"That's Lai with your Uncle Hung." Lai had written to them that September to say Mil was now a grandmother. She had not wanted to mention anything before the baby's birth in case something happened. But once Hung Charles Wheaten entered the world, Lai let them know. She even brought him for a visit the following year, in time for Hien and Beau's wedding.

"Uncle Hung lives in Viet Nam now. Is that where his mom is?"

Another hard memory that the Lord redeemed. "When Saigon fell, many were trapped and could not leave. Lai saw what was happening in advance. She sent Hung to us, but she did not get out. They sent her to a reeducation camp for five years. When she was released, she was not healthy enough to travel, so she stayed there."

"Is that why Uncle Hung went back?" Jemma leaned in, her

sweet face propped on her fists while her elbows stood anchored to the table.

"Partly. He also learned about farming from your Papa Beau. He wanted to take the knowledge he gained and help others in Viet Nam."

The little girl straightened. "Oh! So that's where our family got started helping people to learn about farming and taking it to other countries."

"That is right. Papa Beau named it Plows of Peace because the initials made the name I called Gramma Mil's husband: Pop."

"So, what about this photo, Bà?" Apparently, all her questions about Uncle Hung were answered. Jemma moved on.

"That is from our wedding. We were married the next spring on May twenty-fifth. Your Uncle Steve Riley came home from Viet Nam to walk me down the aisle."

"You looked beautiful, Bà. I love your dress."

Hien loved it too. Thea not only made it, she designed it with Hien in mind. "That is my favorite dress of all times. I would give it to a daughter, but I have only sons."

"I would like to wear it, Bà."

"Maybe you will, sweet girl. We will see."

Jemma turned the page and pointed to another baby photo. "Who's that?"

"That is your Uncle Owen. He was born a year later. We named him for Papa Beau's best friend, Jerry Owen. Your daddy, Riley, came four years after that. Owen grew up to marry Stephanie and Riley married your mama, Susan. Owen and Stephanie have one son and two daughters, Jesse, Niki and Alli. Riley and Stephanie have three girls, Dia, Olli and..." Hien pretended to forget.

"Jemma!"

"Oh, that is right. Jemma." She winked at the little girl. "Your cousin Jesse married Andi, and today they are bringing their baby home to meet his Bà." Hien closed the photo album and kissed Jemma on top of her head.

"Mom, I think I see them pulling in the drive. Are you ready? Stephanie, they're here!" Owen's voice reflected his excitement. This was his first grandchild.

Hien got up from the table and made her way to the rocker—the same chair where Mil rocked Hung and Owen and Riley. It was one she had rocked her sons to sleep while she prayed over them. And when they married and brought grandchildren home to her, she rocked each one of them—Jesse, Niki, Alli, Dia, Olli and Jemma. Five girls and one boy to carry on the Salem name, military tradition, and farming passion. Six grandchildren to teach about the love and faithfulness of Jesus. And now a great grandson.

Oh, she was blessed.

The only part to bring her a twinge of sadness today was that Beau and Mil were not there to greet this new addition. They said goodbye to Mil in 1999 and then, last year, Beau left her side to go home to Jesus. He waited for her there. One day she would see him again.

The front screen door opened. For the briefest of moments she thought it was her Beau coming through the doorway, but it was Jesse. Tall and handsome, following his lovely wife, Marissa, whose grandparents were her good friends, Jerry and Connie. Blessed. She was so blessed. "Bring that little one over here. His Bà needs to cuddle him."

Jesse placed his four-day-old son into her waiting arms.

Hien leaned over, inhaling the sweet scent of new baby.

Jesse knelt next to the chair. "So, Bà. What do you think? We've named him David Joshua Salem."

"That is a strong name."

"We know. For now, though, we'll call him Davy."

"Sweet Davy boy." Hien continued to cuddle him. Then the words came. "Sweet boy, you have a bright future ahead. May you be blessed with strength, courage and a true sense of who you are in Christ Jesus. May your words and actions all be pleasing and acceptable in God's eyes. May you be filled with Godly wisdom that cuts through rhetoric and lies. May you always remain close to God, filled with His presence. A man after God's own heart. And may hundreds of thousands know of your integrity and honesty as you live out the life your Heavenly Father has for you. May you be blessed as you have already blessed our family, David Joshua Salem." She kissed his head.

"Is it time, Bà?" Jesse glanced at her.

"Yes, it is time. Owen, would you bring it to the table? I think you should do the writing. Your father would want that."

Her Owen, not as tall as Beau but almost the spitting image, brought the book from the mantel to the table. With his Stephanie beside him, he pulled out a black ballpoint pen from his pocket, and opened Pop's old Bible to the front where the generations were listed. After a few turns he found the correct page.

Hien watched him inscribe the name of his first grandchild —David Joshua Salem—and the date of his birth, October ninth, 2018. He brought it for her to see. She nodded her approval while a tear absorbed into the baby's blanket.

"Dinner is ready." Riley's wife, Susan, called from the dining room with perfect timing.

"Here, let me take him, Bà." Jesse lifted the bundle from her arms and gave his mother a turn with her first grandbaby.

Owen held her elbow. He guided her to the chair at the head of the table and held it for her. All waited until she sat before taking their seats, with hands folded and gazes her way.

"Let us pray. Father, I—" Emotion stole her breath.

Owen, on her right, covered her hand in his.

She could almost feel Beau's touch. It was enough. He was with her in spirit. "Father, we are so blessed by Your hand. You are so good to us. May we always recognize Your bounty and forever be grateful. We give thanks for this meal, for our family being together, for our newest addition, and for every step you have led us to take. Thank You. In Jesus' Name, Amen."

The family echoed "Amen" and began to eat.

Hien leaned back and closed her eyes, listening with her heart beyond the sounds of cherished voices and clinks of utensils on plates. Somehow, through that beautiful cacophony of family around the table, she heard the strains of music. Beau played "Good Vibrations," just for her.

And it was good.

<<<>>>

Acknowledgments

____

Dear Reader,

About the Author

Jennifer Lynn Cary likes to say you can take the girl out of Indiana, but you can't take the Hoosier out of the girl. Author of The Crockett Chronicles trilogy, she makes her home in Arizona with her husband of forty years where she enjoys sharing her tales of Kokomo with her grandkids.

You can find her at www.jenniferlynncary.com

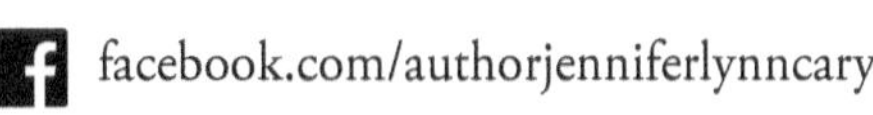 facebook.com/authorjenniferlynncary

Sneak Peak of Wedding Bell Blues: The Relentless series Book 2